Published by Dangerous Words Publishing
Cover by Covers by Combs

ENTERED IN THE ALIEN BRIDE LOTTERY

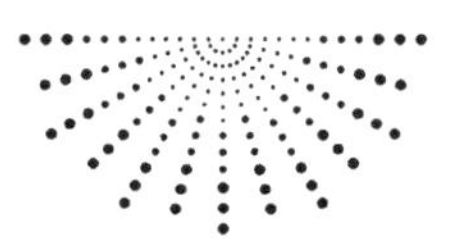

ABOUT ENTERED IN THE ALIEN BRIDE LOTTERY

There are about a million ways to end up in the Alien Bride Lottery. But all it takes is one.

Every unmarried female human over the age of twenty-one gets entered once a year. You can also accept extra entries for legal infractions—instead of paying a parking fine, for example, you can request an extra entry. Lots of women do that. I mean, why not? The chances are astronomical that your name will get chosen to be one of the hundred or so women who get shipped off to space every year.

And even if your name is drawn, the odds are slim that you'll match up with an alien who's looking for a mate.

Most of the lottery-drawn women come back to Earth every year and resume their lives as if nothing changed.

But some don't.

And no matter what, getting drawn in the lottery means you have to compete in the Bride Games.

Guess that's where I'm heading now.

I only hope I can avoid catching the eye of one of the giant, rainbow-hued brutes whose mission is to protect Earth—and who can claim me as a mate.

All because I was Entered in the Alien Bride Lottery…

CHAPTER ONE

NATALIE

There are about a million ways to end up in the Alien Bride Lottery.

Every unmarried female human between the ages of twenty-one and thirty-five gets entered once a year. You can also choose to accept extra entries instead of dealing with the courts for various legal infractions—instead of paying a parking fine, for example, you can request an extra entry. Lots of women do that. I mean, why not? The chances are astronomical that your name will get chosen to be one of the hundred or so women who get shipped off to space every year.

And even if your name is drawn, the odds are slim that you'll match up with an alien who's looking for a mate.

Most of the lottery-drawn women come back to Earth every year and resume their lives as if nothing changed.

But some don't. We Earth women mostly manage to ignore that part. At least, I always did.

So there I was on my twenty-first birthday, out with my college friends for my first legal drink, worrying a little about the midterm exam in my biology class the next week.

Not worrying about aliens.

Mostly, I had my eye on David Stephens, the sax player for the band that Jasmine, my roommate, had convinced to play tonight.

"Hey, Earth to Natalie." Jas waved her hand in front of my face. "If you don't stop eye-fucking him and start trying to get him into your actual bed, *I* might go hit on him just so someone does."

I rolled my eyes. "I'm not his type. He's pretty much made it clear that he's not that into me."

"Oh, bullshit. He's never said any such thing." She took a long drink of her whiskey and Coke. I shuddered—whiskey was probably my least favorite alcohol in the world. Jas eyed my own barely touched drink on the table between us. "No wonder you haven't worked up enough nerve. You need to down your girly drink, then march your sexy ass over there and hit that."

I laughed aloud but picked up my vodka and cranberry and downed it in two gulps. "It's going to take more than that, girlfriend."

"Oh, please, you're a lightweight. Already slurring your words." Jas hopped off her stool and grabbed my hand. "Come on. Let's go talk to him. You have to at least thank the guys for playing tonight. Their break is almost over."

"Okay, okay." I stumbled behind her and was still laughing when all the lights went on in the bar. Everyone froze as the giant televisions on either end of the main room turned on and flipped to an image of a Khanavai male with bright green skin and a shock of white-gold hair in a buzzed mohawk.

The Lottery Director and Bride Games Administrator, Vos Klavoii.

"Hello, people of Earth." He flashed a smile so white it should have been on a toothpaste ad. He'd been drawing the lottery names once a year for as long as I could remember. Not on any schedule that anyone had ever been able to determine, though. Instead, when they were ready, the Khanavai took over every communication device in the world and transmitted the Lottery Drawing.

Over the next few days, the entire world would be watching the most intense reality show ever filmed.

This time, it started at twelve-thirty in the morning, the day after my birthday.

Along with everyone else in the bar, I stared wide-eyed as Vos Klavoii began his usual pre-drawing patter, starting with recapping the treaty that started it all.

"For the last half-century of your Earth years, the Khanavai have protected your planet from the ravages of the Alveron Horde. And all we ask in return is that you send unmarried females for our warriors. That's right, brides for the soldiers who keep you safe and secure in your home."

As he spoke, Vos spun the barrel of an old-fashioned wire raffle-ticket drum, as if he were really going to draw a name out. The enormous screen behind him showed a giant image of the lottery's logo—a hot-pink oval with THE ALIEN BRIDE LOTTERY on it in black—superimposed on a turquoise screen. The colors were garish, like everything about the lottery. Possibly like everything about the Khanavai, given the rainbow hues of their skin coloring.

"This Bride Treaty keeps humanity safe. And the women who are joined with our warriors live happily ever after," Vos continued.

"Yeah, right," Jas muttered. "Nothing like leaving behind everyone and everything she ever cared about to make a girl happy."

I glanced at her and nodded in agreement, but quickly turned my attention back to the television. The Alien Bride Program made for gripping TV, at least. Like most of humanity, I'd be glued to a set all the way through the Bride Games, no matter how long they took.

"You're in the drawing now, right?" David spoke quietly beside me. I hadn't even seen him headed toward me—that's how engrossing the lottery was.

I fought not to jump, instead turning to look at him as I waved a hand airily. "Yeah, but everyone knows you never get chosen your first year."

"Good," he whispered, slipping an arm around my waist and resting his hand on my hip. "I'd miss you."

My grin at that couldn't be contained. I caught a glimpse of Jas's thumbs-up out of the corner of my eye. Ignoring her, I leaned into David.

"It's time for our first drawing," Vos announced, stopping the machine and pulling out a ticket with a showman's flourish. I assumed the tickets were epaper, blank until drawn and then electronically imprinted with the new bride's name at the last moment.

"Angelica Evatt," Vos announced. A picture of the alien bride-to-be flashed up on the screen behind him, along with her basic stats—date of birth, city of residence, and the last six digits of her Lottery ID number, just to be sure. Not that it mattered. She had a Khanavai ID chip implanted behind her right ear, just like the rest of us, acting as a universal translator, but also allowing the aliens to keep tabs on every human on the planet. Even if she tried to run, they'd find her.

"Congratulations, Angelica!" Vos exclaimed cheerfully.

David leaned even closer, putting his lips against my ear. A shiver rolled up my spine as he whispered, "This is going to take forever. Let's get out of here and go celebrate your birthday properly."

"Definitely." I hopped off the stool and gathered my purse, giving a little wave to Jas to let her know I was going. My roommate waggled her eyebrows at me, mouthing "Have fun" as I fell into step next to David.

My heartbeat thundered in my chest. I couldn't believe this was happening. After four years of lusting after the guy, we were finally hooking up. "I'm going home with David Stephens" echoed over and over in my mind like a drumbeat, and I couldn't quit grinning.

We were almost to the door when Vos sang out, "And our second lottery winner is Natalie Ferguson."

Wait. That's me.

My brain stuttered to a stop and I stumbled, then quit walking, still staring at the exit.

So close to escape.

Running was useless.

It had to be a different Natalie Ferguson. My name wasn't totally unique. That's why they gave us Lottery IDs. And showed pictures on the screen. My stomach churned. Then a whisper went up around me.

Finally, I forced myself to turn around.

Everyone in the bar was staring at me.

Fuck.

I dragged my eyes up to the screen.

And there it was. My driver's license picture staring back at me. My mouth dried, and I opened it to say something. Anything. To protest that there was no way that could be me, that no one got their name drawn the first time they were entered. I didn't have any parking tickets or anything. One single entry.

That's all it had taken.

But before I could say anything, a cone of light appeared around me. The bar wavered in my sight and my hand pulled away from David's, even though I was holding onto it as tightly as I could.

"I'm sorry," I managed to say to him, tears springing to my eyes.

And then I was transported off my planet. Out of my life.

And into my own personal hell.

The Khanavai Bride Games.

CHAPTER TWO

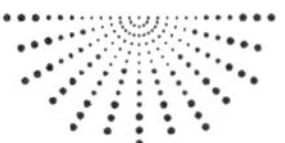

CAV

I frowned at my commanding officer. "Wait. I've been *what*? Um…Sir," I added as an afterthought.

When Commander Dren had called me in for a meeting, I had been expecting him to tell me I'd been accepted into the dark ops program.

"Your name was drawn in the Bride Lottery, Lieutenant. You're going to be mated." Dren beamed at me as if I'd won something precious. I guess in his mind, I had.

Most of my fellow officers would feel the same.

But I didn't want a mate right now. I wanted to learn spycraft. Join the elite squads that carried out clandestine missions in enemy territory.

Commander Dren read my response in my expression. "This *is* an honor, you know." His voice wasn't unkind—after all, he too was a warrior. "The ops program will still be here when you return. And Command Central likes promoting mated officers. This will be good for your military career." He slapped a hand on my shoulder. "Now go pack a bag. You've been granted leave for this, and your shuttle leaves soon."

I put on my blandest soldier's expression. "Yes, sir."

But as soon as I hit the corridor that led from the commander's office to my own quarters, I let my true feelings shine through. Apparently, that meant I looked ready to kill. Every soldier who caught a glimpse of me scurried away as quickly as possible.

By the time I'd finished packing my bag, I'd resorted to muttering a constant string of curses.

I'd managed to refrain from asking Dren if another officer could be granted the honor of an Earth bride. I knew better. It was my duty to sire heirs, to keep the Khanavai race alive. To make sure we had warriors for the next generation.

That thought led me to switch over to cursing the Alveron Horde in general. It was their fault the Khanavai only produced males. The vile monsters used chemical warfare. Even the Earthers knew that poisoning one's enemies was a horrific move. And they'd been well on their way to destroying their planet when we'd intervened to save them.

Lucky for them, their women were compatible with our men. Otherwise, we might have let the otherwise insignificant planet go.

I sighed as I slung my single bag over my shoulder.

I would do my duty. But I didn't have to be cheerful about it.

THE SHUTTLE RIDE was short and uneventful. Luckily, I hadn't been far from the station where the Bride Games were held. Flying with other pilots always made me want to chew off my fingernails. Not out of fear—no, our pilots were the best trained in the universe. But out of sheer boredom. I'd much rather be piloting the ship myself, even if it was only a shuttle.

As I stepped out into Station 21's main thoroughfare from the station's docking area, I took a deep breath.

Time to act like a civilized Khanavai.

I grinned at the thought. There were races out in the galaxy who might argue that the phrase "civilized Khanavai" was a contradiction in terms. They were wrong, of course. We could be as civilized as anyone—as long as we weren't provoked.

A slight buzzing alerted me to a message, and I glanced down at the communication device I wore strapped to my wrist. The disembarkation specialist, a tiny nonbinary Poltien with a shock of blue hair from its left nostril, had promised they would have my quarters ready before I hit the Promenade.

Not quite—but close. It would have taken the Poltien longer to reach the main recreational area of the station, and I'd learned to make allowances for lesser creatures.

Like, I assumed, I would have to make allowances for my new Earther bride.

I shook off the irritation that came with the thought and followed the com's directions to my quarters.

As I passed by the various shopfronts, I found myself noticing the few humans who moved among the crowds. Particularly the females.

With the exception of their generally bland coloring—most of them fell into some shade from pale pink to dark brown—they were attractive enough, with soft, yielding bodies. As a young soldier, I'd even tried a few at the holo-pleasure suites. If the holo designers were to be trusted, human women were also warm in all the right ways.

At the thought, my cock hardened.

Perhaps not all the duties associated with taking a mate would be irritants.

Once in my quarters, I activated the viewscreen to show the latest Lottery Drawing. It had been years since I'd watched the Bride Games, certain that I was a long time away from ever having to participate in them.

Perhaps it was time to begin paying more attention to what might be expected of me.

With nothing to do until I reported to the Games Director, I stretched out on the double-sized bed, a perk of being a *groom*—the ridiculous human word for a male about to be mated.

As Vos Klavoii drew name after name and images of the women flashed up on the screen, I reached down to touch myself, wondering what it would be like to bury myself in that one with the bright blue eyes. Or the one with the puffy lips. How might it feel to have those lips wrapped around my cock?

I stroked myself, imagining the feel of a human woman surrounding me. Perhaps this would be the last time I would have to take matters into my own hands. The thought of an Earther girl's mouth sliding down over me made me throb. I closed my eyes, swallowing a moan as I climaxed.

I opened my eyes, concentrating again on the images of the human women on the screen.

They were all equally lovely, I decided. Any of them would do. I would accept whichever bride was matched to me, fuck her, impregnate her, and report back for ship duty.

And perhaps Commander Dren was right. Command Central would promote me into the Special Ops program once I had fulfilled my genetic duty as a warrior of the Khanavai.

Satisfied with my decision, I rolled out of the enormous bed and moved to the sanicleanse unit to wash.

After all, I would soon be meeting my new mate.

I DRESSED in my formal uniform to report to the Bride Games area of the station. The closer I got to it, the stranger everything around me looked.

I had expected many of the Khanavai to be overdressed—after all, Earthers were reportedly much more susceptible to fluctuations in temperature than we were, and they had spent millennia protecting their bodies from the unpredictable weather of their planet. Rumor had it many of them were uncomfortable with nudity.

So of course most of the Khanavai wore excessive amounts of clothing. Even my tribal chavan, wrapped around my waist and falling almost to my knees, and my traditional vandenoi leather strap, worn across one shoulder, meant that I wore less than most of the other warriors headed toward the Bride Games in a steady stream.

Some of them even wore human-style suits. I shuddered at the thought of so much fabric scratching against my skin. How did the men of Earth fight in such restrictive outfits?

Moreover, the closer I got to the games suites, the more muted the colors became, almost as if they were behind some kind of shadow. Signs for the Bride Lottery—advertisements, the Earthers called them—adorned the corridor walls, purporting to show Khanavai warriors. But these, too, were in muted colors, failing to show the full glory of our males.

And their genitals were covered by the Bride Lottery logo, as if we were ashamed to show ourselves to our potential mates.

Their nudity taboo at play, I suspected.

I rolled my eyes. I would have much to teach my mate.

And any moment now, I would catch sight of her. I found myself gazing eagerly ahead, hoping to catch sight of the Earther females, one of whom would be my supporter, my subordinate, the mother of my children and the keeper of my home as I took to the stars, roaming far and wide to protect our world—and all worlds—from the ravages of our enemies.

Maybe this mated thing wouldn't be so bad after all.

CHAPTER THREE

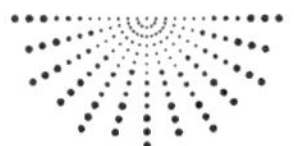

NATALIE

I came out of the transporter heaving. A tiny alien with pure white skin, a rill of skin on its back like a lizard, and a long braid of orange hair hanging out of one nostril bounced around me, squeaking.

"Oh no, this one's ill, too. Please call maintenance for a clean-up." It rose on its toes so it was at face height with me—as long as I remained bent over, clutching my stomach. "Are you going to survive? We need to get you to makeup and wardrobe. As soon as you stop vomiting," it added, crinkling its nose in distaste as its rill lifted and lowered several times, making it look remarkably like a cross between a lizard and a sailing ship.

A Poltien, I thought. That's what these creatures were called. I didn't know enough about them to be able to tell at a glance if it was male, female, or one of the non-gendered versions. A nonbinary, I remembered from my Introduction to Galactic Life course.

I wiped the back of my hand across my mouth and breathed in and out several times until the nausea had passed. "I'll be okay."

"Then follow me this way, please." The Poltien scampered ahead of me. As we walked away from the transportation room, I saw several other potential brides vomiting.

This part of the Bride Games had never been shown on Earth.

I still couldn't believe I was here.

I mean, I guess I knew on some level that I'd gone into the lottery. I had friends who'd gotten married right before they "came of age," as the lottery officials put it, just so they could avoid getting drawn.

Until now, I had thought that was a little excessive. Who wants to be married at such a young age? I had tons of better things to do with my life. After all, it wasn't like you could have it annulled if your name didn't get drawn. No—since the arrival of the Khanavai warriors and the host of other galactic species who had shown up after them, we were expected to try to make our marriages last.

Five years. That's how long a Lottery Bride had to stay with her alien mate. And it was the minimum length a married couple on Earth had to stay together, too.

Fuck. My. Life.

And the farther we moved along the corridor, the more intense all the colors became. I wasn't sure if I'd vomited out all of the alcohol in my system—but I was definitely working on a hell of a hangover.

"Is there anywhere I can brush my teeth?" I finally asked the Poltien leading me.

"Of course," it answered in its high-pitched voice. "There are ablution services in your Bride's Quarters. We're almost there."

Thank God—or whatever deity might be listening. I needed a toothbrush more than I needed anything. Except maybe to go home.

For an instant, I flashed on David's expression as I was transported away from him, his green eyes sad, his face stricken.

No. I can't go there.

I simply had to get through the games, convince everyone there that I was particularly unsuited to be a Khanavai warrior's bride, and go home. Back to my life. Back to my studies. Back to David. My life would be normal again.

And I will never again have to worry about being drawn in the Alien Bride Lottery.

I brightened up at that thought. Once chosen, forever safe. My name would never again go into the drawing.

The Poltien led me around a corner, and I was so lost in my thoughts that I nearly crashed into the giant man coming from the other direction. The Poltien had scampered around him, but I stumbled to a stop barely an inch away from slamming my face into his chest.

Well. Okay. Into his upper abdomen.

He grabbed my shoulders to steady me as I tilted my head back and looked up, up, up into his bright purple eyes.

Holy crap, he's huge, was my first thought. *And so blue!* came next.

All that came out of my mouth was a squeak worthy of a Poltien.

"Are you all right?" the giant turquoise man asked me in a deep, rumbling voice. I had to fight the urge to place a hand on his broad chest to feel it vibrate as he spoke. I glanced over to the enormous hand holding my shoulder, then followed his arm all the way up to his bulging blue biceps, where my gaze snagged. This time, my own hand was halfway toward the muscle before I realized it and forced my wayward fingers back down to my side.

"Um. Yeah, I'm okay." My voice came out all breathless and girlish, and I gave myself an internal smack. Quit acting like a besotted fool, I reprimanded myself.

"She is late." The Poltien, having realized I was no longer following it, had turned around to retrieve me. "And you are not supposed to be in this area. All warriors are to be in the Grooms' Quarters. Not wandering around the Bridal Suites."

The Khanavai warrior flashed her an unrepentant grin, and I nearly swooned. Good lord, but he was gorgeous.

"I must have gotten turned around." But he ruined his explanation by tossing a wink at me.

My heartbeat sped up and I swallowed hard. *Don't get too excited,* Nat, I warned myself. *The goal is to get kicked out of the games, not flirt with the first alien you see.*

"My apologies." The warrior abruptly released me and took a step back. Cold air rushed into the space his warm hands had just covered, and for an instant, I felt bereft at losing his touch.

As the warrior executed a sharp bow, though, I gathered my wits—at least enough to mutter, "No problem," and step around him.

I followed the Poltien once more, but I couldn't help glancing back one last time, only to find the beautiful alien man staring thoughtfully after me. When he caught me looking, he smiled, this time revealing a deep dimple in his turquoise cheek. I whipped my head back around and focused on my surroundings.

I would not let one alien hottie distract me from my plan.

We made it to my Bridal Suite moments later, and this time when I glanced back behind us, the warrior was gone. I couldn't decide whether the sigh I heaved was of relief or disappointment. Probably a little of both.

"These will be your quarters," the Poltien said, opening the door onto a room decorated in shades of white ranging from eggshell to antique, and included a princess-style vanity with a matching stool, a single bed with a white lace spread, and a white chintz chair in a corner next to a perfectly white side table. The whole thing practically screamed Bridezilla.

"This is...nice," I finally said.

"The lavatory is through that door and there are new clothes in the closet." The Poltien pointed to doors on the left and right sides of the room. "Makeup and wardrobe will be here in one standard station hour. Please be ready."

"But—" I began as it backed out of the room. "How long is a standard station hour?" I finished my sentence by speaking to the closed door.

"Guess I'll find out soon enough," I muttered to myself.

I headed toward the door the Poltien had indicated was the lavatory, hoping it wouldn't take me long to figure out how to work any alien technology.

I yawned widely. It had been almost one in the morning when I'd been stolen from my night out. I had no idea how long it had taken to transport me to the station. No matter, though—my internal clock was screaming that it was time for me to go to bed.

First, though, I desperately needed a shower.

CHAPTER FOUR

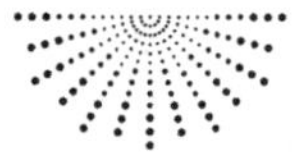

CAV

I settled into my seat in the warriors' viewing room, watching the screen avidly as I waited for Vos to introduce the woman who'd barreled into me in the hallway.

The instant I touched her, I knew. The instinct came from deep within me.

This one is mine.

I would kill any man who tried to take her from me.

Then her eyes had met mine, so wide and surprised, and she had spoken in that perfect, submissive voice.

At the memory, an unbidden growl rumbled in my throat.

One of the other warriors still standing in the room cut his gaze in my direction. "Saw something you liked, brother?"

I sized him up, then waved one hand in the air dismissively, not wanting to give away any more than necessary. "Perhaps. We'll see."

He moved closer, offering the abbreviated Khanavai salute—a fist to the chest in two quick thumps, one with the side of the fist by the thumb, then a second with the closed fingers toward the chest.

I returned the salute, reading the insignia on his vandenoi strap. "Special Ops, huh? I'm waiting for word on my own application."

"Zont Lanov," he introduced himself.

"Cav Adredoni," I replied. "Stationed on the Jalzinian."

He lit up when I mentioned my ship. "Earth defense, huh? Nice. I haven't worked any ops out here yet, but I'm hoping to go undercover on Earth someday. Command Central thinks an Earther mate will be good practice for that."

"Undercover? I didn't know we ran any ops on Earth."

He shrugged. "Only a few. It's not like they have any tech we need. But there are always rumors of Horde infiltration. So far, they're the only species we've found with DNA similar enough to ours to mate. We can't allow the Alveron Horde to poison them as they did us."

I nodded somberly. Once we'd discovered that Earth held the answer to reviving our population, the Khanavai had begun protecting the small blue planet with a ferocity usually reserved for our home planet.

"So apparently Command Central thinks you need an Earther bride, too?" Zont continued, changing the subject back to the more pleasant aspects of our connections with Earth.

I shrugged. "No evidence my groom's spot is anything more than a coincidence."

Zont threw his head back and roared with laughter. "There is no such thing as a coincidence, brother—that's something you'll have to learn if you're going to join Special Ops."

I stared at him for a moment. "So you believe I've been sent to take a mate as part of my request to join Special Ops?"

"Almost certainly. It's the kind of thing Command Central would do."

I leaned back in my chair and stared at the screen, watching the parade of potential brides being interviewed by Vos. Very well. If this was a ploy by Command Central to aid my career in Special Ops, I'd take the challenge.

You've already chosen your bride, a small voice inside me noted.

Fine. I had every intention of taking that bride in particular.

And nothing would stand in my way.

ALMOST A FULL STANDARD station hour later, my mate had still not appeared on the screen, and I had grown tired of watching bland human women simper at me from the screen. Apparently, most of them had heard of Khanavai warrior prowess and were eager to find a mate.

Who could blame them? After all, we were infinitely better than their minuscule human males.

Beside me, Zont leaned forward, apparently engrossed in the show of women parading in front of him. "They're all beautiful, are they not?"

I huffed in irritation. "I have not yet seen the one I plan to take as my own."

"Sometimes it's difficult to choose just one beauty from such a bounty." Zont's tone suggested he thought he was agreeing with me. I didn't correct him. Better to keep my plans secret for now—I wouldn't want the Special Ops officer to decide he wanted my mate for his own.

When I didn't respond, he glanced at me. "It might be easier to choose from a wide selection in person. Perhaps we should make our way to the arena, instead of sitting up here in the video room?"

I blinked. "I didn't realize that was allowed."

Zont raised an eyebrow and his tone turned conspiratorial. "We're Special Ops. We don't play by the rules."

He'd included me in that group. I liked that. With a grin, I stood. "Then by all means, let's go find our brides."

Returning my smile, Zont said, "Your first Special Ops mission. I'm delighted to have you onboard."

We made our way out of the vid chamber, Zont leading. "Do you know where the arena is?" I asked.

"Actually, yes. I managed to get a complete map of the station before I headed this way."

Of course he had. "I should have known."

Zont flashed his ready smile. "Never enter enemy territory without some idea of the terrain. Basic engagement rules."

I nodded. He was right—even first-year cadets knew that much. If I hadn't been so shocked by my sudden change in fortune, I might have considered doing the same thing. It was, after all, rather like what I'd done when I attempted to reconnoiter the Bridal Suites.

He led us down a series of corridors that wound through the station, past the Promenade and into the workers' quarters, an area that didn't even try to hide its utilitarian nature. The station walls there were unadorned gray metal, the rivets holding it in place out in plain sight. "Are you sure this is the way?" I finally asked.

"It is if we don't want to get intercepted and sent back to cool our heels in the Grooms' Vid Room." He turned a corner and opened an unmarked door to a back stairwell. "No one uses these unless there's an emergency that shuts down station power. This will take us to the arena level." He swung around the metal handrail and began taking the steps down two at a time.

About thirty flights later, we came to the bottom of the stairwell. Zont held up one hand, gesturing for me to wait. I found myself slipping into battle mode—perfectly quiet, every sense on high alert. When Zont waved me forward, I slipped through the open door and slid along the wall behind a high screen Zont followed, then moved in front of me.

From the other side of the screen came the chatter of dozens of female voices, ranging from husky to almost shrill, blending together to create waves of sound that washed over me. I paused to soak it in, then inhaled deeply to take in a feminine, almost floral scent.

A particular kind of euphoria suffused my entire body, the kind I usually associated with winning a battle. A chemical release that kept Khanavai warriors joyful when we fought.

And this was a kind of war. They might be called the Bride Games, but really, we were battling for the chance to be united with human females who were perfect for us. I'd been told, but never before believed, that the battle-joy also served to cement mate bonds.

I was beginning to think it might be true.

Zont moved past the screen, which was replaced by blue curtains, almost a match for the color of my skin. He motioned for me to survey the territory, then pointed at a small gap in the curtains. It was a smart move, as the curtain would provide better camouflage for me than it would for him, with his bright pink coloring.

I moved closer to peer through the gap.

Human women moved across the arena floor, some alone, others in groups of two or three. Across the enormous space, I saw several lined up to give their initial interviews, while others sat in tiny chairs around equally small tables, chatting and eating. I could smell the sweet aroma of fruit mixed in with the scent of the women themselves.

The femininity was almost overwhelming.

I was about to pull back and report to Zont when a small, pale hand ripped the curtain back, and I came face-to-face with the very woman I'd been searching for.

CHAPTER FIVE

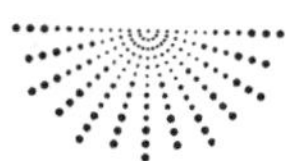

NATALIE

I don't know how long I slept. It felt like more than an hour, though it still wasn't long enough. A sharp knock at the door woke me, and I sat up groggily.

Two aliens entered the room—one Poltien and another, much taller alien whose species I didn't recognize. This one was obviously female, with two large breasts in the normal human spot, and what looked like a third one between and slightly below the others. She had silvery hair bound on top of her head with twisted strands falling to her shoulders in complicated loops, and matching silver tattoos across her otherwise perfectly white skin.

"Finding bras must be a total bitch," I muttered.

Ignoring my commentary, the silvery alien rushed into the room. "I'm sorry we're late," she said, taking both hands in mine and pulling me up off the bed as she eyed me up and down assessingly. "Hm. Not bad," she muttered, brushing one long fingertip across my cheek.

I scowled at her. "Not bad?"

She blinked. “Oh, I’m so sorry. I meant your skin tone only. I was thinking about what kind of makeup we’d need for the cameras. You, my dear, are lovely. Of course.”

I rolled my eyes. I was fairly certain that after drinking in a bar, vomiting in a transporter room, showering in a weird alien device that didn’t seem to use actual water, and falling into bed without so much as brushing my hair, I was decidedly less than “lovely.”

But whatever. I wasn’t here to catch an alien mate. I was playing to lose.

And if that meant looking terrible, I was fine with it. “Good,” I said aloud. “I would rather avoid wearing any makeup at all, thanks.”

Silvery-chick blinked at me and I realized for the first time that even her pupils were silver. “Are you certain?”

“Absolutely.”

She and the Poltien traded glances. “We’ll see how you feel about it after your first interview, my dear,” the Poltien said.

Good enough for now. If I was lucky, I’d blow my introductory interview and be home on the next outbound shuttle.

”Let’s get you dressed in something more appropriate, shall we?” the Poltien continued.

I glanced down at the white sundress I’d pulled out of the white closet. I hadn’t even looked in the mirror, but I was pretty sure it was completely sheer. Otherwise, I might have tried to keep it, too. ”Fine. Let’s see what you have.”

With a wide smile, the silvery alien opened the door and wheeled in a garment rack with dresses in practically every color available. I’d watched the Bride Games often enough to know what came next. First, they’d take me to the arena to be interviewed. And then they’d whisk me off for a “makeover,” alien-style. I’d never realized how much of the makeup and wardrobe elements were planned behind the scenes first, though.

"What are your names?" I asked as the two conferred over the clothing.

"I'm Drindl," the silvery alien said, pronouncing her name with a sound like a ringing bell in a way I was sure I'd never be able to reproduce.

"And I am called Plofnid," the Poltien said, its nostril-braid waving as it spoke. I'd always wondered what the significance of the hair from one nostril might be, but the Bride Games broadcast never focused on the various assistants beyond an occasional interview about what they did for the brides or which brides and grooms they were rooting for.

"I think this one," Drindl said, holding up a sleek burgundy evening outfit with a split skirt and a fitted bodice. "You'll be able to move well in it, and it will accentuate your curves nicely." She glanced back and forth between the dress and me. "The highlights in your hair will pick up the color, too. It's perfect."

My hands reached out of their own accord to touch the silky fabric. She was absolutely right. I would look stunning in it.

"No," I announced. "I hate it."

I didn't, of course. But I didn't want to win this damn reality show.

Playing to lose, I reminded myself.

I moved to the garment rack and began flipping past the dresses, muttering to myself the entire time. "No, no, no..." Then I paused. I held my arm up next to the dress to see how the color looked against my skin. Then I pulled it off the rack entirely, gazed down the skirt, checked out the bodice, and finally held it up triumphantly. "This is the one."

Drindl and Plofnid gasped, covering their mouths with their hands and glancing at each other in dismay.

The dress was a bright, turquoise blue—similar to the skin color of the guy I'd run into earlier, I thought, but then banished the idea from my mind. The fitted skirt flared out at the bottom in a mermaid style that would be virtually impossible to walk in. The sweetheart neckline had a ruffle made out of the same material that flared at the bottom.

And the rest of it—every bit that wasn't ruffle or flare—was covered in turquoise sequins that flashed a hot pink whenever I brushed against them.

It was perfectly hideous.

And it was definitely made for a blonde Barbie-doll type with a tan. It would clash with my dark hair and pale skin in ways that would make Jas wonder if I'd lost my mind.

Assuming she was back home watching on TV—and I found myself hoping she would be. Tears welled up in my eyes as I thought of my life back on Earth.

Drindl, catching sight of my tears, mistook the reason for them. "Oh, darling," she called out in her bell-like voice. "There's no need to cry. If you love the dress that much, you should absolutely wear it."

"Oh, yes," Plofnid echoed. "Let's try it on you and get it fitted."

I turned to hide my smile from them.

The two aliens got me into the hideous dress and tucked and pinned until it fit me to their satisfaction.

"Now," Drindl said, "you'll find your interview suit on the right-hand side of your closet. If you'll put it on, we can style your hair, and you'll be ready to head to the arena."

I put one hand to my head. As I suspected, my dark curls had gone totally frizzy as I slept. "I love my hair exactly as it is."

I saw Drindl swallow as she took in the wild corkscrews of hair sticking out in all direction. "I see."

"The natural look is in these days." I spoke as if confiding a great secret. Drindl's skin turned even paler, if possible. "No," I continued, opening the closet door, "let me just pull on this interview suit and I'll be ready to go."

In the closet, there were actually three suits—one black, one white, and one a dark blue, all cut to flatter the brides' figures. I knew from viewing the Bride Games all these years that contestants usually wore the white or black one during non-Game activities.

Play to lose.

I was starting to enjoy it as a motto.

I pulled the white one out. "This," I said happily, pulling on the skirt and then the jacket.

"Let me at least give you a little blush," Drindl said faintly.

"No. I want the Khanavai warriors to know exactly what they'll be getting with me," I replied cheerfully, digging around in the bottom of the closet until I found a pair of ugly, clompy boots.

Plofnid whimpered in distress.

"I'm ready. Let's go." When neither of my stylists moved, I swept past them, out the door and into the hall, my boots making satisfying thumps as I walked. "Which way?"

Drindl gathered herself with visible effort and joined me. "Down the hall and to the right. Step into the first chute you see. It will take you to the arena. Vos is interviewing the brides there. You'll see the line. Just join in at the end."

"Great." I smiled a huge smile and waved goodbye, then turned and left as Plofnid joined Drindl in the hall and the two watched me, their expressions forlorn.

The chute looked like a giant version of those tubes at bank drive-throughs, and it swept me downward as soon as I stepped into it. My stomach dropped and I swallowed against another bout of nausea.

I can do this.

When the opaque cylinder circled open again, I stepped out into a giant, high-ceilinged room with dozens of women and giant seats rising on one side of it, like a deranged stadium in Wonderland.

I glanced around the room, looking for Vos. But before I saw the host of the show, I caught a glimpse of what looked like a face just withdrawing behind a turquoise blue curtain.

Without even thinking about it, I rushed over and yanked the curtain back, revealing the same alien I'd run into in the hallway earlier.

"I knew it was you!" The bright blue alien blinked those purple eyes once as he stared at me, apparently startled to be caught watching us.

Then, before I could say anything else, he reached out, wrapped an arm around my waist, and dragged me up so my chest was pressed against his and my heavy boots dangled in the air.

Without a word, he pressed his lips to mine in a kiss.

CHAPTER SIX

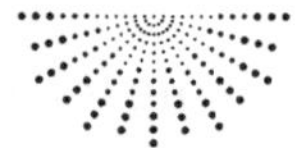

CAV

I pulled the human woman behind the curtain with me, letting it fall completely closed behind her. Her lips against mine felt as soft as they looked.

Slowly, I began moving my mouth against hers, running my tongue lightly over the seam of her lips until they parted, allowing me entry. At the taste of her, sugary-sweet and slightly minty, I growled deep in my throat, a sound of possession. If her mouth was this delectable, how might the rest of her taste?

Her body molded to mine perfectly, and I slipped one arm down to clasp her ass, its fullness filling my hand. I wanted her closer, needed her skin against mine.

She placed her palms against my chest, the touch of them cool against my overheated skin.

If I'd been able to, I would have taken her there, made her mine, completed my ownership of her so no other warrior would ever touch her.

For a heartbeat, everything was perfect.

Then she kicked me.

The thump against my knee sent a sharp pain shooting up and down my leg. Her boots were thicker than I would have anticipated, and my knees buckled with the pain—luckily, since she followed up that kick with others. I drew back in surprise, blinking and tightening my hold on her.

"What the Zagrodnian hells, woman?" I hissed.

"Put me down, you...you blue beast!" she practically shouted. "What do you mean, what the hell? That's my line." By now, she was kicking with both feet, and about half her shots were landing, so I dropped her to the floor—but I didn't let go of her. Now that I had her, I was never letting her go.

Well, not until she used those inordinately heavy boots to stomp on my feet.

Not that she was likely to hurt me while I wore my dress uniform. My boots were bigger, stronger, and better fortified even than the ones she wore.

She figured that out quickly enough, and changed her aim once again, this time in an attempt to connect with my shins. She wasn't battle-trained, though, and telegraphed her next move clearly enough that I was able to dance out of the way without letting go of her waist.

A snort behind me reminded me of Zont's presence, and I glared back at him. "Why don't you do something useful?"

Zont covered his mouth with one hand, his eyes dancing above it. "Looks like you have everything under control, brother" he managed to gasp out, his eyes streaming with suppressed laughter.

"I said, let. Me. GO." The woman pushed her palms against my chest, straining as far back over my imprisoning arm as she could.

That kiss had been perfect. Why was she so upset?

A horrible thought hit me. "Promise not to run away if I let you go?"

"I'm not going to promise that."

Wait. Was she somehow...not interested in me?

"Tell me your name. If you tell me your name, I'll let you go," I said.

She glared at me suspiciously but finally answered. "Natalie Ferguson." As I released her from my iron grip, she muttered, almost as if to herself, "It's not like you couldn't find out, anyway."

I rolled her name around in my mouth, tasting the texture of the unfamiliar combination of sounds. "Nat-alief-ergu-son."

The look she flashed me was as full of venom as a Tarble's attack-pouch. "Just Natalie will do."

Natalie. Her name was almost as lush as she was. "It's beautiful."

She puffed out her cheeks and blew out a breath as she shook her head. I hadn't taken any courses in Earther non-verbal communication, so I wasn't sure if this was a way of expressing thanks for the sentiment. If so, her expression didn't convey the same message, and I'd been given to understand that human and Khanavai facial expressions were remarkably similar.

Without another word, she spun around and marched through the break in the curtains, out to the main arena. I moved to follow her, but Zont put a restraining hand on my arm.

"We're less likely to get kicked out if we watch from the stands," he suggested.

I peered out through the curtains. "Looks like she's headed over for her interview."

Zont snickered. "Then by all means, let's go watch."

His amusement at my decision to take the human Natalie as a mate left me scowling as I followed him to the stands, staying behind the curtain as long as possible. After that, we simply strode across the arena floor as if we belonged there. No one asked any questions as we made our way to the section in the stands nearest the interview area.

"Will we be able to hear her?" I asked as I dropped into a seat next to Zont.

"Standard audio-visual mode," he said aloud, and a holo-viewscreen activated in front of his seat. I followed his example, delighted to discover that the Bride Games had installed the latest technology. Not surprising, since the Bride Games were the most popular entertainment in Khanavai space.

I waved my hand to move through the channels focused on the arena below until I came to the interview section, then split the screen between the actual interviews and an image of the bride contestants in line for their turn.

My Natalie stood at the end of the line, arms crossed and a fierce expression on her face.

She's more beautiful than an Anderovian Nebula.

Zont glanced at me. "Decided on that one, I see."

"She's mine." I spoke simply, but I knew it to be the absolute truth.

"I'm not sure she's aware of that yet." Zont's tone was mild, but I could hear the laughter bubbling up under his voice.

"It doesn't matter if she knows it yet or not. By the end of the Bride Games, I will make sure she knows it."

"Hmm."

I glanced over at my companion, but he was studiously examining some of the other brides in line. I decided to let his skeptical noise pass without comment. "See anyone you like?"

He shrugged. "They're all lovely. But no, there isn't yet one who's caught my eye."

A moment of sympathy flashed through me. It must be difficult for him to be choosing a bride without knowing for certain which one he wanted.

The line inched forward as the next bride moved up to be interviewed. I tapped my foot impatiently, then realized I was echoing my Natalie's impatience as she stood waiting her turn.

Without warning, my screen went blank for a moment. When it came back on, it showed Vos Klavoii standing in front of an image of an Earther cityscape. "Warriors and women," he began, "Earthers and Khanavai, we have an exciting new development in this year's Bride Games. Apparently, one of our contestants has run. That's right—for the first time in all the years we've been holding the lottery, a bride has, as the Earthers sometimes say, gone on the lam."

A gasp went up at the announcement and the brides on the arena floor began chattering among themselves.

"A runner?" Zont looked thoughtful. "How did she manage that?"

On the screen, Vos continued talking as the screen behind him changed to show a pretty Earther with long blonde hair, dark green eyes, and an engaging smile. "Amelia Rivers is now a wanted fugitive on Earth. She's originally from Dallas, Texas, but was most recently seen in Las Vegas, Nevada." He pitched his voice a little lower. "For those Khanavai watching, that's in the United States, a country in what the Earthers call the North American continent."

Get on with it. I want to see Natalie's interview.

I tried to contain my impatience as Vos continued talking, outlining several other facts about the runaway bride.

"Las Vegas," Zont said slowly. "Isn't that the pleasure city?"

Who cared? It was almost Natalie's turn to be interviewed.

I sighed in relief when Vos finally stopped talking and the screen went back to its previous view.

And then my Natalie stepped up to the interview space.

CHAPTER SEVEN

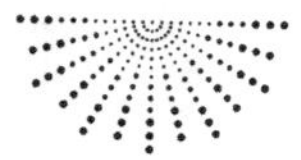

NATALIE

My mind was still reeling from the information that a bride had run when I stepped up in front of the giant green-screen background.

"And now let's give Lottery Bride winner Natalie Ferguson a warm Khanavai welcome!" Vos Klavoii's cheerful voice followed by the canned recording of a bunch of male voices roaring almost cut through the strange mental haze I found myself in. I gave a distracted nod to the host.

"So tell us, Natalie," he continued, "what are you thinking right now as you join the Bride Games?"

I answered without thinking. "I'm wishing I had thought to run."

My response shocked Vos into an unusual-for-him silence. He spluttered for a second before finally saying, "But becoming a Khanavai warrior's bride is an honor."

"For other women, maybe," I shot back. "But I liked my life back home. I want to finish my college degree, get a job, and then maybe find someone to settle down with. Maybe. I'm not sure I want to get married at all." The longer I spoke, the quieter the arena got.

Shit. I probably shouldn't be saying all this. But I needed to get it out.

"What about your planet's treaty with the Khanavai? Their agreement to protect Earth?" Vos's voice dropped, became more intimate. I knew it was a calculated move, an example of showmanship designed to lure me into his confidence, but I found myself leaning toward him, anyway. "What about the warriors who are willing to give their lives to keep you safe? Don't they deserve some reward?"

At his last line, I jerked away from him again. "I'm not some prize to be given away on a whim."

Vos laughed aloud, turning back to face the camera. "You heard it from her, warriors and women. Natalie Ferguson is no prize."

I glared at him for a moment, then simply walked off the small set. Anger flared through me at him, at the situation, at all Khanavai in general. When I saw Drindl and Plofnid waiting for me, I scowled at them both. Drindl began fluttering and singing out instructions in her bell tones, but I ignored her and kept walking toward the nearest elevator tube.

I was almost there when something drew my attention to the stands, a prickling on the back of my neck telling me someone's eyes were on me. There, in the seats, sat the blue alien who'd kissed me. He watched me intently, his intense gaze holding mine for a long second until I managed to break the connection.

What the hell was his deal, anyway?

That's when my two handlers caught up with me.

"We're headed to the makeover stage now," Plofnid told me, reaching up to take my hand and pull me toward the transportation tube.

"Who is that?" I asked, jerking my chin toward the stands. "The blue one."

"Oh," Drindl sighed. "That's Cav Adredoni. One of the grooms. He's a Lieutenant in the Earth Defense Force. One of this season's most eligible bachelors."

Drindl wrapped one arm around my shoulder. "It'll be okay," she said, her high voice consoling. "You'll be able to overcome any negative impression you made during your interview."

I scowled but didn't bother answering. If I'd made a bad impression, I was glad of it.

Not that anything in the blue alien's expression suggested he was put off by my words.

I shoved the thought down and kept walking.

It's not like I care what he thinks, anyway.

THE MAKEOVER ROOM, like the small bedroom I'd been given earlier, was decorated in varying shades of white, with lots of lace and other bridalesque touches. The only color in the room came from a series of posters featuring Khanavai warriors posing behind ovals featuring the Bride Lottery logo.

I rubbed my temples with the fingers of both hands, hoping to scrub away the incipient headache threatening to form. I flopped down in the makeup chair Drindl indicated. "Fine. Let's do this."

In the mirror in front of me, I saw Drindl and Plofnid cast each other hopeless glances. I almost hoped they saw me as unredeemable. If they couldn't do anything with me, then maybe the Khanavai warriors would feel the same way and I could go the fuck home sooner rather than later.

I brushed my hand over my eyes, willing away the angry thoughts as I sat down in front of the mirror at the Earth-style hair and makeup station.

Of course, it wasn't really a mirror. I'd seen enough Bride Games to know that it was recording everything that happened. The grooms would be interviewed, and everything would be cut and mixed in post-production to highlight the drama of a new group of brides being chosen as mates for the Khanavai warriors.

If I thought it would do any good, I'd pick a fight with one of the other brides.

But I knew better.

Hell, after my interview, I was probably short-listed as a final candidate. I knew better than to draw attention to myself. The best way to disappear from the games was to be boring. Bland. A giant nothing.

Apparently, the Khanavai warriors liked their women feisty.

Yuck.

Behind me, Drindl and Plofnid conferred quietly—probably trying to figure out how to make that horrific dress of mine look good despite my best efforts.

"We are ready," Drindl finally trilled out in her Tinkerbell voice. Standing behind me, she pulled my hair back out of my face, showcasing my face. I looked pale, a slight greenish tinge to my skin. Nothing like a Khanavai's bright turquoise color, of course. Just enough to make me look unhealthy.

She tapped a few buttons on the control panel attached to the cart beside her, and an image of the sparkly turquoise blue dress revolved in the top right corner of the mirror-screen as Vos's voice narrated.

"Natalie Ferguson has chosen this mermaid-cut dress in Khanavai blue by our very own designer Krelix," he said. I noticed he left out the usual accolades about how gorgeous I would look in it, and I had to push down a snicker. "Drindl," Vos continued, "What will you and Plofnid be doing in your makeover?"

Plofnid pulled up a short step stool to be able to reach the top of my head. "We'll be adding a wash to her hair, both to bring out the shine and to tame these wild curls of her," the small alien said.

"And I don't want to give away too much," Drindl said, "but we'll be giving her a dramatic evening look."

"Well," Vos said in his deep, smarmy tones, "I can't wait to see what you do with the woman who wishes she'd run."

I rolled my eyes. I was never going to get past that, was I?

With a flourish, Drindl spun me around so I couldn't stare miserably into the mirror-cam any longer. "Let's get going!" she said, and I realized she was as much of a showperson as Vos.

"Sounds great," I muttered, and Plofnid threw an irritated glance in my direction.

So what? Could I help it if I wasn't thrilled about being stolen away from my home planet and dropped into my idea of hell?

Still, it wasn't the stylists' fault. I should probably manage to be nicer to them.

Maybe.

I blew out a breath as they rolled me over to a hair-washing station, dropped the back of my chair down, and settled me over a basin.

This could be worse, I tried to console myself. *I could be here hoping to win.*

CHAPTER EIGHT

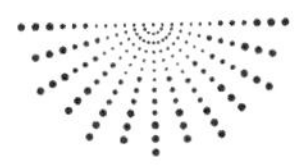

CAV

M*y mate wishes she had run.*

I couldn't get the thought out of my head. Even when Vos Klavoii called all the grooms together to go over the Bride Games schedule, I found myself worrying about my chosen mate's words.

Vos had gathered us in the arena stands, where we would stay during the brides' first official act of the Bride Games—The Bridal Pageant. In previous years, I'd heard that it was based on some old Earther tradition, a beauty pageant. It seemed unnecessary to me, but there were other grooms who had not yet seen a bride they hoped to mate with.

After the pageant, the brides would retire for the evening, during which time their tracking software would be upgraded to read their every emotion and physical reaction. While that was going on, each groom would mark his top three bride choices, and if their DNA was a match, the grooms would be allowed to participate in the games in order to win the right to mate with the bride.

Really, it was as much a competition for us as it was for them, though apparently the brides didn't see it that way.

Bored with Vos's droning on about the rules of the Bride Games—something that every Khanavai warrior knew by heart—I turned on my seat screen and began flipping through the brides in the database.

Three. That was the magic number. Only rarely did a groom fail to make a genetic match with at least one of his chosen brides.

Of course, the best matches were those between True Mates. Not everyone experienced that, however—some simply made a life the best way they could. Even that wasn't so bad once they engaged in mating sex. It was entirely possible to become something close to True Mates through the binding ceremony and sexual bonding time that came afterward.

Human brides were particularly susceptible to creating a True Mates bond with the Khanavai.

Not that I needed the bonding sex. I already knew who my true mate was. I flipped to her screen, listening to her melodious voice as I replayed the moment that had let the entire universe know that she had no interest in mating with a Khanavai warrior.

Natalie Ferguson.

"You're completely set on her, aren't you?" Zont asked from his seat beside me, and I realized I'd said my mate's name aloud.

I leaned over to take a look at his screen to see which brides he'd been perusing.

"Amelia Rivers?" I asked, one brow raised in surprise. "The runaway bride? Can you even choose her?"

Zont grinned. "She's still in the program. And she's the one I want."

"You're going to have a quark's eye of a time of it with that one." My chosen mate might wish she had run—but at least she hadn't actually done it. "How do you know for sure that you're compatible?"

"I have my ways. I pulled her DNA last night, and we are a perfect match. I've put in a request with Command Central to allow me to hunt her as part of this year's Bride Games." He grinned, flashing the sharp canines his region was known for.

My eyes widened. "That's quite an effort to put into simply getting a mate."

Zont rubbed his hands together. "I do enjoy a challenge."

"Maybe I'm not right for Special Ops, after all."

Zont's roar of laughter interrupted Vos Klavoii's instructions, and the host glared up at the two of us. Zont waved an apology, but the quelling look Vos gave him didn't stop the other warrior from leaning over to me to say, "You've chosen the only other Earther female who announced that she doesn't want to be here. You cannot tell me that you don't like a challenge, too, brother."

"When do you leave for Earth?"

"When the pageant ends, Vos will interview me. As soon as that's done, I can take a shuttle down to the planet." A gleam in his eyes suggested he couldn't wait to get going.

I didn't blame him.

The longer we waited for the brides to show up to do their pageant, the more irritable I became. All I wanted to do was get on with seducing my mate. Preferably without the possibility of any other warrior adding her to his list of three.

I had finally stopped looking at the other brides' profiles. I had known from the moment her scent had led me to her in the brides' quarters that she was the only one here I could possibly mate with.

It was Natalie Ferguson...or no one.

The thought sent a spike of rage racing through my chest.

No. No other warrior would end up mated to my Natalie.

I blew out a breath, trying to funnel my anger into constructive planning. The schedule for this set of games was particularly evocative. Every year, the Games Commission worked to make the contests more sensual. The more readings they could take from the contestants, the better the final matches would be.

"At last," Zont muttered beside me, and I glanced up to see the brides gathering near the entrance. I hadn't even noticed when Vos had stopped explaining the games and left to host the upcoming pageant.

"There are almost four hundred potential mates this year," I reminded him. "You can't leave yet."

"No, but the sooner they get started, the sooner it will be over, and I can go capture my own mate." Zont's eager expression brought a smile to my face. I knew exactly how he felt.

The pageant itself was simple. Each bride stepped up onto the stage, stated her name, and added any skills she had that might be interesting to a Khanavai warrior. Then she turned slowly, allowing the grooms to examine her and giving the DNA scanners time to both take her measure and send her scent floating over the grooms. Because no matter how beautiful a female might be, everyone knew that in the end, our scent receptors often recognized our mates before our brains did.

As the old Khanavai saying went, the cock follows where the nose leads.

Which reminded me. "What if," I asked Zont, "you get to Earth and discover your chosen bride smells all wrong?"

The other warrior shrugged. "Then I'll bring her back to take her rightful place in the games." His gaze shifted to his screen, where

Amelia Rivers' image still floated. "But it won't," he added quietly. "I am as certain that she is mine as if I had scented her already."

I couldn't help but nod. Everything about my Natalie had drawn me to her. The way she smelled like Vardish spun sweets, the lush curve of her hips, the heated touch of her lips against mine.

The way she kicked you when you picked her up to kiss her?

I shushed the voice inside my head. But it continued whispering to me, telling me as each woman moved up to the stage and then departed through the exit on the other side that my task might not be as simple as I hoped.

My internal voice's quiet undermining of my confidence continued until I finally caught sight of Natalie moving through the door and onto the stage.

My eyes widened, taking in every last detail of her pageant-wear.

"She chose Khanavai blue," I said aloud, my heart leaping in my chest at the honor she'd done me. Her dress matched my skin tones perfectly.

"And a lot of sparkles," Zont added drily, holding his hand up in front of his eyes as if warding off the flashes of light arcing off her dress.

"Even her skin is dusted in Khanavai blue. And her hair, too." I knew I sounded overawed, but I couldn't help it. Her stylists had pulled her dark curls atop her head in a design like a Khanavai jungle bloom and dusted it in the colors of my people.

"With even more sparkles." Zont met my glare with a grin.

"She's perfect." I longed to fist the flower of her hair in my hand, then pull it from its careful updo, leaving it tousled.

As she stepped up to the microphone and leaned in, I waited to hear her beautiful voice again.

"Natalie Ferguson," she said in a clipped tone, then stepped back again.

"Anything you'd like to add to that?" Vos asked jovially. She simply shook her head, her lips pressed tightly together. If I hadn't known better, I would have said she looked angry.

Okay. So she didn't sound as breathless as she had either of the times I'd spoken to her.

Did she really wish she had run?

No, I reassured myself. That couldn't possibly be true. Otherwise, she wouldn't have chosen to honor me—and by extension, all Khanavai—by wearing a dress in my color. Moreover, if the information on my screen was correct, it was a dress that had been designed by a stylist from my own planet.

As she slowly turned around on the stage, our screens sent out what was supposed to be her scent, sending it wafting across our seats. It was certainly close. But not close enough. I would have known the difference anywhere.

Soon, I promised silently, willing her to meet my eyes as she moved off the stage.

Soon, we will be together.

CHAPTER NINE

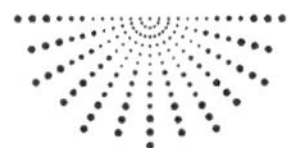

NATALIE

"The Khanavai Spanking Ceremony?" I gesticulated wildly at the schedule I was reading, waving my hand through the words floating in front of me, practically screeching as I did so. "What the ever-loving hell is *that*?"

Drindl and Plofnid glanced at one another, the Poltien's nostril-braid quivering as it blew out a resigned breath. "I knew you weren't going to like that," Plofnid muttered.

"Come eat your breakfast, and we'll tell you all about it." Drindl waved one elegant, long-fingered hand toward the rolling table they'd pushed into my room.

"That's nothing I've ever seen on the Bride Games before." I scowled at the all-white place settings in front of me as I took a seat.

"It's one of several new additions to this year's games." Plofnid moved around the table, removing covers and revealing enough food for four women.

Or maybe one Khanavai warrior.

An image of the gorgeous blue warrior—Cav Adredoni, I reminded myself—flashed in front of me, and for a hot second, I imagined what it would be like to share a meal like this with him.

Quit it, Natalie. Remember, you're playing to lose.

Well. That should be easy enough now. Any man who thought he could spank me was going to find out immediately that he'd picked the wrong Earth girl to lay hands on.

"Did you just growl?" Drindl asked, her eyes widening as she watched me pick up a croissant.

"Did the matches come through this morning?" I had seen enough of the Bride Games to know the basic pattern. Arrival interview, pageant, matching, several games...and then the final round.

I pushed aside what I knew about the final round. I was not going to have mating sex with any of these brutes.

Not even the big blue one?

Again, I shushed my inner voice.

"That was definitely a growl," Plofnid added. "Perhaps some coffee? It's direct from Earth."

A ping sounded at the viewscreen pretending to be a window out onto an Earth ocean this morning—a view chosen, I suspected, to help keep me calm.

"There are the matches now," Drindl sang out, her incipient frown smoothing away as she pushed a few buttons. "Oh, look!" Clapping her hands in delight, she gestured at the screen. "Not one, but three Khanavai warriors have chosen you as a potential mate."

My stomach dropped at her words, the pastry in my mouth turning to a lump I couldn't swallow as I stared up at the screen. Taking a quick swallow of orange juice to wash it down, I stood and moved to stand next to the stylist.

Given the way he'd picked me up and kissed me—*without my consent, dammit!*—I had expected Cav Adredoni to try to match with me. But I had hoped for a genetic mismatch.

Yeah, right, the annoying voice in my head snickered. *Don't forget, you kissed him back.*

I glanced longingly at the butter knife next to my coffee, wondering if lobotomizing myself would shut up the voice.

Not sharp enough.

No. With my luck, I'd end up with nothing but that voice in my mind.

With a sigh, I pulled up the profile of one of the other two Khanavai warriors who had successfully matched with me.

The Khanavai coloring had something to do with the regions they'd originated from on their homeworld, but I had no idea which ones were which—only that they came in a rainbow of shades, all so bright they almost glowed.

The first one was Eldron Gendovi, and he was bright red with dark black hair. His skin tones reminded me of a Mustang convertible a high school boyfriend had rented to take me to the prom my junior year. Like all the Khanavai warriors I'd ever seen, Eldron was absolutely ripped. He wore—or rather, barely wore—one of their skimpy kilt-like uniforms, the sash across his chest covered in some kind of writing. He stood with his muscular arms crossed over his cherry-colored chest, gazing into the distance as if staring down an enemy.

His profile included his picture, some statistics that I didn't understand, and a long list of battles won.

Covering my mouth with one hand, I flipped to the next image. Tiziani Mencono. This guy was banana yellow and completely bald.

Thinner than either Eldron or Cav, he was still so big and muscular that he'd outclass any human male anywhere on Earth. For a brief second, an image of what he must look like naked flashed through my mind.

"Banana," I said from behind the hand still covering my mouth.

"Pardon?" Plofnid asked, raising one eyebrow.

"Banana," I said again, imagining what a bright yellow man with an erection might look like. Laughter bubbled up in my chest and spilled out, pushing past my hand and hanging in the air around us as my stylists stared at me blankly.

Their expressions only made me laugh harder, until I was doubled over clutching my stomach, tears of laughter streaming from my eyes.

I tried to sit down, aiming for the edge of the bed, but I almost missed—so instead, I allowed myself to slide down to the floor, still howling and laughing.

As suddenly as it had started, though, my laughing fit stopped, and I was left with only the tears. They were quickly followed by huge, gulping sobs. Plofnid and Drindl fluttered around, trying to find ways to get me to stop crying, but I couldn't.

This is really happening.

There were women this morning who had not been matched by any Khanavai warriors. They were going home tonight, back to their lives. Back to Earth.

I wasn't. In fact, there was a good chance I would never get to go home. Not for good, anyway.

I had seen the Bride Games often enough to know that being matched to three of them was a bad sign. My chances of ending up permanently attached to an alien had not just tripled. No. After the matching, the odds of being mated went up exponentially.

I was now...I did some quick math in my head...*twenty-seven times* more likely to end up mated to a Khanavai warrior than I had been when I set foot on this station.

I am so fucked.

And not in a good way.

IT TOOK Plofnid and Drindl almost an hour to wipe away all the traces of my morning tears—and that was after I stood in the shower for as long as they'd allow.

Now I sat in front of the camera-mirror again, this time quizzing them about the "spanking ceremony" I was going to have to endure.

"It's not as terrible as it sounds," Drindl tried to reassure me, her crystalline eyes widening earnestly.

Plofnid snorted derisively, sending its nostril-braid swinging.

Drindl drew herself up to her full height, offended at her partner's skepticism. "It is a mating ritual with a long history among the Khanavai."

"Humans don't even spank children as punishment any longer," I said with a scowl.

"I should hope not!" Drindl's cheeks turned an odd shade of gray—her version of blushing, I decided as she continued speaking. "This is a form of Khanavai foreplay. It's not meant to punish or even as correction."

Foreplay? Oh, hell no.

"It's not often used for punishment, anyway," Plofnid added.

I knew it!

"Then why do it?" I asked.

"It's a reminder of the bride's position in the relationship." Plofnid moved around to pull a brush through my hair.

"Her position? What—ass in the air?"

Drindl tittered at my comment, her tinkling laugh almost infectious. I couldn't help but smile.

"Seriously," I continued. "There's nothing about spanking that isn't degrading. It's antiquated and demeaning."

And maybe a little kinky, the traitorous voice inside my head added.

I ignored it, just as Drindl and Plofnid ignored the comments I made aloud. Finally, I heaved a sigh. "Okay. What is my role in this? And how will it work with three matches?"

"First, you'll be meeting your matches for a luncheon. A chance to get to know one another. Then you'll be expected to undergo the spanking ceremony with each suitor. There will, of course, be an appropriate resting period between each one."

"Oh, God," I groaned. "Today is going to suck."

"Not at all," Drindl assured me. "Sucking comes later in the games."

I whipped my head around to stare at her, and she let out the bell-peal of the belly-laugh she'd been holding in until I realized she was joking.

Dropping my elbows to the counter in front of me, I stared at my reflection. Even knowing that I was speaking straight into the camera—and therefore to all the viewers back on Earth who were hanging on every detail of the Bride Games—I had to remind myself of my goal.

"I am playing to lose. I *will* be going back home."

Drindl and Plofnid shot skeptical glances at each other.

Fine. They could think whatever they wanted. I'd show them.

When all this was over, I'd be going home again.

No matter what my handlers believed.

CHAPTER TEN

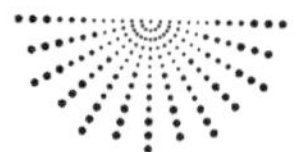

CAV

Luncheon with Natalie.

I was practically salivating at the idea of it. Not of the food. Of my mate. I couldn't wait to be close enough to her to draw in her scent again. Touch her skin. Run my fingers through her hair. My cock grew hard at the mere thought.

But my next thought put a damper on my rising excitement. There would be two other Khanavai warriors there. Warriors who believed they might be able to lure my mate from me.

Worthless sandworms.

I'd show them.

But more importantly, I'd show her—show her that she was meant to be mine, and I hers. My Natalie. My mate.

And then the spanking ceremony. Oh, gods and goddesses, I couldn't stop thinking about that. It was the first time that particular Khanavai tradition had ever been incorporated into the Bride Games—apparently out of respect for human sensibilities.

But the other two Khanavai who had matched with her would be allowed to touch her. Place their hands on her.

A growl rumbled in my throat, my ancient warrior genes bringing out my competitive side.

"No." I spoke the word aloud, even though there was no one else to hear me.

The other warriors could not have her. I couldn't allow it. Natalie Ferguson was mine, and that was all there was to it. I simply had to make sure she realized it.

But I was beginning to realize that even if she felt the same attraction toward me that I felt for her, she wasn't as ready to accept it as I was.

I had to laugh at myself. After all, I had started out not wanting a mate at all. Now, I couldn't think of anything more important to me.

The realization froze me in place on my bed in my Grooms' Quarters room, where I'd been flipping through the schedule of events I'd just received.

Nothing is more important to me than winning my mate.

Was that really true?

It was, I realized. Even earning a place at the ops program was no longer as important to me as making sure I left the Bride Games with my mate by my side.

A mate who didn't want to be here at all.

I found myself rubbing my eyes in frustration. Yes, the judges would be awarding score points during the games. But the final decision rested with the brides. They could not be forced to stay. *Natalie* could not be forced to stay.

She could, however, be wooed.

That was exactly what I am going to do. No matter what it takes.

Before I decided on an exact course of action, though, I needed to get a better sense of my competition. I pulled up the list of matches and examined them more closely.

Eldron Gendovi was a former commander in the military's ground forces. His red skin tones suggested his ancestors came from the mountainous regions of Khanav Prime, and his people were known for being fierce fighters with hot tempers, quick to anger—but also quick to forgive.

Perhaps if I could provoke him, his display of anger would frighten Natalie away from him.

But that wouldn't make her any more likely to turn to me.

His position as commander also suggested that he had strong control over his emotions. He was still a relatively young man, though several years older than I was. If he tended toward violent outbursts, he wouldn't have moved up in the ranks so quickly.

He would be a formidable foe.

I turned my attention to Natalie's other potential match.

Tiziani Mencono, a civilian guardsman from the jungle regions of the planet. Part of me wanted to dismiss him out of hand. What bride in her right mind would choose a civilian? But his people were known for their sneaky, underhanded tactics. There was no telling what he might do to gain her trust.

In fact, the yellow-skinned Khanavai were reportedly overrepresented in the Special Ops program, their cultural training having prepared them to act as spies already.

I wished Zont hadn't already headed down to the planet to begin his search for the runaway bride. It would have been nice to confer with him about Tiziani's potential weaknesses.

Really, though, it didn't matter that Zont had already taken off. Tiziani wouldn't be any easier to defeat than Eldron.

I settled in with the computer interface, determined to see what I could dig up on my two foes before we met in battle—figuratively, at least for now—to compete for Natalie's favor.

WHEN I WALKED into the luncheon room later, the other two Khanavai competitors had not yet arrived. I had planned that, allowing myself the chance to choose the seat at the table that gave me the best chance to command the room. I chose the one facing the door, so I would see Natalie as soon as she walked in—and more importantly, so she would see me before either of the other men.

Of course, since the table was round, taking control of the room was more difficult than I had anticipated. I suspected this had to do with Earth traditions, since humans were more concerned with things like equality and egalitarianism. Among the Khanavai, rank mattered. Had we been battling for a Khanavai female, Commander Eldron would have been seated at the head of a table, I would be seated at the foot as the warrior with the second-highest rank, and Tiziani, as a civilian guardsman, would be seated to one side, assuming he had been allowed to participate at all.

Then again, no Khanavai female would be seated at the table at all. Our customs had begun to change with the integration of human women into our culture. The first Khanavai Bride, Princess Ella, had insisted upon it. And Prince Khai, the warrior who had set up the Bride Agreement with Earth, had adored his mate so much that he had agreed with her.

Oddly enough, every Khanavai warrior mated to a human female had experienced a similar shift in views. Our mating bond was too strong not to influence our behaviors. And so only the old, unmated warriors remained to insist upon the value of our heritage.

Having met Natalie, even for only a few moments, I could see why human women held such fascination for—and sway over—their Khanavai mates. We were hardwired to ensure our mates' happiness and well-being. If being allowed to participate in political discussions and sit at the warriors' tables made our human mates happier, then it was a small price to pay.

I was still pondering this shift in our culture when the other two warriors entered the room together, ushered in by one of the servants. The bride was always last to enter the luncheon, a tradition that had developed over the years since the Bride Games had begun.

New worlds lead to new traditions. It was something my father had said to me more than once. Then again, he had been able to win one of the last fertile Khanavai women on our planet. It had been an easy thing for him to say.

I hoped I could prove him right when I took Natalie back to Khanavai Prime with me.

Standing to give the traditional warriors' greeting, I held my closed fist, thumb inward toward my chest, a little longer than was customary, eyeing first the yellow Tiziani Mencono and then the red Eldron Gendovi. "Greetings," I said to them, "and may the gods favor our endeavors on this day."

It was an unusual statement to make in such a circumstance, as it was generally a prayer before battle. But the other two murmured the reflexive response. "May the gods favor you, as well."

Tiziani's face clouded as he realized that he'd just offered a prayer for my success, but Eldron smiled as he took a seat to my right. Tiziani sat across from him, leaving the seat immediately in front of the door available for Natalie.

"It is a pleasure to meet you." Eldron nodded at us both, then turned to me. "I have learned many good things about you today."

"And I you."

Thus we established our ability to take our opponents' measure. Having watched the Bride Games televised over many years, I knew that Vos and his team of commentators would be discussing the social undercurrents in the room as we waited for the bride to arrive.

Unwilling to appear rude, I turned to include Tiziani in the conversation. "I understand you are a member of the civilian guard?"

"I am a retainer to the southern continent's Royal Residence and am responsible for the prince's safety when he is there." I managed not to roll my eyes. Not that Tiziani's job wasn't important. But given the war with the Alveron Horde, the current prince rarely traveled outside the capitol, and when he did, a retinue of military guards traveled with him. Tiziani was trying too hard to overcome the deficit that came of holding a lower position than either of ours. He would have done better to simply acknowledge that he was a guardsman.

He would lose points with the judges for that.

Good.

I glanced at the commander out of the corner of my eye, but he simply nodded politely at Tiziani's statement, almost certainly gaining style points.

Less good.

But so be it. I opened my mouth to speak again, but the door opened and the two people who had been appointed Natalie's guides—a Poltien and a Blordl—opened the door. The Blordl announced in her trilling voice, "Here comes the bride," a phrase lifted from Earth mating rituals and used to introduce contestants whenever a new game began.

The three grooms stood, waiting for Natalie.

My breath caught in my chest. She was absolutely breathtaking, in the truest sense of the word. Sweeping in past her two assistants, she gazed around the room without speaking, then moved to pull her chair out. Her scent wafted to me, and my cock hardened at the mere smell of her.

Beside me, Commander Eldron inhaled deeply, then frowned.

That was impolite. He might lose the style points he had gained.

Then he stepped forward and took Natalie's hands in his own. She jerked as if trying to pull away from him, then froze, her eyes wide as she gazed up at him.

Gravitiniax Goat Suckers. I hadn't even considered that by positioning myself across from her, I had limited my ability to reach out and touch her.

"My dear," the commander said, bowing over her hands. "I am very sorry, but I'm afraid I have some bad news."

CHAPTER ELEVEN

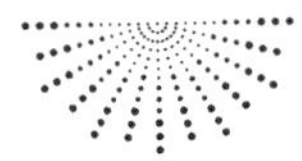

NATALIE

B*ad news? Oh, God. What is he talking about?*

I froze and stared at the cherry-red man with the dark hair bending over my hands. I was terrified of what he might say. That he had decided he was going to take me right there on the table? Or kidnap me? Whisk me away to his planet, never to be heard from again?

No. That was ridiculous. Some part of me knew it was silly, but I couldn't help worrying over every exchange at this luncheon. I glanced at the other two men.

Dammit. I couldn't even remember anyone's name, other than Cav's.

The red guy was something with an E. Edward? Edmund? No. Something alien. Shit. Eddie. Red dude Eddie. I'd just call him Red Eddie. In my head, at least.

The yellow guy was...Banana-Man. That's all I could think of.

Banana-Man was glaring at Red Eddie—or whatever his name was.

Cav, on the other hand, was watching me for my reaction. And as soon as I realized it, I calmed down. My heart fluttered in my chest a little. Somehow I knew that if Red Eddie got carried away, Cav would jump in and save me.

Suddenly, I was able to catch my breath. "What is it you need to tell me?"

Red Eddie's voice dropped, sounding sad. "I'm afraid the synthesized chemical composition of your scent-markers did not do you justice."

Synthesized scent-markers? What the hell was he talking about? I glanced at Cav, hoping he would help me, but he had begun frowning, and now his gaze flickered between me and Red Eddie.

I really should have paid more attention to the details of previous Bride Games.

"You are very lovely," Red Eddie continued. "But I'm afraid I must tell you that we are not a match, after all."

"We're not a match?"

Red Eddie met my gaze sadly and shook his head. "I fear not."

All of my breath left my body in a rush of relief, and I scrabbled at the chair next to me, grabbing the back and sinking into the seat.

Red Eddie followed me, kneeling on one knee before me, as if he were proposing.

Actually, this is an anti-proposal. Thank goodness.

One down, two to go.

"I do hope I have not distressed you too much, Miss Natalie," Red Eddie continued, using my first name as was considered polite in Khanavai culture.

"No," I managed to say, waving one hand weakly. "Not at all. Thank you for letting me know so quickly. I appreciate not having this ordeal drawn out more." I was rambling.

Drindl and Plofnid jumped in to save me. "No problem," Drindl trilled. "We're so sorry your match didn't work out." She took Red Eddie by the arm and opened the door to usher him out. Plofnid stomped past me to follow them, muttering something about false matches ruining the show.

They shut the door behind them, leaving me trapped in a room at a table with the two other aliens.

It's just a meal, I told myself. *I've been on worse dates than this.*

But none where the stakes were quite this high.

Play to lose, Natalie. Play to lose.

The door opened again, and servers began bringing in plates of food—both Earth dishes and Khanavai delicacies.

We'd been trading with the Khanavai long enough that some of their food had made it down to Earth, even if it was rare for the aliens themselves to visit planet-side. So at least I recognized several of the options.

The waiters stopped to offer various portions, and I accepted a little bit of everything, including the food I had never tried before. Might as well expand my horizons while I was here.

As long as I got to contract them all the way back to Earth when this whole Bride Games farce ended.

All I wanted to do was eat in silence. But I knew my friends back home were watching, and I couldn't bring myself to be rude to these two guys. It wasn't like they were personally responsible for bringing me here. Not exactly, anyway.

"Your information card says that you are still a student," the yellow guy said. What the hell was his name? If I had to go back to Khanav Prime with some guy whose name I didn't even remember and who made me think of bananas every time I looked at him, I might just decide to space myself, instead.

"I am. I'm majoring in biochemistry." They both stared at me blankly. "I'm studying the effects of ."

Assuming I don't end up trapped in a forced marriage to an alien.

"I am a guardsman at the Prince's Residence on the southern continent," Banana-Man said.

Oh, thank heavens. Apparently, he was one of those guys who asked a question only so he could answer it himself. That could be useful. If I could get him talking about himself, maybe I wouldn't have to say anything at all.

"I'm wondering," Cav said, tilting his head to address Banana-Man, "how often has the prince been in residence in, say, the last five years or so?"

Banana-Man whipped his head around to glare at Cav.

Interesting response. I didn't know what kind of significance the question might have. After all, I hadn't ever really anticipated being here. I knew some girls studied Khanavai culture as if their lives depended on it. But those were the ones who generally volunteered for the Bride Games. All I wanted to do was go home.

"His Royal Highness may not have been in residence often, but we are expected to keep his home in perfect order for when he does arrive." Banana-Man's tone had turned haughty, as if he were offended.

Ooh. This could be interesting.

I took a bite of my food and settled in to enjoy the show. I almost wished I had popcorn. Someone needed to introduce the Khanavai to *that* tradition. I might not know a lot about Khanavai culture, but I had watched enough of the games on television in previous years to know that there was some kind of verbal sparring going on.

I wished I had Vos Klavoii's commentary running over everything that was happening.

Yep. I definitely liked watching the Bride Games more than I like participating in them.

"Oh, I'm certain of it," Cav said. "Just as those of us on patrol have to keep our ships ready to fight the Alveron Horde at any moment."

Oh. I got it. Cav was a soldier and Banana-Man wasn't. I had forgotten how much that meant to these warriors.

Okay. Maybe I could play this game, after all.

I picked up a long strand of some Khanavai pasta-like thing that was slightly sweet and a little sour, took a bite, chewed and swallowed, and then leaned forward. "Tell me, Cav, as a military man, are you away on missions quite a lot?"

The corner of his lips tilted upward, revealing a dimple in my blue suitor's cheek. "That is often the case, yes. Of course, Command Central prefers for mated warriors to spend more time on the home front."

"Really? I didn't know your commanders cared so much for your happiness."

"It's less about our happiness than about Khanavai survival. That's the whole reason for the Bride Games," Cav replied. "Our job is to repopulate our planet. They certainly wouldn't want to send me on too many missions until I had plenty of time to make sure I helped with that." He leaned toward me, that sexy grin and the heat in his eyes matching up with his emphasis on the word help in a way that left me in no doubt of what he meant.

Heat flashed through my belly, and my nipples tightened at the thought of spending time with Cav, doing nothing but having tons of sex.

Dammit, Natalie. You are here to lose, not to get laid.

How many times was I going to have to remind myself of that?

Banana-Man jumped in. "Of course, as a guardsman, I would always be home."

I didn't even bother to glance at him. Cav's gaze held me entranced.

"And there are some officers who are granted special permission to bring their mates aboard with them," he said, his tongue darting out to lick his bottom lip. "So as to ensure plenty of mating time."

My gaze kept dropping from his eyes to his mouth. Suddenly, I couldn't quit thinking about that kiss in the hallway.

He was gorgeous, and he was teasing me. And damned if my body wasn't responding — more than I ever wanted it to. If I had been here to actually find a mate, I could have fallen into that stare of his forever.

Instead, I dragged my attention away from him by sheer force of will.

"Tell me," I said to Banana-Man, "what is a typical day at the Prince's Residence like?" Not that I cared, but I needed to find a way to block my body's reaction to Cav. Besides, as long as Banana-Man was talking, I didn't have to. All I had to do was make encouraging noises periodically while I shoveled food into my mouth. I didn't even taste it. For that matter, I didn't hear anything that Banana-Man said.

Because although I could pretend to be fascinated by Banana-Man, my entire attention was riveted on Cav. Just a few feet away from me, Cav reflected every bit of my physical right back at me, like a furnace burning hot enough to make me break out in a sweat.

Yes, he was sexually attractive. Fine. I could admit that. But it wasn't enough. I had a degree or three to finish—and for that matter, dates to finish with David.

I murmured something noncommittal to Banana-Man's long-winded description of the exact times and routes he took around the palace when he did his guard duty.

This man would be mind-bogglingly dull on any planet.

I glanced up and saw Cav watching me with a wicked gleam in his eye—one that I was certain did not bode well for me. As the blue alien opened his mouth to say something, I shot to my feet, my eating utensils clattering onto the plate in front of me.

"This has been a lovely luncheon," I said, brushing my white pants free of creases. "I understand I will see you both later today."

Dammit. Don't remind them about what games come next.

Cav flashed that mischievous grin of his—the same one he'd given me in the hallway earlier. One that said he knew what I was doing, and I amused him.

Banana-Man just looked confused.

I really need to figure out his name before I see him again.

"The pleasure has been all mine," Cav said, executing a perfect bow. If not for his bright blue skin and enormous size, he could have passed for a gentleman in one of those historical dramas my mother had loved to watch when I was younger.

Banana-Man scowled and finally stood, as well, copying Cav. "Yes," he said shortly. "A pleasure."

I turned and opened the door behind me, sliding out into the hallway and shutting the door. I leaned my head against the doorframe and breathed in deeply.

It had not been my most graceful exit ever. But at least I had cut the lunch date short. They couldn't make me stay, right?

I headed down the hallway back toward where Plofnid and Drindl had been, hoping I would find them soon.

Everything on this station was filmed, right? Surely someone would let them know to come get me.

After all, I had a spanking ceremony to prepare for.

CHAPTER TWELVE

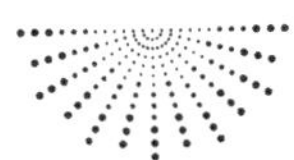

CAV

S*he will be mine.*

Tiziani had obviously bored Natalie with his overly specific details about his job as a guardsman. Her reaction to me had been very different, particularly when I discussed mating. She was interested in me, no matter how often she proclaimed that returning to her planet was her true goal.

I was halfway there.

All I had to do was coax her to me.

By that afternoon, I was convinced that I could win her before the day ended.

Plofnid and Drindl had invited me to join them in the green room for their viewing of the spanking ceremony. I knew that was a good sign. The handlers always ended up having quite a bit of sway with the judges and the brides. Inviting me to join them signaled Drindl's and Plofnid's approval of me as a mate for Natalie.

Assuming, of course, it wasn't part of the program planning to have them invite me. I certainly wouldn't put it past Vos and his team to create drama where little existed.

As I walked into the room, my heart pounded. Tiziani and I had drawn lots, and he had won the chance to be the first to participate in the spanking ceremony with Natalie. Just the thought of him touching her firm, round ass sent shivers of rage racing through my body.

He never should have matched with her. Even if they were physically compatible—which I didn't actually believe—they were obviously not intellectually compatible. He had no sense of humor, whereas Natalie, despite her obvious anxiety about participating in the Bride Games, was overflowing with humor.

She was absolutely perfect.

And I did not want any other male touching her.

By the time I moved to join Plofnid and Drindl on an overly soft seating arrangement, my jaw ached from clenching it.

Drindl took one look at me and patted my hand gently. "All will be well, warrior Cav. You'll see."

I certainly hoped she was right.

I glanced around at the other groups sitting on the too-soft furnishing —mostly handlers, but a few warriors here and there.

The name "green room" had always confused me, as it was not green at all. In fact, the walls were boring and white, designed to focus everyone's attention on the viewscreens that took up most of the wall space.

Everything in here was recorded. For that matter, practically everything in the entire station was. The humans who watched the Bride Games back on Earth were under the illusion that it was a live show. But an entire army of technical workers combed through video images to put together the most appealing entertainment they could think of. Because of that, there was actually about a two-hour delay between *filming*—the strange word humans used for creating visual images digitally—and broadcasting the games back to Earth.

I only knew those specifics because one of the warriors who had gone through primary training with me had been obsessed with human entertainment, including the Bride Games. Not for the reason most Khanavai were interested—the hope of one day participating and being awarded a mate—but because the technical details fascinated him.

Here in the green room, though, we were watching the games in real time. To get through all the games, they often had to be filmed simultaneously, so there were sometimes up to five different games running simultaneously—even though back on Earth, the humans would view them sequentially.

And they were watched just as eagerly on Khanav Prime, as well as the various Khanavai outposts, I had to admit. I had spent many years catching portions of the games in between shifts aboard various ships I had been assigned to during my military tenure.

Now, however, the last thing I wanted to do was watch my bride manhandled by a terminally boring guardsman.

"Oh! There she is!" Drindl sang out, pointing at the viewscreen that opened directly across from us.

Plofnid sat straight up, its legs stretching out in front of it barely reaching the edge of the cushion. It twirled its nose-braid around one finger nervously. "How do you think Natalie is going to react to this?"

Drindl shrugged. "I'm not certain." She turned to me. "Did you watch any of the earlier spanking ceremonies?"

I shook my head briefly, focused intently on the screen displaying Natalie walking into a room not unlike this one, but with barren walls instead of viewscreens and a single chair in the center of the room, slightly raised on a dais as if it were a throne in a palace. Its cushions were red, almost the color of human blood. The color of Commander Eldron, come to think of it.

I couldn't help but hope the commander found a bride at some point. He was worthy of one. Tiziani was not.

After the door closed behind her, Natalie took several steps into the chamber and glanced around. With a shrug, she moved over and sat in the thronelike chair, smoothing down the short skirt of the blue knit dress she wore. The fabric brushed the tops of her thighs. The chair didn't dwarf her as much as the seating arrangements in the greenroom dwarfed Plofnid, but she still looked like a Khanavai child sinking into the soft padding of the chair.

Or at least, she would have looked like a child, if not for her luscious curves.

I wanted to gather her in my arms, sit down on the chair with her in my lap, and hold her close. An ache settled in my chest unlike anything I never felt before. I had heard all my life about Khanavai protective instincts, but I'd never experienced them until now. No more, at least, than those instincts could be roused by a youngling in danger or the like.

This was something different. It was a determination to protect her from harm. It was the bond between mates flaring to life.

And all I'd done so far was kiss her.

On the screen, Tiziani walked into the spanking room.

"That's my chair," he announced, his nostrils flaring at the perceived insult of Natalie taking his place.

She stared at him coldly for a long moment. "I am not here because I want to be."

"But you are here. In my seat."

"I don't know much about this spanking ceremony," she said, a slight quiver in her voice betraying her nervousness. "Just that it's supposed to remind the bride of her place in the relationship?"

Tiziani nodded. "Yes. To ensure that you understand your place as a subordinate in our culture."

Irritation flashed across Natalie's face and I couldn't hold back my snort of satisfaction. Tiziani had just stepped in a flaming pile of etav droppings. He wasn't simply a boring windbag. He was a *stupid* boring windbag.

Natalie crossed her arms and leaned back in the chair. "I think maybe we should change the ceremony."

Tiziani's eyes narrowed. "Change it? This is the way it has been for thousands of years."

"Nonetheless, I think this time, I should spank you."

"What good would that do? I will not be the subordinate when we mate."

Natalie's jaw tightened, and the cameras zoomed in on the hard look she gave him. "Maybe not, but I'm not going to be 'the subordinate,' either. Because we're never going to mate." She all but sneered the last word, and I chuckled, proud of my feisty bride.

"You are required to participate in all the games," Tiziani intoned, clearly quoting from the guidelines and bylaws—perhaps from the original Bride Alliance Treaty itself. "According to paragraph one-point-seven, subsection eight, every bride chosen in the lottery will complete all games to the judges' satisfaction."

Her folded arms tightened over her chest. "I'm not doing this," she said. "It is barbaric and horrific."

Tiziani took a threatening step toward her. "You might need a spanking more than any female I've ever met."

It was all I could do not leap through the viewscreen and drag him away from my Natalie. She was far too precious to allow him to put his hands on her.

From her seat beside me, Drindl patted my hand again.

But it didn't matter. That brute was threatening my mate.

A low growl escaped my throat.

Drindl leaned over to whisper to me, probably trying to distract me from my anger. "There have been several brides who resisted this particular game today."

I glanced at her, torn between finding out what had happened and watching the scene unfolding on the screen in front of me.

"It hasn't been pretty," Plofnid interjected, leaning around Drindl so it could see me.

"One of the warriors was even disqualified for being overly harsh," Drindl added.

"Overly harsh?" I hoped I sounded as horrified as I felt. "What kind of warrior would be willing to harm someone so fragile as a human female?"

"I heard that her resistance engaged his warrior instinct, and he hit her so hard that it caused blood vessels under her skin to break. She's covered in..." Drindl closed her eyes, trying to remember the alien word.

"Bruises," Plofnid supplied.

My stomach clenched as I looked back at the screen. Tiziani had begun trying to wrestle Natalie off the chair. No matter that she was tiny, she fought against him fiercely, hanging onto the arms of the throne with both hands and kicking him every chance she got.

I wanted to jump up and cheer for her, but I managed to keep my composure. Right up until she landed a kick straight in his gonads. He doubled over in pain, and even though he deserved it, I winced in sympathetic pain.

Tiziani let out a roar, doubling over, clutching himself for a moment. Natalie leaped from the chair and raced past him to try to open the door, but it wouldn't budge.

"The judges locked the rooms after some of the incidents this morning," Drindl said, her long silvery fingers creeping up to cover her mouth, her eyes wide as she fretted over Natalie.

"Personally, I think that was a terrible idea." Plofnid shook its head in dire warning. "They should consider the liability."

Tiziani's skin turned such a bright shade of yellow that it practically glowed, and veins popped up all over his body, throbbing visibly. With a snarl, he bent over and charged at Natalie, using his shoulder to slam into her stomach and knock the breath out of her. Then he wrapped his arm around her waist to pick her up off the chair, ripping her grip away from the arms. He spun around and sat down in the chair with a thump, grasping her struggling form and pushing her down until she was draped over his knees.

Tiziani held her down with his forearm and flipped her skirt up to expose her round butt. She wore nothing but a scrap of underclothing, a choice I assumed had been made by the Games Administrator for their prurient appeal.

Tiziani raised his hand, and a growl began rumbling deep in my throat. He brought his palm down against her ass, his bright yellow hand making contact with both cheeks at once. A loud *crack* sounded through the room.

Natalie screamed in pain and redoubled her struggles. The growl that had been working its way up my throat burst out as a full-blown roar.

A haze of purple clouded my vision, and I realized I was standing without having any recollection of getting to my feet.

Tiziani raised his hand again. "You will behave in a manner befitting my mate," Tiziani thundered. "The mate of a royal guardsman!" His hand cracked down again.

Natalie was right. This was barbaric—at least the way Tiziani was doing it.

I will not allow him to hurt my mate.

"Cav, where are you going?" Drindl's high-pitched voice followed me as began moving. I ignored her and strode to the door, throwing it open and breaking into a jog as I headed toward the game rooms.

Drindl and Plofnid gave chase, scampering around me like buzzing, squeaking, irritating insects—until I turned and snarled at them both. They both skidded to a stop and stood frozen in fear.

"Do not follow me," I ground out.

They didn't.

Good, I thought. *No more interference.*

CHAPTER THIRTEEN

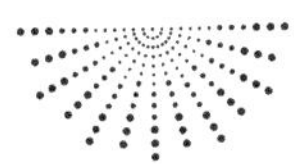

NATALIE

I could not believe this was happening to me. As they had coaxed me into wearing this ridiculous outfit and tried to tame my riotous curls, Plofnid and Drindl had assured me that the spanking ceremony would be fun. Entertaining. More a game than a punishment.

But here I was, bent over the knee of Banana-Man, enduring the most painful, humiliating thing that had ever happened to me.

Yeah, I had figured out his name. But after this bullshit? He was going to be Banana-Man forevermore. The next time Vos put me on camera, I was going to announce the obnoxious windbag's name to the whole universe.

And I was going to make sure this motherfucker never touched me again. Just as soon as I got away from him.

His huge hand slapped down on my ass for a second time, and an unwilling scream ripped from my throat. Tears sprang to my eyes and I fought harder than before to get away from him. But my torso was pinned against his legs and no matter how hard I kicked, I couldn't reach him with my feet.

Yeah. I was definitely going to have some choice things to say to Vos the next time he interviewed me. I couldn't believe the Khanavai Bride Games Administrator had arranged to have me locked in a room with this monster.

Still, though, I was more angry than frightened. It would be bad PR for the Khanavai to allow me to be injured permanently.

Or worse.

Wouldn't it? Surely they wouldn't let him take this much farther.

Banana-Man's hand lifted high above my stinging ass, preparing to deliver yet another blow. My shoulder brushed against his lap as I tried to push my way free, and I realized I had just felt his erection.

Bile rose in my throat, the acid taste of a sudden wash of true fear running through me.

The Human-Khanavai Bride Alliance Treaty said that no woman could be forced. Not to marry, not to have sex. We could only be convinced, either by individuals or during the Bride Games.

I was being convinced of something all right, but it wasn't to have anything to do with this beast ever again.

I was trying to figure out if I could reach myself around to get my mouth close enough to any exposed skin to bite him. Preferably hard enough to draw blood. The threat of being hit again momentarily outweighed my revulsion at the idea of putting my mouth anywhere against Banana-Man. If I could bite him hard enough to distract him, maybe I could get away.

And go where?

I ignored the mocking voice in my head and kept fighting. I was still struggling, trying to find a way to get my mouth to his exposed calf above the top of his military boot when the door to the spanking chamber crashed open with the screeching sound of tearing metal.

I turned my head to the side to discover another pair of Khanavai military boots standing in the room.

"Help!" I screamed, before I even realized who it was. Some part of my mind remembered that in an emergency people responded more to cries of *Fire!* than they did calls for help, so I even threw that in. "Get me out of here! Fire! Help!"

That's when I realized it was Cav. I followed the line of his legs up to his enormous muscular torso, until I met his gaze with my own, my eyes pleading.

The blue Khanavai warrior let out an inarticulate bellow. He dove toward me and with one hand, snatched me off of Banana-Man's lap. With the other hand, he lifted Banana-Man out of the oversize chair and tossed him all the way across the room. The yellow alien hit the wall with a giant, metallic bang that echoed around us. His head snapped back and hit again, and Banana-Man slid down into a crumpled heap on the floor.

I wanted to cheer. Instead, I threw my arms around Cav's neck and began babbling, alternately begging him to save me and pleading with him not to hit me. "Get me out of here. But don't do the spanking ceremony. Please, don't do that. I can't take it. No more. That is not foreplay. Get me out of here."

Cav lifted me to cradle me in his arms like a child. With one hand, he gently rubbed my back. "Don't worry, little one, I will never let anyone hurt you again."

He strode out into the hall and away from the scene of my degradation. To my utter humiliation, I burst into tears.

Cav continued whispering soothing noises to me, nonsense phrases that still seemed comforting in the safety of his arms, and kept moving.

"Please don't take me back to any cameras," I finally sniffled. "I don't think I could stand it."

"I'm not." His deep voice rumbled in his chest underneath my cheek. "I'm taking you to part of the backstage area that never gets filmed." He paused at a doorway. "But we're about to go through the public area, just for a little while."

I nodded and let my hair fall to cover my face, pressing my forehead against his chest to hide my face.

Part of me knew it was stupid to trust any of the Khanavai. At this point, I was convinced they were all brutish beasts. What kind of culture believed it was foreplay to beat their partners?

And yet I felt safe with Cav.

He carried me effortlessly through the space station, the noises around us getting quieter and quieter the farther we got away from the main thoroughfares and the filming areas.

By the time he took me into a quiet, dark stairwell, my sobbing had subsided to the occasional hiccup. When we got to the top step, he simply sat down, holding me in his lap.

A long moment of silence stretched between us until I finally wiggled a little to let him know I was ready to crawl off his lap.

This wasn't an appropriate way for us to be sitting together, anyway. It was far too intimate for me.

I sat gingerly, my ass still sore from the beating Banana-Man had given me.

"I'm very sorry Tiziani hurt you," Cav said. "That was dishonorable. He should never have been allowed to touch you without your permission."

"They locked me in." Even though I knew Cav hadn't done it, I still sounded accusatory.

The giant blue warrior next to me nodded. "That was a very poorly done of them."

"What the hell is wrong with your planet?" I demanded. "You beat your women for pleasure?"

Cav shook his head sadly. "When the spanking ceremony is done correctly, it can be very erotic—for both participants."

"I don't believe you. Anything that hurts is *not* sexy."

One corner of his mouth tilted up, and that slightly wicked gleam reappeared in his eyes as he gave me a sidelong look. "If it hurts, it's not being done right," he suggested, his voice dropping even lower. "And I would never hurt you. Not under any circumstances."

"I can't go back into that room. I won't." My voice started to rise, beginning to turn shrill.

Cav reached over and gently grasped one of my hands in both of his, holding on loosely enough that I knew I could pull away at any moment. "I agree. That would be far too traumatic. I think we should find Vos and his people and let them know that we are requesting a different game."

"Can they do that? Will they?"

He shrugged. "They can do anything they want to. It's just a question of whether or not they will."

"Whose idiotic idea was it to have all you giant alien men striking human women?"

"Certainly not mine." He traced the outline of my hand with one of his enormous fingers, and his touch was gentler than I would have imagined possible.

We sat there for a long time in silence as I tried to regain my composure.

"Okay," I finally said shakily. "Let's go make the request."

"Are you sure you're recovered enough to deal with talking to the Games Administrator?"

"Oh, yes. I have a *lot* of things I want to say to him."

A soft chuckle emanated from Cav. This was a completely different man from the one who had ripped me out of Banana-Man's arms and tossed the other alien into a wall. That one had been enraged. Violent.

Protective.

This version of Cav was also protective—just not furious.

So maybe the two versions were not completely different.

He stood and held out his hand to help me to my feet. My legs shook, my eyes were puffy, and my ass still stung, but I would survive. I suspected I would feel a lot better after I had the chance to give the Bride Games designers a piece of my mind.

"I think maybe they were trying to inject some more excitement into the games," Cav speculated as we made our way out of the stairwell.

"More exciting? Why would they want to do that?"

"The Bride Games have been getting more competitive every year. Initially, these games were simply a way to make sure the brides were matched with the best possible mates. They were not originally intended to be entertainment."

"But once they became entertainment," I continued, figuring out where he was going with the idea, "they had to keep viewers coming back year after year. So the edgier the games, the more viewers?"

"Exactly." Cav led me down a series of long corridors decorated in the bright shades the Khanavai preferred. It took us quite a bit longer to retrace our steps than it had taken us to get there in the first place. I glanced down at Cav's muscled thighs flashing out from beneath his kilt-like uniform. I had to take three steps for each one of his. And given how angry he'd been, there was no telling how quickly he'd been moving when he rescued me.

I also hadn't realized that Cav had taken me through some of the *most* public areas of the station.

When we stepped out into a kind of food court, a wall of food scents hit me, and my mouth started watering. I hadn't eaten much of my lunch, and I was beginning to come down from the adrenaline-spike of trying to fight off Banana-Man.

Cav glanced down at me. "You hungry, little one?"

"Actually, yes, I am," I realized. "Thirsty, too."

"Wait for me here. I'll get something." He ushered me to what was probably a cozy two-person table for the Khanavai but could have been a dinner table for four back on Earth. I dropped down into the oversized chair as Cav walked toward one of the stalls circling the central area.

He returned with another plate of the Khanavai noodles I had enjoyed at the luncheon. Somehow, I wasn't surprised he had noticed which food I had liked.

"I will pay you back for this," I promised.

"For that? You eat so little, I promise it won't matter."

He slid into the chair across from me, placing his own plate of food down. I was about to take my first bite when all the viewscreens in the courtyard came to life around us,. And they all showed the same scene: me, held down on Banana-Man's lap as I struggled, and he slapped my exposed ass twice.

I sat down my utensils, suddenly not hungry anymore.

The scene played through twice, but the second time it kept going, right up to the moment Cav thundered into the room. The image froze on a close-up of Cav's furious expression. Then Vos appeared in the frame. “Stay tuned for an exciting rescue attempt as Cav Adredoni attempts to rescue Natalie Ferguson from a spanking ceremony gone wrong.”

“Fuck.” The word whooshed out of me.

Cav raised one dark blue eyebrow at me.

“I guess you were right,” I said. “They were looking for better television.” I dropped my head into my hands, resting my elbows on the table.

“I think we should take this with us,” Cav said, gathering our plates and moving to a self-packing station.

God. This was humiliating. Miserable. Everyone back home would see it. Hell, probably every human and alien in the universe was watching it right now.

Could anything possibly make this any worse?

I should have known better than to jinx myself, even with a thought.

CHAPTER 14

CHAPTER FOURTEEN

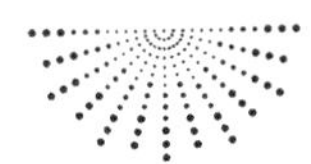

CAV

"Of course you can request a different game." From behind his desk, Vos smiled brightly. Beside me, I felt rather than heard Natalie heave a relieved sigh.

"All you have to do is announce your engagement to one another."

Natalie stiffened. "But we're not engaged."

"What happened in the game room yesterday was unfortunate," Vos said, as if Natalie had never spoken. He stood up and moved around his desk to lean back against the edge. It was a calculated move designed to emphasize his power over us as we sat in the two chairs he had motioned us into when we entered the room, ushered in by his secretary.

I repressed the growl that threatened to escape.

"Cav coming in and sweeping you off your feet was a heroic move in any culture." Vos picked up a small decoration from his desk, a painted metal rendering of Earth and Khanav Prime, with the Bride

Games station in between them, providing a link between the two. "It made for amazing television. Our rates were incredible yesterday. Everyone in the entire known universe is pulling for you two kids."

I bristled at his words. Vos might be older than I, but in Khanavai culture, I outranked him. It was all I could do to keep from launching myself over the desk and attacking him. Only the knowledge that it would not go well for me if I did kept me from it. When the military had seconded me to the Bride Games, they had essentially transferred command to him. I'd signed an agreement to treat the Games Administrator as if he were my commanding officer.

And I was nothing if not an obedient soldier.

Most of the time.

Vos continued talking. "What we need now is a happily ever after. Women on Earth will eat it up. The Khanavai warriors will look up to you, Cav, and Natalie, you will be the envy of every bride from here to Alpha Centauri and beyond."

Natalie crossed her arms and glared at the Games Administrator. "And what if we refuse?"

Vos gave a delicate shrug. "Then the games will continue as scheduled. Including your roles in them."

My stomach clenched at the idea of subjecting Natalie to another round in the spanking room. Besides that … "Will Tiziani be allowed to continue participating?"

Vos gave me a knowing glance. "That depends on what the two of you decide, I suppose. Every drama needs a villain." The smile he gave us could have belonged to one of those villains.

"I will not accept Tiziani as a mate."

"No one expects you to."

"What if I don't accept Cav, either?"

My stomach sank at her words. Having met her, touched her, I didn't know how I could ever leave the space station without her.

I had never heard of a mate-match discovered during the Bride Games not working out. I had to wonder if it had happened, though. Vos's devotion to creating drama and giving the viewers the happy endings they craved made me wonder how many times the truth behind the Bride Games had been covered up. How many other couples had been blackmailed into announcing an engagement or making a claim to romance that didn't exist?

And how often had a Khanavai warrior met his mate, known that they belonged together the way I knew Natalie and I did, and gone home alone, without a bride, anyway?

How did someone even recover from that? The mere suggestion of it was enough to clog my throat with misery.

"In previous years, you have allowed brides to eliminate suitors," Natalie pointed out.

"Indeed we have. But never under such dramatic circumstances."

"So this is all about getting the right ratings for your television show?" Natalie's voice shook with barely suppressed rage.

"Not entirely." Vos brushed nonexistent lint off his purple suit. "We work very hard to ensure that our contestants are happily matched."

"As long as we continue to help you get good ratings, at least," Natalie muttered.

"See? I knew you were a smart woman." Vos pushed himself off the corner of the desk and strolled back to his seat—an oversized version of an Earth-style executive chair. "You have one hour to make a decision," he said briskly. "If you announce your engagement, we will move to the wedding planning portion of the games." His smile turned predatory. "Otherwise, you'll be expected to report to the game rooms." He glanced down at the epaper on his desk, shuffling through some of it. He flicked his fingers once, an obvious dismissal, and the door opened.

His secretary stepped in. "I'll show you the way out," the human male said.

We followed the secretary all the way out into the primary corridor. "Do you know how to get back to the games area from here?" he asked.

"I do," I said shortly, not even bothering to thank him as he returned to his office.

Alone in the hallway, Natalie and I stared at each other for a long, silent moment, her eyes searching mine as if to find an answer there.

I knew what I wanted. But I couldn't make up her mind for her.

She finally broke the silence. "What do we do?

"That has to be up to you entirely," I said. "I would be thrilled if you decided to skip straight to wedding planning. But if you would rather return to the games, I will accept that, as well."

"You will?"

All I wanted to do was bury my hands in her hair and pull her to me for another kiss. But I wanted her to want to be with me as much as I wanted to be with her. "If we go back to the games, I promise I will not hurt you. And I will spend every second I have trying to convince you that we belong together."

The column of her throat moved as she swallowed nervously. I wanted to stroke the pale skin there, follow a line down to her chest, to the swell of her breast.

Slow down, I admonished myself. It would do no good to get myself overexcited about any of this. Not until I was certain of Natalie's consent.

"Maybe we should go talk about it."

"We still have not eaten," I reminded her. "We could take a little time to discuss this."

She nodded. "Let's go back to the food court and see what we can come up with."

I still carried the food we had gotten in the food court. But by now, it had grown cold and inedible. I dropped it in the nearest waste receptacle, listening to the whoosh of the station's recycler whisking it away. I turned to Natalie. "Let's go pick up new plates of sandworms and see what we can come up with."

She froze, her eyes huge. "Did you say sandworms?"

"Yes. I thought you liked them."

"Those were worms? I was eating *worms*?"

I laughed. "They are a delicacy on Khanavai. Once they're dead, anyway. The live worms are disgusting."

A shudder ran through her entire body. "I don't think I could eat them again now."

"What did you think they were?"

"Some kind of pasta."

"Pasta? What is that?"

"Long, thin noodles made of grains. We boil them until they're soft. They have a similar texture to your… sandworms."

"Sounds bland. I've had some of your Earth grains. I could hardly taste them at all."

"We put various sauces on them. Just like you did with that dish." She obviously couldn't bring herself to say the word *worms* again.

I chuckled. "That's not a sauce. Sandworms are cooked in their dying excretions. That's what gives them such an amazing flavor."

This time, Natalie's swallow seemed more convulsive than nervous. "Maybe I could just get some coffee. Do they sell that at the food court? Earth coffee, I mean. I don't want anything made from worms or bug guts or something."

This time I was the one who shuddered. "Coffee? That bitter, dark drink? And you think sandworms are foul?"

"Coffee is fine if you put cream and sugar in it."

"Wait. Isn't cream made from cow-squeezings? That's much more disgusting than sandworms," I teased.

"Cow-squeezings? Oh, God. I'm never going to eat or drink anything again."

It was good to be able to make her laugh. By the time we reached the food court again, we were ten minutes into our hour to decide.

Natalie sat down with a cup of Jalevian tea, first having quizzed me on the ingredients used to create it.

She shifted uncomfortably in her seat, a reminder of her experience with Tiziani. "I can't believe Vos gave us that ultimatum."

"I can," I said darkly. "I'm beginning to think the Bride Games aren't as straightforward as they've always been made out to be."

"Oh, I'm sure of it." She rubbed her hand across her forehead. "I don't know you. We've barely met. I can't agree to marry you."

I inclined my head once, just enough to let her know that I accepted what she said. "Then we have no choice but to return to the games."

"The thought of that makes my stomach hurt," Nathalie confessed.

"I will protect you."

"You can't be there every single moment."

The growl that I had been holding in ever since Vos made his offer once again threatened to escape. "Tiziani will not have another chance to hurt you. I swear it."

And if he tried, this time I wouldn't simply throw him across the room. I would rip him to shreds with my bare hands.

CHAPTER FIFTEEN

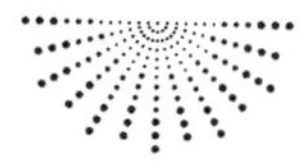

NATALIE

I *just have to get through this nightmare once more.*

I mean, the other things that had happened today hadn't been quite so bad. The luncheon ...well, it was over, at least. Cav rescuing me, our time together since then—those things had been good.

And after we finished this stupid spanking ceremony game, the worst would be past.

They had sent us to a different spanking room from the one that Cav had ripped the door off of that morning. This one had a purple chair instead of a blood-red one. Otherwise, they were exactly alike. My heart started pounding as soon as we walked in, and Cav glanced around the room assessingly.

"That chair is a terrible set-up for the spanking ceremony," he announced.

"What?" That was not at all what I had expected to hear from him.

"Oh, I'm sure it appeals to the old-school Khanavai, the ones who don't want to give up any of our old traditions or accept any new ones. That's ridiculous. Khanavai and humans have been intermarrying now for, what, almost sixty of your Earth years? Our cultures are bound to overlap and intermingle, changing both."

"Makes sense." My voice was trembling. I couldn't stop thinking about what came next, even though Cav was clearly trying to help me overcome my anxiety.

"Anyway," Cav continued, "modern Khanavai warriors do not spank their mates."

"They don't?" I squeaked.

"Well, only for fun." He gave me a slow wink, but that dimpled grin of his made it less seductive and more cute.

I shook my head at myself. Hard to believe I had gone from finding Cav enormous and terrifying to thinking of him as *cute* in such a short time.

"Okay, then," I asked, forcing my voice to remain steady this time, "what do we do? If we're not going to use the chair, I mean."

Cav dropped to the floor, crossing his legs in what we had in my childhood called crisscross applesauce.

"Come sit across from me," he said, leaning forward to pat the cold metal floor in front of him. As I followed his instructions, he turned around and removed the cushion from the seat of the chair, ripping it away when he discovered it was attached. Then he rolled it up and put it beside me. "Stretch out on your stomach. Use that to pillow your arms and head."

I did as he said, but when he scooted closer to me, my entire body tensed up.

"I'm not going to start yet. I'm just getting us both ready." His deep voice took on a soothing cadence.

"Okay." My voice squeaked and I bit the inside of my lips to keep from making another noise.

Cav drew my skirt up to uncover my ass, and this time only my butt cheeks clenched up.

Setting his enormous palm against my practically bare ass, Cav murmured, "Relax. I'll give you plenty of warning before I start the ceremony. Let's simply talk for a while."

His hand was warm and soothing, and he began rubbing in gentle circles.

"I don't know what to talk about." My voice came out sounding breathier than I intended it to.

"You said you were studying biochemistry. What does a biochemist do, exactly?" His hand continued its gentle, hypnotic motion across my ass—which was feeling a lot warmer and less painful than it had when he started.

"Well, it depends," I said, finally beginning to truly relax. "I want to go into cancer treatment research. For all our medical advancements—including the ones brought to us by the Khanavai—cancer still takes far too many lives every year."

"Mm," Cav murmured. "Among my people, too. We've eliminated some kinds, but far from all."

"So that's my goal. I'm one year away from finishing my degree, and if…" My voice trailed off. *If I don't get stuck going to Khanavai, I can still follow my dream.*

Cav didn't ask me to finish the sentence. I think he knew where it was headed. "What made you want to go into that field?"

"My father died when I was eight from a fast-growing brain cancer. By the time anyone knew he had it, it was too late to do anything about it. He was gone in less than a month."

"I'm so sorry."

I shrugged, the motion pulling my skirt up even higher. "Thanks. It's okay. It was a long time ago. But I'd like to help make sure that never happens to anyone again."

"Is your mother still alive?"

Oh, God. My mother. She was watching this. I cringed in embarrassment.

"I'll take that as a yes." Cav went back to smoothing my skin with his hand.

"Yeah. She lives in Denver with my younger sister." God. Was Julie watching this, too? I needed to change the subject, and fast. "You're a captain in the Khanavai space-fleet, right?"

"Right now, yes. But what I really want to do is attend our Special Ops program."

"Special Ops. Is that like spies and stuff?"

"The Khanavai version, yes. I applied this year and was almost certain to get in. This year's class began yesterday."

"Then why did you agree to participate in the Bride Games?"

He shrugged, his hand still rubbing my ass cheek. "My commander encouraged it. Besides, I might not ever get another chance to find a mate." I couldn't help but wiggle my butt a little under his ministrations. "Anyway," he continued, "I'm allowed a one-time enrollment deferment. I can always go next year."

"Why can't you defer more than once?"

"Command Central believes that demonstrates a lack of commitment."

I rolled my eyes. "Militaries. Making stupid decisions on every world."

Cav laughed aloud, then gently patted my butt, like I might a dog's head. "Okay. Stay relaxed and calm. Don't move. I think we're ready for my version of the spanking ceremony."

"You promise it's not going to hurt?"

"I promise." He uncrossed his legs and stretched out beside me on his side, propping himself up on one elbow and keeping the other hand moving in gentle circles over me. "I'm going to be very careful. I won't get you anywhere Tiziani bruised you. You may feel a sting, but it won't actually be painful."

"Is this like how doctors say you're going to feel a 'pinch,' and then it hurts like hell?"

The soft chuckle was deep in Cav's chest this time. "That's not my plan."

"Okay," he said, his voice turning hypnotic again. "Think of your favorite place, the place you feel most relaxed and happy."

That was easy. Having grown up in Colorado, I loved the mountains. I imagined a glacier-formed meadow, deep in the Rockies, stretching out in front of me springtime, covered in wildflowers.

"That's it." Cav's hand cupped my ass, and two of his enormous fingers slipped between my thighs to brush against the outside of my panties.

My nipples hardened at the touch, the realization of how close he was to the core of me sending a shiver through me.

He did that several times, and I writhed a little, embarrassed to realize that my panties were getting soaked—and he could definitely tell.

With Cav, the spanking ceremony was a slow, gentle seduction.

I swallowed, fighting my body's reaction to him. And then, when I'd almost decided he wasn't going to spank me, after all, he lifted his hand and gave my left ass cheek a smack. It wasn't exactly gentle—I heard the sound of it crack through the room. I squealed and jerked, but his hand was right back where it had been, smoothing my ass and stroking my pussy outside my panties.

His touch rubbed away the slight sting. And when he did it again on the other cheek, I actually giggled.

What the hell was this? I couldn't believe I was enjoying a man—well, a male, at least—hitting my ass.

But Drindl and Plofnid had been right. This wasn't punishment.

It was foreplay.

When he moved back to the first cheek, my core clenched, not out of fear, but expectation. This time the slap did sting a little more, but it didn't bother me—it felt more like…waking up my whole body. I was certain he wasn't going to bruise me.

He wasn't going to hurt me.

"I'm going to do this five times on each side," Cav told me, never losing that deep, relaxing cadence to his voice. "Am I hurting you?"

"No," I confessed. "That's not what I'm feeling."

"Mmm," he rumbled, deep in his chest.

After the third round of ass-slaps, he reached up underneath me from behind to cup my mound, the tip of his middle finger circling my clit. My breath caught in my chest. No one had ever made me feel like this before. Like every nerve was alert, aware, ready for his touch—and yet also completely relaxed. When he lifted his hand for the fourth round, I found myself arching my back to lift my ass in the air for him, giving him better access.

And by the fifth, it was all I could do not to turn to face him, begged him to take me, right there in front of the cameras.

But I still retained some semblance of dignity. Not much. But some.

After all, my mother and sister would probably see this.

As Cav moved back to simply stroking my cheeks in circles, I tried to regain my composure.

Eventually, my breath no longer trembled out of me, and that ache deep inside my body had receded to a mere throb reminding me that Cav was still right there, still touching me, still staring at me with those intense violet eyes.

Apparently, Cav had tuned in to my body and become as aware of it as I was of his, stretched out beside me, heat rolling off him in waves. Because the moment I decided I was ready to get out of this room, Cav was already there, pulling his hand away and straightening my clothes.

"See? That wasn't so bad, was it?" He pulled my skirt down and smoothed his hand over it, cupping my ass one last time.

I turned to him, my face burning hot, and grinned, my smile teasing. "It was terrible. I hated every single second of it."

As we stood up and prepared to leave the game room, I stole a glance at Cav, who was sporting an erection.

An enormous one.

I swallowed again, this time at the thought of what he must look like naked.

Play to lose, Nat, I reminded myself—for what felt like about the millionth time.

Oh, fuck that.

Great. The tiny voice in my head was back.

Kiss the sexy alien man.

But for once, we agreed.

CHAPTER SIXTEEN

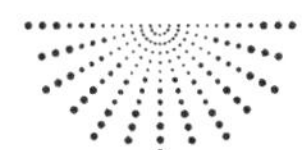

CAV

I want her more than I had ever wanted any female in my life.

My thoughts must have shown in my face, because Natalie closed the gap between us, placing her hands flat on my chest, sliding them up and around my neck. She stood on her tiptoes and ran her fingers up the nape of my neck. She closed her fists, gently grabbing me by the hair, and pulled my face toward hers.

I let myself be led to her, allowed my face to be guided until our lips touched.

I still didn't move. I waited for her to take the lead—not the norm for a male and a female on Khanavai, but I knew that was the only way she would allow this to happen. On her terms. And so I simply breathed. Natalie's mouth opened against mine, and a tiny moan escaped her as she pressed up tightly against me.

Her tongue flicked out against my lips.

That was all the invitation I needed.

With a groan deep in my throat, I wrapped my arms around her, sliding my hands down to that ass I had wanted to grab since the first day I'd seen it. I pulled her in as close to me as I could, close enough for her to feel how hard my cock was, and I swept my tongue through her mouth, kissing her hard and deep, as if I were trying to brand her.

Mine.

She melted against me, molded herself to me, and then responded with all the fiery passion I could have wished for.

It was all I could do to keep from stripping her down right there, bending her over, and filling her, making her mine for real.

The only thing that stopped me was that I knew I wanted it to be her idea. I wanted to make this human woman mine, but only after she made me hers.

Our kiss continued until the klaxon bell telling us filming had stopped began bleating insistently.

Natalie dropped down to stand flat-footed again and covered her ears with her hands. "Dear Lord, how do we shut that thing off?"

"I think we should leave," I shouted, just as the noise stopped, leaving my voice echoing through the room.

With a giggle, Natalie took my hand. "Let's get out of here."

My mate might claim she didn't like the spanking ceremony, but her body hadn't lied to me.

That kiss hadn't lied.

I had to keep her with me just a little longer.

"According to the schedule, we're free until tomorrow morning. Would you like a tour of the station?"

She nodded. "Sure. I was hungover when I got here and didn't bother with any of that."

Good. I didn't want anything to convince her to quit holding my hand. Still, I wasn't exactly sure what she meant. "Hungover?"

"From drinking too much right before I was transported. I was at my twenty-first birthday party." A shadow crossed her face.

"What is it?"

"I'm just wondering what all my friends are doing back on Earth."

"Have you contacted them?" I led us toward the public areas of the station.

Her steps slowed. "No. Brides aren't allowed to contact people back home until all the games end."

I hadn't known that. I pulled her into the main thoroughfare. "Well, until then, let me show you around. Not that there is that much *to* show you. Most of the station is dedicated to the Bride Games. At least the part of it that we will be allowed to visit today."

Natalie glanced at me. "What are the parts we're not allowed to go into?"

"Those are the segments designated for the Khanavai military. We launch watch patrols into Earth space, pretty much patrolling the entire solar system for any incursion by the Alveron Horde."

"I don't hear your current patrols talked about much back home, just the ways that you saved us before."

We strolled past the food court and into the greenery section of the station, used as part of the oxygenation system, and in some areas, to grow food plants. Here, though, the path we strolled along was lined with tall trees, some from Earth, others from Khanavai.

"It's discussed quite a bit on Khanav Prime. Seems like both our governments would want people on Earth to know the Khanavai warriors are still here keeping you safe."

Natalie nodded. "There's plenty of information about that. Advertisements on television, online discussions, all sorts of places. But just that you're keeping us safe. We don't get much about the specific details."

"That does make sense. Our government doesn't want Earth to learn much about our technology. Our culture is very careful about sharing tech these days—supposedly, that's how the Horde got enough information on us to poison our gene."

Natalie stopped and bent over to touch a flower growing beside the path. "We do have access to some Khanavai tech. There are transporters installed in some cities, and it's possible to buy passage, though it's very expensive. And I'm sure the Earth governments have transporters. There are always meetings going on between leaders without any indication of how they traveled. We all assume it's by transporter."

I was about to tell her how the transporter had ended up in Khanavai possession in the first place, because it wasn't native to us. We hadn't designed it or built it originally. But as I opened my mouth to speak, Tiziani appeared on a path intersecting ours, having apparently come into the garden from a different area, his yellow skin once again glowing brightly in his agitation. He marched directly toward us as directly as an arcnov desert beetle's line in the sand.

Coming to a halt immediately in front of us, he put both hands on his hips, widening his stance as if he were a puff-feather blowbird trying to make himself look larger to his rival.

"I have been doing some research on human tradition," he announced in a tone that suggested we should know the significance of his statement.

I gave it a beat, then two, before I said, "And?"

"It is a human tradition that two suitors for the hand of the same woman may have a duel in order to determine the winner."

I shot a glance at Natalie, who was frowning and shaking her head. "I don't know anything about that," she said out of the corner of her mouth.

"Her hand?" I glanced down to where our fingers threaded together.

"It's an Earth phrase. It means mating." Tiziani's irritation practically vibrated from him. "I am challenging you to a duel."

"What kind of duel?"

"To the death," Tiziani intoned.

"Did you learn to announce things like that in guardsman training?" I couldn't help the derision dripping from my voice.

"A duel to the death? Don't be stupid." Natalie waved her hands in the air in front of her, the motion clearly one of negation. "I'm not going to have you try to kill each other for me." She stepped in front of me, moving between us, then standing on her tiptoes to speak more directly into Tiziani's face. "I have no intention of marrying anyone," she said, her voice firm and clear. "I have said from the very beginning that I planned to go back home. I have been playing these games to *lose*. I don't know why no one is willing to listen to me when I say that."

"I watched the spanking ceremony you had with him," he growled. "I saw how he softened it, acting as if our time-honored ceremony was for titillation instead of punishment. He is no true Khanavai."

"I don't care if he's a true chimpanzee. Even if I were planning to choose someone in these games, it would never be you. Listen carefully. I would never marry someone who hurt me like you did. I still can't sit down comfortably."

"This is not between us," Tiziani said dismissively. "It has nothing to do with you, Natalie. Stand aside and let the warriors deal with this."

Natalie gasped in outrage, her hand swinging up as if to slap Tiziani. Quickly, I dropped her other hand, grabbed her around the waist, and pulled her out of the way before Tiziani could do anything to damage her further. Holding Natalie back with one hand, I extended the other arm to put it against Tiziani's chest. "Fine. You can have your duel," I said to the other Khanavai. "Send me the details via com, and I will meet you this evening."

Finally satisfied, Tiziani nodded once and turned sharply on his heel to head back to the Grooms' Quarters.

Natalie spun on me as soon as he was out of sight. "You can't do that. You cannot kill him just because he says he wants a duel."

I felt a warm glow start deep inside me. "You're that sure I will win?"

"Of course you'll win. That's not the point."

The warmth inside me exploded into a smile. "Then what is the point?"

"I told you. You can't kill him."

"Yes, I can. I'm a soldier. We are taught to kill. I've trained for it since I was a child."

"That's a..." She heaved a put-upon sigh. "Of course you are *capable* of killing him. That's not what I meant. Killing him is a terrible idea."

"You don't think Vos will say it'll make for a good show?"

She dropped her face into her hands.

"I don't give a flying space-fuck what Vos thinks makes good television. Or what he thinks we should do. I will never forgive you if you kill him because of these damned Bride Games." Her voice came out muffled from behind her hands.

I placed one finger under her chin and tilted her face up toward me. "What if I promise not to kill him?"

"You'll be holding back, and he won't, and I'm not sure that you will win under those conditions."

So much for that warm little glow inside.

Still…did that mean she was worried about me? The thought made me want to kiss her again. To make her smile.

To make her happy.

At that moment, I realized that even more than I wanted to make her mine, I wanted to make her happy.

And I know exactly how to do it.

I shook my head. "I won't lose. I promise not to kill him. And I promise I won't let him kill me."

"Why are you going to do it at all?" she wailed.

"Come on." I took her hand in mine again and pulled her back to the games area. "Let's go talk to Vos again. I have an idea."

CHAPTER SEVENTEEN

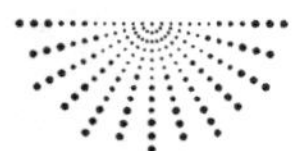

NATALIE

"Two visits in one day. To what do I owe this honor?" Vos remained behind his desk this time, and Cav and I didn't even bother to sit down.

"I assume your cameras caught that little exchange in the garden?" Cav asked, his tone daring Vos to lie.

"Of course."

"Oh," I realized. "That's how Tiziani knew where to find us, wasn't it? You were filming us the whole time." I crossed my arms over my chest and glared at the Games Administrator.

His laugh had always sounded so cheerful and real when I'd watched the games in previous years. Now it made me want to claw his eyes out.

"You two are this year's most favored couple. If you want a job in entertainment when this year's games end, you'll be able to name your price."

I clenched my fists by my side, fighting myself not to pick up the stupid paperweight of Earth, the station, and Khanav Prime he had on his desk and bash him over the head with it.

Cav placed a calming hand on the center of my back, and I instantly felt better.

Fine. I won't murder the Games Administrator.

Not yet, anyway.

"I have a proposal for you," Cav said.

Vos raised one amused eyebrow. "You're supposed to propose to the bride, not to me." When neither of us joined in his laughter, he sat back in his chair and clasped his hands over his stomach. "Do tell."

"Turn this duel Tiziani has requested into a real spectacle. Hold it in the main arena with a full audience. Set it up however you like—"

I opened my mouth to speak, and Cav increased the pressure of his hand on my back. "—but do not allow it to be to the death. That will alienate too many of your human viewers."

Alienate. Interesting translation. I wondered about the connotations of the original Khanavai word.

Vos leaned forward, his elbows on the desk. "I'm intrigued. Go on. What do you get out of this? I assume if you win, you want to be named Natalie's mate?"

He gestured at me as if I had no real part in this conversation. As if I were merely a prize to be given out. I was tired of being treated like an accessory to discussions rather than a full participant.

But Cav was already answering. "No."

This time, both Vos's eyebrows went up in surprise—the first genuine expression I had seen from him since I arrived. "Then what do you want?"

"If I win, Natalie gets to go back to Earth, totally free of any further obligation to you, the Bride Lottery, the Bride Games, or Khanav Prime."

I gasped. Cav had made it clear that he wanted nothing more than to choose me as his mate. So why was he doing this?

Because he cares about me, the tiny voice inside my head whispered.

Vos gave us both a calculating look, then slowly smiled. His amused expression once again made me want to slap him. "And if you lose?"

"I won't lose."

"Come now, Cav. A wager without a penalty is no game at all."

Cav glanced at me, a flicker of anguish flashing through his eyes. Then his gaze hardened, and he turned back to Vos. "If I lose, you do not allow Tiziani to claim Natalie as a mate. Instead, I will agree to be stationed here for a complete Earth year, working for you. Through the next year's Bride Games."

No. That would ruin his chance to attend the Special Ops school.

"On camera?" Vos leaned forward.

"Yes."

"As a returning groom? The first Khanavai male ever invited back to try again?"

"Sure."

"No." Both Khanavai males' heads whipped around to stare at me as if they had forgotten I was there at all until I spoke. I glanced back and forth between them. Then I pointed at Vos. "You make sure this duel is not to the death. Cav winning will make every woman on Earth swoon. And if Cav loses, I will marry him—in the first-ever live broadcast of a Bride Games wedding."

Vos clapped his hands together and laughed aloud, even as Cav said, "You can't do that."

I spoke over them both. "If Cav wins, you get your TV hero, and we get total freedom. If he loses, you get your broadcast version of a happy-ever-after, and Cav and I still get to leave—after the wedding. Either way, this year's Bride Games will be the show to beat for years to come."

There. That should give Vos an offer he couldn't refuse. And no matter what happened, Cav would be able to attend his spy school next year.

Vos set his chin in one hand and tapped his fingers against his mouth as his narrowed gaze flickered back and forth between us. Slowly, he nodded, and then sat up straight. "Agreed," he said briskly. "I will contact Tiziani and tell him the duel has been converted to a game."

"Will he refuse the new terms?" I asked.

"He won't know our terms. There's no need." Vos turned to the viewscreen beside him and began flipping through option. "I will set the duel for tomorrow afternoon and will contact you when the arrangements are finalized."

"I CAN'T BELIEVE you did that," I said, once the secretary had again escorted us to the outer corridor and closed the office door behind him.

Cav's cheeks turned a dark blue, and I wondered if that was his version of a blush. "I couldn't allow that puffed-up Lorishi carrion slug to claim you. Not under any circumstances."

"But you didn't have to make them agree to send me home if you won," I said quietly.

His blue blush deepened, and he gave an embarrassed shrug. "Yeah, I did. I want you to have whatever you most want."

And isn't that the truest definition of love that exists? the voice inside my mind insisted.

"Anyway," Cav continued, "your offer to marry me if I lose is insane. You know Vos will do everything in his power to make sure I can't win."

Now I was the one who shrugged. "If you stayed here through the next Bride Games, you'd lose your chance to go to your spy school. Forever."

His gaze searched mine, and again I pushed back the insistent voice clamoring inside my head, repeating its new definition. *Love: wanting the best for someone else even if it means you don't get what you want.*

Suddenly, the idea of him losing this stupid duel made bile crawl up my throat. Not because I was anxious about having to marry him—oddly, that didn't seem like the horrible fate it had before—but because I was worried Tiziani would hurt him.

For that matter, I was concerned that he might win the duel—for the same reason. Even if he won, he was likely to be injured, and I didn't want to see him hurt.

"Walk me back to my chambers?" I asked.

"Of course." Cav took my hand as if it were the most natural thing in the world. In two worlds.

And maybe it was.

All the way back to my room, I considered what I was planning.

It was probably foolish.

But at the end of the duel, I would either marry this beautiful, kind, thoughtful alien, or I would head home, never to see him again.

And I wasn't even sure which I really wanted.

But I did know one thing.

I wanted *him*.

My body still ached from the spanking ceremony, in all the best ways. So when we arrived at my door, I opened it without letting go of his hands.

He followed me but didn't move otherwise.

If I was going to do this, I needed to be my most forward self. I had never met anyone I wanted to be this open with before. "I want to see what we're like together."

"You do?"

"Yes." My voice dropped down into a range that was pure sex. And I could feel Cav's response to it. The air around us turned electric, causing all the tiny hairs on my body to stand on end.

He didn't move, but his eyes devoured me. "I need this to be your choice," he rasped.

So I stepped up to him, wrapping my arms around him as far as I could, holding his waist and tugging him close to my body. "Believe me, it is." I tilted my head up to him. "Kiss me."

Cav gathered me to him, lifting me off the ground to hold me, his hands cupping on my ass as he teased my lips with his tongue, urging me to open them. I wrapped my legs around him.

It was as good as I could have possibly imagined.

He trailed kisses down my neck, sending chills racing up and down my spine and my arms.

As tightly as we were holding one another, I felt his huge cock getting harder, pressing through his kilt-like uniform, the tip pressing against the core of me.

Damn, I wanted this man. This alien. I had believed I wanted David, back on Earth. But my attraction to the human man was nothing compared to the way my body reacted to Cav.

With a breathless little moan, I pulled my mouth away from Cav's. "This is exactly what I planned when I invited you in."

"I'm glad you did." His eyes were heavy, dark with lust. He leaned in and took my earlobe gently between his teeth, then played with the shell of my ear with his tongue. I moaned, aching for him to touch me even more.

"Are we being filmed right now?" I managed to whisper.

He glanced around the tiny room with its human-sized bed. "There and there," he said, pointing to two spots on opposite walls that looked just like the rest of the room to me.

"Can you do anything about that?"

Cav's grin gleamed in the partial darkness. "Definitely." With a quick step, he moved to the first wall and punched through it, revealing some kind of small electronic setup with a silver orb floating in the center. One twist and he had it out of the wall. He repeated the process on the other side of the room, then took both orbs into the hallway, where he stomped on them, leaving crushed bits of metal strewn across the floor.

"There," he said when he returned. "No more cameras."

"Good," I said, taking his hands and pulling him toward the bed. Then I stopped and began stripping off the short dress Drindl and Plofnid had talked me into that morning.

When I wore nothing but my lacy bra and the tiny thong he'd already seen, I began trying to figure out the closures on his uniform kilt.

With a deep growl, Cav took over, finally unhooking everything and letting it drop to the floor. When he reached for me, though, I stepped backward and sat on the bed, drawing him closer to stand in front of me.

I reached up to take Cav's cock in my hand, rubbing up and down it, feeling the bumps and veins and the sheer size of it. I ran my tongue around the tip, then sucked him as deep into my mouth as I could—which wasn't nearly deep enough, as far as I was concerned.

I would never be deepthroating him, dammit.

I guess Drindl wasn't entirely joking about the sucking ceremony—even if she didn't know it.

The tip of his cock slipped in and out of my mouth several times, growing even larger and harder, before Cav groaned. "You have to stop now, my tiny temptress."

I grinned at the term of endearment. I really would have to learn some Khanavai words.

If he loses tomorrow. If I go with him.

The thought sobered me.

Cav knelt on the floor in front of me. "My turn."

CHAPTER EIGHTEEN

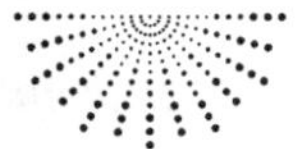

CAV

I knelt in front of her, pushing her knees open, leaning in to inhale her hot fragrance, then slowly licking her wet slit. "I love the scent of your desire." I placed my lips against her, allowing them to brush her as I spoke. "The taste of it. The way you stretch to take me." I reached around and slid my hands along one ass cheek, my fingertips playing her, pulling her closer to me. "And I love the idea of you letting me fill you again and again."

Natalie moaned every time I brushed against her with my lips.

The sight of her sitting there naked made me harder than I had ever been before. "I love you more than I thought it would be possible to love anyone."

I probably shouldn't have said that. But she whimpered and leaned back on her elbows.

"I want you," I said, suckling the bundle of nerves gently, then rotating around it and flicking it with my tongue.

She began bucking against me and I added a finger, sliding it inside her, preparing her to accept me. I moved faster, driving her toward the edge, until she cried out my name as she shattered against me, drenching me in her release.

She collapsed, boneless, still breathing hard. Without giving her time to fully recover, I picked her up and stretched out on the bed, setting her atop me and positioning myself at her opening.

Her eyes fluttering closed, she sank down onto my cock, stretching to take it all. I pumped into her once, then twice, making sure she was soft and ready. Then I grabbed her hips and began lifting her, then bringing her back down to slowly impale her on my throbbing cock.

She whimpered, and I rocked into her, keeping one hand on her but releasing the other so I could circle her clit with my thumb. She squeezed tighter and tighter around me, the pressure of the woman I loved holding me inside her—keeping me deep within her as I made love to my mate.

We came within seconds of each other, our cries echoing through the room as pleasure washed through us in waves.

And that's when my mating cock erupted from the tip, swelling inside her as my first cock softened and receded.

Natalie froze, her eyes wide, and then she moaned in ecstasy.

"You are mine," I growled as I sat up to flip her over, never allowing us to come uncoupled.

"Yes," she whispered. "I am."

As she spoke, I drove myself deep inside her, determined to bring her to her peak once more before I came inside her again—this time with my mating cock. The one that only she had ever known.

And as we began to move again, I knew that this was perfect.

It would always be perfect.

No matter what happened next.

WHEN MY WRIST com buzzed the next morning to let me know Vos was comming, Natalie muttered and rolled over in the bed.

I quietly pulled on my uniform and moved to the lav to relieve myself and splash some water on my face before I commed him back. I didn't want to leave before she woke, so I stayed in there to return the Games Administrator's message, switching out the mirror for a viewscreen. Luckily, his secretary was expecting me and put me straight through to Vos.

The Administrator looked perfectly put together, even though I was sure he'd had a long night. But his white hair was perfectly groomed, his green skin bright and clear. He carefully examined the background in my com-message, and I cursed myself silently for not setting up a sim-back before I'd put the com through.

"Oh, good. You did stay overnight. That ought to push us up in the rankings today." Vos nodded, far too pleased with himself.

"You have information?" I asked in my most military tone, only barely managing to avoid adding a crisp "Sir" to the question.

Vos's laughter echoed in the small lav chamber and I lowered the volume, worried he would wake Natalie unnecessarily. "I do, indeed, Captain."

I waited, holding eye contact with him for a long moment. "Well?" I finally asked. I knew he'd see it as me 'breaking' first, but I didn't care. I wanted to get this over with.

I want to lose. I would win everything I ever desired if I lost this fight.

I shook off the thought. I needed to win so that Natalie could go back home as soon as possible.

I could never live with myself if I lost and she had to go unwillingly with me back to Khanav Prime—or worse, to live as a ship-bride, a human female alone among Khanavai warriors, far from home and always in danger.

No. I will win this battle.

Vos finally answered my question. "Everything is set up as you requested. Tiziani has been informed that this is not a duel to the death. But does not know that his victory will not ensure his ability to claim Natalie as his mate."

"She will be able to make that choice, no matter what?"

"No matter what," Vos agreed.

"Good."

"Your opponent did insist on fighting with the traditional Khanavai swords."

The weapon carried by the Royal Guardsmen. "Of course he did."

A contract popped up on the viewscreen. "You and your...Natalie"—he smirked at me in a way that might have led to having his head severed from his neck had we been in the same room—"should read over the contract. If you have any questions, contact my secretary, Anthony. When you're satisfied, you should sign it and send it back."

I nodded, already scanning the legal language. That was one tradition we had imported from Earth that I did not like at all. In our past, Khanavai warriors sealed binding agreements with a sacred blood oath and then honored those agreements.

Most of the time, anyway.

Fine. Perhaps it was not a bad idea to wrap each other up in these knots of words, binding us to our agreements.

"You should plan to arrive backstage at the stadium at thirteen-hundred hours, Standard Station Time," Vos continued. "If you need directions, contact Anthony. In fact, if you need anything, contact Anthony. I will speak to you again when the duel is done."

He logged off, and I checked the chronometer at the top of the comscreen.

Thirteen-hundred. That meant we still had several hours before I had to be anywhere.

Excellent.

I moved back into the bedroom, determined to wake Natalie in the most pleasing way I could imagine.

BACKSTAGE AT THE STADIUM, I paced back and forth, loosening up my limbs and shaking out my hands.

Not that I wasn't plenty loose already. I had awoken Natalie with a kiss, and we had spent the next two hours discovering everything possible about each other's bodies.

She had been especially fascinated by the wavy bumps running along the top and bottom of my cock.

"What are those?" she asked as she ran her fingers over them delicately and I shivered in delight.

"We call them our mating ridges."

"Human men don't have these."

I grinned. "That's because they don't have our additional mating penis."

"Is that what that was?" She wiggled a little, her eyes going dreamy for a moment.

"It is only aroused by our true mate." I brushed my knuckles against the side of her breast and over her nipple. "You are the only female mine has ever touched."

"Oh." Her voice turned small, worried, and the dreaminess dissipated from her gaze, to be replaced by a little frown of worry creasing her forehead. "I don't want you to get hurt."

"I won't. I told you—I'm going to win and you're going to go home, free and clear of any obligation to the Khanavai."

My assurances didn't smooth her frown away, so I moved downward to distract her again—so much so that we were almost late getting to the stadium. Natalie held my hand all the way there, clutching it as if she might never touch me again.

After this is over, she won't. I shook the thought off and concentrated on the battle ahead. It wasn't that hard to do. All the way there, viewscreens scattered throughout the station blared advertisements for the upcoming fight—starting with replays of the original challenge Tiziani had made. Every time his voice echoed around us, Natalie cringed.

Then Vos's face came on the screen, announcing what he called "the biggest fight for dominance in all the history of the Bride Games!"

Natalie had been right. Vos was turning this into a spectacle like nothing I had ever seen. No matter what happened on the stadium floor today, Vos would be the biggest winner of all.

Except Natalie, I reminded myself. *That's all that matters—making sure Natalie wins by getting what she wants more than anything on two worlds. The chance to go home.*

I was a Khanavai warrior. It was my job to make my mate happy.

And I would do that job.

When we reached the entrance to the stadium's backstage, she pulled me around to face her. As she had done before, she wove her arms around my neck and pulled me down to kiss me—a fierce, possessive kiss. Reluctantly, I pulled my lips from hers, resting my forehead against hers.

"Be careful," she whispered, her sweet breath fanning my face. I inhaled deeply, taking in the scent of her, holding it, inscribing it in my memory. No matter what happened today, I wanted to remember everything about her forever.

She cupped my face in her hands. "Promise me you won't be hurt."

"I promise."

Tears sparkled in her eyes, but she blinked them away and put on a brave smile. "I'll be in the stands with Drindl and Plofnid," she reminded me for the third, or maybe fourth, time. "I'll be cheering for you."

She held onto my hand as she walked backward away from me, our arms stretching out between us until she couldn't hold it any longer, and then she turned and, straightening her back, continued resolutely toward the stadium entrance, squaring her shoulders as she went.

Now, backstage, I could hear the crowd in the stadium, their conversation a muted roar. For an instant, I wished Zont were there to send me off with his unique brand of humor, wishing me luck as I headed toward the entrance to stand in the wings and await my introduction.

But Zont was down on Earth, tracking his own bride—another reason this year's Bride Games were likely to become legendary.

No. All I had was Anthony, Vos's secretary who had arrived with the contract that Natalie and I had completely forgotten to sign.

When he handed the tablet to me, I saw Natalie's name scribbled in her native English letters. I made my sign beneath her, the Khanavai letters bold and stark against her flowing writing. Somehow, that seemed fitting.

"Thank you," Anthony said briskly, turning away. Then he turned back for just a second. "And good luck," he added before bustling away.

I moved closer to the curtains I would enter the stadium floor through. I caught a glimpse of one of the giant viewscreens playing for the crowd.

On it, an image of me kissing Natalie appeared, hundreds of morits tall. It had been taken in Natalie's room the night before. The last thing I saw on the screen was my own fist coming toward the camera to smash it.

Some assistant backstage handed me a sword, and I weighed it in my hand, checking the balance and how well it twirled.

From the viewscreens, I heard Vos announce my name.

This is it.

Time to win.

I strode out into the bright lights and a wall of sound created by the shouting of more voices than I had imagined could ever be on the station at all.

Then I turned, my eyes searching the crowd.

There she was.

My Natalie.

Standing beside Drindl and Plofnid in the very front row, waving and shouting.

This was for her.

I turned to face my opponent.

CHAPTER NINETEEN

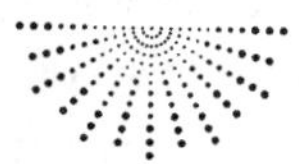

NATALIE

I realized as Tiziani came striding out onto the mat on the stadium floor that roughly half the crowd was cheering for him. That didn't fit what Vos told us about Cav being the favorite, and I had to wonder if the Games Administrator had paid—or perhaps bribed or blackmailed—some of the spectators into rooting for Tiziani.

My stomach clenched as the two Khanavai warriors faced off against each other.

Drindl and Plofnid stood on either side of me, each clasping a hand tightly. My palms were sweaty, but I didn't care. I needed their support.

Beside me, Plofnid sighed dreamily. "He is absolutely beautiful," it said, staring at Cav.

He was. He stood a head taller than Tiziani, muscled and strong. It was all I could do to keep from sighing over him, too. At least, it would have been, if my throat hadn't closed from anxiety.

As Vos raised his hand to begin the duel, and the two began circling one another, I realized that Cav might not have as easy a time defeating the guardsman as he had boasted.

Granted, Cav was bigger and stronger, and he definitely knew how to use the curved, ornate sword he handled. It whistled through the air as he twirled it around in a show of dexterity.

But he had spent his adult life on spaceships, using mechanical weapons—he may have trained his entire life as a warrior, but he had not spent as much time working with the traditional Khanavai swords as long as Tiziani had.

At least, that's what Drindl told me as we waited for the spectacle to begin. She maintained a nervous running commentary on the various bets taking place all over the station, handled through Vos's office, of course. Apparently, gambling on the winner of battles like this was a long Khanavai tradition.

"I bet on Cav, of course," she confided in me.

"I did, too," Plofnid said stoutly. "He is going to squash Tiziani like a Lorishi lightfly and then keep him down like an unbraided child."

Plofnid's staunch partisanship gave me a warm glow inside—but I was still worried.

Now, as the two Khanavai danced around each other, blades slicing through the air so fast I could barely see more than a flashing blur, I found myself standing, pressed against the barrier that kept us all from rushing the floor, leaning over it to watch Cav anxiously. My eyes flickered between his form several feet down and even farther away from me, and the giant Jumbotron-style screens floating in the air.

I wasn't certain how a fight like this could be judged. The two fighters were like whirling dervishes, spinning and lunging so quickly I could barely keep track of who was where. And I had no idea how Cav could possibly find any way through Tiziani's defenses.

But he must have, because suddenly he leaped across the mat, rolling on the floor and coming up under Tiziani's guard, slashing at him once and then rolling away just as quickly. The crowd around me gasped and Tiziani stumbled. Cav started to go for him, but Vos blew the whistle and threw his hands up.

"First point to Cav Adredoni," the Games Administrator announced.

Around me, cheers and boos erupted. I added my voice, screaming, "Go, Cav!" and jumping up and down.

On the viewscreen in the air, Tiziani held his hand to his side, walking in a circle for a moment. When he pulled it away, his hand was covered in a dark, viscous fluid. Khanavai blood.

He snarled at Cav, who gave him a mocking salute.

Vos spoke briefly to Cav, who nodded and turned his back on the mat to walk away for a moment.

Okay. So this would work like some combination of a fencing display and a boxing match? Where they fought for a certain number of points, maybe.

"How many points does it take to win?" I asked my companions.

"Either five points—which means drawing blood—or until one of the fighters can no longer stand," Plofnid explained.

Five points. He only needed four more, and then Could walk away from this.

But scoring the first point didn't help Cav. It only enraged Tiziani, who entered the next round with a ferocity he hadn't shown before.

I realized for the first time that Tiziani's slighter build could actually benefit him. He was less muscular and shorter than Cav, but just a hair faster. He'd spent his life on Khanav Prime, in natural planetary gravity.

I read somewhere once that could make a difference in muscle development. Ship's gravity was never perfect, never quite the same as the gravity on a planet.

So Cav might be stronger. He might even be more used to fighting in station gravity.

But Tiziani's muscular structure had benefited from being a guardsman on the planet.

And he was technically better with the sword. Just as I had feared.

Tiziani scored his first point with a single slash against Cav's dominant left arm, the one he most often used to wield the sword. I gasped, along with half the crowd, while the other half cheered for Tiziani.

I turned around to glare at those closest to me.

Traitors.

Cav's arm dripped blood so dark it looked black from where I stood pressed tightly against the railing, every cell of my body straining to make its way to Cav, to stop this monstrous gladiatorial display. But Cav simply wiped his other hand across the wound and shook blood off onto the floor, splattering it in front of Tiziani. Then he gave the yellow alien a feral smile and flipped the sword into his other hand.

Tiziani's second point came when he feinted right and then spun around to slide the sword across Cav's muscular thigh, slicing away part of Cav's uniform even as he cut deep into the blue alien's skin.

I ripped my hands away from Plofnid and Drindl to clasp them over my mouth. My stomach clenched and I didn't make a sound.

Had Tiziani cut across an artery?

Is Cav going to die out there?

I released a breath I hadn't even realized I was holding when Cav limped away, stopping to pick up the shred of fabric on the ground, using it bind his wound. When he was done, he tested his leg, turned to the audience, blew me a kiss, and twirled around on the injured leg, as if to show that he could.

But I was really worried now. I could not stand here and watch him die. Because no matter what he told me, it was becoming clear that was a very real possibility.

Frantically, I gestured toward Vos, then, when he didn't see me, I jumped up and down, waving my arms over my head to get his attention.

The Games Administrator strolled over to me while the warriors waited. "Yes?"

I glanced up the giant screen, but Vos had turned off the mics.

"Stop this," I begged. "I will marry Cav. You'll get the wedding you want if you just *stop* this."

Vos shook his head. "Absolutely not. You signed a binding contract." He glanced at the warriors, then gave me a vicious smile. "Anyway, it looks like you are going to have to marry your warrior when he loses, no matter what."

My jaw clenched, and it was all I could do to keep from punching Vos in his smug green face.

From his spot on the mat, now splattered with blood, Cav mouth something to me, but without my translator, I couldn't tell what was.

I really need to learn some Khanavai.

Strolling back to the center of the mat, Vos signaled the fight to begin again.

And for the first time, I saw my Khanavai warrior in action—fighting for real, without holding back at all. Tiziani had injured Cav's left leg and arm, hoping to knock his opponent off-balance.

But I saw the moment that something—adrenaline? Battle rage? Or maybe just sheer determination—took over Cav's entire body.

He wasn't performing for the audience anymore. He wasn't even performing for me.

My blue warrior moved through space like a lethal dancer, his sword slashing through the air in front of him as if slicing away the very molecules to give him more room to become the killing machine he had trained to be.

His first strike hit the wrist of the hand that Tiziani used to hold a sword. It jarred the sword out of Tiziani's grasp, and for an instant, I feared Cav had cut off the hand, too.

But instead, the strike simply left one tiny scratch behind, as I saw when a camera from somewhere zoomed in, showing the blood welling from the cut.

It was enough to count as a point.

But Cav wasn't done. With a spin, he kicked Tiziani out of the way and scooped up the other alien's sword. Coming up, he used Tiziani's own sword to slice across his banana-yellow leg in precisely the same spot the Tiziani had cut Cav.

Vos began whistling and motioning for the fighters to separate, but Cav wasn't done. As Tiziani bent half over to clutch his leg where blood poured from the wound, Cav leaped in, catlike and predatory, and brought the crossed swords down against the back of Tiziani's neck, ready to pull them apart and slice the other alien's head completely off.

Like cutting a banana. The thought echoed through my mind, and a nervous giggle escaped me. I clapped my hands over my mouth again, my stomach clenching as I waited to see if Cav would finish the move.

Everyone in the stadium held a collective breath as the scene below us froze into a tableau, echoing with potential death.

Cav held Tiziani there, bent over, for one beat. Then another. And a third.

Then, with only the barest motion, he lowered the swords enough to nip the nape of Tiziani's neck in two separate spots.

No one else moved.

Vos blew his whistle, breaking the spell that held us all in its grasp. All around me, the stadium erupted in noise.

Without even thinking about what I was doing, I climbed over the railing and jumped to the stadium floor, rushing across it to throw myself into Cav's arms.

CHAPTER TWENTY

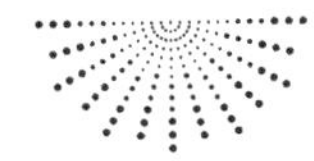

CAV

I caught Natalie as she jumped into my embrace, swinging her around once before she wrapped her arms around my neck and kissed me fiercely.

The stadium and all the people around us faded, the world contracting until it held only the two of us, my senses aware of nothing but the feel of her mouth against mine, the touch of her body as she pressed herself against me.

I could have stayed like that forever.

Eventually, though, Natalie pulled away from me. “Never again.” Tears brimmed in her eyes. “You cannot put yourself in that kind of danger ever again.”

“I was never in any real danger,” I assured her.

“Bullshit.”

It took a minute for my translator to work that one out, and I began laughing when it did. “I assume that’s an expression of disbelief and not a request? Or is it more of that strange food relationship you have with cattle on your planet?"

She hit me lightly in the chest and I lowered her to standing. "I'm serious," she said. "I cannot bear the idea of you getting hurt."

All around us, people were talking, but I ignored them and brushed a curl of Natalie's hair back, tucking it behind her ear. "Oh, my tiny temptress. I am a soldier. I am likely to be in danger again."

She frowned at me fiercely. "Maybe even more often now that you're going to spy school."

"Special Ops training," I corrected her.

"Whatever. Same thing."

That's when it hit me.

I had won.

Natalie was free.

My heart cracked in two.

I swallowed hard to keep the sudden rush of grief from bearing me down to my knees.

No. I was a Khanavai warrior, and I would stand tall, no matter what.

"Anyway," I managed to say in a lighthearted tone, "you get to go back to Earth. You can finish your biochemistry degree. Find ways to save both our people from cancer."

Natalie's eyes grew wide, and then they filled with absolute fury. "Like hell I will." She took a step closer to me and waved her tiny finger under my nose, her voice rising with every word. "There is no way I am leaving you to run off and get yourself killed the first chance you have."

I blinked and took a step back from this tiny ball of fury that had suddenly erupted in my face. "I'm not?"

"Absolutely not."

Just as quickly as it had erupted, all the anger drained from her body, and she sagged, dropping her face into her hands and bursting into sobs.

I stepped back toward her, my hands reaching out to wrap my arms around her, but not knowing if I should touch her. "I won't. I promise I won't run off and get killed."

She froze. Then she turned her tear-stained face up toward me. She studied me with her beautiful brown eyes, her gaze piercing, penetrating. Finally, she nodded as if coming to some decision. "You're right," she said. "You won't."

Utterly baffled by her swift shifts in emotion, I watched in confusion as she spun around in the crowd of Khanavai warriors and human females, her gaze scanning the faces. She finally found who she was looking for. "Vos! Come here."

"Yes?" he asked as he strolled toward us.

"Are you recording?"

The Games Administrator nodded. "I am."

"Then be sure to capture this."

What was my miniature supernova about to do now?

She took my hands in hers and tilted her face up to stare at me intently again. All around us, the crowd began to quiet, sensing something important might be happening.

"Cav Adredoni. I do not want to go home."

Inside my chest, my heart began to knit itself back together, a surge of hope swirling around it, repairing it. A smile began to curve my lips upward. "You don't?"

"No. I want to go wherever you go. I don't care if that's to Khanav Prime, to whatever ship you are stationed on next, or even off to spy school."

"I don't think they allow mates in spy school," I said.

"Then I guess they're going to have to start." Now she was beginning to smile, too.

"So, are you saying you want to be my traveling companion?"

That earned me an eye-roll. "No, you idiot." Around us, people begin chuckling. "I want you to marry me."

My heart exploded in a starburst inside me.

"And I want you to be my mate," I replied.

"Excellent." Natalie turned to look at Vos. "Looks like you're getting your wedding after all."

Then she was in my arms again, and I couldn't tell which of us was kissing the other—only that we were perfectly entwined.

And it would be that way forever if I had my way.

Not that I was entirely certain that I would have my way in much of anything. I suspected my mate was going to have quite a lot to say about how our lives went from now on.

From somewhere behind us, a roar started, then grew. I had just enough time to recognize the sound and turn around to find Tiziani, his face contorted with rage, leaping toward us, his sword spinning around as he prepared to strike.

Everything inside me screamed that I had to protect my mate.

With a roar that rivaled any I had ever made or heard in battle, I spun Natalie out of the way, lowered my shoulder, and dove into Tiziani's midsection, flipping him over my shoulder and onto the ground, where I slammed my boot into the center of his chest, knocking the air out of him and holding him down.

All around us, people stood in shocked silence.

A slight commotion to my right drew my attention, and I watched as Commander Eldron shouldered his way through the crowd, holding the hand of a small, dark-skinned human woman.

"Nice to see you again, Commander," I said.

"You as well." The commander glanced down at Tiziani. "Looks like you have everything under control."

"At least for the moment," I said conversationally, even as the guardsman under my heel began to try to wriggle away.

"You know," the commander continued, as if we were chatting over a meal, "I know Prince Aranov. I think it might be best if I commed him about his guardsman."

"Yes," I agreed. "Perhaps the prince will have some idea how to handle him."

"Oh, no," Natalie interjected. "I have a much better idea."

The commander raised his eyebrows. "Yes?"

"Vos," Natalie said to the Games Administrator, "don't you have a position open?"

Vos flashed his signature smile. "I believe I might, come to think of it."

On the floor, Tiziani began to protest, having regained his breath.

"What kind of position?" Commander Eldron asked.

"I could use an assistant between now and the next Bride Games," Vos said. "And we have never had a failed groom returned to the games. It could be an interesting storyline next year."

"No," Tiziani groaned. "I can't leave my life on Khanav Prime."

The commander shook his head. "Oh, I don't believe you'll be having any say in it." He glanced down at the woman next to him and gave her hand a squeeze. "Besides, it might teach you something about how to interact with Earth females."

He turned then to bow to Natalie. "Congratulations, my dear." To me, he said, "I'll take over here. I think you and your mate have a ceremony to plan."

Natalie and I shared a look. We did have a ceremony to plan—but more than that, I wanted to take her back to her room and show her what it truly meant to be the mate of a Khanavai warrior.

CHAPTER TWENTY-ONE

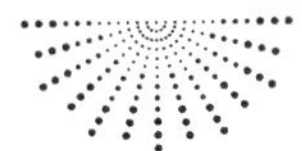

NATALIE

In my room in the bride quarters, Plofnid and Drindl fluttered around me, making sure every detail of my wedding dress was perfect.

Not that it mattered, as far as I was concerned.

The night before, Cav and I had made our vows to each other—with our words and our bodies.

Not that we needed the words. I finally understood exactly what he meant when he said he knew we belonged together.

He was right. We did.

The two stylists finally finished making their final touches and straightening my ivory lace dress.

Drindl stood back and clasped her silvery hands in front of her third breast. "You are absolutely beautiful," she trilled.

Plofnid leaned back and looked me up and down with a critical eye. "Perfect," it announced, tossing its nose-braid back over its shoulder.

"How much longer?" I asked, anxious to finish the public portion of our mating ceremony.

"Not long," Drindl said, casting a conspiratorial glance at Plofnid.

I sighed. As happy as I was to be mated to Cav, I was ready to get this second spectacle over with so we could start our new life together.

I was about to ask if we could head to the stadium when the door burst open and Jas, my mother, and my sister Julie came flying into the room.

I gasped, stunned to see them. My mother threw her arms around me and immediately started crying. "Oh, baby, you don't have to do this."

Jas stood back with her hands on her hips and glared at me. "I can't believe you're going to marry some stranger and take off to another planet."

Julie watched me, her eyes narrowed. "You really want to do this, don't you?"

"I do," I said simply.

Mom dropped her arms from around my shoulders and took my face in her hands, her tears drying instantly. "Really? Are you certain?"

"Absolutely. And I promise I will com all the time. Cav said he would come to Earth with me as soon as we're able to."

"So is that spanking thing as sexy as it looked?" Jas asked. "When Cav did it, I mean. Not that yellow asshole. Did you think he looked like a banana?"

My cheeks heated. "Can we talk about all that later?"

"What are you going to do about your degree?" Mom demanded.

"It's all been arranged with the school. I'm finishing my last year virtually."

"Really? You can do that?" Julie asked.

"Apparently if the Khanavai government wants it, they can make it happen," I told her. A speculative gleam started in her eyes.

"You are never leaving home," Mom said, pointing at my sister.

"That's how we ended up here," Jas told me. "Vos Klavoii contacted us personally and said he knew you would want us to be at the wedding. I guess the Khanavai government really can make anything happen."

"Vos Klavoii is almost as big an asshole as Banana-Man," I replied.

"It's time," Drindl sang out, opening the door and ushering us out.

She and Plofnid led us through the brightly colored station, my best friend and family alternating between chattering and gawking at everything around them.

As we stepped into the backstage area of the stadium, I looked out to the area where Cav had fought with Tiziani just days before. It had been decorated in a mix of Earth and Khanavai flowers, a riotous explosion of color transforming the sterile space into something beautiful.

A perfect mix of both worlds.

I caught a glimpse of my groom, gorgeous and muscular and strong, standing beneath an arch draped with white lace. I definitely detected Drindl and Plofnid's touches in that particular choice.

Jas managed to sneak in a whisper. "You know, David was devastated."

I shrugged. "I feel bad for him. But…"

"But you're in love with someone else," Julie interjected. I hadn't even realized the sixteen-year-old was listening in.

"Guess he waited too long, then," Jas said. "You snooze, you lose."

"I didn't know I needed someone who would fight for me," I said quietly.

Mom reached down and squeezed my hand. "If you're sure about him, then I'm happy for you," she said.

I couldn't tear my eyes away from my mate, waiting for me. "I am absolutely certain."

Vos and his secretary Anthony bustled in.

"It's time," Vos said. "Let's get everyone to your places. Ladies, if you will follow me, I will show you to your seats."

"Tell me exactly how the Bride Games work," Julie said to Vos. "How do you decide who gets chosen, really?"

As he ushered them away, Vos turned back to me. "Best Bride Games ever," he said, giving me a very human thumbs-up.

"And I definitely won," I whispered as they all moved away, and I was left standing alone.

I knew the cameras were rolling and everyone on two worlds was watching.

But as the strains of human orchestra music began playing, and I stepped out into the spotlight that Vos had arranged to have trained on me, none of that mattered.

The only person who mattered was my bright blue alien groom waiting for me, just a few steps away.

And this time, once I reached his side, I would never leave it again.

EPILOGUE

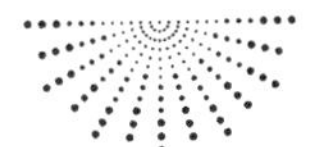

AMELIA RIVERS

LAS VEGAS, NEVADA, EARTH

I knew it was coming.

I'm not sure how, but as soon as the screen on my computer went blank and then spun back up with Vos Klavoii's face smiling brightly at me, I was absolutely certain my name was going to be drawn in the Bride Lottery—the hellish agreement that Earth's leaders had made to sell us to the aliens who protected our planet.

I'd grown up with the propaganda. It was our civic duty. Men registered for the draft, women registered for the Bride Lottery.

Fuck that.

No way in hell was I going to be handed over to some giant man to be brutalized into bearing his children.

So I walked away from everything, instead.

I stood up, pulled on my boots, grabbed my purse and a jacket, and left the Las Vegas hotel room I'd booked for the conference I'd been attending. There was a drugstore nearby on the Strip, so that's where I headed.

All around me, screens showed the alien game show host drawing name after name. As I moved along the sidewalk, dodging the tourists who thronged the city even late at night, I kept my head down, praying I could get what I needed before my name came up.

Inside the store, fluorescent lights buzzed above me as I tossed the things I needed into a basket. A box-cutter. Nail scissors. Alcohol. Needle and thread. Bandages. Hair dye. And at the last minute, a pile of granola bars and a giant bottle of water.

I half-expected the cashier to comment on my choices, but the tall woman behind the counter barely even glanced at the items as she scanned them.

I was practically running by the time I got back to my hotel room, and my hands were shaking as I dumped everything out onto the counter in the bathroom.

What I was about to do was as illegal as it gets. And I was sure there would be physical and mental repercussions, as well. But at that moment, I didn't care.

I'm a doctor. I can do this, even to myself.

Taking a deep breath, I counted to ten as I exhaled. I was a surgeon, and I'd done plenty of minor excisions. My hands stopped trembling, and I reached up to make the first incision about an inch behind my ear, hissing sharply as the pain hit. But I breathed past it and kept going. I'd have to stay steady to cut the wires that led into my brain.

Less than ten minutes later, I dropped my biochip into the toilet and flushed it away. With any luck, authorities would try to chase it down as it washed through the Las Vegas sewers, giving me time to get away.

I stitched up the wound I'd created with the needle and thread. I'd rinsed it all in isopropyl alcohol first, but I'd still need to keep an eye on it for any infection. Luckily, the conference had been rife with pharmaceutical reps handing out sample meds like they were candy. There were bound to be a few antibiotics in there if I needed them.

After I'd taped a bandage over the whole grisly mess, I glanced around the bathroom. It looked like a crime scene with blood smeared across the counter. With a shrug, I moved into the bedroom, trying to decide what to take.

My computer? Phone? God, they'd be able to trace me with those.

Better get a burner phone.

I grabbed the biggest shoulder bag in the room—one with a pharmaceutical company's logo on it, a conference-attendee gift—and threw a change of clothes into it, along with a sample bottle of antibiotics and all my drugstore purchases.

The television was still playing in the background, and Vos had just drawn another name. "Amelia Rivers," he announced.

I turned around as if in a trance. There it was. My face on the screen behind him.

Shit. Time to go.

No time to dye my hair, either. Maybe I could duck into a casino bathroom for that. Or better yet, find a way to do it at the airport—assuming I got that far.

But before I left the room, there was one last thing I needed to do. Moving in front of the bathroom mirror, I lifted up my long, blonde ponytail. Then I used the nail scissors to snip it off. I shook my remaining hair out. It was a shaggy mess, but at least I looked a little less like myself than usual.

I carried the ponytail out of the room and dropped it in a trashcan as I bypassed the elevators and opened the stairwell door.

"Here goes nothing," I whispered to myself as I headed down.

The heavy door closed behind me with a final-sounding click as I walked away from everything I'd ever known.

ENJOYED THIS STORY? Be sure to leave a review!

CAPTURED FOR THE ALIEN BRIDE LOTTERY

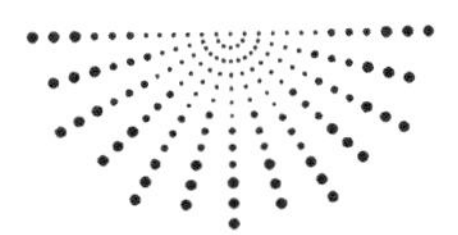

ABOUT CAPTURED FOR THE ALIEN BRIDE LOTTERY

I refused to be in the Bride Lottery—so now I'm a runaway bride.

Somehow, I knew my name was going to be drawn in the Bride Lottery—the hellish agreement that Earth's leaders had made to sell us to the aliens who protected our planet.

I'd grown up with the propaganda. It was our civic duty. Men registered for the draft, women registered for the Bride Lottery.

No way in hell was I going to be handed over to some giant man to be brutalized into bearing his children.

Instead, I cut out my bio-tracker and walked away from everything.

I should have realized they'd send one of those hulking, brightly colored aliens to track me down and bring me back.

Never did I expect that he'd be devastatingly attractive. Or that we'd have to go on the run from the evil Horde trying to destroy both our planets.

Now that we're together, can I ever run away again?

And could he really hand me over to the Bride Games to be taken by another warrior?

Because I think I might be falling in love...

Fans of Grace Goodwin, Evangeline Anderson, and Ruby Dixon will love this steamy new series featuring gorgeous, bright alien heroes and the sassy human women they choose as mates!

Every book in the Khanavai Warrior Bride Games series is a stand-alone romance. Join these brides as they find a whole new world of happily ever afters.

PROLOGUE

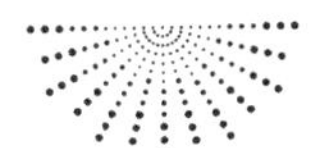

ZONT LANOV

Four solar days. That's how long I'd been on Station 21, hoping to find my mate in the Bride Games.

I'd made my fun where I could, leading my new friend Cav Adredoni on an unauthorized trip down to the arena floor, where he'd certainly found *his* bride, even if she didn't realize it yet. But he'd gotten one whiff of her and instantly known she was destined to be his.

As the old Khanavai saying goes, the cock follows where the nose leads.

Don't get me wrong—I was having a wonderful time. The entire endeavor was almost as entertaining as a trip to the Clavox Pleasure Mines, where the females all have five breasts and can bend in the most interesting and unusual directions.

Well, maybe not *that* entertaining.

But I was enjoying myself.

That's what I kept telling myself, anyway. However, the absence of even one human female who captured my interest—much less my nose *or* my cock—had begun to weigh on me.

Maybe I wasn't destined to find a mate, after all.

Cav and I sat in the audience, our comscreens focused on the bridal interviews below. Bride after bride stepped up to speak to Vos Klavoii, the Games Administrator. The human women were lovely, in their own way.

But none was *mine*.

I had to fight not to heave an irritated sigh. I was on leave from Special Ops, and I would enjoy my vacation, even if I didn't find a mate of my own.

Without warning, all the screens in the stands went blank. I glanced around, instantly on alert for danger. Could this be an attack from the Alveron Horde?

No, I realized as the screens blinked back on, showing Vos in front of an image of an Earther cityscape. This interruption might not have been planned, but it was definitely executed on purpose.

"Warriors and women," Vos said, "Earthers and Khanavai, we have an exciting new development in this year's Bride Games. Apparently, one of our contestants has run. That's right—for the first time in all the years we've been holding the lottery, a bride has, as the Earthers sometimes say, *gone on the lam*."

The palpable excitement in Vos's voice echoed out over the stadium and I had to laugh. This was exactly the kind of thrill the devotees of the Bride Games hoped for every year. A gasp went up at the announcement and the brides on the arena floor began chattering among themselves.

Still…

"A runner?" I spoke my thought aloud. "How did she manage that?"

Cav didn't answer, focused as he was on Vos, who continued talking as the screen behind him changed to show the runaway Bride Lottery winner. "Amelia Rivers is now a wanted fugitive on Earth. She's originally from Dallas, Texas, but was most recently seen in Las Vegas, Nevada." His voice dropped. "For those Khanavai watching, that's in the United States, a country in what the Earthers call the North American continent."

I registered the words, but the image of the human female on the screen held my attention. She was…

Perfect.

The word popped into my mind, and in that moment, I knew it was true. She was perfect—for me, at least.

"Las Vegas," I said slowly. "Isn't that the pleasure city?"

Cav shrugged, too anxious to see his own mate's Bridal Pageant interview to pay much attention to my questions. Fine. I could find out more about Amelia Rivers on my own. I pulled up the program and ran a search for her name.

She's stunning.

And she's mine.

I SPENT that night mapping out my plan of attack and gathering the team I would take with me. A quick consultation with my commanding officer led him to contact Vos to ensure I had the complete cooperation of the Bride Games Administrator.

Central Command did prefer officers who were happily mated. Stable and settled.

I simply had to wait until the Bride Pageant ended, and then I could depart Station 21 for Earth.

It seemed too long a time to spend pacing my quarters, so I joined Cav to watch the brides, arriving just in time to hear Vos instructing the grooms on the rules of the Bride Games.

Might as well keep myself entertained until it's time to leave.

If not for Cav's determination to win his own bride, I would have invited him to join the operation. But he was far too besotted with her to risk taking time away from the Games.

I slipped into the seat next to him and turned on my screen to examine Amelia Rivers once again, even though I had already memorized the brief biography in the program.

"Natalie," Cav breathed as he flipped to her image on the screen.

"You're completely set on her, aren't you?" I asked. For the first time, I truly understood that overwhelming desire to focus on one female.

Cav leaned over to look at my comscreen. "Amelia Rivers?" he asked, sounding surprised. "The runaway bride? Can you even choose her?"

I grinned. "She's still in the program. And she's the one I want."

"You're going to have a quark's eye of a time of it with that one." Cav shook his head. "How do you know for sure that you're compatible?"

"I have my ways. I pulled her DNA last night, and we are a perfect match. I've put in a request with Command Central to allow me to hunt her as part of this year's Bride Games." I couldn't help but grin.

Cav's eyes grew wide. "That's quite an effort to put into simply getting a mate."

I wanted to laugh aloud—there was no effort too great to gain this woman—but I simply rubbed my hands together. "I do enjoy a challenge."

"Maybe I'm not right for Special Ops, after all." Cav's voice turned dejected.

My roar of laughter interrupted Vos Klavoii's instructions, and the Administrator glared up at the two of us. I waved an apology, but still leaned in to whisper to Cav, "You've chosen the only other Earther female who announced that she doesn't want to be here. You cannot tell me that you don't like a challenge, too, brother."

"When do you leave for Earth?"

"When the pageant ends, Vos will interview me. As soon as that's done, I can take a shuttle down to the planet." I couldn't wait to get going. I leaned back to contemplate how wonderful it would be to have a mate of my own.

Once I tamed her, of course.

Finally, after what seemed an eternity, Vos wrapped up his instructions and the brides began to gather at the entrance to the arena. "At last," I muttered. This was taking forever.

"There are almost four hundred potential mates this year," Cav said. "You can't leave yet."

"No, but the sooner they get started, the sooner it will be over, and I can go capture my own mate."

Cav smiled as the Bride Pageant began, each bride stepping onto the stage, repeating her name, and listing the skills that made her a viable bride candidate. Then she turned slowly to allow the DNA scanners to take a scent sample and send it out over the room.

"What if," Cav asked me, "you get to Earth and discover your chosen bride smells all wrong?"

I shrugged. "Then I'll bring her back to take her rightful place in the Games." I glanced over at Amelia Rivers' image, still up on my comscreen. "But it won't," I added quietly. "I am as certain that she is mine as if I had scented her already."

Yes, the nose might lead the cock. But I was in charge of them both—and we were all going to Earth.

To make Amelia Rivers mine.

No matter what it took.

CHAPTER ONE

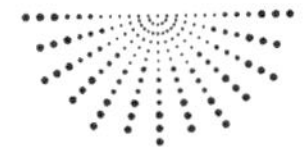

AMELIA RIVERS

I knew it was coming.

I'm not sure how, but as soon as the screen on my computer went blank and then spun back up with Vos Klavoii's face smiling brightly at me, I was absolutely certain my name was going to be drawn in the Bride Lottery—the hellish agreement that Earth's leaders had made to sell us to the aliens who protected our planet.

I'd grown up with the propaganda. It was our civic duty. Men registered for the draft, women registered for the Bride Lottery.

Fuck that.

No way in hell was I going to be handed over to some giant man to be brutalized into bearing his children.

So I walked away from everything, instead.

I stood up, pulled on my boots, grabbed my purse and a jacket, and left the Las Vegas hotel room I'd booked for the conference I'd been attending. There was a drugstore nearby on the Strip, so that's where I headed.

All around me, screens showed the alien game show host drawing name after name. As I moved along the sidewalk, dodging the tourists who thronged the city even late at night, I kept my head down, praying I could get what I needed before my name came up.

Inside the store, fluorescent lights buzzed above me as I tossed the things I needed into a basket. A box-cutter. Nail scissors. Alcohol. Needle and thread. Bandages. Hair dye. And at the last minute, a pile of granola bars and a giant bottle of water.

I half-expected the cashier to comment on my choices, but the tall woman behind the counter barely even glanced at the items as she scanned them.

I was practically running by the time I got back to my hotel room, and my hands were shaking as I dumped everything out onto the counter in the bathroom.

What I was about to do was as illegal as it gets. And I was sure there would be physical and mental repercussions, as well. But at that moment, I didn't care.

I'm a doctor. I can do this, even to myself.

Taking a deep breath, I counted to ten as I exhaled. I was a surgeon, and I'd done plenty of minor excisions. My hands stopped trembling, and I reached up to make the first incision about an inch behind my ear, hissing sharply as the pain hit. But I breathed past it and kept going. I'd have to stay steady to cut the wires that led into my brain.

Less than ten minutes later, I dropped my biochip into the toilet and flushed it away. With any luck, authorities would try to chase it down as it washed through the Las Vegas sewers, giving me time to get away.

I stitched up the wound I'd created with the needle and thread. I'd rinsed it all in isopropyl alcohol first, but I'd still need to keep an eye on it for any infection. Luckily, the conference had been rife with pharmaceutical reps handing out sample meds like they were candy. There were bound to be a few antibiotics in there if I needed them.

After I'd taped a bandage over the whole grisly mess, I glanced around the bathroom. It looked like a crime scene with blood smeared across the counter. With a shrug, I moved into the bedroom, trying to decide what to take.

My computer? Phone? God, they'd be able to trace me with those.

Better get a burner phone.

I grabbed the biggest shoulder bag in the room—one with a pharmaceutical company's logo on it, a conference-attendee gift—and threw two changes of clothes into it, along with all the sample packages of meds, including more than one antibiotic, and my drugstore purchases.

The television was still playing in the background, and Vos had just drawn another name. "Amelia Rivers," he announced.

I turned around as if in a trance. There it was. My face on the screen behind him.

Shit. Time to go.

No time to dye my hair, either. Maybe I could duck into a casino bathroom for that. Or better yet, find a way to do it at the airport—assuming I got that far.

But before I left the room, there was one last thing I needed to do. Moving in front of the bathroom mirror, I lifted my long, blonde ponytail. Then I used the nail scissors to snip it off. I shook my remaining hair out. It was a shaggy mess, but at least I looked a little less like myself than usual.

I carried the ponytail out of the room and dropped it in a trashcan as I bypassed the elevators and opened the stairwell door.

"Here goes nothing," I whispered to myself as I headed down.

The heavy door closed behind me with a final-sounding click as I walked away from everything I'd ever known.

I MARCHED DOWN THE STRIP, moving as quickly as possible. The farther away from my own hotel I got, the better it would be for me. I swung into a casino hotel, one of the smaller ones, and hid in a bathroom stall, dying my hair a dark burgundy red.

Yet another blood-red scene I'm leaving behind.

No one came in while I rinsed out the excess dye in a sink, and at the last minute, I stripped off my white button-down shirt, balled it up, and ran it through the dyed water, just in case anyone at the conference remembered what I'd been wearing that day.

When I squeezed the excess water out, the shirt was a weird shade of pink with darker burgundy streaks running through it. I pulled a t-shirt out of my bag to wear and held the now-pink shirt under the hand dryer.

I blotted my hair and dried it, at least a little, under the air-blower for hands. I surveyed the results in the mirror.

I definitely didn't look like myself any longer. I looked exactly like the rebel I had never been, not once in my entire life.

Now I have to get out of Las Vegas.

I had already abandoned my plan to head to the airport. I couldn't fly—they were too careful about checking IDs. Same with renting a car.

Buses, I decided. Maybe Greyhound would be less stringent with their ID requirements.

When I walked through the hotel lobby and stopped to ask the concierge for directions to the bus station, he barely glanced at me before offering me a map and the information I'd requested. He might remember me later, but it was a random stop, so it might be months before anybody figured out they needed to talk to him in particular.

Luckily, the bus station was within easy walking distance. I hated to blow any of my limited cash on a taxi. I slipped my still-damp shirt over my t-shirt and walked with my head down, avoiding eye contact with anyone else.

The bus station in Vegas was cleaner than I anticipated. Not that I'd ever ridden on a public bus before. I ground the heels of my hands into my eyes, suddenly feeling tired.

Maybe it would be easier to give myself up, go through the Bride Games.

The thought made my stomach clench.

I'm just tired, I told myself. It was well after midnight by this point. I'd feel better once I got out of Vegas.

At least the desert air had mostly dried the shirt I'd dyed.

A single bored ticket agent manned the counter, tapping at the keys with long, pointed fingernails painted a bright blue that matched the streaks in her hair.

"Hi. When does your next bus leave?" I tried to sound nonchalant, but I could feel my anxiety threading through my voice.

The ticket agent frowned at me. "Where are you headed?"

I shrugged. "Wherever the road takes me, I guess." I knew it was a stupid answer, but I was trying to channel my inner hippie-child. The one who'd never existed—but who might be the sort to dye her shirt to match her hair and take an impromptu trip on the next bus out of town.

She gave me a long look but went back to clicking keys on her computer. "We have a bus leaving for Chicago in about twenty minutes."

Chicago. That was the kind of place I could get lost in. Barring that, if I started worrying about getting caught, I could get off at any stop along the way and switch to another bus line.

"I'll take it."

She didn't blink when I gave her my name. I guessed she hadn't been watching the Bride Lottery. I almost sighed in relief when she handed me my ticket.

But as I reached out to take it, she held on to the other end for a second longer than she had to. "Good luck, Ms. Rivers," she said quietly.

My gaze flew to hers, and I realized she did know who I was. My heart began beating frantically in my chest. "I'm sorry?" I managed to choke out, as if I didn't understand what she meant.

"I hope you get away," she murmured. "They shouldn't be able to take us." Then she let go of the ticket and resumed her bored façade. "Have a nice trip," she said aloud in her professional ticketing agent voice.

I didn't start feeling safe until the bus pulled out of the station. My fellow passengers ignored me, settling down into their seats, most of them attempting to nap.

Adrenaline still coursed through my veins, my heart pounding harder than it ought to. I didn't know where I was going, not ultimately, and I wasn't sure I'd be able to hide from the Khanavai Bride Lottery indefinitely—but I was determined to try.

Rumor had it there were other races out in the galaxy, ones who didn't require the equivalent of a human sexual sacrifice to coexist.

The only ones we were certain of were the Alveron Horde—the aliens who had attacked our planet, leading the Khanavai to offer to protect us in exchange for human brides—and the Khanavai themselves.

Until we managed to develop better spaceflight technology, I was essentially trapped on Earth.

I never thought I would feel as if my entire planet were a cage.

At least it's a big cage.

Surely I can find somewhere to hide.

CHAPTER TWO

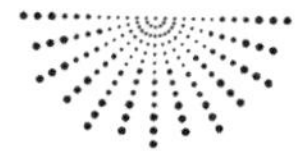

ZONT

I stood in the dry desert air beside an open tunnel that led into the Las Vegas sewer system, watching as human law enforcement officers milled around in search of any sign of the woman I hunted. While they worked to prove what I had already determined —that she had never been anywhere near this spot—I flipped through a stack of e-papers, learning what I could about my quarry's background.

Amelia Rivers.

This report was a little more in-depth than what I had been given at the Bride Games on Station 21. There, I had found out that she was twenty-eight years old, light-haired, and trained as a medic.

This report expanded on that information. She had never married, and she had grown up in the northern hemisphere of the Earth in the United States state of Connecticut.

But when ran, she had been in the human pleasure city of Las Vegas.

Vos, the Bride Games Administrator, had not mentioned what she'd been doing there.

As far as he was concerned, Amelia Rivers was just another runaway bride, a potential crack in our two planets' Bride Alliance, the agreement allowing Khanavai warriors to claim human brides—we took unmarried human females in exchange for protecting Earth from the ravages of the Alveron Horde.

That I was willing to hunt down Amelia Rivers and bring her back was enough for the Games Administrator. With my assistance, he would keep our treaty safe.

And to the Khanavai, the Bride Treaty was everything. At this point, almost an entire generation of Khanavai warriors had at least one human somewhere in their genetic history.

There had even been some rumors of human-Khanavai mixed females being able to reproduce—amazing, given what the Horde had done to our DNA. Humans were exactly what our people needed to keep our culture alive.

But I had seen more than another bride-shaped savior of our people when her image flashed on the holographic viewscreen in front of my seats in the stadium.

Amelia Rivers was not simply another bride. Not only another mate for one of our people.

No. She was *my* mate. *My* bride. The human female for me.

The only one for me.

I had known it as soon as I saw her, in the same way that all Khanavai knew their mates. Well, almost. I would need to scent her to cement the bond, but as far as I was concerned, that was a mere technicality.

And she might not realize it yet, but I suspected the same kind of sixth sense—sixth for humans, anyway—was exactly how she had known to run before her name was ever even called in the Bride Lottery.

Now I knew even more.

She had grown up with wealthy Earth parents, raised largely by servants—they called them "nannies" on Earth, which oddly enough was also a name for goats, a kind of common herd animal. And also sometimes a nickname for grandmothers.

Earth language is truly bizarre. I shook my head and continued reading.

Amelia had attended the best schools available, but unlike many of her wealthy classmates, she was not willing to spend her life in idle entertainment.

Instead, she strove to become the best at everything she did.

So when she had gone to Earth medical school, she had chosen to become a surgeon.

Of course, what she didn't know was that her field would be obsolete within the next decade.

Cutting people open in order to repair them. Utterly barbaric.

Her parents arranged to pay for Amelia to be excused from the Bride Lottery year after year, claiming exemptions and bribing officials to keep their daughter free of Khanavai entanglements.

Right up until they got caught.

From everything I had learned so far, Amelia did not know her parents had paved her way to remain free of the Bride Lottery. Like so many other women, she simply assumed it was luck or fate.

But now, fate had intervened in another way—specifically, in me. I was her fated mate, though she didn't know it yet.

And I was going to track her down and make her mine.

At least, that's what I thought when I landed on Earth.

I had spent my entire adult life in the military, training to become a member of the Khanavai Special Ops team.

We were skilled in tracking and hunting, in eliminating our enemies, and in protecting our allies.

I knew how to function in virtually every kind of terrain from here to Andromeda Five. I was used to foes who were smart, canny, wily.

But apparently, I wasn't ready for an adversary who *cut out her own tracker* and flushed it down the waste receptacle. Speaking of barbaric. I shuddered. "Why would she slice open her skin to remove her communicator?"

The tiny human male standing next to me with his hands on his hips looked me up and down with a derisive snort. "She's not the first runner your kind has dealt with, is she?"

My frown turned into a scowl. "She doesn't need to be afraid of us."

The law enforcer shrugged. "Doesn't mean she has to be excited to go with you, either. I understand this lady's a doctor. A surgeon. Plenty good at cutting, I expect. Seems like maybe she has a life here she wouldn't want to leave."

His wide-legged stance was aggressive, and I realized as I compared him to the other human males standing around that he was, in fact, bigger than most of them. More muscular, probably stronger. There was a distinct possibility that he would be considered a fine masculine example of the species, with dark eyes and skin that was one of the darker shades on the boring beige-to-brown spectrum that humans tended toward.

He's nothing compared to a Khanavai warrior, of course, but perhaps impressive among his own kind.

Part of me wanted to slap him down, remind him of Khanavai superiority. But there was a chance I would need human assistance in this particular hunt. Especially since the bride at the end of it was meant to be mine.

Knowledge of the local customs could be useful—especially since no one on the impromptu team I had hastily assembled specialized in Earth culture.

Besides, they were all in orbit on the shuttle Vos had given me in exchange for allowing the entire hunt to be filmed by the silver ball currently hovering beside me, noting every moment of this exchange.

I might as well attempt to garner goodwill—both with this law enforcer and the viewing audience of both worlds.

After all, I might know Amelia Rivers was mine. But she was still technically a Bride Games contestant—I would need Vos to sign off on our pairing before this was over.

A ping on my wrist communicator alerted me to a message coming in —one of the perks of having been able to commandeer a military team to work with me on this. I was particularly pleased to have found Wex, the communications officer who had been given leave to work on the Bride Games transmission. He was technically still military, so I had added him to my team.

Now Wex's words scrolled across the screen: **Vos offering a bounty for bringing Amelia Rivers in safe. At least three other hunters heading planetside to claim the bounty**.

Great. In addition to tracking down my runaway bride, I'll have to eliminate the competition, as well.

I wondered briefly if any of the other bounty hunters were after Amelia herself, or if they simply wanted the monetary prize that came with capturing a human woman who fled the Bride Lottery.

I turned my attention back to the dark-skinned police officer. "Tell me about the various modes of transportation she might have taken out of your pleasure city."

He snickered, shaking his head and squeezing the bridge of his nose with two fingers before glancing up at me. "Just the usual. Planes, trains, and automobiles. She couldn't get very far walking."

I held up the plastic bag containing her now ruined and befouled communicator chip and examined it with distaste. Without her implant, I had no way to track her directly.

Time to engage in some old-fashioned tracking.

Turning away from the enforcement officer, I keyed my wrist communicator's vocal recognition program. "Get me an analysis of all potential transportation methods out of the pleasure city of Las Vegas on Earth, along with a detailed analysis of which method the fugitive was most likely to have taken."

Wex's response came almost immediately. "Without sufficient parameters, this could take some time."

I snarled, and out of the corner of my eye, I saw the human officer take a step backward, away from me.

Good. The humans needed to learn to respect the Khanavai.

Just as I would teach Amelia to respect us. To respect me.

Once I caught up with her.

CHAPTER THREE

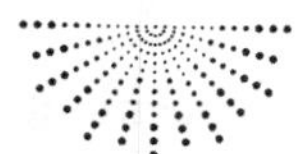

AMELIA

Abandoning all my electronics in Las Vegas had left me desperate for information, but at the same time, I was afraid to try to find out too much from other passengers. So at the first stop, I'd bought a couple of preloaded generic epaper news and novel collections to entertain myself during the trip.

The very first news headline was all about me.

Runaway Lottery Bride, it screamed in bold letters as soon as I opened it.

I snapped the cover closed on the bold text, fighting not to glance around and see who was watching. When I realized no one was paying any attention to me, I opened it up again and scanned the headlines to see what the news sites were reporting.

I spent three full days on that bus ride. The itinerary said it was a two-day trip, but we had numerous, excruciating delays. It was a long and miserable trip. And every time I updated my epaper at one of the stops, my picture was plastered all over the front page. At the first stop after I realized exactly how big the story about me had become, I bought sunglasses, huge ones that covered half my face. They were terribly out of style, but dark and anonymous. I kept them on constantly, as if blocking out light so I could sleep.

For part of the way, from Green River, Utah, to Denver, Colorado, I ended up with a seatmate, an overly chatty woman from a Chicago suburb who, luckily for me, only wanted to talk about her grandchildren. Even she gave up trying to talk to me after several rounds of me responding with only, "Yes," and "No," and the occasional grunt.

I almost bailed in Denver, where we had to transfer to a different bus. But my seatmate chose another victim, and I was left to myself again.

Denver was also where I bought and loaded a vid upgrade for my epaper reader. For one thing, I figured if I was going to be successful at this hiding business, I would need to keep up with what the news was saying. But even more than keeping abreast of my Most Wanted status, I decided earbuds would serve as a solid deterrent to any other chatty types I met along the way.

It turned out I was the top of the vidnews stories, too. Well, at least most of the time. The third day, the big story was the Station 21 wedding between Cav and Natalie, topping off the Bride Games season as a resounding success.

But that brought the talking heads on the news right back around to me. Apparently, when she had done her initial interview with Vos Klavoii, the Games Administrator, Natalie had said on interplanetary television, "I wish I had thought to run, too."

When I heard that, it was all I could do not to groan aloud.

I clicked from there into a vid interview with several young women excoriating me for having run. And from there, I went down the rabbit hole, reading and watching all the articles and vids I could find.

The current president of the United States had publicly chastised me for being willing to start what he called "an interplanetary incident" and a "diplomatic nightmare for the entire planet."

That made my stomach hurt. Setting off an interplanetary disagreement had never been my plan. I didn't want to ruin anyone else's life. But I *never* wanted to get married. I wasn't one of those little girls who planned her perfect wedding. For as long as I could remember, I had wanted to be a doctor. And most of all, I did not want to be under anyone else's control again—not now, not ever.

My breaking point, at least when it came to consuming news about myself as Earth's most famous Runaway Bride, came when one popular news personality asked what I assumed were rhetorical questions. "Why would Amelia Rivers run away? Why not go to the Bride Games and simply refuse all her suitors? Why not marry someone else for the requisite five years and then get divorced? Why go on the run at all when there are so many other options?"

Part of me wished I could just reach through the epaper screen and slap him across the face. Not that doing so would have been productive, but it might have made me feel a little better. I turned my face to the window and stared out at the blur of the passing landscape from behind my ridiculous glasses.

I couldn't quit thinking about those questions. I imagined myself answering all those questions and more.

Why not marry someone else and get divorced after five years?

Because the idea of a loveless marriage horrified me. In fact, the idea of any marriage at all horrified me.

Besides, everyone knew that about half those fake marriages—the ones designed to keep a woman firmly on Earth—ended up being investigated by the Khanavai-Earth commission. And the penalties of being caught out were harsh.

I certainly didn't want to go to prison for my imaginary fake loveless marriage.

Of course, there's no telling what would happen to me if I were caught now.

In retrospect, maybe a fake marriage would have been a better idea.

But I had been too busy going to med school, finishing my residency, getting the rest of my work done to become first a doctor, and then a surgeon.

And a five-year marriage didn't protect anyone. There were plenty of stories about divorced women being dragged off to the Bride Games. No woman was safe until she was past easy childbearing age.

Why not go through the Bride Games and reject all the suitors?

That answer seemed obvious to me. I'd read the studies. The Khanavai might say they scented their mates—whatever the hell that meant—but statistically, women with skills that might be useful to the Khanavai were chosen as brides almost ten times as often as those who did not have similar skills.

Hell, even Natalie what's-her-face was studying biochemistry, according to all the stories I'd read. She was smart and accomplished and would be an asset to the whole damn planet of Khanav Prime.

There was no way I would go through the Bride Games and not be inundated with Khanavai suitors. Once that happened, it seemed there was no way out. Less than one percent of women who were chosen by Khanavai warriors turned down the offer to become their "mates."

God. I even hated the word they used for their partners, their wives. *Mates*. Yuck. It was animalistic and degrading.

I didn't know what kind of coercion the Khanavai were using, but when even someone as obviously staunchly opposed to an alien match like Natalie ended up married to one of them—in a giant, televised show of a ceremony, no less—there was something weird going on.

Ultimately, I did not trust the aliens. I didn't believe that they had shown up to protect us from the Alveron Horde with no ulterior motives, I didn't believe that their magical mate-scenting abilities were real, and I definitely did not believe that every bride who left with them went of her own free will.

My mother had always said I had a suspicious mind. It made me a good doctor, adept at sorting through all the clues a patient could offer and then figuring out what was wrong with them.

That same suspicious mind also made me a horrible choice for the Bride Lottery.

Of course I ran.

I would rather be a fugitive for the rest of my life than end up stranded on another planet with some giant husband I barely knew, unable to ever come home.

Because I was certain that's what happened to these women. Suspicious mind or no, nothing about the Bride Lottery added up.

A couple of the vid channels even did spotlights on one of the Khanavai grooms who had come down to Earth to hunt me down. I didn't bother to read anything about it other than the lurid headlines, and I certainly didn't watch the vids.

Khanavai men were hunting me down. That was all I needed to know. I was terrified enough already. Reading up on the war accomplishments of a giant alien who wanted to force me to marry him was not likely to make me feel at all better.

I just about gave myself a headache thinking about all of it. That's when I switched over to reading ridiculous mystery novels. The problem with those, of course, was that I always figured out the mystery within the first few chapters. But the stories were a diversion from the relentless news about the Bride Lottery, the beautiful bride on Station 21, and the Runaway Bride back on Earth.

By the time we hit the Chicago Greyhound station, all I wanted was to sleep in a full-size bed and to take a long, hot shower. Not necessarily in that order.

It was late morning in Chicago—a full twelve hours after we'd been scheduled to arrive—and the sun was shining brightly outside, so at least I had a reason to wear my ridiculous sunglasses. I considered waiting until the bus was almost empty to exit, but then at the last minute, decided I would be better off exiting in a clump of people, just in case anyone was watching for me.

Not that I expected anyone to be here looking for me—my choice to run to Chicago had been impulsive and last-minute, so there shouldn't be anything to lead them to me. Whoever *they* might be.

But as soon as I stepped off the bus, I knew exactly who *they* were.

They was an enormous, surprisingly gorgeous, hot-pink-skinned Khanavai male with dark hair and overly developed chest muscles—which I could tell because he was shirtless. Possibly because no one on Earth made shirts big enough to fit him.

Startled, I glanced down the rest of him. Apparently, we didn't make pants big enough, either. He wore what we had all come to recognize as a traditional Khanavai warrior's uniform. A kilt-like skirt with a belt and a cross strap made out of some kind of leather, decorated with various symbols of prowess in war.

That was another reason I hadn't wanted to get involved with the Khanavai—they were too warlike. I had been to war zones when I traveled briefly with Doctors without Borders, and I'd seen what war did to people.

I was a healer, not a fighter. I did not want to be involved with anyone who wielded weapons. In fact, I wasn't even willing to date police officers here on Earth.

No. If I were ever to get married—which I wouldn't—I wanted someone gentle and kind.

I couldn't have spent more than two seconds taking in his appearance. But I completely froze during those two seconds, and apparently, that was enough to catch his attention.

Even worse for me, it was enough to catch the attention of another set of multicolored aliens scattered around the station as if they were trying to blend in. Like that was possible, given their size and colorations.

All four of them began to converge on me, apparently tipped off by my reaction to them—which seemed odd, since I certainly wasn't the only Greyhound passenger staring at the aliens in our midst.

For all I knew, the big pink guy—presumably their leader, given all of the pins and medals and other symbols he wore on his leather cross strap—gave them orders to capture me by any means necessary.

"Shit," I muttered to myself, ducking into a women's bathroom directly inside the entrance to the bus station building and hoping it would be enough to keep them from following me.

It wasn't, of course.

Seconds later, I was surrounded by leering aliens in all the colors of the rainbow.

CHAPTER FOUR

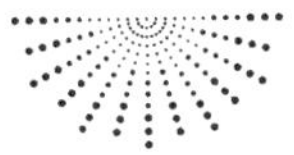

ZONT

I spotted the bounty hunters as soon as I entered the bus station in the human city of Chicago. It was difficult to miss them—no Khanavai on Earth had the benefit of blending in.

I had no idea how they established Amelia Rivers' location. As soon as my team hit the ground in the pleasure city, they began retracing her steps.

Wex had been the one to track her to a bus station—apparently a relatively common mode of travel on Earth. I didn't completely understand it. Why would Earthers still use such slow modes of transport when there were much faster means of getting around the world? Maybe not as fast as the methods the Khanavai had developed, but still, better than crawling along the planetary surface in a wheeled contraption designed to fit more people inside than could possibly be comfortable.

As soon as Wex passed on the information he gained from something called a *ticket agent*, I departed Las Vegas for Chicago. My team was still in the pleasure city in case the intel Wex had extracted from the ticketing agent was wrong. I told them to wait there and continue investigating any credible leads.

Now, I stood here waiting, planning how to introduce myself to my mate and dismissing the bounty hunters as utterly irrelevant. The slight anxiety I felt at finally meeting Amelia served to heighten my awareness. The bounty hunters didn't have a chance.

I saw her the instant she stepped off the bus. Even from a distance, I caught her scent wafting toward me.

Mine, a deep, primal part of me growled.

The aerial vidglobe that had followed me through my entire search buzzed around my head like an annoying bug.

She had chopped off most of her golden hair and turned it a shocking red color, similar to some of my own people's skin tones. She also wore eye coverings that reminded me of something insectoid—and remarkably similar to images I'd seen of the eyes of the Alveron Horde.

Despite those changes designed to fool onlookers into thinking she was someone else, I knew her instantly.

I was still frozen in place, drinking in the sight of her, when the bounty hunters closed in.

My mate was no fool, I was glad to see—she immediately ducked through a nearby doorway, confusingly labeled *Females,* according to my visual translator. I hadn't realized any form of gender discrimination was still allowed on Earth.

I burst into motion a half-second behind the bounty hunters, who followed her without pausing.

Screams erupted from the *Females* room, and several human females burst through the open doorway, forcing me to pause or risk mowing them down.

By the time I got inside the strangely elongated space with several small doors to boxed-in spaces, the bounty hunters had surrounded her like a pack of Lorishi canine predators. One of them held her by the arm as she struggled to free herself. He turned to his leader with a lascivious grin and said, "When we get her up to the ship, can we use her?"

That same primal part of me sent a deep growl crawling up my throat. "She's mine."

The leader, a red Khanavai male with no battle honors on his traditional vandenoi leather strap, threw his head back and laughed. "We got here first, *groom*." The last word came out with a sneer. "You'll have to wait to claim her on the station. After we claim the prize money." He turned to the blue male who held her. "And after, as Jole said, we have a little fun."

I took a threatening step forward, my voice rising. "That's my mate you're talking about."

A mate who had continued to fight against her captor the whole time we were speaking. *Good girl,* I thought as I nodded at her, hoping she could sense my approval.

"She's not your mate yet, *splavot*," the leader spat out at me, using the most derogatory term he could come up with—one for a mateless male.

A purple haze of rage colored my vision, and I took another step toward them, my weaponless hands curling into claws. "Let me save you from these animals," I said to Amelia, holding out my hand.

She shrank away from my offer, her eyes wide, terror rolling off her in palpable waves.

Oh, Zagrodnian hells. Right. She had removed her tracker, which also served as a translator. She had no idea what any of us were saying.

I couldn't imagine she would trust me any more than she would trust any of these monsters—especially since all she'd seen was another Khanavai male barging into this…what? Sacred feminine space? And then I'd growled and thundered. No wonder she was frightened.

Still, a tiny part of me wailed inside at the realization that my mate had not recognized me as instantly as I had recognized her.

Deal with it later, Zont, I admonished myself.

Digging deep into my memory, I pulled out a few words of the dominant Earther language for this zone—something I had learned when I was studying to apply to be stationed on Earth, even though it wasn't strictly necessary, since universal chipping for humans was a requisite part of the Bride Alliance.

At this moment, I was glad I had taken the time to do the extra work.

I stretched my hand out toward her again, giving it a little bounce. "I save…" I scrambled for the correct pronoun for a human female. "Her. I save her."

For the first time since I'd entered the *Females* room, Amelia stopped struggling for a brief moment, her brows creasing in confusion. "What?"

"I save her. I save Amelia."

"You'll save me?"

You. That was the pronoun I'd been searching for.

A vague recollection from a class on human body language prompted me to shake my head from side to side as I said, "Yes."

"Well, which is it? Yes or no?" Amelia redoubled her struggles.

This time I held my head perfectly still. "Yes. I save you."

By now, the three bounty hunters had drawn their bladed weapons—the Bride Alliance did not allow any other weapons to be brought to Earth—and pointed them at me.

I hadn't thought Amelia's eyes could grow any larger, but her realization that the other three Khanavai males were arrayed against me proved me wrong.

I managed to dredge up one more Earther word to shout at Amelia as I sprang into motion, sweeping the legs out from under the blue male who gripped her arm.

"Run!"

My move to free her from her captor's grasp exposed my right side, leaving it unprotected as I came up and drew my own sword in one smooth motion, and the leader of the group swung at me, hitting my side and sliding his sword along one rib. Pain, bright and sharp, flashed through me.

The third hunter took a jab at me as I spun away from the one who had managed to open up a slice in my side.

Grabbing the wound, I pressed against it, pushing hard in case it was deep. The exhilaration of the fight kept me from feeling the pain of it too much, though. With one booted foot, I smashed the original attacker's sword hand, crushing his fingers under my heel with a satisfying crunch.

I glanced up at the door long enough to see Amelia Rivers pause to glance back at me worriedly. Then she was gone, and I was left behind fighting the two remaining bounty hunters while the third pulled up to a sitting position and cradled his hand, tears running out of his eyes.

These males were not warriors. They had no sense of how to carry on fighting when injured. As soon as I realized they were amateur fighters, I knew it wouldn't take me long to beat them.

Then one of the remaining two—the green one, not the red leader—realized that Amelia had disappeared. Without a word, he spun toward the door and raced out, chasing her.

I don't have time for this.

With that thought, I spun my traditional Khanavai sword one-handed and struck out at the leader.

He pulled back quickly enough to keep from getting killed, but not so fast that he was able to avoid my blade entirely. I caught him on the shoulder of his sword arm and hit it hard enough that the blade sank into the joint, sticking briefly in the bone when I tried to pull it back out.

The red leader let out a wail as his weapon clattered to the ground.

I let go of my wound and grabbed the bounty hunter's discarded blade, my fingers on the hilt slippery with blood from my wound.

Armed now with two blades, I pointed one at each bounty hunter. "Don't follow me."

They both glared at me sullenly, but neither made any move to come after me as I backed toward the door. As soon as I hit the main room of the bus station, I paused to survey the enormous space, searching for Amelia and the green Khanavai bounty hunter who had followed her.

I didn't see them at first, but a feminine scream echoed through the room, and something clattered loudly. Whipping my head around, I caught a glimpse of Amelia going down under the green Khanavai male as he tackled her. In their chase, they had ended up on the far side of the terminal, knocking over tables and chairs—tiny, human-sized things—that any self-respecting Khanavai male should have been able to leap over.

A moment after Amelia hit the floor, she yelled again, and this time I could make out words.

"Help me!"

The primal part of me that had been growling at every male who came close to Amelia burst forth like a wild animal let loose from a cage, and I responded with a wordless roar of rage.

Lifting both my sword and the bounty hunter leader's smaller blade into the air, I leaped forward, brushing tiny humans out of my way as if they were annoying Blovitia flies.

I would kill the male who had dared touch my mate.

CHAPTER FIVE

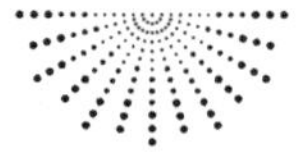

AMELIA

As the green Khanavai holding me figured out what was happening, he dropped my arm and raised his hands in the air, his sword clattering to the ground as he began backing away from the rampaging pink alien charging toward him.

The pink Khanavai descended on the green one like some kind of avenging angel, speaking to him in the Khanavai language, something that sounded to me like an old-fashioned record player being played backward, the lyrics garbled and incomprehensible, but somehow entrancing.

The other two Khanavai men who had accosted me in the bathroom came staggering out, both patently injured, but equally obviously determined to join their partner in any battle against the pink one.

Seeing where I was looking, Pink Guy's gaze followed mine. He spat out something harsh to Green Guy, who dropped to his knees and clasped his hands behind his back. Frowning irritably, he swatted away the small silver globe that hovered in the air around him, darting this way and that. I finally realized it was almost certainly a recording device for the Bride Games.

Shit. Now the entire world—the entirety of two worlds—will see me. Everyone will be watching for me.

Then Pink Guy turned to me and said something unintelligible, but he pointed at the ground as he said it—clearly, he was ordering me to stay where I was.

I don't take orders well. Surgeons rarely do—we're used to being in charge in the operating room, working either as the sole surgeon or at least as part of a surgical team trained to work together, with people we recognize as equals.

No matter how unbelievably gorgeous he might be, this was just some alien warrior.

He doesn't have control over me. He isn't in charge.

So the instant his attention turned back to Green Guy, who still knelt on the floor, I began inching away, ending up far enough out of his line of immediate sight that I felt safe to turn and dash toward the door.

The cheerful sunshine outside made me glad I wore my sunglasses, even though it was nothing compared to the blazing brightness of the sun in the Nevada desert.

I glanced frantically to the left, then to the right, uncertain where to go next. Then I realized it wasn't important. It didn't matter where I went, as long as it was away from the aliens trying to capture me—presumably to transport me to Station 21 where I would be forced to take my place in the Bride Lottery and participate in the Bride Games.

The first chance I had, I ducked down a side street. Seconds later, I heard a shout in Khanavai from somewhere behind me, followed by my name.

Good. At least I'd lost them. For the moment, anyway.

Finally taking a look around, I realized that I had ended up in an alley of some sort, created to cut between two streets.

There wasn't anywhere to hide here, so I continued to the end of the tiny lane, peeking out around the edge of a building to make sure none of my potential pursuers were there.

All I saw was a mostly empty sidewalk with a few humans walking briskly to their destinations, so I chose the direction that would take me as far away from the bus station as possible. As I moved, I pulled out the oddly dyed shirt I had stuffed in there.

It was wrinkled and smelled funky, and it didn't cover my now-distinctive hair, but at least it might disguise my clothing so that anyone reading a "last seen wearing" bulletin might not realize it was me.

My stomach clenched at the thought. If that really had been a camera drone filming everything that happened, everyone in the world would have plenty of visual images of me. Cutting and dying my hair had been for nothing.

Fuck, fuck, fuck.

I ducked into the first convenience store I saw, hoping to find something, anything, to cover my hair.

Lucky for me, a few Chicago White Sox caps hung sadly on a stand at the end of one aisle. I snagged one, ripped the price tag off, and jammed it on my head, tucking as much of my hair under it as I could. When I took the price tag to the front, the woman behind the counter took one look at me, and her mouth dropped open. I realized I'd been recognized.

A tiny, old-fashioned television on the counter was running a news clip about me. I leaned around the price scanner to see an image of Pink Guy running through the Chicago Greyhound station like a lunatic. The image panned from him to me and back again, and a ticker scrolled across the bottom of the screen, spelling out exactly what happened.

Fuck. Again.

The Bride Games superfans were going to go wild for this shit.

I am never going to get away.

I shook the thought off, grabbed a couple of bills out of my wallet worth far more than the cap cost, and dropped them on the counter

"Just give me half an hour," I begged. "Keep the change."

The store clerk nodded uncertainly, but I supposed that was the best I could hope for: someone who kind of agreed not to sell me out to the aliens who wanted to take me away and breed me.

A whole string of curse words ran through my head, but I simply whispered, "Thanks."

I took a deep breath, reminding myself that I was tired and dirty and frightened, and that just because the aliens had tracked me to Chicago after I traveled on a bus that required government identification, it didn't mean I wouldn't be able to get away otherwise.

I had talked myself down by the time I pulled open the glass door that let out to the street.

As I stepped out onto the sidewalk, I came face to face with the gorgeous pink alien who had been hunting me. Or rather, I slammed face-first into the chest of the super-hot, hot-pink alien, who caught me by the shoulders.

He did try to save you, an inner voice reminded me.

Shut up, I told my inner voice.

This close to him, my nose smashed into his skin, he smelled incredible. Like pine or sandalwood. Something earthy, which struck me as funny, given that he wasn't from Earth at all.

I tilted my head back to raise my gaze up to his face—and up, and up, and up.

His turquoise eyes gleamed back at me with something that, on a human, I would have called suppressed amusement.

But who knew if these aliens really felt things the same way we did?

There had been a lot of discussion on the news and on various video sites about how similar they were to us, ever since they had arrived and the first Khanavai bride had married their prince.

But I wasn't sure I believed it, any more than I believed the business about such a huge percentage of the brides being perfectly happy to go away to Khanav Prime with their Khanavai spouses—the ones they had met only days before.

Then the hunter's mouth stretched into a wide, impossibly beautiful smile, and I almost swooned.

Pheromones, I decided, trying to engage my critical thinking skills to avoid being duped by my body's reaction to this guy. *It has to be pheromones.*

Nothing else could account for my sudden urge to grab his face and pull him down to kiss me.

Oh my God, I'm thinking like a besotted idiot. I took a small step backward to try to put a little distance between my nose and his bare skin. He continued holding me lightly by the shoulders, however.

"Amelia Rivers," he said, his Khanavai accent making my ordinary name sound like something exotic. "You. Safe."

He tilted his head in a slight jerking motion that probably meant something to the Khanavai. I hadn't ever bothered to learn much about their culture.

I nodded. "I'm okay."

He examined me up and down, frowning. "No hurt?"

This time I shook my head. "I'm not hurt."

"Is good." He spoke in a firm tone, as if challenging me to contradict his claim that the fact that I wasn't hurt was good.

I wasn't about to do that, of course.

"Amelia go Zont."

Zont. That was the name he had used for himself earlier.

"You want me to go with you?"

He stood perfectly still as he replied, "Yes," his voice as decisive as it had been when he told me it was good I wasn't hurt.

I supposed I could go with him. He would protect me from the other Khanavai who were after me, at least. Unless he wanted to drag me up to Station 21.

I could always try to get away from him.

In any case, I couldn't run right now. He was much stronger than I was, and he hadn't let go of my shoulders yet.

I checked my reasoning, trying to decide if my inclination to do as he suggested—or ordered, I guess—had more to do with the overwhelming pheromones he was giving off or with logic.

At that moment I couldn't tell.

Maybe it would be better to try to get away.

Maybe I could convince him to release me.

I had just opened my mouth to suggest that when a strange, high, buzzing noise caught my attention. I had only ever heard that particular noise on old vids from decades ago. Videos of the only time any of the Alveron Hordeships had gotten through the Khanavai blockade to attack Earth.

Zont was already scanning the skies above us.

I recognized the shape of an Alveron Hordeship from those old vids. It came screaming out of the sky, diving toward us.

And for the second time in less than an hour, Zont yelled one word at me. "Run!"

CHAPTER SIX

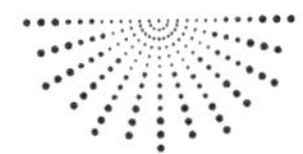

ZONT

As when she had ducked into the *Females* room, my mate did not hesitate. When I ordered her to run, she spun on her heel and took off down the Earther walkway beside the street.

The aerial vidglobe was spinning wildly, taking shots of me, of Amelia Rivers, and of the Alveron Hordeship in the sky.

I set out after Amelia, easily overtaking her with my longer stride. As I ran, I keyed in communications to my team on their ship. "Alveron Hordeships over Chicago. Send notification to Command Central. Request immediate assistance. Repeat: I request immediate assistance." I practically shouted the instructions into the com unit I wore on my wrist.

I realized I was about to outpace Amelia and paused long enough to grab my mate around the waist and toss her over my shoulder. We could make better time, even when I was burdened with her, then we would if I had to wait for her to catch up to me.

Half an Earther city block ahead, I saw what I was looking for—an entrance to a building that was wide open, a sign with an arrow pointing to it that read *Parking*.

I dashed into the covered space, a darkened area full of cars—those wheel-based conveyances that humans still insisted on using to crawl across their planet.

Not until that moment did I realize that Amelia was pounding on my butt with her tiny fists and yelling, "Put me down! Put me down, you…you beast!"

"Not quite yet," I told her, even though I knew she couldn't understand Khanavai, and I couldn't think of the Earther words to say what I wanted her to know. So speaking to her didn't do any good, but I couldn't help myself—I needed to tell her that what I was doing was for the best, even if she couldn't understand me when I said it.

"Dammit, you giant pink…*man*! Put. Me. Down!"

I ran up a paved ramp, deeper into the heart of the *Parking* building. I checked my wrist com for any response from my team, but something about this giant, cavernous space blocked out part of the signal. I tapped the sound off, leaving it set to vibrate against my skin if anything came through.

The word *garage* sprang into my mind, a space where Earthers hid their vehicles to keep them from being damaged by weather or taken by other humans.

From outside the garage, I heard the sound of drones separating from the Alveron Hordeship.

I had heard that sound before, and it still sent chills racing down my spine. I listened for the sharp whine of the drones moving closer and began searching for a place to hide.

The semi-indoor space was shadowy, with vehicles taking up most of it.

As the drones got closer, I spotted a tall, gray, boxy vehicle, and slid into the space between it and another equally large conveyance, this one red, ducking down just in time to conceal us as one of the drones darted into the parking garage.

With Amelia still slung over my shoulder, I dropped to one knee, then slid her down until I held her cradled in my arms, resting on the knee of my other leg.

She inhaled sharply, and if the fierce indignation of her expression was anything to go by, prepared to deliver a blistering rebuke for my inappropriate behavior in picking her up to carry her.

At that moment, she was the most beautiful female I had ever seen. Her eyes glittered with self-righteous anger, the skin of her previously pale cheeks flushed a pink that rivaled my own skin, and her lips—I didn't have the right words to describe them. Nothing seemed descriptive enough. Lush, full, enticing. All of that and more

Despite the danger I knew we were in, for a moment my entire attention focused in on her mouth.

Her tiny, pale pink tongue darted out to lick those amazing lips, and it was all I could do to keep from groaning aloud with desire for her.

"You—" she began.

I had to make her be quiet. But I couldn't think of the word to say to her. I had known it once upon a time, but it was as if my grasp of Earther language had completely disappeared in the flight from the Alveron Hordeship. We could not alert the drones to where we were hiding. We would be lucky to avoid their attention as it was.

So I did the first thing that popped into my mind.

I kissed her.

This time, I did groan deep in my throat. She tasted as sweet as she smelled, as amazing as she looked. She tasted like Lorishi shellfruit, its dark, sweet inner juice worth the work it took to get it out of its hard outer husk.

And although I'm certain my kiss startled her initially, she softened into it almost immediately, her arms snaking up to wrap around my neck, her mouth going pliable. I teased her lips gently, flicking my tongue against them until they parted for me, allowing me to enter her mouth as I so desperately wanted to enter her body.

She leaned against me, and I wrapped my hands around her waist, pulling her up closer to me. Her soft breasts, constrained by far too much fabric, pressed against my bare chest.

My cock hardened, aching and throbbing with my need for her, pushing up against the fabric of my chavan.

For a moment, Amelia gave as good as she got, her tongue tangling with mine, her fingers sliding up the nape of my neck and threading into my hair.

I could have lost myself in that kiss forever. But the sound of the Alveron Horde drones reminded me where we were. When I ended the kiss and pulled away, she stared at me briefly with a gaze that looked almost drugged, her eyes unfocused, her lips slightly swollen from the kiss.

Quiet.

That's the word I was searching for.

"Quiet," I whispered. "Alveron." I accompanied my words with a gesture in the direction the drones were approaching from.

Amelia's eyes widened and she clamped one hand over her mouth. She bobbed her head up and down, and I finally remembered that *that* was the actual physical gesture for *yes* among Earthers in this region. Side to side was *no*.

A *nod*. That's what they called it. I nodded my head in return, acknowledging hers.

We needed to get out of here. This was no place to be.

Anyplace under an Alveron Horde drone attack was no place to be.

I turned my eyes toward the top of the vehicle we crouched behind.

Hearing the drone move away, I gently moved Amelia onto the ground and made a motion asking her to stay where she was. She nodded and didn't move, so I hoped she understood. Then I raised up just enough to peer through the two translucent insets on the car in time to watch the drone head up to another level. As I watched, my mind supplied the word *windows*; apparently being on Earth was helping me remember more of what I had learned from my studies than I had expected.

The drone disappeared up the ramp and I started to duck down again, but something inside the vehicle caught my attention.

The control panel.

For all that Earthers still relied on individual transportation pods like this one, they had adopted some of the Khanavai technology. What my people had allowed them to use, anyway.

For one, they no longer filled their cars with tanks full of explosive propellants to make them run. Now, their transportation control systems were configured like miniaturized versions of every spacecraft I had ever flown.

And I had been at the top of my class in avionics in my Special Ops training.

It wouldn't take much for me to commandeer one of these vehicles and use it for my own purposes.

I had just begun thinking about what I might use for tools to complete my goal when the drone came soaring back down the ramp.

Inspiration struck.

Carefully, I drew my sword quietly from the scabbard I had tucked it into.

Holding a hand out in another "don't move" gesture to Amelia, I risked one more peek through the windows to chart the drone's movements as it slowed, shining a light into the darker spaces between the cars it passed.

I had to time this perfectly.

CHAPTER SEVEN

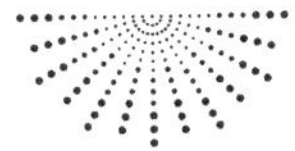

AMELIA

Zont crept to the end of the SUVs we crouched between, peering around the bumper to check the position of the drone. I didn't know what good it would do to attack it with a sword, but I hoped he'd disable it enough for us to be able to sneak out past any others that might be around.

But then Zont started spinning that giant, weirdly curved sword of his around in a circle, one-handed, until it was cutting through the air with a whistling sound that almost rivaled the sound of the drone's engines. He leaped out from behind the gray SUV, and extended straight upward, slamming his sword into the drone so hard that it would have knocked it across the garage like hitting a baseball out of the park, had it not been for the fact that the sword cut partway into the drone and stuck there.

Zont laughed aloud and said something that sounded triumphant, if garbled.

As soon as the drone was out of the picture, the aerial globe vid recorder dropped down from where it had been hiding, presumably in the concrete supports that ran along the ceiling of this floor to hover in front of my face.

I assumed it hadn't followed us at all.

Oh, God. That kiss was recorded. My face flushed hotly.

Then all that blush drained away and I went cold when I realized the judges for the Bride Games, those shadowy figures who made all the final decisions about final mate matches, would almost certainly use that against me.

How could I say I didn't want Zont when I was on vid passionately kissing him?

With one hand, I reached up and rubbed my forehead, trying to get rid of the tension I felt forming there.

Maybe with the Alveron Horde invading for the first time in half a century, the whole Bride Games thing would be suspended for a while.

Yeah, right. A girl could dream.

Zont brought the disabled drone down to the ground and put his foot on it to hold it while he ripped his sword out of it. The tiny camera drone that had been following him all along chose that ill-fated moment to buzz up in front of him, and with what sounded like a muttered curse, he smashed it with his sword, too. It tumbled to the ground, making a sad beeping noise for several seconds before it died, all its lights fading out slowly.

I almost felt sorry for it.

When Zont turned to glance at me, his eyes were full of some kind of battle fury, and I shrank away.

His expression instantly turned contrite, and all that rage dropped away. He held out his hand for me to take and said, "Amelia safe."

I believed him.

It was absolutely insane, but I believed him.

As soon as the camera and drone were both down, I scrambled to my feet as Zont turned to examine first the gray SUV and then the red one we stood between.

"Wait," I suggested. "The camera probably got images of both of these." My gesture took in both the red and the gray SUVs. "If you're planning to steal one of these—that's what you're doing, right?—we need to get one the vid drone didn't see."

His eyes narrowed as he considered my words, and then he nodded sharply once.

"Another level?" I pointed upward, and he nodded. He sheathed his sword, gathered up the disabled drone and the camera globe, and then held out his free hand.

It made me nervous to take it. What did holding hands mean to Khanavai men? But when I reached out and set my hand in his, he wrapped his large warm fingers around it, and I felt comforted.

We moved up to the next level. I worried that the Alveron Horde drone might have gotten images of these, too, and sent them back to the attack ship. But that could apply to every car in here, and I wasn't willing to step foot outside without at least the minor protection a car might offer.

On the second level, Zont made a beeline toward the brightest car available—a cheerful red sportscar that probably cost as much as I made in a year, even as a surgeon.

"Not that one," I insisted. "We need something that will blend in. Something boring." I scanned the lot. "That one." I pointed to a small gray Mazda with a tiny dent in one fender. "It's not flashy and I've seen a million of them around."

Still standing by the red sportscar, Zont said something incomprehensible, but clearly, he was protesting my choice.

I stopped moving toward the Mazda, put my hands on my hips, and glared. "Do not try to mansplain my own culture to me. Would you please just trust that I know what I'm talking about? We'll stick out in that one, and the owner will throw a fit when he finds out it's gone. This one will be harder to track."

Zont grumbled, but he followed me.

Watching Zont hotwire a car—one of the new ones, advertised as utterly theft-proof because of all the Khanavai technology imbedded in it—was somehow one of the sexiest things I'd ever seen.

That had always been a weakness of mine, seeing accomplished men doing work they excelled at. But any attraction I'd ever felt to any other guy was nothing compared to the sudden wave of heat that rushed through me as he took the drone apart, pulled out what looked to me like a tangled mess of electronic components, and fashioned them into a device that he used to send a signal that first unlocked a nearby sedan, and then started it.

Sexy muscles. A willingness to step in and save me every chance he got. Brains—he had to be smart to be able to work with machines, take them apart and put them back together the way I did with broken bodies. Competence. No, more than that. *Excellence* in his field.

And, oh God, he could kiss.

Everything about him seemed absolutely perfect.

Even if he was a hot-pink alien from another world.

I am in so much trouble.

Before we got in the gray SUV and left the garage, Zont checked the com watch he wore on his right wrist, an advanced version of the kinds many people on Earth had begun to use. He tapped it and frowned.

How much of our technology is really Khanavai in origin?

I hadn't thought about it before, but our planet was more intertwined with theirs than I had realized.

How much of the surgical equipment I used regularly came from another planet?

Intertwined.

The word flashed through my mind again, this time bringing up images of Zont's arms wrapped around me, his tongue in my mouth, his...

Stop it, Amelia.

The inner admonishment didn't help. I needed something to distract me from my own thoughts about the man—*the alien*—currently trying to make his wrist com work.

"Let me see your wound." I should have checked it earlier, but we were too busy running and hiding.

He turned to allow me to examine the cut in his side. It was an ugly gash, red and raw and far too long for me to be happy about, but it wasn't terribly deep, and it was clotting well.

"You could use some stitches in that," I said. "But it can wait a little longer."

"Yes," he agreed. "Go now. Sew later."

Sew? Where did a Khanavai warrior learn that word? I shook my head to clear the thought, and Zont misunderstood my intent.

“No?” he asked, his tone turning dark as a frown beginning to form between his brows.

“Yes,” I corrected, ready to get as far away from the site of the Alveron Horde attack as possible. “Go now, sew later.”

He grunted his approval and we got into the Mazda.

I didn’t even ask where we were going.

I probably should have.

CHAPTER EIGHT

ZONT

Earther cars were not made for Khanavai warriors.

Amelia showed me how to push the seat back as far as it would go, and still, my knees bumped against the control panel.

When I sat up straight, the top of my head brushed the ceiling of the car. So I huddled into my seat, hunched over, my elbows almost on my knees, which were themselves folded up and pressed against the control panel.

It was remarkably uncomfortable.

We had a few false starts and stops as I learned how to work the controls and drove down the ramps leading us out of the parking garage. Amelia gasped and gripped a handle above the door on her side—perhaps made for that purpose?—a couple of times, but we made it out safely.

Of course, there were a few conventions about human driving that I didn't know. Amelia pointed them out, however.

"You're supposed to drive on the right side of the road, not the left," she said, her voice rising a little at the end of her statement as another car came directly toward us.

"But the driver is on the left side of the conveyance," I muttered. "This makes no sense."

"Whatever your grumbling about, just stop. I am tense enough as it is without listening to you bitch about things I can't understand."

I glanced at Amelia briefly. The bandage over the insertion point behind her ear highlighted just how much we needed to find a translator for her.

When she caught me staring at it, she fluffed her Khanavai-red hair to try to cover it.

"Keep your eyes on the road," she instructed.

The streets were mostly empty, save for a few cars moving about, like the one that tried to run into us simply because I was on the wrong side of the road.

The human walkways were similarly abandoned, doors shut, and in many cases, covered with horizontal slats.

Blinds, that's what they called those. I remembered it because the word was connected to not being able to see, and not being able to see was called *blind* in this Earther dialect.

I drove in random directions for a while, my primary goal simply to get away from the last place the Alveron Horde had seen us. I didn't know if they were after me in particular, but I had learned from hard experience that it was always best to assume the worst when it came to my people's enemy.

I would have to determine our final destination eventually.

Leaning forward, I scanned the skies through the vehicle's front window.

Nothing.

Whatever the Alveron Horde had been doing in the Chicago skies, their Hordeship was nowhere to be seen at the moment.

My wrist com buzzed against my skin, and I glanced down at it.

A voice message from Wex.

Deciding it was safe enough to stop for a moment, I turned the wheel of the car sharply to enter a paved area with the building set far back from the road. The car made a screeching sound, and Amelia echoed it. After a glance ascertaining that she was frightened rather than hurt, I ignored her, instead scanning for enemies before halting the car. A few empty vehicles dotted the open space, another designated spot to leave human vehicles.

"Why are we stopping?" Amelia asked anxiously.

I waggled my wrist com at her, and she nodded in comprehension.

When I tapped in the instructions for the com to play the message, Wex's voice came out against a backdrop of battle sounds. My heart rate increased just hearing it.

"We would love to come help you, sir, but we are under attack in Las Vegas right now. I repeat under attack—" Wex's voice was cut off in the middle of his next sentence by an explosion, and then the com gave me nothing more but static on the message.

I checked for any other messages. Nothing.

Was that explosion an indication that my crew had been destroyed by a Hordeship? I had to find out. But I had no way of doing so—not without giving away my own location.

I did some quick calculations. If I was right, the ships that attacked Chicago would have had just about enough time to make it to Las

Vegas after it left Chicago, arriving in time to cause whatever it was that had made my team lose contact.

I banged my hands against the steering wheel in frustration, and it made an ominous cracking noise.

Amelia reached one of her small, slim hands over to rest atop mine, which were currently clenched around the steering wheel. "What happened?"

As if I could tell her. My frustration increased, and I waved my wrist com helplessly.

I tried to pantomime it as I spoke. "Alveron." I made a flat plane of my hand and streaked it through the air. "Las Vegas." I stopped my hand and dropped it quickly, opening it as I made an exploding noise.

"The Alveron Horde attacked Las Vegas?" Amelia asked, her expression startled.

I shrugged, hoping I was remembering the human gestured for uncertainty correctly. Then I patted my chest. "Zont team. Las Vegas."

"Your team is in Nevada and got hit by them?" Amelia gasped.

I nodded my head slowly, exaggerating the gesture, tapped my temple, and shrugged. "Yes?"

"Are you saying you think that's what happened?"

I nodded again. "Yes."

"That's horrible." Amelia slipped her hand down to my forearm, where she gave it a little squeeze of sympathy.

When she withdrew her comforting touch, I felt strangely abandoned.

I tried to send out a message to Station 21, but the wrist com's range, while certainly better than anything Earth had, wouldn't reach quite that far.

The Alveron Horde probably took out some of the relay systems Earth had in place.

I growled in frustration and realized Amelia was watching me with worried eyes. "Is good," I tried to reassure her.

What can I do?

I was stuck on Earth with my mate who was a runaway Bride Lottery candidate, in a car stolen from a nearby garage, and almost certain to be searched for soon, either by Earth officials or by the Alveron Horde, if they'd realized I was here. I couldn't get in touch with anyone higher up, and my team had been almost certainly shot down, perhaps even killed.

I should have felt daunted by all of this.

Instead, as I considered all the problems I faced, elation ran through my veins.

This was what I had trained for. I was a Special Ops soldier. We lived for setbacks like this.

Granted, most of the training had assumed my back-up team would be available, but I knew how to get by while I looked for them.

First, I had to go back to Las Vegas. I wasn't about to abandon my team—even if they were a temporary crew.

Leaning forward, I pulled up the vehicle's automated map features and began working out the coordinates I was looking for.

Amelia peered closely at the screen, too.

"Seriously?" she demanded. "Las Vegas? Why should we go back there?"

We desperately needed to get her some way to understand me when I spoke.

"You're going to Las Vegas? Isn't that where your team just got shot down? Isn't that what you're telling me?"

I nodded decisively at her.

"Zont save team."

"That's all well and good," Amelia said. "But can you drop me off somewhere along the way? I don't think it's a good idea for the two of us to make a cross-country drive when Alveron ships are attacking major cities."

One sentence in her little speech hit me pretty hard. *Just drop me off somewhere.*

There was no way in hell I was willing to let Amelia get away from me. Not after what it had taken for me to get the chance to come down here and find her.

I shook my head forcefully. "Amelia. Zont. Go Las Vegas."

Amelia scowled at me, crossing her arms over her chest. I immediately recognized it as a defensive move. Something I was saying was upsetting her.

"But why do I have to go? I won't be any help while you're fighting the Alveron."

"Amelia, Zont. Mates."

Amelia stared at me with wide, fear-filled eyes. "You can't be serious. We aren't *mates*. We just met—we don't even know each other. We're not married, and we're sure as hell not destined for each other in any way." Then, almost as if muttering to herself, she said, "It was just one kiss. Sheesh."

I reached over and placed my hand over hers, where she was anxiously knitting them together in her lap. I had to find a way to reassure her. "Zont save Amelia. Zont save team."

I didn't know how to make it any clearer than that.

She didn't answer, but she didn't attempt to get out of the car, either.

As we pulled out into the street, I checked the coordinates and the map. Twenty-five hours. I did some quick conversions in my head. Less than two complete solar days.

Amelia settled back in her seat but kept her arms crossed defensively in front of her.

Over a full Earth day until we could reach my team using this miserably slow Earth transportation.

With any luck, nothing else would go wrong between now and then.

CHAPTER NINE

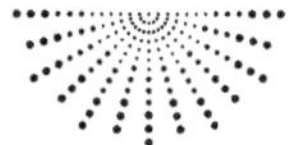

AMELIA

I fell asleep as we left the city.

Despite being anxious about the Alveron Hordeships possibly swooping down, firing at us, and blowing us off the road entirely, the motion of the car and the slow darkening of the sky as the sun began to set soothed me. The crash that came after the surge of adrenaline meant that I slept deeply.

Part of me even admitted as I drifted off that despite Zont's initial issues driving, I felt safer with him at the wheel than I had at any other point during the last three days.

I jerked awake what felt like a long time later, uncertain what dark dream had pushed me out of my sleep.

Almost certainly something having to do with the Bride Lottery.

I wanted to ask Zont what his role in coming to capture me had been. Was he a soldier on a mission? The way he talked about saving his team certainly suggested that. At any rate, he was different from the other three who had accosted me in the bus station. They had seemed less capable, less...

I tried to think of the word that fit. Protective, definitely.

Capable. That would fit, too.

Attractive was a given.

I glanced over at Zont behind the wheel, taking in the planes of his face as he concentrated on the road.

Then I frowned. Beads of sweat popped up along his hairline. In fact, if I looked carefully, I could see stress lines around his mouth, and his arms shook a little as he gripped the steering wheel.

Seeing his strain brought my attention to my own body.

"I need to stop somewhere," I announced.

He frowned and shot a confused glance in my direction.

"I have to, you know...pee," she said.

He said something in Khanavai, but since I didn't understand it, I ignored him.

Seeing a sign on the side of the interstate advertising several fast-food places, I pointed. "Take the next exit, please. There's a place we can stop for a few minutes."

Zont whipped the car onto the service road at what felt like full speed, leaving my stomach behind us somewhere on the highway as I gasped and clutched the handle above the door.

Otherwise, though, he got us to McDonald's just fine with my directions. On the way, we passed a standard array of roadside conveniences—the fast-food places, two chain motels, and a recharging station for cars.

I reached into my increasingly grimy pharmaceutical-rep-provided bağ and pulled the baseball cap out of it as Zont found the darkest corner of the parking lot and pulled to a stop.

"If you need to..." I gestured vaguely toward him, "relieve yourself, there are facilities inside." I paused and looked him up and down critically. "Of course, you're bound to get noticed. Unless you want to end up all over the news again, you might want to, I don't know, go over there." I pointed to a dark patch behind the parking lot where a light had burned out or been broken.

I finished tucking my hair up under the cap and slung my bag over my shoulder, not bothering to wait for a response.

Inside, after I'd used the restroom, I decided to grab something to eat and drink.

I considered just walking out the door on the other side of the building and taking off, getting away from Zont and his mission to save his team.

But something told me those three Khanavai creeps who had assaulted me in Chicago were still out there looking for me. The last thing I wanted to do was end up having to deal with them on my own, while Zont was in Nevada.

So I stayed and placed my order. No one inside the restaurant even blinked at me when I ordered food. I bought three times as much for Zont as for myself under the assumption that someone that big and that muscular burned through a lot of calories in a day.

Especially a day like the one we'd had.

When I got back to the car, Zont was sitting in the driver seat. I didn't know if he'd ever gotten out. His eyes were closed, and his breathing sounded off—a little too shallow, a little too fast.

I placed the bag of food in the floorboard of my side as I climbed in. "What's wrong with you?"

Zont shook his head, but I wasn't sure what he meant—and I wasn't sure I would believe anything he told me, unless it was that he was very ill.

"Let me see that wound again." When he didn't answer I poked him in the shoulder, hard, with two fingers. "Hey. I'm a doctor. Let me see that wound." He sighed and shifted in the seat, holding up his arm for me to take a look at it.

He had seemed to be doing well enough earlier, but now the wound was red and puffy. I probed the skin around it with my fingers, and it was hard—another sign of infection.

It's a sign of infection in humans, I reminded myself. That didn't mean Khanavai healed the same way.

I almost remembered reading something in med school about Khanavai physiology being exceptionally susceptible to some human germs. Supposedly that had been brought under control by the Khanavai medical community.

Then again, the Khanavai medical community might not have fully considered the possibility of an open wound created in a public bathroom in a Chicago bus station.

For the first time ever, I wished I had concentrated more on xenobiology when I had the chance back in med school.

"It should take days for the wound to get this infected." I leaned in closer to examine it, probing around of my fingers again, this time closer to the opened edge. Zont flinched, and I glanced up at his face.

"Okay," I said. "I won't touch it again right now. Let me feel your forehead."

He frowned even more fiercely, but I was in my element, and I had dealt with less cooperative patients than him. "Right now," I demanded.

Not until he bent down to let me place my hand on his broad forehead did it occur to me how ridiculous this was. I had no idea what a Khanavai's normal body temperature might be. It felt to me as if he were burning up, like a furnace turned up high. I might have chalked that up to his alienness, except for the sweat that began rolling down his face. As I stared at him trying to decide what to do, a huge shudder racked his body, followed almost immediately by another one.

Chills.

This was bad. I needed to get him somewhere safe and see if I could help him get through this infection.

You need to get him to a hospital, Amelia. I brushed the thought away. There was still time for that.

At that point, it didn't even occur to me to run. I could have gotten away, I'm sure. He was too sick to follow me. But in this moment, I was a doctor, and he was my patient. I would not leave him sick and alone, possibly dying. I wouldn't have left him dying from anything—much less a wound he had gotten trying to protect me.

"Trade seats with me. I'm taking you someplace where you can get better."

From the tone of the Khanavai words he said, Zont was protesting my announcement, but he made no real move to stop me as I opened my door and moved around to the driver's side. "Scoot over, big guy. Or get out and walk around. Your call."

He swung his legs out, and I expected him to stand up and walk around the car, but when he pushed away from the seat in order to stand up, he staggered into me. I caught him under his arms, stumbling back under his weight, but he managed to steady himself by grabbing the roof of the car and regain his balance.

"Back seat," I ordered him, opening the door and gesturing. "Now."

He managed to stay upright for the amount of time it took to get around the door before he toppled over into the car's back seat. I pushed on his legs to get him to draw them after himself, and then I slammed the door.

In the driver's seat a moment later, I rubbed my eyes before heading back the way we came.

As I retraced our route toward the highway, I berated myself silently. Why hadn't I insisted on cleaning out his wound before we left the garage? What the hell kind of doctor was I?

A surgeon, the logical part of my mind answered. The wound wasn't deep, even though it was long. On a normal human, it probably would have healed up just fine without any intervention at all.

I wasn't used to treating Khanavai patients.

As we pulled into the parking lot of the first hotel, it occurred to me to turn on the radio to hear what was being said about me, about the Alveron attack, even about Zont.

But when I keyed it on, there was nothing but static.

Exactly like the static on Zont's wrist com earlier.

Either we were in some sort of information blackout, or the Alveron Horde had taken out our entire communications system.

I was really afraid it was the latter.

Turning off the radio again, I glanced back at Zont. He was perfectly still, but I could hear his shallow, rapid breathing.

Time to play doctor.

I didn't know where the words came from, but they came with a host of utterly inappropriate images in my mind.

Time to get out of this car and start treating him like a patient instead of a hot guy, I told my overactive imagination, which responded by sending one more image of Zont stretched out on a bed, totally naked, smiling at me.

With a groan, I forced myself out of the car and headed inside. Not until I was halfway across the small lobby did it occur to me that I should have looked for someplace less generic—preferably the kind of place where you could rent rooms by the hour, since I didn't have a credit card on me.

I cursed silently with every step toward the check-in desk. I had to at least try.

A woman slightly older than I was sat on a stool behind the registration desk, flipping through an epaper magazine.

When she glanced up, her eyes widened, and I knew I'd been made.

CHAPTER TEN

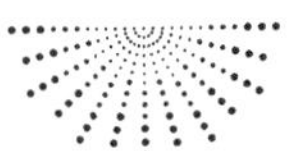

ZONT

Later, I remembered the next three days only in flashes.

The sound of human females talking, their words both sharp and blurred at the same time.

"Thank you so much for this," Amelia said as she opened the car door.

"Seems like an awful lot of trouble to go to for one of *them*." I didn't recognize the second voice, and I couldn't drag my eyes open enough to look at her.

"It's … complicated," Amelia said, and then her voice faded out as everything around me turned black.

The next time I woke, it was to the sound of her voice urging me to drink something. "Come on. You have to take this. That's it, sit up a little."

I swallowed instinctively, felt the cold, fizzy liquid wash down two pills. I coughed a little, and she patted my back until I stopped. Her cold hands felt good against my overheated skin.

I awoke again to a burning pain in my side, and Amelia's soothing voice as she said, "I know this hurts. I'm trying to draw out the infection as much as I can." The heat disappeared for a moment, only to return. "I wish I had a wound vac," she muttered to herself.

I opened my eyes as much as I could, seeing her bright red hair bent over my torso, her tiny fingers massaging the edges of the wound in my side.

It's become infected, I remembered.

Amelia dipped a small square cloth into a plastic bucket of steaming-hot water, then placed it against my side. I drew in my breath on a hiss, the air whistling through my teeth.

Aurelia glanced up at me. "Oh, you're awake. I'm applying heat to soften the tissues and try to draw out some of the infection. And Dee—the woman who works the front desk at night—is bringing some Epsom salts. We're going to have to see if we can soak the wound." Her voice was matter-of-fact, calm, professional. "I've also been giving you antibiotics. We'll keep those up for a while longer." She frowned. "But if this doesn't start improving soon, I'm going to have to take you to a hospital." Her voice lowered and I realized she was talking to herself again. "Consequences and Bride Lottery be damned."

"Do whatever you have to in order to stay away from the hospital," I managed to croak out. "I can take it."

She glanced up at me with a frown, and I remembered she couldn't understand what I said.

Exhausted by the effort it took to speak, I collapsed back against the pillows.

The next several hours were an agony of heat, and cold, and pain. I tossed and turned, feverish, calming only when I heard Amelia's soft voice urging me to be still, to let her do her work.

In my fevered dreams, I was in the deserts of Lorish, a sand rat chewing on my side, over and over again, its tiny teeth, sharp and pointed, gnawing at me. I tried to brush it away, and Amy's hand clamped down on mine. "Stop," she said.

Right, I wasn't in a Lorishi desert. That had happened years ago. Earth. "I am on Earth, in a hotel room, with my mate Amelia. Earth," I muttered aloud.

"That's right, Earth," Amelia said, and for a moment, I thought she had understood my words. Then I realized *Earth* was the only word in my statement that she understood other than her own name.

The next time I awoke, it was to the sound of Amelia's voice as she opened the door. "Thank you so much."

"How is he doing?" That was the same feminine voice I'd heard when we first got here.

Dee, I remembered. The woman who worked at the front desk. Part of me marveled that Amelia had trusted someone enough to help us.

"It's still touch-and-go. The antibiotics, if they are going to help at all, should kick in sometime soon." Amelia sounded haggard and worn. I managed to open my eyes enough to watch her for a few seconds.

She looked as exhausted as she sounded.

This was not how mate bonds were supposed to work. I was supposed to take care of her, make sure that she was safe and cherished.

"The news this morning described the car you're in," Dee said. "You might want to move around back. I will watch him while you're gone, if you want."

"Thanks. That would be great." Then Amelia was gone, and Dee sat down on the bed next to me. I opened one eye to see a dark-haired human woman about Amelia's age.

"Why are you helping us?" I managed to ask, my voice barely above a whisper, glad to talk to someone who could understand me completely. Someone who had not cut out her own translator.

Dee gave me an assessing look. "I'm not helping *you*," she replied, her tone acerbic. "I'm helping *her*. Because I don't think it's right that you guys have the option to take women away from their lives, away from their families, away from everything they love, just because you want to have babies."

I considered what she said, tried to see it from a human perspective. What if someone told me that I had to leave my career in Special Ops? That I had to be torn away from my family, my friends, my entire life, leaving it all behind to go be someone's mate, whether I wanted to or not.

My stomach sank. For all that the Khanavai had set up the Bride Games so that the brides had a voice, we had not done enough to teach human females what their lives on Khanav Prime would be like. We had not given them enough incentives to join the Bride Lottery willingly.

I nodded, acknowledging Dee's statement. "I see what you mean."

She patted my hand gently. "But if she decides to go with you, you take care of her, okay?"

"I will," I promised.

Amelia sailed back into the room. "Car's moved," she told Dee. "Thanks for the heads up."

"You should probably watch the news," Dee said. "I keyed your room for our best vid pack. Don't tell anyone."

The two women shared a conspiratorial smile.

"Thanks again for that, too," Amelia said, nodding toward a bag on a small chest at the end of the bed.

"No problem. I'm headed home. Check in with me tonight if you need anything," Dee said. As Amelia saw her out, I drifted off into sleep again.

Amelia's next ministrations of my wound hurt like the flames of Earther hell, jerking me awake from a dream involving being tortured by the Alveron Horde. I sat straight up with a bellow.

"Well, that's one way to reopen a wound." Amelia's dry tone made me want to smile, but I hurt too much. I glanced down at my side. It seemed less red and swollen than it had, but now it leaked yellow pus.

"Bad?" I asked, my voice still hoarse, as I gestured at the oozing wound.

Amelia shrugged. "Actually, I think it's a little better than before. Getting all this drained out definitely won't hurt." Her glanced flickered toward my face. "I mean, you'll probably feel pain, but it will do your body good."

It felt like an eternity as she cleaned and disinfected the wound, then covered it with bandaging material she retrieved from the bag Dee had brought. I fought myself to remain perfectly still, despite my desire to jerk away from her capable hands. In the end, though, I managed to limit my response to no more than flinching.

She felt my forehead again. "You're still hot. I wish I knew the average body temperature for Khanavai. It would help me know whether or not this fever has broken."

I shook my head. "No."

"No, you don't have a fever? Or no, your fever hasn't broken?"

I stared at her, frustrated by our limited communication.

"Let's try those one at a time. Do you think you still have a fever?"

"Yes."

She blew out a frustrated breath. “Okay, then. It’s time for more pills, anyway.” As she handed them to me to take, she muttered to herself again, “God, I hope I’m not poisoning you or something.”

The comment made me laugh aloud, even though it hurt to do so, and I nodded my agreement.

I TOSSED and turned for several hours, sometimes hearing the news playing on the comscreen, sometimes not. At one point, Amelia woke me to give me more pills and force some foul broth down.

“It’s chicken soup. It’s good for you,” she explained, but I could only take a few mouthfuls of the stuff before I pushed her hand away.

I hated appearing so weak in front of my mate.

My dreams were vivid, nightmarish visions from my past and from an imagined future. I fought the Horde, drove off Lorishi sand predators, was forced to mate with someone who was not Amelia and sent to live on a strange world with customs I didn’t understand.

When I finally awoke from those dreams a final time, the bedclothes were soaked in my sweat, but I didn’t feel feverish any longer.

The room was dim, but a thin ray of sunshine shone in through a crack between two dense fabric hangings over the window.

Curtains, I remembered.

I kicked off the covers, reveling in how much I didn’t hurt. But as the bedclothes landed on the floor, a feminine mumble of protest came from the other side of the bed.

Rolling over, I realized that Amelia had joined me in the bed at some point, possibly simply collapsing from exhaustion. I had vague memories of seeing her slumped over in the single chair in the room—but that position would not have been conducive to sleep.

She rolled over to face me, eyes closed, and settled back into sleep. Her lashes cast deep shadows under her eyes. No, I realized as I watched her sleeping, those shadows were already there, blue-gray reminders of how hard she'd worked to save me.

"Oh, my beautiful healer," I murmured. Overwhelmed by her beauty, her dedication, her sheer force of will, I gathered her into my arms and kissed her.

CHAPTER ELEVEN

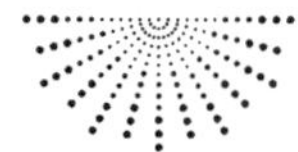

AMELIA

Zont's kiss wove itself into my dream, changing it from a nightmare of pink skin and open wounds to something much more sensual.

I'd spent three full days trying to divorce my feminine side from my medical skills, trying to work on helping Zont's body heal without actually noticing that body.

It hadn't worked.

Even as I cleaned his wound, wiped down his feverish skin, brushed his sweaty hair back from his forehead, I couldn't help but take note of everything about him.

"Sure hope this isn't just some alien man-cold," Dee said dryly, but when she got a glimpse of his wound, her hard eyes softened.

"He got that saving me from other Khanavai," I said, and she nodded.

"Let me know if you need anything."

"Could you go to a drugstore for me?" I gave her a list of the things I'd need and a wad of the cash in my bag. "Keep the rest, if there's any left over." I probably shouldn't keep handing out tips like that, but she'd been kind enough to check me in with a fake name, and she'd get in trouble, maybe even fired, if anyone found that out. Giving her a little extra money seemed the least I could do.

Now, in my dream, Zont held me in his muscular arms, kissing me, his deep voice murmuring a Khanavai phrase over and over in between kisses. It sounded like, "Brinday makavon avoi."

I returned his kiss, allowing my hands to roam over him as I'd been so desperate to—but hadn't allowed myself—while I nursed him.

His back was as strong as I imagined it, and when I allowed my hand to drift down his flat stomach, my fingers brushed the tip of his fully erect cock.

His hiss of indrawn breath was my first clue that this wasn't a dream.

Oh, shit. I jerked my hand back, and my eyes popped open to find Zont gazing at me, his turquoise eyes serious and intense.

"I'm sorry," I stammered. "I was asleep, and I thought…" I scrambled to sit up, looking for the blankets to cover me in my t-shirt and silk panties.

Finally, I woke up enough to realize something significant. "Hey. Your fever broke."

A smile stretched across Zont's face. "Yes," he agreed.

"That's great." I reached up to touch his forehead, firmly in doctor mode again. "Let me see your wound."

He turned a little on his side to give me access. I carefully peeled back the bandage and ran my fingers around the edges again.

"It's healing," I exclaimed triumphantly, blowing out a relieved breath. "Thank God."

I considered what needed to happen next. Food, definitely, and lots of liquids. I'd done what I could over the last few days to keep him hydrated, but he would be starving soon, and he needed nutrition, especially since he'd pushed away the chicken broth I kept trying to get him to eat while he was feverish.

"Wait here," I said, jumping up to head over to the minifridge, entirely forgetting that I still wore very little clothing.

Ignore it, Amelia. We're both adults.

I scooped my jeans off the floor and wriggled into them. Only then did I chance a glance back at him. His gaze followed me intently, his turquoise eyes dark with passion.

Fuck. I was alone in a hotel room with a Khanavai warrior who watched me with lust in his eyes.

And for the first time since this farce of an escape had begun, I admitted something to myself.

I want him, too.

The thought froze me in my tracks for a second, but then I continued to the tiny refrigerator to gather up some of the bland food Dee picked up for us.

He ate and drank everything I put in front of him except the chicken noodle soup, which he sniffed, then pushed away with a grimace.

I picked up that bowl and retreated to the chair to eat the soup and consider my attraction to him.

Was it simply some kind of weird doctor-to-patient transference? Some sort of Stockholm Syndrome effect? Also, I'd just treated him as a patient. Would having sex with him be unethical?

You're overthinking this, I told myself. *It's simply lust. He's gorgeous and he saved you and then you saved him. Sex isn't an unusual way to celebrate everyone still being alive.*

And waking up to him kissing me had done something to me—flipped a switch that I couldn't turn off.

I couldn't quit thinking about him touching me, kissing me...

It's just sex. It doesn't mean forever.

And with that thought, I made my decision.

As he polished off the last of an entire box of saltine crackers, I set the empty soup bowl on the counter next to me and stood. "Come on. Let's get you into the shower."

Panic flashed through his turquoise eyes. I didn't bother to clarify what I meant, choosing instead to simply take his hand and lead him into the bathroom, which suddenly seemed much smaller than it had before.

I turned on the water, holding my hand under the spray until it warmed up.

Then I looked back at Zont and raised both eyebrows. "Join me?"

He moved toward me, and I reached up to pull his lips down to mine until I was kissing him again. Even the taste of him was hot and slightly spicy, with just a touch of dust from our recent attempt to hide from the Alveron Horde.

Pulling me closer to him, Zont deepened the kiss, his tongue tangling with mine in a way that was brand new and achingly familiar—as if I'd kissed him before.

No. That wasn't right.

As if I've been waiting for his kiss all my life.

The shape of his shoulders under my questing hands was identifiably Zont, as well. I would never be able to touch another man and not think of my enormous, gorgeous pink alien with the turquoise eyes and dark hair.

Standing on my tiptoes, I ran my fingertips down the backs of his arms, tracing the sharply defined triceps and sliding my palms down to his elbows.

With a strangled noise in the back of his throat, Zont slid his own hands down my back until they cupped my ass, then pulled me up against him, the heat of his erection burning through his kilt.

No, I reminded myself. His *chavan*.

If he could learn some of my language, I could learn his, as well.

I wound my arms around his neck, taking a step backward and tugging him toward the shower.

"We …talk.. this first?" Zont's actions didn't match his words, as his fingers worked feverishly at the knot I had tied in the front of the t-shirt I had grabbed in the gas station.

"Absolutely not. No talking." With a triumphant motion, I shoved the leather strap—the *vandenoi,* he had called it—from Zont's shoulder, leaving his broad chest and the hard planes of his stomach completely bare.

Making a strangled noise of my own, I moved my mouth to his chest, reaching up to flick my tongue delicately against one nipple, smiling at both the crisp feel of the hair on his chest and the way he both shivered and pulled away from me.

"No," he said, but he was smiling.

"What about this?" I lightly nipped the other one, until Zont pulled my t-shirt, finally unknotted, over my head, using it to trap my arms when I lifted them. Pushing me back toward the spray, he held me still with one arm as he closed his mouth over one breast, using his tongue to play with the nipple through the silky fabric of my bra.

"Oh. I've been wearing that for days. Stop."

He laughed deep in his throat and inhaled, as if he couldn't get enough of the scent of me, as filthy as I knew I was.

Giving up any pretense at attempting to escape, I reveled in the feel of his mouth on me. As he pulled away long enough to push the fabric out of his way, cool air rushed in, stippling the skin of my breast with tiny chill bumps until he once again claimed the nipple, the flick of his tongue echoing my teasing motions earlier.

Zont released me long enough to unhook my bra—he took a few seconds to examine it, then popped it open with a single flick of one hand, as if he'd been dealing with human lingerie his whole life.

He tossed the bra and the t-shirt onto the bathroom floor, then turned his attention to the other breast, kneading it lightly even as he licked and sucked at it.

I moaned at the sensations streaking out from my nipples and through my entire body.

By the time his mouth trailed down my stomach to the top of my jeans, I was trembling. As he licked along the waistband, desire surged through me in a searing wave, rolling from my chest and moving down, as if it had been released directly from my heart. It settled in the deepest part of me, right at my core, as a hot throb of need.

With a deft motion, Zont unbuttoned my pants, sliding them off my hips and catching my silk panties with his thumbs on the way down, dropping them atop the shirt and bra.

I tugged ineffectually at the waist of his *chavan*. "Take this off, too."

One corner of his mouth crooked up. "Demand?"

"A request." I matched his smile but barely noticed as my smile faded at the sight of him when he stepped back and removed the *chavan*. My mouth dried and I met his heated gaze with one of my own.

I stepped back into the shower, under the spray.

In the shower, I showed him how I lathered my hands with soap. Then I slowly, carefully began to wash him, using it as an excuse to discover his body. When I placed my hands on his shoulders to get him to turn around, he followed my wordless directions without complaint.

With one hand, I caressed the tip of his cock, running my hands over it as I'd wanted to since I'd first seen him naked, sliding my finger across the slight wetness there and circling my finger around the head. Then I leaned forward and licked him gently once, all around the tip before taking as much of him as I could into my mouth, sliding down on him until I reached my limit.

His cock jumped as if it was all he could do to keep from spilling himself into me right then. I moved up and down, taking him deep into my mouth and sliding back out, making tiny noises of pleasure as I did, and making his cock jump in time to my motions.

When I slid his cock out and gave it a small kiss, he groaned, and I realized he'd been holding his breath. I glanced up to find his arms outstretched, palms flat against the tiles to hold himself up.

I stood up with a self-satisfied smile and lathered my hands with soap before running them up and down the length of his cock. It grew even harder and longer under my touch—something I wouldn't have believed possible—and along the sides of it, a series of bumpy ridges appeared, typical Khanavai physiology, I assumed, since he watched my hands in fascination and didn't freak out.

I finished bathing him, then let him run soapy hands all over me, reveling in the feel of his skin on mine.

Afterward, we dried each other with towels. His hands were both strong and gentle, even though they were so big he could wrap them around my waist.

Finally, unable to stand it any longer, I pulled Zont toward the bed until he lifted me in his arms and carried me the final few feet.

"You should be too weak to do this," I admonished him. "You're still injured, you know."

He grinned—and continued carrying me.

When he leaned down and deposited me against the pillows, I tightened my hold around his neck. He smiled against my lips and slid one knee onto the mattress between my legs. "I stay."

"Just making sure." I punctuated my words with tiny kisses.

Gently, he pushed me back, his palms spreading my knees apart until he could taste me. With long, sure strokes, he licked and sucked my pussy until I writhed beneath him. The feel of his mouth against me left me wet and panting, aching for more.

"Please." I spoke in the barest whisper.

He paused, hovering over me, holding my gaze.

"Say Zont," he demanded. His voice was scratchy with need. "Zont," he pointed at himself, then at her, "Amelia. Mates."

I paused, torn between the ache at the center of my being that demanded he come into me, and my need to maintain control over the situation.

If Zont isn't my mate, then why am I here? Who could he be to me, if not my mate? Simply the man—the Khanavai warrior—who saved me first from dangerous bounty hunters and then from the Alveron Horde?

Was I in bed with him *simply* because he was attractive?

No. No matter what semi-logical arguments I'd made to myself earlier, that wasn't my style.

Who is Zont to me?

Images of him from the last few days flashed across my mind, fighting the other Khanavai, carrying me into the garage,

Like ice cracking, everything I thought I knew about how I felt about Zont broke apart, tumbling away and letting loose a torrent of emotion walled up behind it.

This man was worth more than a one-night stand. He had saved me. And instead of rushing me back to the Khanavai, he had given me the chance to get to know him. To trust him. He treated me with kindness.

With love.

"Zont," I breathed. "I don't know yet if we're mates. But I am willing to consider it. I swear."

At my words, Zont slid into me with a groan, and I met him, pushing until he touched that innermost part of me, the part that had been aching for him for a lifetime, even if I hadn't known it.

CHAPTER TWELVE

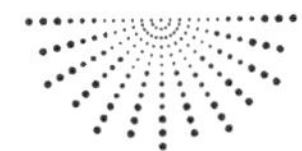

ZONT

I knew we should discuss this first. I had a million things to explain to Amelia, more to tell her. But I was drunk on the taste of her, and when she whispered my name, I was lost.

Admit it, Zont. You were lost from the moment you saw her on the screen, back on Station 21.

As she tightened around me, calling my name, I couldn't hold back any longer, and my first orgasm tore through me, leaving me shaking and spent—for a moment.

Later, I promised himself. *We will talk about everything. Once she has a working translator and can truly understand me.*

Then, without my consent, my mating cock pushed through the tip of my first cock. Taken by surprise, I tried to draw myself out of Amelia, tried to stop myself. But when I attempted to pull away, she clung to my shoulders with her hands and wrapped her legs as tightly around me as possible.

"Oh," she breathed. "You Khanavai recover fast." With that, she began moving against me, her body working mine, guiding us both toward that point of no return.

Unable to resist her tiny, mewling cries, I pushed my mating cock into her, driven by a force stronger than my own will.

She'll hate me for this later.

I knew it was true, but I couldn't stop.

I won't tell her. Unless she chooses me as her mate, I will never let her know this moment bound me to her.

After all, humans didn't have the same mating force. Not exactly.

Right?

Even as I made the promise to myself, I knew it was wrong.

Slipping one hand between us, I slid my thumb against her clit, stroking it in time to our motion, pressing harder every time I trapped my hand between our bodies.

As she shattered around me, my name ripped from her throat, even as my lips claimed hers.

My gaze met hers, and I fell into her eyes, my entire being held as warm and secure as her body held my cock, the entire universe pulsating around me in a moment like nothing I had ever felt before. Groaning, I buried myself deep inside her again, her delicate hands grasping my ass, her legs wrapped around me as she rose to meet me. With every thrust, I claimed her—or rather, I allowed her to claim me.

Still, that primal part of me growled, *Mine.*

The thought drove me to the edge, heat throbbing through me as her slick pussy squeezed my cock, holding me tight even as I drew my mating cock out and thrust it back in, her cries growing louder as I pounded into her, harder and harder. My balls drew up tight against my body and I exploded into her, mixing my mating cum with our earlier orgasms.

Tying me to her forever.

I didn't even realize I had been calling out her name until I held myself above her on my elbows and whispered it into her hair.

"Amelia, my perfect mate," I whispered into her hair in my language, "I love you."

It will all work out, I told myself. *It's going to end up being even better than it could have been otherwise.*

Even I didn't believe my lie to myself.

THE SOUND of Alveron aerials woke me. I didn't know how long we had slept, but I was certain it had not been long enough.

Then, over the sound of the Alveron Horde drones, I heard boots drumming down the walkway.

Reaching over, I shook Amelia awake. Her eyes popped open, and she opened her mouth to say something but quieted when I placed one finger over her lips. When she nodded her comprehension, I tapped my ear and pointed at the door.

She tilted her head, listening to the thumping coming toward our rented room.

Maybe we can learn to communicate without a translator, after all.

Without a word, she sat up and slipped out of bed, pulling on her Earther clothing and slipping her feet into the shoes she had worn.

I did the same, pulling on my chavan and drawing my sword out of its scabbard. I positioned myself at one side of the door and gestured for Amelia to hide in the sanicleanse room. But she shook her head, picked up one of the Earther lamps made of a heavy ceramic substance, and situated herself on the other side of the door.

I pantomimed the door swinging open and hitting her in the face, rolling my eyes and head to indicate how dizzy she would be if that happened.

She stifled a snicker and stepped several morits to the right. At least she would be out of their immediate line of sight if anyone burst through. They'd have to enter the room to see her.

So we were ready when the bounty hunters kicked the door in. It was a stupid move on their part.

They act like they're not up against a trained, seasoned warrior, I thought as I swung my sword into the neck of the first one to enter. He dropped to the floor with a final gurgle.

Amelia blanched but brought the lamp down atop the second bounty hunter's head with enough force to leave him reeling. He stumbled out of the way, and I waited for the third bounty hunter to enter.

Coward that he was, though, their leader had sent his two men into the room and had not followed them. I flattened myself against the wall and scooted over enough to peer around the wooden frame.

I had expected an ambush of some kind. Instead, I found the leader staring up into the sky, his mouth wide open.

One of the Alveron Hordeships streaked overhead, and I jerked back and flattened myself against the wall again with a curse.

"What is it?" Amelia hissed, moving back to her original position against the wall, too.

"Alveron," I said pointing upward, toward the ceiling and the sky outside.

I had assumed Amelia couldn't get any paler than she had when I had almost decapitated the first bounty hunter to enter. But she did.

At least Earthers were aware of the danger the Alveron posed. I calculated our chances of survival if we made a dash for the car, but Amelia had moved it to the rear of the building. We would be exposed for far too long if we left now.

I wracked my brain to come up with any alternative escape route, but everything involved us leaving this room.

If I had been fully aware when Amelia had chosen this place, I would have suggested one of their common houses with rooms that entered into internal hallways rather than onto external walkways.

The sound of another engine flying overhead caught my attention, and my heart leaped in my chest. Could it really be true?

I chanced another peek outside, just in time to see a Khanavai ship tracing the same path the Hordeship had taken.

At that moment, the leader of the bounty hunters raced into the room.

I leveled my sword at him. "Get out."

The leader began babbling. "I can't. That's an Alveron Hordeship outside. Please don't make me leave. I'll give you the bounty, I promise."

I sneered at him. "I don't want the bounty. I want the female."

The red leader unbuckled his sword belt and let it fall to the floor, holding his hands up in the universal sign of submission. "You can have her. I'm unarmed, and I won't hurt you or your female."

Although she couldn't understand what we were saying, Amelia chimed in at that moment. "Sit down on the chair."

The leader followed her directions, and Amelia pulled a small pair of scissors out of her bag.

Interesting choice. I wondered if she was going to try to stab him with them.

Instead, she picked up one of the lightest bed coverings and cut a notch into it. Then she used that weak point to rip a strip of fabric away from the rest of the covering. She used the long strip to tie the bounty hunter's hands behind his back.

Pride filled my chest. My mate was resourceful, strong, smart. Calm in a crisis.

She's perfect.

Above us, the Khanavai shuttle ship engaged the Alveron Hordeship.

In their first shot, the Khanavai ship took out the Alveron Hordeship's control center for the drones, and suddenly, the several drones that had been circling the building we were in dropped to the ground, useless.

The Khanavai had learned the importance of taking out the drones first through hard lessons.

Once the drones were no longer a danger, I stepped entirely outside the door to watch the battle overhead. As long as the Hordeship was engaged in battle, it wouldn't focus on us.

A few moments later, Amelia joined me, her bag slung over her shoulder and my scabbard and belt in her hand. I pointed up into the sky, where the two ships fired on each other.

"Red dude is tied up," she reported. "Should we try to get out of here while everyone else is busy?"

Good idea. I took her hand, and we began racing around the building toward the car.

As we reached the back of the building, the Khanavai ship got in a lucky shot. The Hordeship exploded midair, raining down debris and crashing in a fiery burst over a nearby field.

Even running around the small building had all but depleted my strength. My legs shook, and my head spun.

I stood several morits from the vehicle Amelia and I had commandeered and watched as the Khanavai shuttle—the same one I had brought from Station 21—settled to the ground.

Looking for something to support me, I stumbled toward the wall of the building, finally leaning against it to keep me standing upright.

My people had found me.

Rescued.

We were finally safe.

CHAPTER THIRTEEN

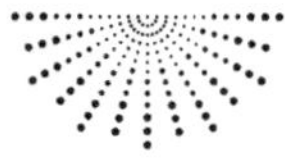

AMELIA

Zont suddenly slumped back against the wall as if he needed it to hold him up.

The ship, so much bigger than they looked on any of the vids I'd ever seen, touched down in the almost-empty parking lot.

Lines appeared around the hatch as it unsealed, and then it popped open. Five helmeted and armored Khanavai soldiers ran out of the ship, guns like none I'd ever seen before in their hands, shouting at the two remaining bounty hunters, who instantly dropped their weapons.

As the swords clattered on the ground, the leader of the Khanavai, another bright blue alien, pulled off his helmet and called out as he stalked toward us, his terrifying ray gun—or whatever it was—pointed directly at me.

When he called out again, it became clear to me that he was either asking me a question or giving me an order.

But without my translator, I didn't know what he wanted.

I froze, convinced in that moment that I was about to die. Without a word to me, Zont pushed away from the wall and raced over to the blue Khanavai warrior.

Convinced he was once again putting himself in danger to save me, I broke free of the hold my terror for myself had on me, ready to rush in to try to save the pink man who had done so much to keep me from harm.

But instead of meeting in a deadly clash, the two Khanavai embraced, and then stepped back and did some weird salute thing involving thumping their chests with their fists.

My legs went weak as I heaved a sigh of relief, and this time I was the one slumping back against the wall.

As the Khanavai men were greeting each other, a woman with a riot of wild curls such a dark red they were almost burgundy and wearing a black pantsuit stepped into the doorway of the ship, took a deep, happy breath, and stepped down the gangplank leading to the ground.

She glanced around until she saw me, then waved. "Hi," she called out. "I'm Natalie. That big blue guy over there, the one I'm guessing forgot to introduce himself, is my husband Cav Adredoni."

I stared at her suspiciously, still half-certain she was a human cop, here to arrest me after tricking me into believing she was friendly.

She glanced over her shoulder at the ship. "And thank God we don't have to use the transporter to get back to Station 21. That shit makes me puke every damn time."

"Look," Natalie said a few minutes later, after she'd used the bathroom in the hotel room where I'd nursed Zont back to health. She glanced around at the mussed sheets on the one bed in the room with raised brows before continuing. "I'm pretty sure I was sent down here to convince you that mating with a Khanavai warrior is the very best thing that could ever happen to you."

She gave a small smile and shook her head as she leaned back against the dresser at the end of the bed, delicately pushing aside the bowl that held the dried remains of my chicken soup. "I can't do that. I'm not going to try to convince you of anything. Overall, I think Khanavai men are probably pretty much like Earth men. Some of them are absolutely amazing. Loyal, strong, protective, kind."

She paused. "Let's get out of here—grab anything you want to take with you, okay?"

I nodded uncertainly but rushed around the room and gathered up everything I'd brought in with me.

When we stepped outside, Cav and Zont stood close together, their words running together as they discussed...whatever it was they were discussing in their own language.

I felt like I was in some twisted version of reality, where men spoke a language I couldn't even understand, and this twenty-something girl was suddenly in charge of the rest of my life.

And I went to med school for this?

I had to force back the tears that threatened to erupt at the thought.

We stepped outside, and the smile that seemed to always lurk behind Natalie's expression widened. She waved at her husband, who waved back. Then she turned to me and wrapped both her arms around one of mine, hooking elbows and tugging a little to get me to walk with her.

We headed toward the ship and Natalie continued talking. "So. Like I was saying. There are lots of good Khanavai guys. But there are plenty of assholes among the Khanavai, too. I met one real jerk—he was a groom in my Games." Her voice dropped. "Yellow. Like a giant banana. Can you imagine what his cock must look like?"

Trying to follow her conversational threads was likely to give me mental whiplash.

"Anyway. You'll meet another asshole when we get up there. Vos Klavoii has said he wants to talk to you."

Vos Klavoii. The Games Administrator.

Shit. I was really and truly going to end up in the middle of the Bride Games, wasn't I?

I'd definitely want to bring the conversation back around to that—but I had some questions I wanted to ask Natalie first, though. "Are you happy?" My voice came out sounding almost desperate, so I tried to modulate it. "You're married to Cav because you want to be? They didn't try to coerce you in any way?"

She threw her head back and laughed aloud. Even though it had been only a week since I left the hotel in Las Vegas, it felt like it had been centuries since I'd heard anyone laugh. It was a good sound—bright and clear and true.

"Oh, they tried all kinds of coercion. But in the end, Cav and I chose each other. We're good together." Again she glanced up at her new husband, and I could see love shining from her eyes.

But she's so young, that overanalytical part of my brain fretted. *What if she doesn't know what she's talking about?*

"Are you worried about going to Khanav Prime?" I asked.

"Oh, hell yes. Terrified. But Cav will be with me, and he's promised that if I'm miserable there or in any of his postings, we can come back to Earth."

"You believe he'd keep his word?" This time, I didn't even try to hide the incredulity in my voice.

"Absolutely." Well, she certainly sounded sure.

"Do you think it's likely that you'll take him up on that offer—to come back to Earth, I mean?"

Natalie made an uncertain noise. "Oh, I don't know. I kind of doubt it. I wouldn't want to put Cav in the same kind of situation that I'm terrified of going into. Honestly, we're probably going to end up posted on a ship. He's training for Special Ops soon, and when that's over, he is going to request an analysis position on one of the battleships close to the Alveron Horde borders—but only if I can go with him."

"So you're certain they're not going to arrest me? Send me to alien prison?"

"Are you kidding?" Natalie snorted. "Vos was certain that he'd had the top-rated Bride Games season ever, in all the years anyone has been running it. Then, you took off—and actually got away. For a whole *week*. Cav and I got married, and now Mia and Eldron are having to go through a whole series of new Bride Games all by themselves, just to satisfy Vos's appetite for ratings. Bringing you up to Station 21 and making you participate in the Games? It's like he's died and gone to heaven."

Even I had to snicker at that.

Her expression turned serious. "Don't get me wrong. Vos is a scheming prick. He will do everything he can think of to get you to fall into his plans, anything that might serve his purposes. And his purposes are ratings. Period."

My body went tense at the thought of participating in the Bride Games. It was my worst nightmare come true.

Natalie must have sensed my anxiety rising. "But you can also negotiate with Vos. That's what Cav and I did. It worked, too. We both ended up getting exactly what we wanted." She paused for a moment, then added quietly, "You just have to outthink him."

Before I could respond, Dee walked out of the lobby, her arms wrapped around her stomach as if giving herself a giant hug, her expression utterly stricken as she saw me walking by.

I broke away from Natalie to race over to Dee. I threw my arms around her. "It's okay," I said. "I'll be all right. I promise. Thank you so much for all your help."

She returned my hug tightly. "If you ever get back and need anything, come find me," she whispered.

Tears sprang to my eyes. *I hope to hell I haven't gotten her in trouble.*

One of the Khanavai warriors who had accompanied Zont's ship called out something in their garbled language.

"Time to go," Natalie said.

I broke away from Dee and brushed a hand over my eyes, wiping away my incipient tears.

"I'll make sure she's okay," Natalie said to a visibly worried Dee.

Then I turned and headed toward the Khanavai ship.

Toward my uncertain, terrifying future.

The exact one I'd been trying to avoid.

CHAPTER FOURTEEN

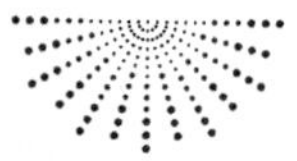

ZONT

While we were on Earth, I believed I could convince Amelia to accept me as her mate.

But now, as we took off and headed to Station 21, my hopes plummeted. Amelia sat in her seat with her hands twisting in her lap, fingers twining together over and over, like restless colrav snakes about to strike.

A sense of dread rose in me, twisting my stomach into knots as we got closer to Station 21. For a moment, I wondered if I was somehow picking up on Amelia's worries. But really, I was mostly concerned about Amelia's reaction to the Khanavai space station.

No, I finally decided. I had plenty to be worried about.

Back on Earth, I had only enough time to sketch in the barest details for Cav. I assumed he had orders to report back to Command Central, and I needed an opportunity to give him the entire story.

He knew, of course, that all communications have been disrupted. I wasn't likely to face the repercussions for having gone off-grid with a Bride Games candidate.

Unless, of course, they discovered I had mated her without either their permission or hers.

I shuddered at the thought of having Amelia ripped away from me so soon after I'd found her.

I definitely needed to tell Cav the whole story.

There was no privacy on the shuttle, however, not with all of us strapped in and headed to Station 21.

My anxiety wasn't lessened by our arrival. As we walked through the brightly colored corridors to the main concourse, Amelia stared at everything with wonder—a common enough response from humans, but somehow, I'd expected Amelia to be different.

When she stopped to frown at a comscreen replaying Cav and Natalie's wedding, I felt better—as if seeing her critical faculties in action, even in so small a way, might make her more likely to accept me as her mate.

Cav and Natalie accompanied us to Medical, where Amelia was taken to have a translator reinstalled and a receptionist led me back to have my wound treated.

The technician took one look at the still-open wound and started clicking his tongue in dismay. "Earth injury?" he asked. When I nodded, his mouth twisted into an expression of mild disgust. "I hate these. You'll end up with a scar, you know."

He didn't wait for me to respond, instead taking the scanning instrument and aiming it at the cut in my side.

"You realize this was recently infected?" His tone was accusatory as he glanced at the readings on the comscreen he pulled up in front of him. "And you are full of an obscene amount of antibiotics." He shook his head as he picked up a repair wand and began running it over my injury. "Earther medics," he muttered. "Fucking barbarians."

"Hey." I grabbed his wrist, squeezing a little harder than absolutely necessary to force him to stop and look at me. "That's my mate you're talking about."

His startled gaze turned up toward my face. "What?"

"My mate. She's the Earther medic who saved my life with those barbaric techniques you're denigrating right now."

He raised the hand that I didn't hold in a gesture of surrender. "I'm sorry—no offense meant. I didn't understand the circumstances, obviously."

I was not entirely pacified by his response, but at least he knew he needed to apologize.

Releasing his wrist, I held my arm up higher. "Go ahead."

As usual, the healing wand stung at first, then itched, and finally healed all the tissue, leaving me feeling as good as new.

Well, almost. This time, as the technician had warned, there was a scar. "It's an effect," he explained, "of the damage done, the infection, and the…." His voice trailed off, and I knew he meant the methods Amelia had used to save me.

I nodded my understanding and left the exam room without another word.

Back in the outer office, I rejoined Cav and Natalie in waiting for Amelia.

"Interesting scar," Cav said.

I lifted my arm and twisted to examine it, then sighed.

Well, at least I'll have something to remember Amelia by after she finds out I mated her, and she runs screaming into the arms of the first suitor who isn't me.

And here I thought I'd lost my sense of humor.

I rolled my eyes at myself and settled back in a chair to wait.

"GETTING a new implant hurt less than taking the old one out," Amelia said to Natalie, who made a sympathetic noise.

"I'm glad to hear you're not in any pain."

Amelia whipped around at the sound of my voice. "Oh. I..." she paused. "I guess I got so used to you not speaking in complete sentences, I kind of forgot that was because of my missing translator."

I gaped at that, not sure how to respond.

From beside my mate, Natalie snickered. "Oh, wait, Amelia. Looks like you might have spoken too soon."

That elicited a faint smile from Amelia, but I was glad she didn't laugh outright. Cav's mate seemed far too prone to levity for my current tastes.

Amelia, on the other hand, was suitably serious. Not that she didn't have a sense of humor. I'd seen it. But she took the right things seriously.

You used to have a sense of humor, you know, my inner critic told me. *Not all that long ago.*

Then again, not all that long ago I hadn't almost died from a single cut of a sword. Or mated an Earther without her explicit consent.

I'm far too fucked to think anything is all that funny.

A tall, red Khanavai warrior stepped into the room, leading a tiny human female—smaller even than either Nathalie or Amelia. This female's skin tone was toward the dark brown end of the beige-to-brown range of human skin tones. Her long, dark hair fell in curls down her back. She wore a bright red dress that matched the skin tone of the soldier she walked with.

"Zont, Amelia, I'd like you to meet Commander Eldron Gendovi and his bride, Mia."

"Only a prospective bride thus far," Commander Gendovi replied.

"Nice to meet you, Sir," I said as I gave the traditional Khanavai salute—a fist to the chest in two quick thumps, one with the side of the fist by the thumb, then a second with the closed fingers toward the chest, ending with a flourishing bow.

Commander Gendovi gave the abbreviated version, skipping the bow at the end. The gesture drew my attention to the number of awards he wore on his vandenoi strap. Given his medals—including the Royal Khanavai Order of Service, the highest honor possible—I suspected he was more important than he pretended to be.

"The commander specifically asked to meet with you and Amelia," Cav said. "Especially since he and Mia are about to have to go through a round of Bride Games themselves."

I turned a startled glanced toward Cav. "You think they'll make us go through the Bride Games?"

"Probably," Commander Gendovi said with a nod. "I wasn't able to get us out of it. No matter how many favors I tried to pull in."

I heaved a sigh. I desperately needed to tell Cav what I had done. I started to pull him aside then and there, but we were interrupted by the arrival of Vos Klavoii's assistant, Anthony.

A small but incredibly efficient human male, Anthony bustled into the concourse hallway. "Oh, good. You're all here. Please follow me to Mr. Klavoii's office."

It looked like I wasn't going to be able to tell Cav anything anytime soon.

"Remember what I told you," Natalie whispered cryptically to Amelia.

What had she told my mate?

As we fell into line to follow Anthony to the main Games Director's office, I hung back to be at the end of the line.

Amelia and Natalie slowed and dropped behind me, irritating me in ways I couldn't express while we were on the station. It went against everything I believed to allow them to walk behind me. I couldn't protect them if someone attacked from behind. Not that I expected us to run into trouble— this was Station 21, after all. But all my military training told me that one soldier needed to be in the front, one to the rear.

You're safe here, I reminded myself.

For now, anyway—right up to the moment that I told someone about my mating cock coming out to play with Amelia.

Amelia stuck close to Natalie's side, and I couldn't help the stab of envy that came with realizing she felt safer with the other human woman than she did with me.

Even after everything we had been through together.

When I accidentally mated myself to Amelia, I was certain I could walk away from her if necessary.

Don't lie to yourself, Zont, my conscience prompted me. *You were certain you could get her to accept you as her mate.*

My conscience was a damned nuisance.

But it was right, I realized.

It had never occurred to me that I would have to fight against any other grooms hoping to claim Amelia as their own.

I was Special Ops. Chosen from the best of the Khanavai Space Fleet. Trained to be even better. The very best of the best.

And about to lose my mate in a stupid competition.

I ran my hand down my face, from eyes to chin.

Fuck. I was in serious trouble. This, as the human saying went, *sucked*.

Anthony led us into the Games Director's outer office. "Please wait here."

He disappeared into the inner office and returned a few moments later with Vos Klavoii himself.

"Please, come into my office," Vos said, opening the door and ushering us inside. "We have some issues to discuss."

CHAPTER FIFTEEN

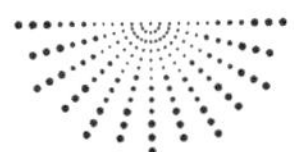

AMELIA

"You have to be kidding me." I stared at Vos Klavoii—probably the most well-known figure on all of television—with my mouth hanging open in shock.

"I never kid." Vos's voice was completely serious, different from his onscreen persona.

"Repeat those options to me, please." I tried to keep in mind what Natalie had told me about him. *He's an ass, but he can be negotiated with,* I reminded myself. *As long as it's in his best interest—and increases his ratings.*

"Your choices are simple," Vos replied, his voice too prim for my tastes, but also somehow commanding. This was a man who was used to getting his way, no matter what it took. "You may choose to accept Zont Lanov as your mate, as he was the only groom to put in a formal request to court you during the Bride Games, even after you fled."

The sneer that accompanied his words made me wish I had a hotel lamp in my hands to bash over his head, but I simply nodded. "I see."

"Or you may choose the second option. If you choose that route, you will participate in the full range of Bride Games, along with Commander Gendovi and Mia Jones."

I considered the options. I had promised Zont I would seriously consider being his mate. But going through the Bride Games meant the possibility of going back home at the end. And not home to an Earth where I would always be on the run, but home to the life I'd had before. A life with a thriving medical practice, friends, a place of my own, a life I had built.

A life I loved.

A life without Zont.

The Games Director gave me just long enough to let all that run through my head, but before I could say anything, he held up one hand to stop me. "There is, however, as you humans say, a catch."

"Of course there is," I muttered. From where she still stood beside me, Natalie elbowed my side. I grunted but didn't say anything else.

"In order to compete in this special edition of the Bride Games, you must first reject Zont Lanov as a suitor."

Everyone in the room gasped—except, I realized, Zont, who stood stock-still, staring at the ground, waiting for my response.

"Either way," Vos continued, "you will be filmed choosing someone. And I do not foresee you leaving Station 21 without a Khanavai mate."

"Why?" I finally managed to ask.

"Which part would you like to have explained?" Vos asked, a small smile playing around his mouth.

If I'd had my lamp from the hotel room, I might have done more than try to knock him out with it. I might have used it over and over on his smug face.

"Why do I have to reject Zont to participate in the new Bride Games? Why do I have to take any Khanavai mate at all?" My voice came out sounding strained, as if it had to battle the anger in my throat to get out.

Vos's expression turned hard. "Because you ran. By jeopardizing the Bride Alliance between Earth and Khanav Prime, you have drawn the Alveron Horde's attention to Earth."

"What do the Horde attacks have to do with me running?"

Vos shrugged. "To the best of my knowledge, no one has determined the exact connection yet. But the ship they sent to Earth focused only on those areas where you were discovered—Las Vegas, Chicago, and a small settlement in the otherwise barren land known as 'Nebraska.'"

Barren land of...? No. Focus on what's important, Amelia.

"And you must leave with a Khanavai warrior," Vos said, "because both our governments must be reassured that you will not be a problem any longer."

"I..." I stumbled over my words. "I need time to think about this."

Zont spun on his heel and left the room without saying anything. My stomach dropped, and I tried to follow him. But Cav grabbed my arm. "Let me," he said.

I nodded, uncertain what I would even say to Zont, anyway.

"You may have the time you need." Vos tried to make his tone magnanimous, but it came out smug. He was all too pleased with himself.

"Come on, Amelia," Natalie said, taking me by the arm. "Let's go for a walk while you decide what to do."

She drew me out of the room, casting a glare back at Vos as we left.

When we were almost to the door to the outer office, Vos called out after us, "You have until tomorrow morning to make your decision."

Natalie let out an actual growl in response but managed to keep it under her breath.

"I don't know what to do," I wailed as soon as we were out of the Administrator's office. "I need more time."

"Shh," Natalie patted my shoulder as she made soothing sounds. "Let's get away from this hallway. Vos's office gives me the creeps."

She led me down toward the main concourse and to a food court area, where she bought some kind of hot tea and gave it to me to sip. "Would you rather sit or walk?"

"I don't know," I replied listlessly.

"There's a hydroponic garden nearby. It's a good place for thinking." I followed her through what seemed like a maze of corridors until we emerged in a space full of greenery—and other colors, too, a riot of plants from both Earth and Khanav Prime, and possibly other places, too.

Natalie dropped down onto a bench. "I'm going to sit right here. You can sit with me, go for a walk, talk or not, whatever you want."

"I think I'd like some time alone."

She nodded. "You got it. I'll be here whenever you're ready to come back."

I stepped onto the path leading into the densest part of the vegetation. After days surrounded by people—at the medical conference, on the bus, in the car with Zont, and ever since the Khanavai shuttle had picked us up to come to the station, it was nice to be alone with my thoughts for a while.

I knew I was too exhausted to be making life-altering decisions.

Doesn't look like I have any other choice, though.

Tears welled up in my eyes, blurring the flowers and plants around me into something that resembled a Monet painting.

I brushed the tears away, determined to consider what to do next.

A rustling in the plants to my right drew my attention, and a bright yellow Khanavai pushed past me on the path, muttering obscenities as he went.

I remembered Natalie discussing a yellow Khanavai groom. *Can you imagine his cock? Like a giant banana.*

I wondered briefly if that was the same guy.

Jesus. This whole place is like a fucking circus.

I glanced at the yellow guy's retreating back. *Complete with clowns.*

Actually, come to think of it, I was pretty sure that was the role I was expected to play—entertainment for the masses.

More like a human sacrifice.

The thought made me snort in laughter, even through my tears.

Okay. So my options were to "mate" with Zont or to choose someone I knew nothing about. And I already knew a lot about Zont. He was protective, for one thing.

Even when he'd been sent to Earth to find me, he had saved me from other Khanavai and protected me from the Alveron Horde. He'd been willing to drive halfway across the country to save his team.

I would never have to worry about anyone hurting me.

And the sex was amazing.

When I considered it that way, it didn't seem quite as awful as it had when I'd been faced with it in Vos's office with the Administrator leering at me.

Maybe Zont could even help me find a way to practice medicine on Khanav Prime. There were brides there, right? Surely they needed human doctors sometimes. And most Khanavai these days had at least some human DNA. Perhaps I could specialize in treating human ailments new to the Khanavai.

Okay. I could do this.

Even if the thought of leaving my life made my stomach hurt.

But I had been willing to leave my life behind to go on the run. Maybe this wasn't so different, after all.

Time to go find Zont.

CHAPTER SIXTEEN

ZONT

I left Vos's office with Amelia's words echoing in my head.

I need time to think about this.

I should have expected her reluctance, I suppose, but hearing it aloud still hurt. I had to wonder if capturing my reaction on vid for his show had been part of the reason Vos had arranged for her to say it in front of me.

I hit the horticulture area in full stride, marching into the greenery as if I had someplace to go.

I was halfway down the entrance path when I heard Cav calling my name from behind me.

"Zont! Hold up!"

I paused, but reluctantly, and waited for the blue Khanavai warrior to catch up with me.

"What the Zagrodnian hells are you doing?" Cav demanded.

"You heard her. She needs time to think about it." I didn't meet my friend's gaze. Instead, I turned and began marching down the path—a little more slowly this time, though. Apparently, I didn't really want to be alone, after all.

"Are you kidding me?" Cav said. "You knew from the moment you saw her picture that Amelia Rivers was the woman you wanted."

I shrugged. "If we're true mates, shouldn't she feel the same way? If I know from the very beginning, why doesn't she?"

Cav stopped, planted his feet on the path, put both hands on his hips, leaned his head back, and roared with laughter.

I scowled at him. "Quit that. What's so funny?"

When Cav didn't answer, I rolled my eyes and walked away from his laughter.

"Hey, I'm sorry, I'm sorry." He caught up with me again and fell into step beside me. "It's just that human women are not made the way we are. They don't have the inborn sense of what man would be perfect for them."

I glanced at him out of the corner of my eye. "I'm not sure I believe you. I have read some of their literature. There are all sorts of stories about human women falling in love at first sight."

"Have you noticed how many of those end up with one or both of the couple dead?" Cav countered. "I mean, have you seen any of the vids of *Romeo and Juliet*? That's supposedly one of their great love stories, and everyone involved in that little love affair ends up dead from either stabbing or poison." He snorted. "Does that sound like a culture that believes in the ability of humans to choose their own partners wisely?"

I had to snicker. "Maybe not. But we have been together for *days* now. She should have learned something about who I am in that time."

"You mean in all those days together when first, she couldn't understand a single word you said, and you were sick and dying?"

This time, I was the one who stopped in the middle of the path. "You know, I didn't necessarily want someone to challenge me right now."

"Oh. So you were looking for—what? Commiseration?"

The corner of my mouth twitched up. "Maybe."

Cav slapped me on the back. "Sorry, my brother. You will not get that from me. Remember, you have chosen a female from a completely different planet as your mate. You cannot expect her to abide by anything resembling logical rules."

I grunted something that might have been a sound of agreement.

"Besides, you told me you *like* a challenge."

I cut my eyes toward him. "Says the warrior who chose the human female who said she wished she had thought to run."

"Somehow, that doesn't cut very deep coming from the male who went after the female who actually did run."

We walked along in silence for a bit longer.

"You know," Cav said contemplatively, "even human males complain about their females being overly emotional."

And if she's emotional now...

I groaned aloud, stopping in the middle of the path and dropping my head into my hands.

"What?" Cav asked.

"I have done something really, really stupid," I admitted. "Something that, if Amelia finds out about it, might be an even bigger obstacle to us mating than her running away from the Bride Lottery in the first place."

Cav frowned at me. "What could you have done that would be that bad?"

"So, back there on Earth, while we were in the hotel…" I paused, my stomach clenching at the thought of saying the next words out loud.

Cav waited patiently for several seconds, before finally prompting me. "What happened?"

"It was after I had been ill but before you got there. She took me into the lav. We got into the sanicleanse together. And then…" My voice trailed off.

"Are you trying to tell me you fucked her?" My friend fought to keep from smiling.

"Well, yes. But that's not all. After I came," I paused, inhaling deeply to try to draw in the courage to say the rest of it.

Comprehension began dawning on Cav's face. His voice dropped to a horrified whisper. "Your mating cock?"

I nodded, feeling the heat of a blush turning my cheeks from their normal bright pink to something closer to Commander Gendovi's color.

Cav's eyes grew wide as he stared at me. "Please tell me she knew what was going on."

I shook my head mutely.

"Oh, warrior brother of mine. You have stepped in a flaming pile of etav droppings."

"I know," I agreed miserably.

We turned off onto a side path, heading deeper into the garden.

"You know you have to tell her, right?" Cav stopped, stepping in front of me to look me in the eyes. "And before she makes any kind of final decision."

"I know."

Cav back into step with me, his brow furrowed. "However, telling her might not be as bad as you fear."

"What do you mean?" For the first time since I had accepted what I'd done, hope flared in my chest.

"Human physiology is not like ours. Their females don't respond to mating cock the same way that a Khanavai female would. A human woman isn't bonded to you the way you are to her."

"I already knew that."

"But think about it. Because it's not something that happens to them—at least, not on the same level and to the same degree as it would have with one of our own kind—there is not a taboo around it in human culture as there is on Khanav Prime."

"That's true." Maybe things weren't looking quite so bleak, after all.

"In fact, Natalie didn't even *know* about the mating cock until we were together. She had never heard of it."

I flashed a shocked glance at him. "What? Are you sure? Is that something that our government has been hiding from the humans?"

Cav shrugged, "I'm not sure that they have been hiding it, so much as not talking about it."

"Why wouldn't they tell humans about it?"

"I think it might be something that is such a given on our world that it never really occurs to us to discuss it. So maybe it never occurred to our government to consider it important information."

"That's...possible." And it was considered such a personal, private matter between mated pairs that the only time conversation about mating cocks came up was between couples who were mated to one another. And of course, in our sexual education courses—where we were taught at a young age that sex was natural and normal, but that the mating cock was to be reserved for one's true mate—a rule that was easy enough to abide by, since one's mating cock only made an appearance in the presence of that mate.

I shook my head in wonder, stunned at the thought that more than an entire generation of human women had grown up knowing about the Khanavai, but not about our mating cocks.

As we rounded another corner, a yellow Khanavai male practically barreled into us as he rushed down the path.

"Watch where you're going—" he began, then stuttered to a stop when he saw Cav.

"Hello, Tiziani," Cav greeted the other male pleasantly.

The yellow male snarled, but he managed to reply, "Hello." Still, he bowed up, his chest expanding, and his muscles clenching.

"Don't even think about it," Cav said. "It was part of the Bride Games, and those are over. You lost."

Tiziani growled deep in his throat, but he stepped aside to let us pass.

I glanced between him and Cav, then said to Tiziani as we walked by, "Smart move, brother."

The yellow Khanavai glared after us until we rounded the next corner.

"Rival during your Games?" I asked.

"Only in theory," Cav replied. "He never had a chance."

We walked silently for a while before I turned back to our previous conversation. "You're right. I need to tell Amelia what happened."

"And all the repercussions of it," Cav said.

I sighed. "There aren't any repercussions for her," I pointed out.

"But it's not fair to her if you don't tell her what the repercussions will be for you." Cav paused. "*Before* she makes her final decision."

He was right, of course, but it also didn't seem fair to tell her that if she chose someone else, I would spend the rest of my life mateless and alone. "Seems like a lot of pressure to put on her."

"Maybe," Cav acknowledged. "But I still think she deserves to know."

"Yeah." I stopped and turned around in a circle, realizing that I had been so caught up in our conversation, so engrossed in my own anxiety, that I had lost track of where we were.

Some Special Ops officer I had turned out to be.

"Can you get us out of here? I think I have something I need to go tell my mate."

"Of course," Cav said, smiling.

The closer we got to returning to the main part of the station, the more I knew Cav was absolutely correct. Amelia might not choose me. I knew that, and if it happened, I could come to accept it, eventually. But I had to give her all the information I could so that she would be able to make a completely informed choice.

No matter how much it terrified me.

CHAPTER SEVENTEEN

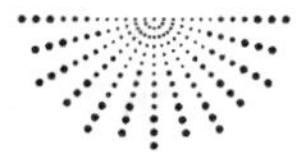

AMELIA

Zont was nowhere to be found when we began looking for him. Cav either, for that matter. Natalie and I made a loop around all the public areas of the station, then circled back around to where we started, just in time to see both Khanavai warrior males exiting the garden.

When she saw them, Natalie cracked up laughing. "Of course you would bring him here," she said to Cav. "This is where I brought Amelia to think, too."

Cav wrapped his arms around her and kissed her on the forehead. "It's pretty much my favorite place in the station. Other than our quarters, of course."

She thumped him on the chest. "Behave. And, since you mentioned it, take me back to those quarters. These two have something to discuss, I think."

As they walked away, Natalie gave me an encouraging wave, and I was pretty sure I heard Cav mutter, "Oh, you have no idea how much they have to talk about."

I turned away from watching them to find Zont staring at me intently.

We both spoke at the same time.

"I need to tell you something."

"I want to talk about this."

We both stopped speaking, and then we both laughed.

"I really want to say this first, before you say anything," I told him.

"Let's sit on the bench," he said, gesturing for me to lead the way back to where I'd talked to Natalie.

"The thing is," I said, twisting and hooking one leg up onto the seat in front of me so I was turned completely sideways to face him, "my parents had a miserable marriage."

Zont frowned. "They were unhappy in their mating?"

I laughed. "That's putting it mildly. Yes. They were very unhappy."

"That doesn't happen among the Khanavai," Zont said. "There's a reason for it, too."

I put my finger up and held it against his lips. "Let me finish, okay?"

He nodded, and I continued.

"I don't know if you're aware of this, but I come from a very wealthy family."

He nodded. "It was in the report I read about you."

Well, that was one good thing about this Bride Lottery thing. It wasn't like any Khanavai would be trying to marry me for my family money.

"She stayed married to him because divorce wasn't something that happened in our family." I paused and swallowed. I'd finished my tea some time ago, but now I wished I had kept some for this conversation. "I spent my entire childhood wishing that my parents would get divorced because I was convinced they would be happier with other people."

Zont frowned and leaned toward me, focusing intently on my words.

"And I know that your people don't do divorce, either."

He opened his mouth to say something, and I held my hand up again.

"It has always been important to me that I not end up like them. So much so that I had no intention of marrying anyone ever."

This time, he leaned back, and I thought perhaps I detected hurt in his eyes. But I forged ahead, anyway. "That's why I ran. I never wanted to get married at all. And in my experience, marrying for the wrong reasons—whether they were political, or because of wealth, or even because someone is lonely and wants someone else around? It's a terrible idea." I paused, trying to think what else to say.

Zont nodded slowly. "I think I understand," he said.

"You do? Really?" I sighed in relief.

"Yes. You don't want to risk an unhappy marriage for any of those reasons, so you're going to go through the Bride Games to find the best possible match for you." He didn't meet my eyes as he said it, and he chewed on his bottom lip for a second before blowing out a sigh and starting to stand up.

I put my hand out to touch his leg. "That's not what I'm saying at all."

Zont dropped back onto the bench with a huff of air, and I couldn't tell if he was relieved or irritated.

"Then what are you trying to say?"

"I'm not exactly sure. I guess… I'm just trying to tell you that I'm scared of this. The idea of making the wrong decision terrifies me at the best of times. During med school, I froze more than any of my classmates. It was bad enough that my professors were afraid I would never actually become a doctor." I paused. "But I got over it. And I learned that sometimes, when you're faced with two equally bad options, you just have to choose one and deal with the outcome."

"So mating with me is a bad option?"

My gaze flew to his face. I was worried I'd find anger there—the kind of anger I had seen all too often on my father's face when he was speaking to my mother.

Instead, I saw the beginnings of a smile playing around his mouth. Not the kind of smile Vos had given me earlier, but something gleeful, relaxed, maybe even joyful.

And definitely amused.

"That's not it." I reached out and flicked my fingers against his thigh in a mock slap. "No. Everything I know about you tells me that you are good and kind, the kind of man that, if I were inclined to marry anyone, I would be searching for." I paused again, my voice dropping. "But I am frightened out of my mind of making a commitment like that."

He nodded, his expression growing thoughtful. "I have something to tell you, too."

This time, he paused so long that I prodded him. "Yes? What is it?"

He was so serious that I feared he might be about to tell me something awful, like he already had three secret wives at home on Khanav Prime and couldn't marry me, anyway.

That would be just my luck.

"First I need to explain something about Khanavai physiology. Have you ever heard of the mating cock?"

I blinked at him, taken aback by the question. "You mean a penis?"

He shrugged. "Sort of. It's not quite like anything human males have."

I blinked, thinking about our night together. "I didn't notice anything particularly unusual. Unless you mean the ridges on your penis." I retreated into the most technical terms I could find, taking comfort from slipping into my medical persona.

"That's part of that," he said. "The mating cock… appears…in the presence of our true mate."

My eyes grew wide. "The Khanavai males have a second penis?" I tried to imagine where it might be stored.

Zont grinned, his cheeks turning an even darker pink. "Technically, yes. It's considered very private, something we don't discuss with others except in our original early sexuality coursework—and then, of course, with our mates."

"So the fact that it didn't—what was it you said? *appear*?—when we had sex, does that mean that we're not true mates?"

If anything, his blush deepened.

"I don't care about that," I said, trying to comfort him. "If we can try to have a real relationship, one that's based on trust and caring about each other, then I don't need that part of it."

"That's not what I'm trying to say at all," he echoed my earlier words back to me. "It *did* appear."

"It … oh." I turned to face forward, leaning back against the bench. "You mean when we… ohhh," I said, finally realizing what he meant. "So that second time, you didn't simply recover quickly? It was actually a *second…*"

"Exactly."

I turned the new information around in my mind. "So what does that mean? Are we already mated? Am I already bonded to you somehow?"

"Not exactly. As far as our scientists have been able to determine, human females react differently to a mating cock than a Khanavai female would. While being with me when I…use…my mating cock might make you more inclined to be my mate, it won't bind you to me —it *didn't* bind you to me—the way it would have a Khanavai female."

I exhaled a breath I hadn't even realized I was holding, not sure if I was happy or sad to learn that. "Okay, then, so we're not —" I stopped in the middle of my sentence and turned to face Zont again. "You said it doesn't work that way for *me*. What about for you?"

Zont didn't look me in the eye. He stared at the station floor for a long moment before he finally answered. "It bound me to you."

"What does that mean?"

"It means that no matter what you choose, I am mated to you."

"Can it be undone?"

He laughed, but all the joy I'd seen in his smile earlier was missing from the sound. "No."

"So you're stuck with me forever?"

"Or without you." He shrugged one shoulder. "You can choose someone else. I cannot."

"So if I decide to go through the Bride Games and choose someone else, what will happen to you?"

"My mate would leave with some other male. And I would go back to what I was before—except this time," he said, his tone both matter-of-fact and a little sad, "I would no longer have the hope of someday finding a mate and having a family."

"I see." My voice had gotten very small as I added yet more information to my considerations.

Zont's entire future depends on me.

For the first time since I heard my name called during the Bride Lottery drawing, I stopped to consider what all this might mean for someone else.

"Come with me," I said, coming to a decision. "We need to go talk to Vos again."

My heart started pounding hard as Anthony showed us into Vos's office.

"So," Vos said as we came to stand before his desk. "Have you come to a decision?"

I opened my mouth to answer, and the entire room tilted sideways.

For a second, I thought I was having some kind of stroke, maybe brought on by the stress of the last week, but then I realized the entire station was shaking, the ugly decorative items on Vos's desk sliding off onto the floor with a crash.

I grabbed Zont, trying to stay upright, as klaxons began blaring through the entire station and a military sounding voice ordered people to report to their stations. "We are under attack. I repeat, Station 21 is under attack."

CHAPTER EIGHTEEN

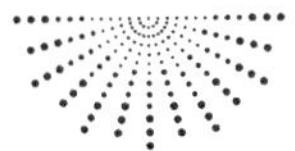

ZONT

I heard the next blast as it hit the station. And I recognized it immediately.

The Alveron Horde. They were attacking Station 21 directly.

Did that mean that something had happened to the outposts that were supposed to guard us? For that matter, how had even a small Horde-ship gotten past them and down to Earth? I had not been paying careful enough attention, too wrapped up in my own mating issues.

And now, here I was on Station 21 as a groom, not even assigned to a specific unit. I didn't have a battle station to report to.

I could, however, protect Amelia. I grabbed her, pulling her toward the doorway, hoping to be able to stow her someplace safer than this office.

"Wait. What about Vos?" she asked, her tone worried but not panicked.

I glanced back at the Games Administrator, only to find him huddled beneath his desk. I had never thought much of him—any male who served his military time making television shows wasn't worth much attention, as far as I was concerned.

But as I watched, a third volley hit the station so hard that the wall of Vos's office caved in, dropping on top of the desk and almost flattening it, with Vos still beneath it.

Vos's scream echoed through what was left of his office.

My analytical brain kicked in instantly, and I began trying to determine the safest room in the station. *We're lucky there hasn't been a hull breach yet—not one that we know about, anyway.*

"We have to get him out," Amelia said, flipping into what I was beginning to recognize as her doctor mode and pointing at the pile of rubble mostly covering Vos.

"I'm not sure he's worth it," I told her, trained to make a call about which soldiers to leave behind on a mission.

She flashed a horrified glance in my direction, then shook her head. "He doesn't have to be worth it. We still have to save him. I took an oath."

"So did I," I sighed, and moved toward the desk with her. Vos might technically be part of the Khanavai military, but he was basically a civilian, not a fighter.

Vos was pinned down under the old Earth wooden desk he'd had sent up here, probably at great cost to the Khanavai government. It was all I could do to keep from saying that ending up crushed under it served him right. But Amelia was right—we needed to at least try to save the smarmy bastard.

I started to push against the wall to see if I could shift it—or at least most of the weight of it—off the desk.

"Wait," Amelia called out. "I need to check something first."

I nodded and backed off for a moment while she bent down, murmuring gently to the Games Administrator. "Okay, take a deep breath, breathe with me. In and out. Slowly. There you go. Don't hyperventilate." Once she had him somewhat calm, she began checking the points where the desk pinned him down.

"Call Medical," Amelia instructed me.

I tried, but all I got was static. "I can't reach them."

"I guess it's up to us, then." She continued murmuring to Vos as she checked his vitals.

As she did that, a crackle came through my wrist com. "Where are you?" Cav asked.

I keyed my com to respond. "Vos's office. He's pinned down. Amelia is trying to help him."

"Be there in five," Cav replied, and cut the com.

When I turned my attention back to her, Amelia was explaining something to Vos. "So I'm going to have to tie this off. It's going to hurt, and I'm sorry about that. But if I don't, you're likely to bleed out entirely when we move this desk off you."

Vos whimpered but nodded his comprehension.

Amelia glanced up at me. "We need something to make a tourniquet with. I need to be able to tighten it around his leg, right here." She pointed to a spot on his thigh.

I crouched down to take a look. Part of the desk had splintered off and gone straight through the director's upper leg, literally staking him to the floor.

"I don't know if it's in an artery," Amelia murmured, "or if it's just gone through the muscle, but I want to make sure we can save his life."

I tilted my head, the gesture suggesting that we move away from Vos for a moment. "Can you save the leg?"

She shrugged. "I won't know until I see it. But every moment we spend talking about it is another moment that he might be losing that limb."

Without asking any more questions, I stripped off my sword belt and handed it to her. "Will this work?"

She played with the buckle for a moment, figuring out exactly how it worked. "This is perfect. I might need you to help me tighten it up enough before you try to lift anything off of him."

Cav entered the room at that moment, Natalie behind him. "I understand you might need help moving some things," Cav said.

"Oh, good, You're here. Perfect," Amelia said, moving back toward Vos and handing out assignments as if she had been born to it. "Natalie, you hold his hand while I get this tourniquet on. Cav, stand there. Be ready to lift the wall and then the desk when I tell you. Mr. Klavoii? Can you hear me?"

Vos opened his eyes, his skin having turned an ashy shade under the natural green of his complexion. "I'm here."

"Okay. Keep breathing, nice and slow, just like we talked about. Like this." She demonstrated, ostensibly for Vos, but she held Natalie's gaze as she did so, and as soon as she stopped, Natalie took over encouraging the director to breathe with her.

Sliding the belt under Vos's leg caused him to cry out, and Natalie continued breathing with him as Amelia talked him through exactly what she was doing. "I'm going to tighten the belt now. It's going to hurt, so you hold onto Natalie's hand." She tugged the belt as tight as she could, then gestured for me to come help tighten it further.

Vos's screams echoed through the room even more loudly than they had before. Sweat popped out along his brow line, and I marveled at Amelia's ability to remain calm, to keep talking to him even when it was clear he wasn't listening. Her voice was soothing, professional, direct.

"Okay," she said, "first, we're going to see if we can get this wall out of the way." She glanced at Cav and me, and we both pushed against the metal, shifting it a few inches at a time. Vos screamed the first two times we moved the wall, and it jostled the desk beneath it—and his impaled leg. Then he passed out, and I, for one, preferred it to hearing his screams.

Once Vos was unconscious, Amelia cut off her calming patter and turned all business. "Okay. Now you two lift the desk and move it as quickly as you can. Natalie, I want you to put your hands here, and lean all your weight on it, yes, right behind the belt. We want to cut off as much blood flow as we can right now, at least until we can get him to Medical. They might be able to save his leg—and I don't want him to bleed out before we give them that chance."

Cav and I situated ourselves, ready to lift the desk, and a giant shudder went through the entire station as it took yet another round of fire.

The office walls creaked but held this time.

"Now. Lift the desk now," Amelia ordered.

We lifted the desk, and the spike that had gone through Vos's leg came out with a wet-sounding *pop*.

"Okay, now we need to move him," she said to Natalie, who stood up long enough to grab Vos under one arm while Amelia grabbed the other. Together, they pulled him back, out of the way of the desk.

Cav and I dropped the desk on the floor with a thump, and Natalie went back to leaning on Vos's thigh.

Vos mumbled and moaned but did not awaken.

Probably for the best.

I stepped in. This part I knew. Getting people out of danger—that was my specialty. "Let's get him to Medical."

Cav and I each took a side, carrying him with his arms draped over our shoulders, our arms around his waist, and each with a hand under his knees. Amelia raced beside us, keeping the tourniquet tight to slow any bleeding, while Natalie rushed ahead to tell the medical technicians we were coming.

Medical was in chaos, but a technician met us at the door and called some of his people over to take Vos from us.

Amelia went with him, the two of them discussing blood loss and arteries and other medical issues that might arise.

"How can I help?" she asked the medical technician. "If you need any, that is."

"We definitely need the help," he replied, his voice fading as they disappeared into the clinic.

I watched Amelia go, pride swelling in me.

I might not know yet what she had decided, but no matter what, she would always be my mate.

CHAPTER NINETEEN

AMELIA

It took the Khanavai military response six hours to wipe out the Alveron Hordeships that had attacked Station 21.

Because I spent all night and half the next day in Medical helping tend to the wounded, I didn't learn this until the next day.

In fact, I came off the Medical shift only because Dr. Javant told me I had to get rest, or I was going to end up doing more damage than good.

He was right, but as I walked out of Medical, I realized I had no idea where to go.

I staggered toward the food court, where I picked up a cup of something like coffee—the Khanavai version of it, anyway. I was just taking my first sip when two aliens—one tall and silvery with three breasts, and the other short with a braid hanging out of one nostril—came rushing toward me.

"It's you, isn't it?" the tall silvery one trilled.

"Of course it is." The short braided one bowed, and I nodded a greeting, finally dredging up the species name for both of them.

A Poltien and a Blordl.

"I'm Amelia Rivers, if that's who you're looking for."

"Yes," the Blordl said. "I'm Drindl. Natalie sent us to find you. We have been waiting, but we must have missed you when you came out of Medical."

"And I am Plofnid," the Poltien added. "We can show you to your quarters. I suspect you need some sleep."

"That would be glorious. But first, do you know where Zont is?"

The two glanced at each other and my heart clenched. Surely nothing had happened to him while I had been off saving other people? I didn't think I could forgive myself if that were the case.

"He's already asleep in your quarters," Drindl said.

I glanced between the two of them. "Our quarters? And whose idea was that?" I knew it couldn't have been Vos's—he was still under sedation. We had managed to save his leg, but only barely. He would probably walk with a limp forever, but at least he would be able to walk.

Drindl's laugh sounded like the chime of bells. "It was Natalie's plan. She said that she knew what you would choose."

Plofnid scowled its disapproval. "But we can arrange different quarters for you, if you like."

I considered it for less than a hot second. "No, I think taking me to my quarters now would be perfect."

The room they led me to was dark, and I could hear Zont breathing heavily as he slept. I tiptoed into the bathroom and figured out how to use the shower unit, then carefully crawled in under the covers next to him. I didn't even bother to look for nightclothes. I was that tired.

As I stretched out in the bed, Zont's arm reached out to snake around my waist and pulled me back to him. I snuggled into the warm comfort of his embrace.

"Glad you made it here," he murmured.

"I am, too."

Then we slept through the whole day and most of the next night.

When we finally woke, Natalie and Cav had both left messages on Zont's wrist com.

"Vos wants to see us," Zont told me as I sat up in bed and stretched.

I rolled my eyes. "I don't have anything to say to him."

Zont grinned at me. "Aren't you supposed to let him—and me, too—know what you decided?"

I laughed. "You mean you haven't guessed yet?"

He dove for me, grabbing me and rolling me over on top of him, then pulling me down into a deep kiss.

A kiss that was promptly interrupted by a buzzing on Zont's com.

"Now, dammit," Cav said.

"Okay, okay." Zont keyed off the com and sighed before giving me one more kiss and setting me on my feet.

There were clean clothes in the closet, and I pulled on a black pantsuit remarkably like the one Natalie had worn down to Earth to pick us up.

As we walked through the station, hand in hand, I took in all the damage that had been done by the Alveron attack. Throughout the entire station, the bright colors of the walls had cracked, showing gray metal beneath.

It was a wonder we hadn't suffered a hull breach, and all died.

"Well," I said. "It's not like the Bride Games can go on in the middle of all this."

"The Bride Games are still on," Vos said petulantly as he sat up in his hospital bed.

"The station is a wreck, sir," Anthony told him, his tone anxious.

"There must be spaces on the station that were not destroyed."

"Well, yes…" His assistant's voice trailed off.

"You are in no shape to host another set of Bride Games," I said. "And I say that as your doctor, not as someone you wanted to blackmail into participating."

Vos turned his glare on me. "Everyone is expecting there to be another set of Bride Games. We have been advertising it."

"After the Hordeships were destroyed, I spoke to Commander Gendovi," Zont interjected. "There's some indication that the Alveron Horde might have intercepted the Bride Games transmissions and determined exactly how important they are to us."

I turned my startled gaze to him. "Really? Is that why they were following us on Earth?"

Zont nodded. "It's quite likely, yes. As the only bride off the station, you were an easy—or at least easier—target."

"Is Gendovi certain that's what happened?" Vos asked.

"Of course not," Zont said. "We're still looking into it. In the meantime, the commander has suggested postponing the next Games."

"We'll see about that," Vos muttered. "He can't shut down the Bride Games just because he doesn't want to go through them."

As it turned out, Vos was right.

Despite their concerns that the Alveron Horde might have been tapping into transmissions not meant for them, Central Command was unwilling to cancel the Bride Games entirely—not least of all because doing so would be akin to breaking the Bride Alliance between our two planets, something the commander told me himself the next time I went in to check on Vos.

Commander Gendovi didn't stay long, though—Vos was in high spirits and working to rope everyone into his next show.

"So I need to know," the Games Administrator said to me when the commander was gone, "what have you decided?"

I finished checking his leg with the Khanavai instruments that Dr. Javant had taught me to use. "It looks like you're healing very well," I said.

"Do you choose Zont or do you choose to participate in the Bride Games?"

I leveled a serious look at him. "I saved your life, you know."

I started to move away, and he grabbed my wrist. "We cannot allow the Alveron Horde to see that they have had any effect on us."

For the first time, I thought maybe I saw something in Vos beyond his determination to gain ratings. "Is that patriotism I'm detecting?"

The Games Administrator huffed and looked away.

"I choose Zont," I finally relented enough to tell him. "And if you want to, you can broadcast our mating ceremony—another wedding—to appease your viewers until the station is cleaned up enough for more Bride Games."

Vos's face brightened, but I held out a hand to stop him from speaking.

"But nothing extravagant. No one can be there except Cav and Nathalie, Commander Gendovi and Mia, Plofnid and Drindl, and

Zont's team." I narrowed my eyes at Vos. "And no matter what kind of excitement you have planned for the next Bride Games, you had better make sure that Commander Gendovi and Mia end up together, if that's what they want." I tapped his injured leg for emphasis, and Vos flinched. "Got it?"

"Agreed," Vos said, more than a little reluctantly.

"Good." I walked toward the door but paused to look back. "You should arrange for your vids to be there tonight. We have already made arrangements for the ceremony."

Vos's mouth fell open, and I winked at him.

Then I went to find Plofnid and Drindl to help me prepare for my wedding day.

CHAPTER TWENTY

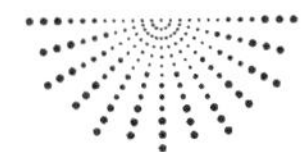

ZONT

Natalie had insisted on us observing some ridiculous human tradition that involved a groom not seeing his bride on the wedding day. "But we saw each other this morning when we got out of bed," I protested.

Natalie simply laughed. "Too bad. We're not counting that. You don't get to see her for the rest of today. Not while she's getting ready. Not until she comes down the aisle."

"We don't have an aisle," I pointed out. "We have a room."

Now I stood in that room, one of the few undamaged spaces in all of Station 21. Someone had decorated it in a riot of flowers, covering nearly every surface, even the walls.

I suspected Plofnid and Drindl. They apparently *loved* weddings.

I didn't like the idea of this being broadcast. If Central Command was right, we had opened ourselves, and Earth, to invasion—*re-invasion*—

by the Alveron Horde, simply by broadcasting so often from Station 21.

But Central Command disagreed with my assessment. They were quite certain that both humans and Khanavai needed the distraction that another mixed-species wedding could bring them.

So I stood in a brand-new uniform chavan, waiting for my human bride. My team stood in Khanavai guard formation, ready to back me up if her family intervened, as tradition dictated. I repressed a snort at the thought. I had asked Amelia if she wanted to wait until her parents could arrive for the wedding, and she rolled her eyes. "God, no. We can go visit them someday. Maybe. If they behave."

As I shifted from foot to foot anxiously, I thought of that morning, after we left Vos's Medical room.

It would be burned in my memory forever.

Amelia had taken my hand and tugged on it, so we fell behind Cav and Natalie. As we passed the station garden, she stopped at the bench where we had discussed her fears of marriage the day before. There, she turned to face me, taking both my hands in hers and staring up into my eyes.

"Yes," she said.

"Yes?" I repeated, afraid to even hope that she might mean what I thought she did.

"I will be your mate." She waited for me to respond.

But I couldn't. Emotion clogged my throat, kept me from saying anything at all.

"Have you changed your mind or something?" If not for the light dancing in her eyes, I would have assumed her question suggested she was worried.

I shook my head. "No."

"Oh, hell." She reached up and rubbed behind her ear. "Is there something wrong with my translator? Are we back to yes-and-no questions only?"

A smile spread across my face. "No," I said.

This time, she laughed aloud. "So you're willing to marry me?"

I nodded. "Yes."

"Today?"

"Yes."

She laughed again and shook her head. "Okay. But *you* have to tell all our friends. I need to make sure you can actually talk before I agree to any lifelong kind of thing."

I joined in her laughter, and we turned to catch up with our friends.

Now, my heart pounded as the music began to signal the start of the ceremony.

Natalie and Mia came in before Amelia, dropping petals on the floor in an odd act of floral destruction.

Human customs really were very strange.

Then Amelia stepped into the doorway, vidglobes floating around her, and I gasped.

She could have shown up in the same jeans and the strange, streaked shirt that almost matched her hair, the same clothes she'd worn for much of the time I'd known her, and I would have thought she was the most beautiful female on all of two worlds.

But in a long, satin ivory dress, with her hair curled into tiny ringlets and adorned with white and blue k'feldaflet flowers, she absolutely took my breath away.

Cav stepped up and offered his arm to escort her the short distance to me.

Drindl and Plofnid took up the rear of the tiny procession, both wearing blue, as well—Drindl in a dress similar to the other bridesmaids', Plofnid in a perfectly tailored, blue, miniature, human-style suit.

At the last minute, Dr. Javant pushed Vos Klavoii in on a floatchair.

The ceremony itself was simple—a mix of a human marriage rite and a Khanavai mating ceremony. As the senior officer attending, Commander Gendovi officiated as we promised to love and honor each other. And in the Khanavai tradition, we swore to protect one another, allowing our infinite love room to grow.

When it was over, Commander Gendovi told me I could kiss my bride, but he was too late—I had already started.

AFTERWARD, Plofnid and Drindl rushed out while everyone else was congratulating us, only to return with a small army of station employees bearing a table, chairs, and a meal for all of us to share, including an astounding number of bottles containing a pale, fizzy Earther alcohol.

Amid the festivities, Commander Gendovi turned to me. "I had a conversation this afternoon with Command Central," he began. "And we have a proposal for you."

I tilted my head to indicate my interest. "Yes?"

"We are considering opening up a permanent station on Earth for a Khanavai diplomatic corps. We think you might be a good fit to act as our military liaison."

"Me? Really?"

The commander's eyelid shivered down in a barely perceptible wink. "We would also like to have a Special Ops presence there."

Amelia leaned around me to speak to the commander. "Would this be a long-term posting?"

"Why yes, yes it would." Gendovi smiled, a tad smugly.

I glanced at my new bride, checking with her before I replied, but I already knew the answer. "I would be happy to take the position, sir."

Later, as we danced on the small floor Drindl and Plofnid had arranged to provide, my new mate—*wife*, in Earther terms—whispered to me, "So tell me about this mating cock of yours?"

I grinned. "Well, for one thing, it only appears after the first orgasm—and only with our one true mate."

"I think you should show me."

"I agree." I took her hand and announced our departure. We were followed by a shower of floating soap bubbles—another strange Earther tradition—and then finally, Amelia took off her shoes so we could dash back to our quarters.

As soon as the door shut behind us, she began kissing me passionately, deeply. Her fingers ruffled through my hair and I slipped my hands behind her waist, hauling her up against my chest with a hot growl of desire.

The embrace was perfect. Even as my craving for her swirled through my veins, my mind was clear.

We fit together. Like a perfect puzzle.

Gently, I pushed her toward the bed, my pulling her closer to me, my lips teasing against hers to deepen the kiss even further. My tongue slipped from between my lips and flicked at hers, demanding entry. Her mouth opened to accept me into her, her head dropping back as I took over, the heat of our kiss moving through me in waves of arousal.

My cock hardened, and a soft moan escaped my lips as Amelia's hand moved down to slide over the length of me.

Amelia flashed a wicked smile, sinking to her knees in front of me. I watched, transfixed, as she reached up under my chavan, stroking the length of me. After a moment, I unbuckled my belt and unhooked the closure of my ceremonial uniform, letting it drop to the floor in a pool around my ankles. My cock sprang free, standing tall and proud, my mating ridges fully erect along the sides.

Her mouth slowly opened so her tongue could slip out and drag gently across the head of my cock teasingly. She let out a soft moan at the taste, making my cock throb and pulse. She enveloped the first few inches of me, pursing her lips and sucking on the head, then sliding down to take more of me into her mouth. I gasped, and she glided up and down, then gazed up at me, trailing gentle kisses along the length of my cock.

"Mm, you feel nice," she murmured, gripping the base of my cock with her hand and rubbing her cheek up and down the path she'd just kissed.

I groaned at the softness of her cheek against the hardness of my cock and pulsed against her. My cock thickened more and throbbed inside her mouth, my balls aching for release.

Oh, gods and goddesses. If she kept this up, I wouldn't be able to last nearly as long as I'd like to. She pursed her lips around the head and sucked even harder than before, her tongue flicking across the slit and almost sending me over the edge.

Then she pulled away long enough to say, "First you come with your regular cock, then your mating cock comes out to play?"

"Mm-hmm," I managed to say. "Yes."

"Then don't hold back. Please."

"I won't. But first…" I stepped back and held out my hands to pull her to her feet. Then I picked her up and carried her to the bed.

She laughed aloud. "What are you doing, Zont?"

"I want to taste you."

"Oh," she breathed. "Yes, please."

Before I set her down, I pulled up her beautiful ivory dress, revealing her soaked panties. Hooking my thumbs in the elastic, I pulled the scrap of fabric down—breaking it in the process. I didn't even apologize. Instead, I tossed it away and ran my hand over her ass. She let out a throaty moan as I took my turn to kneel before her. Gently, I pushed her knees apart and leaned into her, my tongue circling her clit.

Amelia melted back against the mattress, tilting forward to give me better access. The taste of her made me harder than ever, and as I slid first one, then two fingers inside her, the hot wetness of her nearly undid me.

Her sweet taste surrounded me, infused itself into me.

My love. My mate.

I worked my fingers into her as I sucked and licked. And when she bucked against my hand and mouth as she came, it was all I could do not to plunge my cock into her right then.

I was glad I hadn't when, a few seconds later, she stood and turned around so her back was to me, twisting her head to kiss me and offering me the back of her neck. I ran my lips along her shoulders, savoring the shivers I sent through her. Then she leaned forward just a little and gave me another one of those wicked smiles of hers.

"Oh, gods and goddesses. Yes, please," I murmured aloud. Gently, one hand in the small of her back, I pushed her forward until she was bent all the way over, her hands braced on the bed.

She was so tiny, so much shorter than me, that I had to hold her hips and lift her legs off the floor so she could kneel on the mattress to bring her sweet, hot pussy to the right height. I pulled her back toward me as my own hips surged forward to begin pressing my shaft into her.

Her inner walls clenched down around me, the muscles rippling along my cock, squeezing me tight even before we moved. I took my time allowing my shaft to disappear into her, giving her time to adjust to my size.

My hands tightened gently on her hips as I began to pump, every insistent thrust of my cock shaking her body, her head rising and her back arching each time my hips thrust forward. "Yes," she growled, her voice hoarse with arousal. "More. Please, more."

Even her words added to the ecstasy building inside me, drawing my balls tight against me as I fucked my mate, the one female who could draw this much passion from me. My cock began to jerk inside her, emptying my first orgasm into this amazing, brilliant, beautiful human woman, and I called out her name even as I clasped her tightly against me.

Amelia shuddered against me, and I let go of her hips with one hand to reach around and circle her clit, over and over, until she screamed my name.

This time, when I told her, "I love you, my mate," she knew exactly what I was saying.

CHAPTER TWENTY-ONE

AMELIA

We were both shaking when Zont withdrew from me, then picked me up and gently placed me to lie on the bed before lying down beside me.

But I knew we weren't done.

I draped one leg over him and leaned my head against his chest as he wrapped his arm around me.

Running my fingers along the hard planes of his abdomen, I fluttered them around his cock, which I could already see was changing shape as I touched it.

"Wow," I said in utter fascination as his first cock—the only one I had seen so far, slid back, the slit at the top widening to allow a second, very different cock to emerge, first as a small appendage—but one that grew.

And grew.

And, oh my God, it was huge.

"It's *purple*," I said, my tone betraying my utter fascination. "Are they all purple?"

"All what? Mating cocks?"

"Yes." I reached out and touched the tip, and it jerked toward my hand. I slid down his body to get a closer look.

Zont laughed so hard he had tears running down his face before he could speak again. "I don't know. I haven't seen any other mating cocks—not outside of pictures in sex education classes, anyway. And those—" He paused. "Come to think of it, yes, they were all purple."

"Mm." I answered him absently, intent on exploring this part of him I'd never seen before. "And it's connected to a different kind of testicle?" I ran my hand to the base of the mating cock and felt the swelling there, definitely apart from his balls. I stroked it to test the sensitivity.

Zont moaned softly. "I can't decide if you're asking as a doctor or as my mate."

Surprised, I glanced up at him. "Both, of course." I went back to exploring. "So no one else has ever touched it before?"

"Only you." His voice sounded strained—probably because I had begun to slide my hand up and down his mating cock.

"And that means no one has kissed it before?" I dropped tiny kisses down the rippled shaft.

"No."

"I'm the first one to lick it?" I flicked my tongue out to slide it from base to tip.

"Gods and goddesses, Amelia. You're going to drive me insane."

I sat up and pushed him back against the pillow, swinging my leg over him so that his cock rested just at my entrance. "That's the plan."

"I was afraid of that," Zont rasped.

And then I was riding him, the sounds of our passion mingling, driving us both higher and higher, until we crashed over the edge together, his mating orgasm setting off something primal inside me, shattering me into a million pieces...

And then bringing me back to myself, back to Zont. Back to the only place I ever wanted to be. The one place—the one person—I would never run from.

As I collapsed on his chest and he wrapped his arms around me, I tried the phrase I'd been holding onto for this moment, having memorized it the day Zont had said it to me. "Brinday makavon avoi."

My new translator worked, creating an odd echo in my head as I said the words in one language and heard them translated into English.

The words did mean what I suspected.

So I said them again.

"I love you, my mate," I whispered to my Khanavai warrior, in his own language. "I love you."

"I love you, too," he responded in English. "Forever."

EPILOGUE

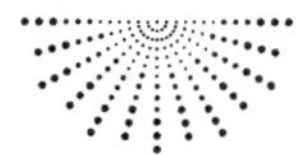

MIA

s I watched Zont and Amelia exchange their vows, I swallowed hard, glancing up at Commander Eldron Gendovi, wondering if maybe he really could save me.

Oh, God. I hope so.

Tears sprang to my eyes, and I blinked them away before he noticed.

What should I do?

Running wasn't an option. Amelia had tried that, and she'd ended up here on Station 21, mated to and marrying the alien who had chosen her.

At least she'd had the option of either agreeing to be with Zont or going through the Bride Games. Vos Klavoii hadn't given me a choice in the matter—he was determined to have another series of Bride Games with several grooms vying for my affections.

Of course, Eldron and I hadn't had sex, and rumor had it that Amelia and Zont had been together before they even made it up to the station, that he had actually mated her without her knowledge—whatever that meant. The Khanavai were pretty cagey about how the mating process worked. When I'd asked Eldron about it, he'd simply caressed my cheek and said, "I promise I'll tell you all about it. But not until we're officially paired."

Every single day since I met him, I had thought about that moment in the corridor outside the hangar, when I had been about to board the Earth-bound shuttle.

I thought I'd escaped being given to an alien warrior. I was wrong.

God. I was less than an hour away from washing out of the Alien Bride Games.

None of the Khanavai warriors had chosen me, and I was scheduled on the next shuttle off the filming station.

My secret was still safe.

I mean, I'd been on television. The whole world had seen me participating, even though I tried to keep a low profile. But I couldn't count on not having been seen. When I got back home, I'd have to run.

Again.

Change my name, get new ID cards.

Get a new translator-tracker.

Again.

I shuddered at the thought of another back-alley procedure. They were dangerous at best, and I knew I was risking getting caught by the authorities by going back.

Worse, taking the risk of getting a new tracker might put me right back on the Bride Lottery list.

But then a bright red alien passed me in a hallway. A whole long line of women waiting to board the shuttle, and a Khanavai warrior had stopped, sniffed the air, and turned to scan all of us.

I ignored him, staring at the floor and huddling down into myself, trying to avoid any attention at all—just as I had during the entirety of the Bride Games up until now. Even during the pageant and interviews, I had mumbled my responses, hoping to make myself as boring as possible.

But the cherry-red giant made a beeline toward me. He placed one finger under my chin and gently raised my face so he could look me in the eye.

"You're beautiful," he whispered. Then he leaned down, those luscious lips of his aiming for mine.

And the next thing I knew, we were all over each other. He picked me up and I wrapped my legs around his waist. His tongue plundered my mouth, leaving me gasping, his kiss making my head spin.

I inhaled the scent of him, something dark and heavy with a swirl of sweetness to it, like chocolate or coffee. Everyplace his body touched mine—which was everywhere—sparks of sheer lust shot through me, spinning me into a world where only the two of us existed.

If not for the shouts and cheers of the other brides in line, I probably would have let him fuck me right there.

Instead, I reluctantly pulled away from the kiss, and he set me on my feet.

When he said, "Come with me," and held out his hand, I followed him.

One of the vidglobes had caught it all, and it had been broadcast live—complete with commentary from Vos Klavoii, as I'd learned later.

Now, the memory of his kisses sent a shiver down my spine, and Eldron glanced down at me, taking my hand in his and bringing it up to his mouth long enough to drop another spine-tingling kiss on it.

I smiled up at him, unwilling to let him know how anxious I was.

Bad enough that my name had been drawn in the Bride Lottery.

Now, even though they were supposedly over, I was back in the Games. And not the usual ones, either—a whole new set of challenges, just for me.

Guess it'll make for good television back home.

I sent up a silent prayer to any god who might be listening that I could resist my attraction to Eldron long enough to get back to Earth, to the people I love.

Back to the people I needed to save.

And that I would be able to keep him from learning my most desperate secret.

The odds aren't looking good, though.

ENJOYED THIS STORY? Be sure to leave a review!

CLAIMED FOR THE ALIEN BRIDE LOTTERY

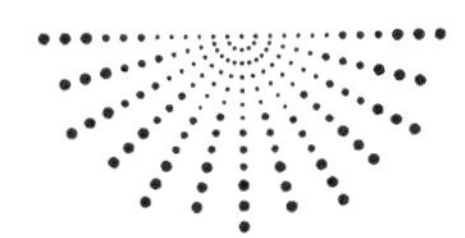

ABOUT CLAIMED FOR THE ALIEN BRIDE LOTTERY

I thought I'd escaped being given to an alien warrior. I was wrong.

I was one hour away from washing out of the Alien Bride Games.

None of the Khanavai warriors had chosen me, and I was scheduled on the next shuttle off the filming station.

But then a bright red alien passed me in a hallway—and the next thing I knew, we were all over each other.

Bad enough that my name had been drawn in the Bride Lottery.

Now, even though they're supposedly over, I'm back in the Games. And not the usual ones, either—a whole new set of challenges, just for me.

Guess it'll make for good television back home.

I just hope I can resist him long enough to get back to Earth, to the people I love.

And that I can keep him from learning my most desperate secret.

The odds aren't looking good, though…

Readers adore this hot series featuring gorgeous, bright alien heroes and the sassy human women they choose as mates!

Every book in the Khanavai Warrior Bride Games series is a stand-alone romance. Join these brides as they find a whole new world of happily ever afters.

CHAPTER ONE

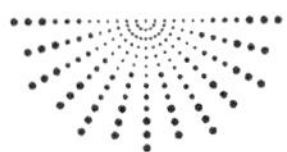

MIA JONES

My name—the one I have now—never should have been drawn in the Alien Bride Lottery.

The back-alley surgeon who replaced my ID chip promised me it was clean, loaded with the information that I had already been through the Games.

I guess that'll teach me to trust the word of someone who made a living as a criminal, illegally replacing the chips our world government required all humans to have implanted.

But the night I was transported up to Station 21, I wasn't at all worried.

I was, however, hot, sweaty, and irritated.

"If you needed unbuttered toast, you should have noted it in the order," I snapped at Kitty, the waitress on the other side of the passthrough to the kitchen—the one who was currently glaring at me over the plates under the heating lamps.

"*Noted it in the order*?" she repeated with a sneer, one hand on her hip. "Who talks like that?"

I rolled my eyes and snatched the toast off the plate under discussion, replacing it with unbuttered toast. "There."

Turning away without waiting for a response, I moved back to the grill. Kitty took the plate with a huff, and as soon as she was gone, I inhaled deeply and blinked away a tear.

I shouldn't be here at all. I trained at *L'école de Cuisine du Chef,* the single most prestigious culinary school in Paris. I should have been in a five-star restaurant in New York or London or Los Angeles, astounding patrons with my delectable, edible creations.

Instead, I was in a crappy diner in Atlanta, slinging hash browns and frying eggs.

But it beat the hell out of the alternative.

Yeah—this is infinitely preferable to what I ran from.

As I finished plating the last meal from the grill, voices rising from the dining room caught my attention. Wiping my hands across my apron, I made my way out to the front room to see what was going on.

"It's the new Bride Lottery," Kitty announced excitedly, clasping her hands under her chin as she stared up at the television.

I frowned. "Those poor girls."

Kitty raised one eyebrow. "What do you mean, *those poor girls*? They are so lucky. They never have to work again. All they have to do is sit and be beautiful for their alien husbands." She struck a pose. "Can you imagine how wonderful it would be to do nothing but spend all day being waited on hand and foot?"

"You don't know what happens once the cameras are turned off," Wanda, one of our regulars said.

I moved over to pat her soft, wrinkled hand. "That's right, Wanda. I don't think we know nearly enough about the Khanavai. I bet they're not as perfect as they pretend to be on TV."

"I remember the first time they showed up," she said—not the first time we had all heard the story, but I paid polite attention, anyway.

"The Prince sure was pretty," she reminisced. "And for the first couple of years, him and his princess were all over the news. It was like a fairytale. Then they just up and disappeared. Hardly ever heard anything at all about their prince again."

"So you think we shouldn't trust them?" Kitty asked the old woman.

"Not even a little bit."

"But it's not like all that many women end up with Khanavai husbands," Joey, our busboy reminded us. "A whole lot of women get chosen every year in the Bride lottery, and then a whole lot get sent back down to Earth."

"Some of them don't," Kitty countered. "Some of them gets swept off their feet and taken away to live happily ever after."

I managed to contain my snort of derision, but only barely.

Happily ever after doesn't exist. It's a trick designed to convince women to give up their entire lives for somebody else.

At least, that was my experience.

"Ooh. Vos Klavoii is about to draw another name!" Kitty called out.

I decided to take a seat in the dining room. After all, no one was going to be ordering anything much until the drawing was done. I might as well take a break. I was practically dead on my feet. Working the 3 a.m. to 10 a.m. overnight shift well into the morning was good, because it meant I could get Josiah to bed at Rebecca's and then be there when he woke up from his morning nap the next day. We might have to change that once he started school, but for now, it meant that we were home together for most of the day.

That didn't leave me much time for sleeping, though.

But we were safe.

Someone would have to be watching us pretty closely to be able to tell where we lived. And if they found that out, they'd have to be watching even closer to figure out where Josiah spent his nights.

I stifled a yawn as Vos Klavoii, the bright green game show host who ran the Bride Lottery and Bride Games, continued his mindless chatter about this year's crop of brides.

Crop. He might as well come out and say it—he thinks human women are grown to be brides for Khanavai males. Like we're not worthwhile on our own.

This time, my jawbone cracked as I gave a giant yawn.

Sitting down probably hadn't been a good idea. I was about to drift off to the sound of everyone enjoying the Bride Lottery drawings when the sound of my own name—the one I used now, anyway—jerked me awake.

"Mia Jones," Vos repeated, flicking his fingers toward the eboard behind him as he waited for the bride's picture to be flashed on it behind him.

No. It can't be me. This is not a terribly uncommon name. There must be at least twenty others with the same name, I reassured myself.

"We seem to be having some technical difficulty," Vos said, his game-show host demeanor not breaking for even a moment. I wondered if he slept with that smile pasted on his face.

All around me in the diner, everyone began jumping up and down and shouting.

"It's you, Mia, it's you!" Kitty grabbed my hands with both of hers and pulled me up out of the chair as if we were suddenly best friends.

I tugged my hands out of hers. "You can't know that. It might not be me at all. Anyway, I'm not eligible for the lottery."

My coworker stopped her silly dance. "Why wouldn't you be?"

My breath stuttered to a halt in my chest. *How can I answer that?*

No one here knew I had a child, and I was not about to tell them.

For that matter, I wasn't even Mia Jones. I was just playing a part: Mia, a little shy, a little talented in the kitchen, trying to get by as best I could.

That's all they needed to know.

Wanda peered deep into my eyes as if reading everything there, then turned to the others. "That's none of your business," she announced. "Maybe her name was already drawn before."

"Nah. She's lying," Kitty decided. "She just doesn't want a hottie alien husband. Because she's insane. Clearly."

Vos was still on the screen, his green skin glowing almost a neon color as he chattered away about the history of the Bride Games in an attempt to fill time while they sorted out their technical difficulties.

"Oh, here we go," he finally said. "It looks like we are getting the feed through, finally. I hear they're sending it over right ... *now*."

My entire world narrowed down to that one moment, the eternity in the second between Vos announcing the picture was on the way and the picture actually showing up.

When it finally came on the screen, I wished that I could have stayed in that second forever.

It was me.

Somehow, the Bride Lottery registration had gotten my name and new ID number and had drawn me in the Lottery.

Cold washed through my limbs and my vision flickered in and out.

I have to get out of here, have to run. A drumbeat started in my head. *Get back to Josiah. Get us out of here. Save him.*

The transportation technology picked me up when I was halfway to the door, dashing across the room and ripping my apron off as if it held my tracker. I don't know where I thought I would go. There was no one on Earth who could save me, no place I could hide. I was acting on pure instinct.

The very last thing I saw as I was transported to Station 21 was the outline of Vos Klavoii's face fading until only his smile remained.

Like an evil, green, Cheshire cat.

CHAPTER TWO

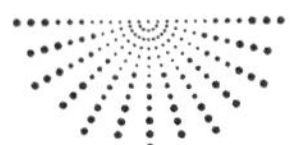

ELDRON GENDOVI

"The Alveron Horde has been far too quiet lately," I insisted. "They are planning something. I know it."

"No, they're not. The Horde has been defeated." General Clovad sighed and shook his head. "I understand your concerns, Commander Gendovi, but they're unnecessary."

My jaw clenched, but I managed to simply nod. "Yes, sir."

"However," the general continued, "just in case you're right, I'm going to embed you in the Bride Lottery program this year."

I had already begun to excuse myself, so his words took me by surprise. "Embed me?"

"Not officially. If you're wrong, I don't want to terrify anyone. But on the off-chance that you're right, I think it would be a good idea to have you close to our best source of viable mates."

Of course, that would be the general's primary concern. Rumor had it that his own Khanavai mate—one of the few females remaining of our species on the planet—was dying. And the general, who had married not from love, but from political necessity, already had his eye on replacing her with one of the young Bride Lottery humans.

Still, I was smart enough not to bring that up.

“If they have anything planned,” he continued, “I suspect it will be at the height of this year’s Bride Games—and we will have you there.”

“If I may ask, sir—you’ll have me there as what, exactly?”

The general’s eyes lit up. “As a groom, course. You might as well get a mate while you’re there.”

Three weeks later, I was still convinced the Horde was planning something. The longer we went without hearing any news from The Darkness—the part of the galaxy the Horde had claimed—the more comfortable the upper brass got. And the more nervous I became.

The Khanavai had gotten more lax over the years as the Alveron Horde failed to attack year after year.

I did not believe that we were safe from the ravages of the Horde. And I definitely didn’t believe the space station where we filmed the yearly Bride Lottery and Games was safe.

So here I was on Station 21, pretending to search for a bride.

Only Vos Klavoii knew my real mission. He’d been clear. I had to make my bride-hunt convincing—anything else, and he would have to boot me from the show, possibly too soon to do any good if the Horde did attack.

I glanced around the tiny room I had been assigned as my groom’s quarters.

This was a young man’s game. I was at least a decade older than every other groom here.

I didn’t fit in.

Luckily, I didn't have to. I simply had to continue participating until I was absolutely sure that the Horde didn't have something up their alien equivalency of sleeves.

I had no interest in actually becoming a groom.

Besides, my research suggested that the Bride Lottery and Games had been a terrible miscalculation on the original Khanavai explorers' part.

Not that they weren't immensely popular now—they absolutely were. But when we, as a species, had first arrived on planet Earth, we had been watching various entertainment programs for years. Earthers had been so naïve that they had blasted their entertainment out into space to be picked up by anyone who happened by.

We had half expected, given the content of the entertainment, that humans would have blown themselves to bits already by the time we got there.

As it turned out, although Earthers really were easily as violent as their television shows had suggested, they weren't *quite* so likely to wipe themselves out entirely.

No one knew that yet, though, when Prince Khan had arrived half an Earth century before. He and his team had saved Earth from the Alveron Horde attackers, then dropped in on the planet to introduce themselves and ask for payment for protection: genetically compatible female mates to replace the ones the Horde had genetically poisoned.

When Prince Khan's research team put together the proposal for the Bride Lottery and Games, however, they made one tactical error. They thought human reality shows were, in fact, real.

The Khanavai assumed the entertainment they had intercepted and studied was somehow indicative of Earthers' actual, true courting rituals.

As it turned out, Earther females did not usually participate in games to win their spouses.

Not even kissing games.

Not competitively, anyway.

Mostly.

No one on Prince Khan's team had realized that salient fact soon enough, so as part of the treaty between Earth and Khanavai Prime, the Khanavai had set up a game show during which human brides competed for the honor to mate with a Khanavai warrior.

As it turned out, human women were not uniformly thrilled with the idea of catching their mates like fish, as one early contestant had succinctly put it.

I'd had to look up what fish were and all in all, I was rather glad we didn't have them on Khanavai Prime. No matter how delicious human women seemed to think they were, they appeared to be slimy and scaly.

And unflatteringly floppy.

No. We were definitely not fish to be caught.

Now that the Bride Lottery was fully enmeshed in their culture, of course, many Earther females had begun to look forward to it. But that early reluctance explained the Lottery portion of the agreement. The Bride Alliance Treaty specified that human women could not be mated against their will, but they could be convinced.

Early on, it took sorting through a lot of women to find one who was both willing to leave her world and compatible with one of our warriors.

Now it was much easier—but the Bride Lottery lived on as tradition.

Anyway, I thought smugly as I stretched out on the single bed in my quarters, I wasn't actually looking for a bride. I was looking for any way the Horde could break through our defenses.

Spying on my own people wasn't my idea of a good time, but I knew it had to be done.

A ding from my com let me know that a message had arrived.

It wasn't the information I was waiting for, though. I had been hoping for more details about the station's weaknesses, as the general had promised.

Instead, I received a catalog of all the human women whose names had been drawn.

Oh, well, I thought. *I might as well entertain myself while I wait for the real info I need.*

Paging open the com file, I began flipping through the images of the various women.

Humans all looked the same. They were all some shade of beige or brown, and all so uniformly, terrifyingly tiny.

I had to wonder how our warriors kept from damaging their new spouses during the mating rituals.

The thought made my skin crawl.

No one that small should ever be taken as an ally.

And definitely not as a mate. I was about to close the file and go back to my brooding when something caught my eye.

Two human women—complete opposites, but equally beautiful. One with amazingly pale skin, so pale I could almost see the veins through it. And the other was equally as dark, her skin the shade of the black lava rocks of the Trashanta plains.

Then again, maybe this assignment wouldn't be so bad, after all.

CHAPTER THREE

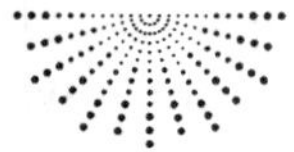

MIA

"No. Really. I'm not supposed to be here." My voice broke as I begged the Poltien who had greeted me to let me go back home. "You don't understand."

The Poltien's hot-pink nose-braid shivered as its owner inhaled in an obvious attempt to remain calm.

"You are required to be here. You are certainly not the first bride who has begged to go home."

"I'm not who you think I am."

The Poltien turned a sharp gaze in my direction. "Defrauding the Lottery Commission is a serious offense," it warned me.

Crap. I needed to get out of here, back home to Josiah. But I couldn't get caught having switched out my tracking device. And I sure as hell couldn't get caught pretending to be someone I wasn't for the Bride Lottery.

There must be a way out of this.

"Do you have anything more to say?" the Poltien asked.

I shook my head meekly, changing tactics midstream.

It would be better if I didn't say anything at all. The Khanavai were bright, flamboyant, violent warriors. I just needed to be the most closed-in version of myself I could come up with. That was my best bet for losing fast enough to get home, maybe in as soon as twenty-four or forty-eight hours.

Becca would have seen what happened, and I trusted her to keep Josiah. She'd be confused, since women with children weren't supposed to end up participating in the Bride Games. But she knew I would never leave Josiah for long.

Play dumb, Mia Jones. It's your best bet.

I grew up watching the Bride Games with my mother, before she passed away. We spent hours every year enthralled by beautiful women from all over the world as they moved through Station 21.

My favorite event was always the Bride Pageant.

I used to dream that I would someday get to be one of them. I imagined myself choosing the perfect red dress, twirling around on the stage and capturing the gaze—and adoration—of one of the Khanavai warriors.

And now that I was here, I felt none of that magic. Instead, my stomach clenched into a tight fist inside me.

I have to go home.

I had no idea how to manage it.

"My name is Thorvid," the Poltien leading me out of the transporter room introduced itself.

All around us, other short Poltiens and a few tall, willowy, three-breasted Blordls led potential brides out of the transporters, taking them away to be dressed for the pageant as the Khanavai grooms gathered to watch the show.

If this had happened even six years earlier, I would have been giddy with excitement.

But not now.

Actually, I wouldn't have ended up here even if this name and number had been drawn back then.

"I'm Mia Jones," I replied shortly.

"Most brides have two assistants," Thorvid explained as it led me through a series of hallways. "But my usual Blordl partner is back on her home planet, having a baby. So I'm afraid you're stuck with just me."

"That's fine," I said, only half my attention on the conversation. "I don't really expect to be here very long."

Thorvid shot a confused glance in my direction. "Why not?"

Shit. I shouldn't have said that. I gave a little negating shake of my head. "I just don't think any of the Khanavai warriors are going to be very interested in me." I spoke like it was a certainty, even knowing I wasn't safe from being chosen, as if just saying the words could perform some kind of magic to get me home sooner.

Thorvid stopped in the middle of the empty hallway and turned to gaze at me appraisingly. "Well, I wouldn't say you're the worst choice someone could make."

In my former life, I might have been offended by the remark. This time, though, I simply laughed halfheartedly. "No," I said, "I'm probably not the worst possibility."

But not the best, either, I added to myself. *Especially if the one choosing is worried about violent exes.*

Thorvid showed me into my room in the bride's quarters. On television, these rooms had always looked magical—light and airy, everything decorated in white with lots of lace.

In person, it looked almost a little tacky. "Very … bridal," I observed, taking a seat at the mirrored table by the wall.

Thorvid snickered. "It's starting to get a little outdated, I think. But what do I know? It's not like fabric with lots of tiny holes in it comes from *my* world's traditions."

"What kinds of marriage traditions *do* the Poltien have?" I asked, suddenly curious to realize that I had never heard anything about how the genderless race reproduced.

Thorvid's face flushed the same color as its nose-braid. "We need to go ahead and start getting you ready for the pageant," it announced brusquely, opening a closet door and pulling out several swaths of fabric to hold up against my face.

Right. The pageant was the first level of choosing.

If I can make it through that without catching the eye of any Khanavai males, I can get back home to Josiah.

Of course, assuming he was watching, Frank would have figured out where I was living—in terms of the town, anyway. I would never be able to go back to the apartment Josiah and I had been living in.

But with any luck, he wouldn't have figured out where Josiah was staying. No one at work knew where I lived, or even that I had a child —much less who kept that child when I was gone. I could get into town, grab Josiah, and get back out before Frank had time to track us down.

Right?

Even with all his resources, there was a chance I could still escape.

We could still escape.

And what if you can't? a tiny voice in the back of my mind whispered.

No. I wouldn't think like that. I had never given in and I wasn't about to start now.

"... red?"

"I'm sorry?" I had completely lost track of what Thorvid was saying to me.

"For your formal dress for the pageant," Thorvid said. "I think a dress in this shade of red. It looks beautiful next to your dark skin."

Thorvid wasn't wrong. The shade it had chosen from among the fabric swatches was my best color.

And it would also make me stand out. "No. I want to wear something more... traditional."

The Poltien frowned. "Okay. How about something in a bright yellow?"

"No. I want a black evening gown."

A pained expression fluttered across Thorvid's face. "Are you sure? You're beautiful." It brushed my hair back from my face. "A little tired around the eyes, maybe. But a color like this could brighten up your whole expression. And a Khanavai warrior could change your life. I've seen it happen."

If only I'd had that option six years ago.

But I hadn't. And now, I didn't have any choice but to try to get through this quickly and get back home. "I am absolutely certain."

Those were my goals: minimize my time in front of the cameras, don't cause any scenes, don't do anything to get me noticed.

With the exception of the cameras, I'd had the same goals for the last two years. Only this time, it was life or death.

Just get through this and get back home.

"Yes, I'm sure. Please," I finally said. "A simple black evening gown. Nothing fancy. Nothing that will garner too much attention."

With a sigh, Thorvid nodded and headed toward the door. "I'll be back in a little while to help you get ready," it said. As it reached the door, though, it paused and turned back.

"Whatever you're so afraid of, you don't have to be. You're safe on Station 21. I promise."

As the door shut behind the Poltien, a single tear shivered on my eyelashes and fell down to my cheek, tracing a path partway down before I dashed it away angrily with the back of my hand.

I might be safe, but Josiah wasn't.

And if anything happened to him while I was gone, I didn't think I would be able to survive it.

CHAPTER FOUR

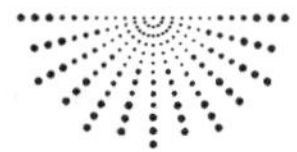

ELDRON

Skipping out on the grooms' events probably wasn't the best way to maintain my cover.

Still, it wouldn't necessarily hurt me. After all, the Games Director knew why I was really here—and it wasn't to find a bride, no matter how much I might secretly want to do exactly that.

While all the other grooms were watching the Bride Pageant, I was prowling around backstage, checking to see if I could figure out any ways the Alveron Horde could have infiltrated the games.

Part of the problem was that I didn't know what I was looking for, only that I had a deep conviction that the Horde was planning something nefarious.

Of course, the Horde was physiologically so different from us—and from humans—that it was unlikely they'd be able to pose as either Khanavai or human.

At least, that was what we assumed.

To the best of my knowledge—and I had top-secret clearance, so my knowledge was among the best—no one had ever seen a member of the Horde alive.

For that matter, we were not certain that the husks we recovered from downed Hordeships were the driving intelligences of the attacks. By the time we got to the ships and pried them open, all that was left inside were shells, like ones from the bugs that humans called locusts. Paper-thin remains that crumbled at the slightest touch.

Our scientists had speculated that the Horde was controlled by a single intelligence, like the queen of a hive. If that was the case, then presumably that single intelligence could be outsmarted. We simply hadn't figured out how yet.

The best we had managed to do was drive the Horde back.

We hadn't even shared all of this information with our human allies. For that matter, relatively few Khanavai knew it. And if we could find a way to defeat the Horde once and for all, no one would ever need to know.

In the meantime, the long quiet spell since the last Horde incursion was making those of us who studied them for a living very nervous.

Regardless, though, there aren't any Hordeships or giant bug aliens backstage at the Bride Games.

Just crowds of human females, I suddenly realized, many of them staring up at me with wide eyes. The effect of all those human gazes on me was unnerving.

Even the scent of them was overwhelming. I caught bits of fragrance ranging from a hint of Lorishi shellfruit to the smell of rain in the Darinsk forests, to the rank scent of Klarvi sour mash.

I have to get out of here. As I turned to make my way to the lift, however, I caught a whiff of something entirely different—something enticing and sweet.

My heart leaped in my chest and a deep, possessive part of me growled, *mine.*

Maybe I could find a mate here, after all.

I froze, trying to find it again in a sea of smells. Slowly, I turned in a circle, my head tilted back in an ancient, predatorial stance while I teased out all the smells around me. The human females standing closest to me began backing away as if recognizing a hunter in the midst of prey.

The tantalizing scent was gone.

I ached to follow it—as the old saying went, the cock follows where the nose leads. But I couldn't figure out where the scent had come from.

My cock had nothing to follow.

For another second, I searched the crowds, hoping to see something that would spark a recognition in me.

Nothing.

Rather, there were dozens of attractive human females. But not one of them called out to my soul.

Maybe it had been my imagination. An effect of wishful thinking on an overactive imagination.

With a sigh, I headed back to the lift.

Moments later, as I made my way into the stands where I could at least pretend to be interested in the pageant going on below, everyone's screen went blank for a moment. When they switched back on, they all showed Vos standing in front of an image of an Earther cityscape. "Warriors and women," he began, "Earthers and Khanavai, we have an exciting new development in this year's Bride Games. Apparently, one of our contestants has run. That's right—for the first time in all the years we've been holding the lottery, a bride has, as the Earthers sometimes say, gone on the lam."

A gasp went up at the announcement and the grooms in the stands began whispering to one another.

That's interesting. I wonder how a human woman will fare on Earth trying to get away from Khanavai-level technology.

As I settled into my seat, the next bride stepped up onto the dais for her interview.

"And now let's give Lottery Bride winner Natalie Ferguson a warm Khanavai welcome!" Vos Klavoii announced cheerfully. She gave a distracted nod to the host.

"So tell us, Natalie," Vos continued, "what are you thinking right now as you join the Bride Games?"

"I'm wishing *I* had thought to run," the dark-haired human in the unflattering blue dress replied.

Vos went silent, then spluttered for a second before finally saying, "But becoming a Khanavai warrior's bride is an honor."

"For other women, maybe," Natalie Ferguson shot back. "But I liked my life back home. I want to finish my college degree, get a job, and then maybe find someone to settle down with. Maybe. I'm not sure I want to get married at all."

The arena grew entirely silent, and I found myself chortling at her replies.

"What about your planet's treaty with the Khanavai? Their agreement to protect Earth?" Vos's voice dropped and Natalie leaned in toward him. "What about the warriors who are willing to give their lives to keep you safe? Don't they deserve some reward?"

At his last line, she jerked away from him again. "I'm not some prize to be given away on a whim."

Vos laughed aloud, turning back to face the camera. "You heard it from her, warriors and women. Natalie Ferguson is no prize."

Natalie glared at him for a moment, then walked off the small set.

Now, *she* was interesting.

And as the synthesized version of her scent floated across the grooms' seating area, I caught a hint of what I'd smelled earlier.

Not quite the same. But close. Could the synthesizing process have changed it so much that I wasn't recognizing it?

Perhaps.

In that case, I should probably meet her.

I hesitated, uncertain whether to turn the pretense that I was looking for a bride into something more real.

Or maybe I should go to the space survey deck to see if they had completed the new scan of the observable skies that I had ordered when I first arrived.

I wasn't sure about Natalie Ferguson—but her smell enticed me. If she was the source of the scent I'd caught earlier, I needed to meet her. I held my finger over the option to choose her, trying to decide why my stomach clenched as I considered taking her as my mate.

Could I live with her forever?

I shook my head. Why wouldn't I be able to? The Khanavai had a long tradition of choosing mates for life.

I sighed. *This is a side effect of your fears about the Alveron Horde,* I told myself. It had nothing to do with reality—just like those fears.

I shouldn't worry about whether or not my mate would be perfect for me. The Bride Games had a long history of making perfect matches.

But the things I valued—my long history of battles won against the Alveron Horde, my strength, my power, my military command, my influence on Khanav Prime? Those were not the things human women were said to value.

No. Human women valued softness. Kindness. The ability to compromise and make decisions together.

I shouldn't be here.

At the thought, I gave a bitter laugh. My very anxiety about choosing a mate felt like softness.

Maybe I do belong here, after all.

Shaking my head, I swiped through the display and chose Natalie Ferguson as a possible mate.

CHAPTER FIVE

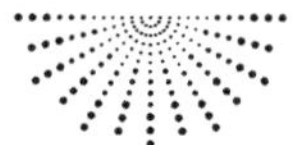

MIA

I *cannot believe she said she wishes she'd run.*

Didn't she know saying something like that would just draw more attention to her?

I didn't want to be here, either. But I was going to take the exact opposite approach. Instead of making a big deal about how much I wanted to go back to Earth, I was going to be a nobody. I wanted to be sure no one even remembered my name.

When Thorvid came back into my room with the plain black gown I requested, I had it style my hair in a simple ponytail clasped at the back of my neck with a plain black band.

"It's so boring," the Poltien complained. "You have such beautiful dark curls. We could do something truly interesting with your hair."

I gave it a severe look. "Absolutely not. Nothing *interesting,* whatever that means. I want to look elegant and classic."

That, I had decided, was going to be how I got out of this mess.

It hadn't taken Thorvid very long to finish getting me ready, especially once I had insisted on minimal makeup. My Poltien handler had been disappointed, I could tell from its crestfallen expression as it surveyed the results in the mirror.

I reached out and patted its hand. "Since we have some extra time before the pageant starts, I need a favor."

Thorvid shot me a suspicious glance.

"Nothing that will get you in any trouble. I promise."

"What is it?"

"I need to make a com call back to Earth."

Thorvid crossed its arms over its tiny chest, its nose-braid shivering in disapproval. "That's not allowed."

"I know. But I promise I'm not calling anyone I shouldn't be. It's just—I was with a girlfriend when my name was drawn, and I know she's got to be worried about what's going on with me now." Mentally, I crossed my fingers. I needed to be able to contact Becca. I had to let her know that everything would be okay.

"A girlfriend?" Thorvid raised its eyebrow suspiciously.

"Just a friend. I promise." Unbidden, tears sprang to my eyes. "I need to tell her that I'm doing well."

Thorvid's expression softened. "I'll see what I can do. Wait here."

The Poltien left the room, leaving me alone with my thoughts. Several hours had passed on Earth, but Josiah was almost certainly still asleep.

Becca, too, for that matter. She might not even know what had happened yet. But I had to be sure that she knew Frank might come looking for us, to make sure she didn't go around my apartment trying to find me—or worse yet, contact the local police.

Every time I thought about Josiah being so far away from me, sick dread roiled through my stomach. I swallowed it down for the umpteenth time.

By the time Thorvid came back into my room, I sat with my hands clasped, wringing them around and around—stroking the finger that had once held my wedding band, as if I could wipe away even the memory of it.

In the doorway, Thorvid held up one finger to its mouth, telling me to be quiet. Without a word, the Poltien moved in and tapped some keys on the com in the mirror in front of me.

"That should do it. We're off-camera now—but we'll need to hurry. What number do you need to com?"

I reached past its shoulder and tapped in Becca's number.

She answered in dark mode, suggesting she had been asleep. "Hello?"

"Becca, it's me, Mia. You don't have to say anything, just listen. I am okay, but my name got drawn in the Bride Lottery."

"What?" The lights came up on Becca's end, showing her sitting up in bed with a handheld device, staring at me with wide eyes. Her blonde hair stuck out in messy tufts. She scrambled for her glasses on the bedside table, putting them on to peer at me. "But I thought you couldn't be—"

I interrupted her before she could say anything that would give me away to Thorvid. "I know. I'm not sure exactly what happened. Please, just know that everything is fine. I should be home in a day or so. Can you hold down the fort until then?"

Becca's eyes darted to the left, toward the room where Josiah slept, but she didn't say anything directly about him.

I guess she's taken to heart all my dire warnings about Frank and what he would do to us if he found us.

"Of course," she said. "I'll take care of... everything."

"Thank you. I will try to let you know when I'm headed back if I can—but I'm not certain exactly when that will be."

"I understand."

I heaved a shaky sigh of relief. At least now I could be sure that Becca would take care of Josiah until I could get back. Not that I would have expected anything else. In the two years I had known her, Becca had become my closest friend, a kind of substitute aunt for Josiah. I trusted her implicitly—so much that I had told her the truth about myself.

"If we don't want this com to be tracked, you need to cut it off now," Thorvid said, its tone gentle.

"I love you and I love—" I stopped myself before I said Josiah's name.

"Love you, too. We'll see you soon," Becca said. "Take care of yourself."

I ended the call with tears welling in my eyes. Once upon a time, I had thought there was nothing worse than being trapped, afraid for myself. Now, though, I was beginning to think it might be worse to be trapped and afraid for my child.

THORVID HUSTLED me down to the backstage area to line up for the Bride Pageant. As I stepped off the lift, an enormous, bright red Khanavai warrior brushed past me, and it was all I could do not to stop and stare at him in absolute wonder.

He was giant, muscular and broad, with skin the color of the dress Thorvid had tried to convince me to wear. Just the sight of him made me gasp, and I had to shake myself out of it. *Come on, Mia. Your job is to be inconspicuous, not stare at gorgeous aliens.*

I ducked my head and hurried to the end of the line of women waiting for their turn in the pageant, doing my best to blend in. But not before I saw the warrior pause and lift his head as if scenting the air like a large predator—a wolf or something.

Then he was gone, and a few minutes later, Natalie Ferguson was giving her answer to Vos's question. And while part of me wished I had run, too, I wasn't about to say so aloud.

When my turn came on the dais, I gave half-mumbled, almost incoherent answers. Doing everything I could to project the image of a boring, half-addled idiot that no man in his right mind would want to spend the time with.

It worked, too. By the next morning, all the Khanavai males had chosen the women they wanted as brides.

And I wasn't one of them.

"Now we just have to get you ready to go home," Thorvid said, its mouth twisting in disappointment.

I almost wanted to comfort the Poltien, but when I opened my mouth to say something, all my breath rushed out of me in a whoosh of relief, and I burst into tears.

I was going home.

I would have to run again, just in case Frank had seen me on TV.

But I could do that.

I knew how to run.

Sometimes, it felt like that was all I knew how to do.

But it didn't matter.

I was going home to get my child.

CHAPTER SIX

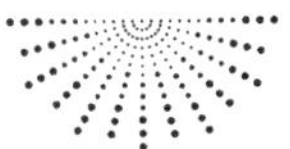

ELDRON

The next day, I made my way to the luncheon room prepared to determine once and for all if Natalie Ferguson was my mate.

In the hallway outside, I met up with Tiziani Mencono. I nodded a greeting and dismissed him in a single glance. He was one of the yellow tribesmen of the Darinsk rainforests on Khanav Prime, and according to the research I had completed on him, he was a mere guardsman in the prince's household on the southern continent.

If it came down to a physical fight between us, I would win. But if Natalie was his true mate, nothing would keep them apart.

When we entered the luncheon room, we discovered that Cav Adredoni, our third competitor for Natalie's affection, had already entered.

Smart move, I conceded silently. In any traditional Khanavai setting, it would have allowed him to take control of the room by choosing an advantageous seat.

Of course, the human penchant for round tables thwarted that plan, forcing him to choose between a seat that gave him a full view of the doorway or a seat that would allow him to be first to greet Natalie when she entered. Adredoni had chosen to view the doorway.

I looked forward to seeing how that worked out for him.

The bride was always last to enter the luncheon, a tradition that had developed over the years since the Bride Games had begun.

Standing, Adredoni gave the traditional warriors' greeting, holding his closed fist, thumb inward toward my chest, a little longer than was customary, eyeing first the yellow Tiziani Mencono and then me. "Greetings," he said, "and may the gods favor our endeavors on this day."

I blinked at his choice to utter what was generally a prayer before battle as a greeting but murmured the traditional response. "May the gods favor you, as well."

As I took a seat to Adredoni's right, I smiled at the younger captain's bold moves. Tiziani, on the other hand, scowled as he realized that he'd just offered a prayer for Adredoni's success. Tiziani sat across from me, leaving the seat immediately in front of the door available for Natalie.

"It is a pleasure to meet you." I nodded at them both, then turned to Adredoni, interested to see what kind of competition he might offer. "I have learned many good things about you today."

"And I you."

Somewhere in a television studio on the station, Vos and his team of commentators were certainly discussing the social undercurrents in the room as we waited for the bride to arrive.

Adredoni showed off his social skills by including Tiziani in the conversation. "I understand you are a member of the civilian guard?"

"I am a retainer to the southern continent's Royal Residence and am responsible for the prince's safety when he is there."

As I had expected, he was a nobody. The current prince rarely traveled outside the capitol, and when he did, a retinue of military guards traveled with him. Tiziani was a pretender to rank. The judges would score harshly for his attempts to show off.

I nodded politely at the guardsman.

The door opened and the two people who had been appointed Natalie's guides—a Poltien and a Blordl—opened the door. The Blordl announced in her trilling voice, "Here comes the bride," a phrase lifted from Earth mating rituals and used to introduce contestants whenever a new game began.

We three grooms stood, waiting for Natalie.

Beside me, Captain Adredoni inhaled, and his entire being seemed to light up from within.

That is how a male finding his mate should look. Could more than one Khanavai warrior have the same true mate?

I took a deep breath, hoping to discover the answer. And then I frowned.

The synthesizers had gotten Natalie's scent…well, not wrong, exactly. But the synthesized version lacked the fullness of the scent that was uniquely hers.

And that scent did not belong to my mate.

Better to end this farce now than allow it to drag on. Reaching out, I took Natalie's hand in my own. She flinched, then froze.

Definitely not mine.

"My dear," I said, bowing over her hands. "I am very sorry, but I'm afraid I have some bad news."

Natalie gasped as if I had mortally wounded her. Surely she hadn't already decided on me?

Then she caught her breath. "What is it you need to tell me?"

I allowed my sadness to infuse my voice. "I'm afraid the synthesized chemical composition of your scent-markers did not do you justice."

Natalie glanced at the other two men in the room, her expression confused. *Bloated blundevins,* I cursed to myself. *A Khanavai female would have known what I was trying to say.*

"You are very lovely," I continued. "But I'm afraid I must tell you that we are not a match, after all."

"We're not a match?"

I met her gaze sadly and shook my head. "I fear not."

Her breath left her body in a wild rush, and she scrabbled at the chair next to her, grabbing the back and sinking into the seat.

Why is she fainting? My mind scrambled for an answer. Was my rejection really that much of a shock to her system? We had never met before—but perhaps she was one of those females who built entire worlds of fantasy around her. Maybe she had decided we were meant to be together and was unable to remain standing at the mere thought of my rejection.

I followed her down to help support her as she landed on the chair and remained kneeling on one knee before her.

"I do hope I have not distressed you too much, Miss Natalie," I continued in my most polite tone.

"No," she said, waving one hand weakly. "Not at all. Thank you for letting me know so quickly. I appreciate not having this ordeal drawn out more."

Her two assistants leaned in, the Blordl drawing me to my feet. "No problem," she trilled. "We're so sorry your match didn't work out."

She opened the door to usher me out. The Poltien followed us, muttering something about false matches ruining the show.

The Blordl shut the door behind us, and I was once again free to follow my hunches about the Alveron Horde's plans to disrupt the Bride Games somehow.

Even if part of me—that deep, primal part that had growled out its possession of the scent backstage—whimpered in sadness that Natalie Ferguson had not been my mate, after all.

At least I have work to do, I consoled myself—and from here, it would be easy to cut through the shuttle bay area to the main offices and get back to that work. "I'm going to the military side of the station," I told the assistants, who murmured their goodbyes, apparently glad they wouldn't have to escort me anywhere.

But as I turned down the main hallway that opened onto the shuttle bays, I found myself in a long hallway full of women.

And once again, that smell—*the scent of my mate*—hit me like a fist to the gut.

She's here, I realized. *Somewhere among all these women.*

And I would do whatever it took to find her.

CHAPTER SEVEN

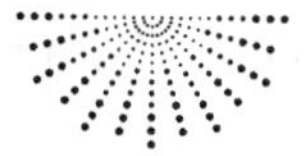

MIA

"Why can't we use the transporter to go home?" I asked Thorvid as it led me toward the shuttle bay.

"It has something to do with the number of destinations required. Too much of a power drain on the station."

I gave the Poltien a side-eye. "And we're not the stars of the show any longer, right?"

It grinned. "Exactly."

"Thank you so much for everything," I said as we reached the end of a long line of women waiting to go home. "I know I wasn't the easiest bride to assist."

The Poltien gave a shrug, its nose-braid swinging with the motion. "It was lovely to work with you. Be careful on the way home."

I waved as Thorvid left, then leaned back against the wall and closed my eyes.

I'll be home soon.

Relief swept through me, and I blew out a relieved sigh.

My eyes were still closed a moment later when a whisper went up among the women who surrounded me.

What now?

I saw him as soon as I opened my eyes. There he was again—the bright red warrior who had been stalking through the crowds of women backstage during the pageant.

He wore one of their skimpy kilt-like uniforms, including a sash across his chest covered in Khanavai text. His dark hair stood out against his cherry-colored skin and his silver eyes almost glowed. He paused in the hallway, lifting his nose into the air again as if catching a familiar scent.

Crossing his muscular arms over his chest, he scanned up and down the line of women as we stared back at him in wide-eyed wonder, falling silent, none of us daring to make a sound in the face of that intense stare.

His gaze swept across the line of women waiting to enter the shuttle. I froze, terrified, feeling like a small forest creature hunted by some giant, monstrous animal.

Before, I had thought he reminded me of a wolf, but his motions were more graceful than that, smoother—he was definitely stalking his prey, but more like a big cat than anything lupine.

He moved toward our line, his long, loping steps bringing him inexorably toward me.

I knew it the moment he zeroed in on me, too. His gaze snapped to my face with an intensity like nothing I had experienced before.

My entire awareness narrowed down until everything around us seemed to fall away. It might as well have been just the two of us standing in that hallway outside the landing bay.

He moved in until only inches separated us, my eyes level—barely—with his chest. I tipped my head back in time to see him bend down to wrap me in his arms. "You're beautiful," he whispered.

His scent, masculine and spicy, something both exotic and familiar, enveloped me, and I found myself drawing it into my lungs as if the smell of him were oxygen—like I needed to breathe in his particular aroma in order to live.

Without my volition, my eyes closed, and I tilted my lips toward his. He claimed my mouth fiercely, hungrily, teasing my lips open and thrusting his tongue inside as if he were staking claim to me.

A tiny moan fluttered in the back of my throat. At the sound, the muscular red alien literally swept me off my feet, scooping me up with one arm behind my knees, the other supporting my back. I wound my arms around his neck, weaving my fingers into his hair, my involuntary response half-terrified and completely passionate.

My entire body ached to get closer, as if he were a safe harbor in the storm that was my life.

As that thought crossed my mind, I remembered the life I needed to return to.

Josiah.

With a gasp, I pulled away from his kiss.

"Put me down," I urged him breathlessly.

With a strange kind of *pop*, the world came rushing back in.

All around us, the women standing in line were shouting and cheering.

The red alien leaned his forehead against mine. "I've been looking for you."

"No." The word snapped out of me by pure instinct. "I'm not who you've been searching for. You made a mistake." I began to struggle, and he placed me gently on my feet.

"Why are you standing in this hall?" His imperious tone left me blinking in surprise, but I answered him, anyway.

"I'm getting ready to leave. I'm going back to Earth."

His eyes widened as he glanced around at all the other discarded brides. "Absolutely not. That cannot happen." His voice rang with authority.

Who was he to say what I could or couldn't do?

"It's happening. I'm going home." I fell back against the wall, retaking my spot in the line—but also using the inner hull of the station to support me, disguising the shaking of my knees.

"We'll see about that." He frowned and glanced around as if trying to find someone in charge. "You." He pointed at the nearest Poltien, who was standing wide-eyed, holding a compad with a passenger manifest. "This woman. What is her name?"

"I can answer that for myself," I announced. "I'm Mia Jones, and I am going back to Earth."

The Poltien looked back and forth between the alien and me and shrugged. "It's not up to me."

"I am Commander Eldron Gendovi. And Mia Jones is going with me."

Panic began crawling up my throat. "I am *not*."

The shuttle bay door opened, and the line of women began moving steadily inside, streaming into the bay to board the shuttle.

The commander reached down and took my hand, managing to hold it lightly but also firmly. He raised his other wrist to his mouth and barked out a code into the wristcom. "This is Gendovi. Get Vos on the com, please."

This cannot be happening. I have to get home to Josiah.

My stomach twisted at the thought of staying here any longer than I already had. But if I caused a scene, it might raise even more questions than were about to be leveled in my direction.

Oh, God. What do I do?

My lips still burned where the commander had kissed me, and part of me wanted nothing more than to throw myself at him, ignore the world around me.

But I couldn't do that. Not if I wanted to make sure no one figured out about Josiah.

Not if I want to make sure Frank doesn't get to him.

My heart sank as my fellow rejected brides filed into the shuttle that would take them home.

What to do? Stay here and deal with whatever had just happened? Or try to fight my way onto the shuttle and get back to Earth?

I had to go home.

I reached up and grabbed the commander's wrist. "Please, you don't understand. I have to get home. It's..."

I was about to say it was a matter of life or death. But I was interrupted by Vos Klavoii, appearing at the end of the hall and hurrying our direction.

"Commander Gendovi!" he exclaimed. "I am thrilled to see that you have found a mate—even if it was at the very last minute."

I opened my mouth to protest, then realized Vos had been followed by several vidglobes, every single one of them focused on me.

All of them sending images of my face back to Earth.

So much for not getting noticed.

I am so screwed.

CHAPTER EIGHT

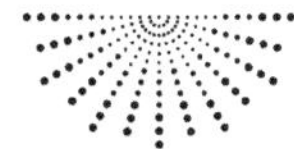

ELDRON

"Are you sure you don't want to simply join the current Bride Games?"

Vos sat behind his desk, his elbows resting on the broad expanse of Earth wood in front of him as he tapped his forefingers together. He had not asked me to sit, but I'd pulled a chair away from the wall, anyway. Station 21 might be Vos's domain, but I outranked him. At worst, we were equals, and I was going to do everything I could to make sure he remembered that.

"I'm positive," I finally replied after staring at him for a few long, silent moments. "I have several tech teams at work scanning nearby areas, particularly the Alveron Horde quadrants, for any new intel. I need to check in with them. Mia and I will simply have a mating ceremony and be done."

I hoped that getting the ceremony over with quickly would help eliminate the expression of sheer terror I had seen on my mate's face when she realized that rather than going home to Earth, she would be participating in the Bride Games with me.

As for whatever reason she had for wanting to go back to Earth? We could deal with that later. I would make sure she had everything she wanted.

There would be no reason for her to ever need to go back to Earth.

Of course, if she were homesick, we could visit occasionally.

Vos narrowed his eyes at me. "I agreed to allow you to join the grooms in this year's games on the condition that if you actually found a mate, you would participate in the Bride Games."

We held one another's gazes for another long moment as I considered whether this was a battle I truly wanted to fight.

Finally, I gave a curt nod. "How would you feel about extending this year's games? Let me finish my work, and then Mia and I can go through the Games separately."

Vos flashed that signature grin of his. "Draw the Bride Games out longer? Fine by me. It ought to bring up the ratings." He paused, an almost evil gleam in his eye. "But we will have a completely different set of games for you and your bride. I'll put a team on it and see what we can find out about her background. We should be able to come up with something… suitably interesting for the two of you."

I wasn't sure I liked the sound of that—but having seen the spanking ceremony that Cav and Natalie had engaged in, I knew I didn't want to participate in the same games they had. Those sorts of foreplay games were far too intimate to be shown to the entire galaxy.

With any luck, Vos and his team would be forced to come up with something a little less revealing.

"In the meantime," Vos continued, "we had to reassign one of your team members. Wex Banstinad, a communications officer, was assigned to Zont Lanov, the Khanavai warrior who has headed to Earth to track down Amelia Rivers."

I ran the names through my memory, finally coming up with a connection. "The bride who ran? A warrior has decided to try to gain her as his mate?"

"Indeed, the bride who ran." Vos's smile seemed genuine, for once. "This is going to be the most exciting set of Bride Games ever."

I rolled my eyes. He wasn't wrong. But having found my mate, I wasn't terribly interested in playing any of Vos's ridiculous games.

Still, I had agreed to participate, and that agreement had gotten me access to Station 21's equipment for my project.

"I'm going to check in with my team," I announced as I stood. "I'll see if I can find another technician to replace Wex Banstinad."

Vos gave a little two-fingered salute and went back to plotting whatever it was he had in mind.

I was not certain he even noticed as I left his office.

CHAPTER NINE

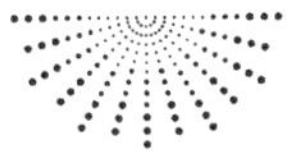

MIA

In my dream, I stood at my kitchen counter, chopping onions as I prepared dinner.

I could tell Frank was angry the moment he strode through the front door, the dark cloud that hovered around him on days like this making my stomach twist and turn with a dread I couldn't even put into words.

Josiah, not even a year old yet, played on the floor at my feet, banging pots and pans together happily, a cheerful sound, but one I knew I needed to silence.

Bending over, I spoke softly to him. "Baby, let's go find another toy for you to play with."

I took the pan lid away from him, and Josiah began crying. I tried to shush him, turning to look for something else he could play with.

But as I stood up, Frank was there, fist raised. "How many times do I have to tell you to make the baby shut up?" he snarled.

His fist came down with a sickening crunch against the side of my face. I heard the sound before I felt it, and even as I landed on the ground, I was thinking, "I have to get the baby to stop crying." The first words out of my mouth were to comfort Josiah. "It's okay, baby, it's okay."

I crawled toward him, the tile on the floor spattered with the blood I spit out my mouth.

Frank's boot—all I could see of him out of the corner of my eye—reared back, aimed at Josiah.

With a burst of energy I didn't know I had, I leaped forward and curled myself around my baby, protecting him with my own body, taking Frank's boot in the small of my back rather than allowing him to hurt my child.

I AWOKE WITH A START, the feel of Frank's boot throbbing in my kidneys and tears streaming down my face.

I could not allow him to figure out where Josiah was.

Of course, I hadn't gotten back to Earth. I was still on Station 21, back in my overly lacy bride's room. The shuttle had left without me while Vos had chattered about fitting us into the Bride Games.

In the end, I had stood by silently as Commander Gendovi drew the Games Administrator aside and spoke to him quietly and urgently. I didn't know what about. All I knew was that I was standing to the side while two alien men kept me trapped and plotted out my future.

But it wasn't the first time I had been trapped. I had gotten away then, and I would get away now. I simply needed to make sure Josiah was okay—and then I would do everything I could to find a way back to Earth.

I was sure that's what had prompted the dream. It was my subconscious reminding me that I knew how to bide my time.

I knew how to run away.

Oddly enough, the situation I was in right now—onboard Station 21 with no clear way home—didn't feel any more stifling than I had felt married to a wife-beating cop, living in New Jersey.

This is just another situation to run from, I told myself.

I simply had to plan.

And to do that, I would need more information. I moved to the com in my dressing-table mirror and messaged Thorvid.

"Could you please tell me how to watch the last several days' Bride Games on this thing?"

THAT AFTERNOON, Eldron commed to ask me to attend a duel with him.

My mouth fell open at the request and I stared at him for a long, silent moment. "A...what?" I finally managed to get out.

"A duel," he repeated. "Is that not what Earthers call it? Two grooms who matched with the same bride are going to engage in combat."

I rubbed my eyes with the heels of my hands. "Um. Duel. As in, to the death?"

Now Eldron was the one who gaped like a fish. "To the *death?*" he repeated. "I should hope not."

"But they are going to fight?"

"Yes. Vos is arranging for spectators, and I would like to attend to give my support to one of the two men. Will you accompany me?"

Sitting alone in my room wasn't getting me very far in my escape plans. Besides, watching the latest Bride Games vids had brought up a rather pressing question—one I suspected I needed to ask Eldron in person.

"Would you come by my quarters first?" I asked him.

I wouldn't have expected someone with cherry-red skin to be able to blush, but I swear Eldron turned even redder with pleasure. "It would be my honor."

By the time he arrived, I had been pacing the length of my room for half an hour. I inhaled, hoping to calm my nerves before I opened the door.

It didn't work. My hands trembled as I waved Eldron inside. "Please come in."

His enormous shoulders took up more of my room than I had anticipated. Even leaning back against the door didn't give me enough space. I tried to figure out how long it would take for me to rip open the door and get out, as opposed to how much time it would take him to cross the room and pull me away from the only exit.

I found myself counting the steps from where he stood to where I stood.

"What did you wish to discuss?" His concerned voice snapped me out of my reverie—but not out of my terror.

It was stupid to invite him in.

"Mia? Are you okay?"

I swallowed, trying to work up the nerve to speak.

"We can discuss anything, my *vanata*."

Just spit it out, Mia.

"They're not going to make us do one of those spanking ceremonies, are they?" My voice shook as I forced myself to ask the question. "Like Natalie and Cav had to do?"

Eldron frowned as he examined my expression. "A spanking ceremony? That is a very old Khanavai tradition—and it is not one that I find necessary in our modern society." He paused, his gaze traveling over my face as if he were trying to read what he saw there. "Especially since our two cultures are becoming more blended every year."

All the air rushed out of my lungs at once. My head seemed to grow lighter, and my vision went entirely white.

When I could see again, Eldron was helping me sit down in the dressing-table chair, his touch tender.

"Why did that worry you so very much?" His voice was as gentle as his hands.

"I need you to promise me you'll never hit me. Not even as a joke or in play. Promise?"

He dropped to one knee before me, as if he were proposing marriage, his voice going even deeper than usual. "I swear I will never raise my hand against you."

"Even if the Bride Games demand it?"

He lifted one fist and tapped his heart twice, once with the end and once with his closed fingers toward his heart, a kind of salute I had seen Khanavai warriors all over the station give one another. "No one could ever make me hurt you. On my honor as a Khanavai, I give you this vow."

Those words were oddly formal.

I wasn't entirely certain what he meant, but I didn't have to be—it was obvious this was the most serious promise he could give me. I leaned forward and clasped his fist in both my hands, bringing it up to my lips and dropping a light kiss on it. "Thank you."

"You are most welcome, my *vanata*." He moved as if he were about to stand, but then paused. "Would you prefer to refrain from attending the duel? If violence offends you..."

"No, let's go. I need to get out of this room."

With a nod, he finished rising and held his hand out to me to help me rise from the chair.

I swear I will never raise my hand against you.

If only I could bring myself to fully trust that promise.

CHAPTER TEN

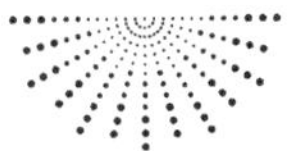

ELDRON

"Tell me about this duel," Mia requested as we made our way to the auditorium. "Who is fighting, and why?"

"You have been watching the Bride Games, yes? That is how you know about the spanking games?"

She nodded, her eyebrows drawing down in a frown at the memory. "I didn't really get past that part on the vids." With a sidelong glance, she added, "I did see the part where you told Natalie she wasn't your mate. How did you know?"

"I could tell from her scent." I considered elaborating, but when she simply nodded, I decided it would be better to explain the Khanavai connection between smelling and mating another time.

"Ah. Well, Cav and Natalie have chosen one another. But Tiziani, the third male in that luncheon—"

"The yellow one?"

"Yes, the yellow one. He accosted Cav in the garden and challenged him to a duel."

"Even after Natalie chose Cav?" Mia's voice turned shocked.

"Some males have very little honor."

"That's for sure." Her murmured words were barely loud enough for me to hear, and I had to wonder if who had shaped her low opinion of males. Had one raised his hand against her? The mere thought of it sent a surge of anger racing through my body, and I had to fight to suppress the growl that rose to my throat.

I would kill anyone who dared touch her in anger.

But no such male is here now, I reminded myself when Mia flashed an anxious glance at me, as if she could sense my rising agitation.

She's your mate, that same inner voice pointed out. *She almost certainly can sense your emotions.*

I gave her a reassuring smile and led her into the arena where Cav would, I assumed, thoroughly trounce his opponent.

As we took our seats, Vos's face came on the screens—both at our seat vids and on giant ones hanging in the air above the arena—announcing this as "the biggest fight for dominance in all the history of the Bride Games!"

My inner warrior bristled at that. After all, we Khanavai were a dominant lot. But I was civilized enough to push the instinctive response aside.

Cav and Tiziani met on the stadium floor, facing off against each other.

Glancing around the spectators, I found Natalie standing and clasping her two assistants' hands. The vidglobes zoomed around her, flashing her anxious face up on the screens all over the arena.

About half the spectators cheered for Tiziani. I had to wonder why. Cav stood taller than the yellow warrior and was obviously the more honorable male.

But they were both trained, one as a soldier, the other as a guardsman, and both handled the traditional Khanavai sword well.

On the screen in front of me, an offer to place a bet through Vos's offices appeared.

"What is that?" Mia asked, leaning in closer to me.

"Gambling on the winner of battles like this is a time-honored Khanavai tradition," I explained. "Bets on the Bride Games alone help fund Station 21. Would you like to bet on one of the warriors?"

She shook her head without taking her eyes off the contestants. "I wouldn't want to risk wasting the money."

I blinked, startled that she would assume I expected her to spend her own currency. "Allow me, then."

"No, thank you." Her voice was quiet, but I could almost taste her reluctance in the air around us, as if she feared being in someone's debt.

Am I sensing her emotions now?

Quietly, I placed a large bet on Cav. If he won, I would gift it to the newly mated pair.

The two fighters began whirling around one another, their blades whistling in the air.

Tiziani was a skilled fighter, but Cav was larger and slightly faster, leaping across the mat, rolling on the floor and coming up under Tiziani's guard, slashing at him once and then rolling away.

Tiziani's fans gasped as he stumbled. Cav, overcome by his warrior's instincts, lunged for him, but Vos blew his whistle, threw his hands into the air, and announced, "First point to Cav Adredoni."

Tiziani held his hand to his side, and when he pulled it away, his hand was covered in blood. The cameras showed him snarling at Cav, who saluted him mockingly.

Mia watched with eyes like saucers.

"Cav needs four more points to win," I explained.

In the next round, Tiziani scored a point by cutting Cav's dominant arm, and beside me, Mia gasped.

"Would you like to leave?" I asked her, but she shook her head without taking her eyes from the fight below.

She's not completely horrified by violence—this bothers her less than the spanking ceremony, I realized.

Tiziani gained a second point with a cut across Cav's thigh, and onscreen, Natalie clasped her hands across her mouth. Next to me, Mia mirrored the other woman's movement.

But when Cav used a ripped part of his *chavan* uniform to bind the wound, blew Natalie a kiss, and twirled around on the injured leg, Mia's hands relaxed.

"I can't stand the thought of Natalie having to watch this," she said as Natalie called the Games Administrator over to talk to him.

"I have faith that the right warrior will win," I assured her, reveling in the kindheartedness of my mate.

I had seen the expression on Cav's face. He would not allow Natalie to be taken from him.

Just as I would never allow my beautiful Mia to be taken from me.

I was right, too. Cav swirled in on the power of his battle rage, spiked as it was by the determination to protect his mate, and within moments, the fight was over—Cav gained several points, took the yellow warrior's weapon away, and ended with both swords poised over the back of Tiziani's neck, prepared to decapitate his opponent.

Everyone in the stadium froze, waiting as Cav held Tiziani bent over for three long heartbeats and then simply nicked the other male's skin.

"Come with me," I said to Mia as Vos blew his whistle and the stadium erupted in noise. Below us, Natalie leaped over the barrier separating her from the floor and rushed to throw herself into Cav's arms. "We should go congratulate the newly mateds."

Leading her down to the floor of the stadium, I held Mia's hand and pushed my way through the crowd, where we discovered that as we made our way to the floor, Tiziani had attempted to attack Cav yet again.

"Why would he do that?" Mia asked in a whisper.

"He is entirely without honor," I said disdainfully. "That cannot be allowed to happen—not without some form of consequence."

"Nice to see you again, Commander," Cav said, one foot holding the other Khanavai down on the station floor.

"You as well." I glanced down at Tiziani. "Looks like you have everything under control."

"At least for the moment." The guardsman under his heel began to struggle and Cav leaned on that foot to hold him still.

"You know," I continued, keeping my tone conversational, "I know Prince Aranov. I think it might be best if I commed him about his guardsman."

"Yes," Cav agreed. "Perhaps the prince will have some idea how to handle him."

"Oh, no," Natalie said, a smile beginning to grow across her face. "I have a much better idea."

I turned my attention to her. "Yes?"

"Vos," Natalie said to the Games Administrator, "don't you have a position open?"

Vos's smile flashed across his face. "I believe I might, come to think of it."

"No!" From his position on the floor, Tiziani began to protest, having regained his breath.

"What kind of position?" I asked.

"I could use an assistant between now and the next Bride Games," Vos said. "And we have never had a failed groom returned to the games. It could be an interesting storyline next year."

"No," Tiziani groaned. "I can't leave my life on Khanav Prime."

Adopting a serious expression, I shook my head. "Oh, I don't believe you'll be having any say in it." I glanced down at Mia and squeezed her hand. "Besides, it might teach you something about how to interact with Earth females."

Turning, I bowed to Natalie. "Congratulations, my dear. To Zont, I said, "I'll take over here. I think you and your mate have a ceremony to plan."

The matched pair smiled at one another and, as they turned to leave, I let go of Mia's hand long enough to help Tiziani stand. "Come with me," I said, pulling him toward the backstage area. "You have a future to plan, as well—though I doubt it will be as pleasant as Natalie and Cav's."

CHAPTER ELEVEN

MIA

I spent the next several days trying to figure out how to get off Station 21 and back to Earth.

Originally, the plan had been for Commander Gendovi and me to go through a series of Bride Games immediately. I had panicked at the thought but luckily—for me, anyway—pretty much everyone on two worlds was completely engrossed in the saga of the runaway human bride and her pursuing alien as it was playing out on Earth between Zont and Amelia. Vos had agreed to put off our games until those antics were over.

He would do almost anything for ratings, I had realized.

But watching Zont as he talked to his team, preparing to hunt down the woman who had tried to get out of being a bride at all had also convinced me of one important thing: getting away from a determined Khanavai warrior who believed he was your mate was just about impossible.

Running from Frank had been easy by comparison.

I spent my nights pacing the confines of my bridal room, trying to come up with a scenario that would allow me to get down to Earth, grab Josiah, get both our trackers replaced, and then get away from North America entirely.

It hadn't occurred to me that I was being watched by vidglobes all the time until the morning Thorvid showed up in my room with a worried expression on its face, its lizard-like rill fluttering up and down on the back of its neck as its nose-braid quivered.

"Do you feel like a caged animal?" the Poltien asked as soon as the door closed behind it.

I blinked, trying to figure out where the question was coming from. "A little bit," I admitted.

Thorvid drew me into the lav, turning on the sanicleanse and punching in a code on the mirror com, presumably to give us some privacy. "Vos called me into his office and ordered me to find out why you have been pacing in your room at night."

I gave the Poltien a blank stare. "Shit."

Thorvid tilted its head back and forth, examining me from all angles. "Defecation? That makes you need to pace? If you are having gastrointestinal difficulties—"

I snorted. "*Shit* was not an explanation. It was…" I paused as I tried to figure out how to explain that I'd been cursing. "It was an expression of dismay."

"Ah. That makes more sense," Thorvid said. "Would you like to explain to me why you're dismayed?"

"Not really. I guess you can tell Vos I suffer from insomnia." I crossed my arms over my chest and tapped my chin with my forefinger. "I need to make him less suspicious of me."

Thorvid mirrored my stance, crossing its own arms over its thin chest as it peered up at me. "The Games Director has instructed me to get you ready for a date with Commander Gendovi. I suggest you bathe, and then we will choose an appropriate outfit for you."

"You really think I should?"

"Yes. You will assuage Vos's concerns about you by going on an outing with the commander." Thorvid gave me an assessing look. "You should probably know that according to recent polls, Commander Gendovi is fast becoming a fan favorite on the Bride Games. Vos is looking for footage that will encourage that impression of him."

And thereby improve the Bride Games' ratings. Right.

"So you're suggesting that I should play up to Eldron if I want to make Vos less suspicious of me?" Could it be that even without knowing what I wanted, Thorvid was on my side?

Yes. The Poltien really was trying to help me, I decided—not as in *help me land a husband,* but as in help me obtain what it was that I most wanted.

No matter what that might be.

I had to blink back tears. It had been so long since anyone but Becca had truly cared about me. I had almost forgotten what it was like to have a friend.

"That is exactly what I mean. Whatever you are planning, you need to be prepared for a variety of outcomes."

That was certainly true. I'd learned not to plan too far ahead as I had gone on the run from Frank. Get everything in order and be prepared to take whatever opportunity presented itself.

"I've grown to like you," Thorvid said. "I don't want to see you hurt."

I opened my mouth to respond, but the Poltien continued speaking. "That said, Commander Gendovi is a good Khanavai male. Whatever it is that you're afraid of, I feel certain he can help. I strongly encourage you to tell him whatever it is that's bothering you. The

Khanavai protect their mates. He will make sure that nothing ever harms you."

Oh, God. Part of me longed to do exactly that—go straight to the commander and tell him about Frank, about Josiah, and beg him to save us.

Don't be foolish, I admonished myself. *You can't afford to be weak. You cannot risk your life or Josiah's in that way.*

"Thank you," I said to Thorvid, not committing to anything. "If you'll excuse me, I think I'll shower now."

With a long, final look at me, the Poltien exited the lav.

My handler had at least one thing right. I wasn't going to be figuring out how to get off the station by hiding in my room.

I might as well get dressed.

As I stepped into the shower, I decided to take at least part of Thorvid's advice.

I would go on a date with Commander Eldron Gendovi. I would play it up for the vidglobes that were sure to be floating around us, filming our every move.

But I would also be using that time to watch for some way out of my predicament. Preferably some way that I could arrange myself. One that didn't rely on anyone else.

There were parts of South America that were still remote by Earth standards. If I could get back to Earth, maybe Josiah and I could disappear there.

I knew, though, as I moved into my room and prepared to allow Thorvid to help me dress, that spending more time with Eldron was going to cause at least one problem.

The longer I was around him, the more I liked him.

Being around him made me feel safe and comfortable—and that was dangerous.

Falling in love with him would be the stupidest thing I could possibly do.

I just didn't know if I could keep myself from it.

But it didn't matter how I felt about the gorgeous, muscular red alien.

As soon as I could, I was getting out of here.

CHAPTER TWELVE

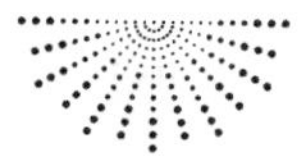

ELDRON

"The Alveron Horde is tracking Amelia Rivers on Earth."

I spun around from where I'd been examining the latest readouts. "How did they get past our scans?"

Lieutenant Drais, Wex's replacement, gave me a sheepish glance. "We weren't scanning that part of the sky—we have been focusing all our attention on the quarter that you directed us to scan."

Simply because we focused on one area didn't mean we should ignore the others. I had to fight back an urge to reprimand Drais.

"We need to scramble help to them," I ordered. "Send down two squadrons for direct combat. And while you're at it, put together enough of a force to create a scanning net around Earth. We are going to need to protect our bride-source planet more carefully from now on, I believe."

"Yes, sir." The lieutenant spun around and began snapping out orders.

I paced back and forth in the command center.

There was something more to this strange move on the Horde's part. I knew, somehow, that this was connected to the creeping feeling I'd been having that the Alveron Horde was planning something.

Why would they go after one person on Earth?

She was one of our brides—and the Horde had poisoned our DNA so that we could no longer breed with our own kind. Maybe they wanted to keep us from mating with humans, too. But that wasn't all that was going on here. I was certain of it.

And speaking of brides, Mia and I were supposed to meet for our first date. I checked my com, relieved to find I still had time before I was supposed to meet her for dinner in the station's common area.

"Our forces have been deployed," Drais reported sometime later. "There is nothing more to be done here at the moment." He shot a glance at me out of the corner of his eye.

Looks like everyone on board the station knows I'm supposed to have a date.

Not surprising, I supposed. I had not intended to find a mate on this trip—but I also had not realized how intrusive it would be to have every move of my courtship broadcast to the entire galaxy.

I had tried to convince Vos to cancel our participation in the games altogether, saying, "Surely the bride hunt on Earth will give you enough material for this year."

But the Games Director had refused, even after General Clovad had given him a call. "These are the most-watched Bride Games of all time," Vos declared. "Your participation will only enhance those numbers."

"Keep me apprised of any news," I now ordered Drais as I prepared to leave the command center. "I will be nearby."

On our third date, Mia insisted on choosing our outing. The last two days, we had participated in what Mia called "traditional date-night activities," having gone for a meal the first time and for a group showing of an Earther vid, which Mia called a "movie."

"This is what Earthers do for entertainment, is it not?" I asked over the com.

She laughed, leaning back in the chair in front of her mirror, but agreed. "Yes. Dinner and movie are as human as…well, I guess as much as betting on duels is a Khanavai tradition."

"So why are you objecting to it?"

"I'm not objecting. I just think we should try something different tonight."

I frowned. "Without a Bride Game to structure it, there is not much to do on Station 21."

"There's a gym, isn't there?"

"There is a physical recreation area, yes."

"And a garden?"

"That, as well."

"Hm. Okay, then. Meet me outside the garden at our usual time, then. Dress casually." As she signed off, I detected a gleam in her eye.

What does my mate have planned?

I arrived at the appointed time wearing one of my usual *chavan* uniforms, but without the *vandenoi* strap with my battle decorations.

Mia arrived before me and was waiting on one of the benches near one of the walkways leading into the garden area. Beside her sat a bag with the Station 21 gymnasium's logo imprinted on the side. She moved it off the bench, leaving a place for me to sit next to her.

"What did you bring?" I asked.

"It's a surprise." She eyed me up and down. "You are a soldier, right?"

"That is the meaning of my rank of commander, yes."

"How much time have you spent training for ground combat?"

I frowned at her. "It has been a while, but yes, I have ground combat training."

"Well then, it's time for more practice." She grinned, and I realized that I had rarely seen her smile. Unzipping the bag, she pulled out two unfamiliar weapons.

"You can't shoot projectile weapons on a space station," I reminded her. "You could damage the hull, and any breach could cause a decompression."

She rolled her eyes. "It's a paint gun."

"A paint gun?"

"It won't damage anything—just make whatever it hits a little messy."

"So the idea is to shoot one another, but with *paint*?"

"Yes. We'll take turns—kind of like hide and seek, but with paint guns."

"Hide and seek?"

"It's a game. One of us hides, the other seeks. We track each other down and the first one to get hit loses that round."

This was nothing like any Earther courting tradition I had ever heard of. "You want to spend our evening together playing a wargame?"

When Mia threw her head back and laughed aloud, I admired her long, slender neck, and her contagious laughter made me want to grab her and kiss her right there.

"This is one of my favorite things to do on my days off," she said. "I go with—" Her face shut down as quickly as it had opened up when she laughed. "I do this sometimes on my days off."

A wave of sick envy rolled through my stomach. *Who else does she play these courting games with?*

I almost asked, but I sensed the question was off-limits. And more than anything, I wanted to see her smile again, so I changed the subject. "How did you arrange for this?"

Her expression lightened. "Oh, you know." She shrugged and waved a hand airily. "I got Vos to tell me who to talk to for the materials. I've been all over the station today planning for this. Oh. That reminds me." She handed me a pair of goggles. "You don't want to get this stuff in your eyes," she warned me. "It stings."

I slipped them on and peered out at her, certain I looked like a wide-eyed fliptiani night bird. Then I took one of the guns from her and said, "I'll hide first. You seek."

"Okay. I'll close my eyes and count to a hundred. And then," she waggled the other gun at me, "I am coming to get you."

It was a better game than I anticipated—and she was much better at it than I expected. She found me quickly during her first round, so tiny and quick that I didn't see her coming.

"You shot me in the back," I objected.

My mate's self-satisfied snicker made me grin, as well. "You really should have been watching your six," she said.

"My what?" I twisted around to peer at my backside. "I don't have six of anything at all back there."

"No. 'Watch your six' means to watch your back. It's like the numbers on the clock."

Involuntarily, I glanced down at my wristcom.

"Not that. An old-fashioned Earth clock. It's a circle and six is at the bottom..." She gave up trying to explain. "Just trust me. You need to pay more attention to what's behind you."

When my turn came to track her down, she surprised me again, leaping out of a stand of yontar reeds that I had automatically dismissed as too small to hide an enemy.

I clearly needed to update my thinking to include tiny humans.

Again, she waited until I was past her to leap out and shoot my back with the bright green paint.

"Watch my six?" I said sheepishly.

"Exactly." Mia turned to head back toward the bench where we had left the gym bag, and I took a moment to admire her ass, shapely in her casual wear—a pair of formfitting pants and a t-shirt that came only to her waist.

Then I took aim and shot that shapely ass with a splatter of purple paint.

Mia squealed and jumped, spinning around and opening fire on me. "Not fair," she yelled out, even as she covered my chest in green paint.

"Oh, I'll show you 'not fair'," I growled through my laughter. I dropped my paint weapon entirely and lunged for her, picking her up and draping over my shoulder as she squealed and kicked. I took a few steps, then swung her down to place her gently on a bed of purple Earth heather. I stretched out over her, tucking one hand under her hip and the other under her head to pull her into a kiss.

As always, she met my touch with equal passion. My cock hardened at the feel of her under me, and she whimpered deep in her throat as she felt it brush up against her through my *chavan*.

Within moments, though, she was pulling away from me—as she had done every time I had kissed her. "That green paint on your skin makes you look like Christmas," she murmured, reaching up to run her finger through the paint on my chest, drawing an Earther's representation of a heart.

I glanced down at myself. "With some interesting purple smudges where it touched the paint on your chest."

"On my *shirt*," she corrected.

"We could change that. I would love to rub this paint all over your skin," I murmured as I ducked down to claim her lips again.

The more time I spent with Mia, the more certain I became that she feared taking a mate at all. It wasn't me—I was certain of it.

She responded to my kisses, but she feared her own response.

I must find a way to change that.

A ding from my wrist interrupted us, and I pulled away from Mia to check my com, groaning aloud when I saw the message. "Vos Klavoii wants us to meet him in Medical in an hour."

She wiped her hair from her brow and frowned down at her soiled clothes. "That should give me time to shower and change, then. I'll meet you there."

CHAPTER THIRTEEN

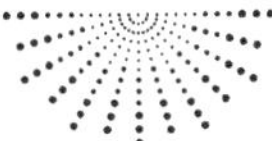

MIA

Back in my room, I took a quick shower, then pulled on a bright red dress that swung around my legs.

As I made my way toward Medical to meet Eldron, I considered how well the day had gone.

Not just the game, though I had to admit I enjoyed that part even more than I had expected to.

No. The game hadn't actually been my goal. I had spent all day wandering around Station 21, ostensibly to gather up supplies for the impromptu paint gun game.

Really, what I had been doing was figuring out how to get away. And also determining whether there were any sneaky methods of getting weapons. Not to use on anyone here—at least, I didn't plan to. But if I could get some kind of weapon off the station and down to Earth with me, I might be able to use them to protect myself and Josiah, if I ever needed to.

I had gotten the information I needed, too.

It had been easy to pretend to be turned around, lost in the station. And I had watched everyone as they had gone about their day, using their wristcoms in place of typical Earth ID badges.

So that was it. All I had to do was steal an official wristcom and use it to make my way off the station.

A bitter laugh echoed in my head. *Like that's going to be easy.*

But at least it was a plan.

ELDRON WAS WAITING for me outside Medical, where he took my hand to lead me inside, where Cav and Natalie stood with another Khanavai male with skin the same hot pink shade as Thorvid's nose-braid. They all gathered around a medbay gurney holding a human woman.

It took me a second, and I did a double-take when I realized the Khanavai male was Zont. That meant…I glanced over at the woman on the gurney. Yep, that was Amelia Rivers, the runaway bride.

My stomach sank at the reminder of how difficult it was to get away from the Khanavai.

Cav was already speaking, introducing us to them. "Zont, Amelia, I'd like you to meet Commander Eldron Gendovi and his bride, Mia."

I stiffened at the description and Eldron glanced down at me briefly. "Only a prospective bride thus far," he said mildly.

"Nice to meet you, Sir," Zont said, doing that chest-thumping salute thing of theirs, but ending with a flourishing bow.

Eldron gave an abbreviated version and did not return the bow. I wondered if that had something to do with their rank.

"The commander specifically asked to meet with you and Amelia," Cav said. "Especially since he and Mia are about to have to go through a round of Bride Games themselves."

I turned a startled glance toward Eldron. I didn't know he had asked to meet them.

Then again, I hadn't even known they were on the station.

Can I really get away from these guys?

"You think they'll make us go through the Bride Games?" Zont was asking.

"Probably." Eldron nodded. "I wasn't able to get us out of it. No matter how many favors I tried to pull in."

Something else I hadn't known.

If I had even the slightest plan to end up marrying Eldron, I would be insisting on having him practice some better communication skills.

Lucky for me, I had absolutely zero intention of sticking around.

Zont looked fairly panicked and grabbed Cav's arm as if to say something, but Vos Klavoii's human assistant, Anthony, bustled into the room.

"Oh, good. You're all here. Please follow me to Mr. Klavoii's office."

"Not us," Eldron whispered to me as Zont helped Amelia off the gurney and the other two couples followed Anthony.

"What was she in here for?" I asked once they were gone.

"Amelia? Implant replacement. She and Zont spent the last week on Earth unable to even talk to each other."

I chewed on my bottom lip. That meant that Medical had replacement chips in stock? I wondered if I could snag one of those before I left, too.

"What are you so thoughtful about, my *vanata*?" Eldron's question snapped me out of my plotting.

"Nothing. Just wondering why Vos would have us come down here then immediately drag everyone else away."

He shrugged. "Almost certainly some scheme that will bring him more viewers."

With a snort, I agreed.

"As long as we're here, though," the commander continued, "why don't we go get something to eat?"

No. I couldn't spend any more time with him—not if I wanted to keep my sanity when it came time to tear myself away from him. "I'm so sorry. I'm more tired than hungry. I think I'm going to go back to my rooms now."

His expression fell, and I had to force myself not to change my mind.

Josiah is waiting for you. You can't get attached.

But it seemed like Eldron was determined to do everything he could to convince me that we belonged together. When we reached my door, he gently drew me into his arms, his mouth slanting over mine in a kiss.

I knew better than this. I shouldn't let his kisses distract me from what I knew I needed to do.

I needed to go back home.

For the first time since I had left Frank, I was torn.

If Eldron was really who he seemed to be—protective, calm, kind—then maybe I could fall in love again.

But what if he wasn't? What if, like Frank, it was all a ruse? An act to convince me, a way to lull me into complacency until I agreed to be with him. And then, once I was really and truly under his control, he would lash out.

I shuddered and pulled away from Eldron's kiss.

"What's the matter, my *vanata*?" He asked, cupping my cheek in his giant red palm.

I shook my head. "Nothing," I murmured, unwilling to voice my fears —if I told him my worries, he might get angry.

That's Frank, I reminded myself. *Just because he would have resented your worries doesn't mean that Eldron will, too.*

"You can tell me anything," Eldron tried to reassure me.

Was that true?

I opened my mouth, inhaling as I prepared to test my theory that Eldron was very different from Frank.

What's the worst that could happen? If he rejected me, I would go back to Earth.

And if he didn't?

Maybe Josiah and I could have a new life. A different one. A life with a protector instead of an abuser.

Just say the words, Mia.

But as soon as I had convinced myself that it was safe to speak, an enormous shudder wracked the entire station, giant cracking noises coming from all around us.

"What is that?" I gasped.

"It's the Alveron Horde. They're attacking." Eldron spoke into his wristcom urgently. "This is Commander Gendovi. Situation report."

An unfamiliar voice echoed from his com. "Two Alveron Hordeships have appeared inside our seventh sector and opened fire on the station."

Eldron cursed fluently, something that sounded like "Gravitiniax Goat Suckers" before turning his com back on. "Scramble the J-32 fighters, just as we discussed. Pattern Phlantox 327. I'm on my way."

He headed toward the door, then stopped as it slid open. "Stay here and wait for me."

I started to object, but he was gone, racing out the door and heading off to fight the battle he had been preparing for.

I can't just sit here and do nothing. I have to help.

But what can I do?

I could imagine Natalie barking orders to help get people moving, and Amelia was a doctor. I, on the other hand, had hardly any skills at all. And most of those were in the kitchen.

I doubt anyone is going to want to eat while we are under attack.

But I had also spent plenty of time cleaning kitchens, I thought as the station rattled and I heard objects falling in the hallways. There would be work for me once this was over.

I also knew how to take orders—years of kitchen training had taught me that.

If people are hurt, Amelia can tell me what to do.

And maybe I'll have a chance to snag a couple of extra tracker chips while I'm there.

Without another thought, I headed toward the medbay.

CHAPTER FOURTEEN

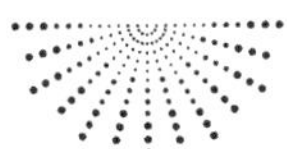

ELDRON

I raced to the lift and made my way up to the battle bridge of the station, a room most humans didn't even know existed on Station 21. For all that we were allies, the Khanavai still very much saw ourselves as senior partners, unwilling to share all our technology.

By the time I got there, the view screens were showing the F7 quadrant—exactly the section sky I'd been having Captain Drais and his men scan.

"What happened?" I demanded.

"Two Alveron Hordeships just appeared out of nowhere," Drais replied. "We've been scanning for days, and our instruments didn't show anything."

"I knew it," I muttered.

The Alveron Horde had been quiet for years—occasionally popping up in the far corners of our territories, but rarely attacking.

The Lorishi home planet had been the one exception to that in ages. Command Central had assumed that the Lorishi had been caught off-guard because no one had been scanning for Horde incursions. I was convinced that wasn't what happened at all.

"They have some new kind of cloaking technology," I repeated aloud.

Just as I have been saying for months.

"Our fighters are leaving the base now," Wex's replacement, whose name I couldn't remember, announced.

I stepped closer to the viewscreens, as if my physical presence could help the fighters as they darted around the two visible Hordeships.

Part of me wished for an Earther vid-style space battle, full of explosions and zapping sounds as the fighters fired on the Hordeships. But that's not how space battles really happened. They were silent and slow, and I only knew for sure that the first Hordeship had been disabled when our instruments told us there was no more energy running through it.

It was just a giant hull floating in space.

The second ship withdrew almost instantly, disappearing as it engaged its hyperdrive. I heaved a sigh of relief. "What do our casualties look like?"

"Minimal structural damage, Commander," Drais reported. "Casualties coming in from several decks, but overall, I think we did pretty well."

"Agreed." I ran my hand across my forehead. Could I have caught this if I hadn't been so engrossed in getting to know Mia?

Maybe it was a bad idea for me to continue this farce of a mating game. But even the thought of letting her go made my heart constrict in my chest.

No. I needed her. Now that I had found my mate, there was no way I could let her go.

Nothing would ever convince me to walk away from her.

For now, though, I needed to focus on how this attack had happened.

"Someone get me a suit," I said. "I'm headed over to the Hordeship to see if I can figure out how they got past all our scans."

"Are you sure?" Drais turned a startled gaze toward me. "We have technicians who can do that for you."

I didn't know how to explain to him that everything about this had come to me by instinct. I hadn't been able to explain to General Clovad how I knew that the Alveron were planning something. And now, I couldn't explain why I knew that I had to be there in person to figure out their new technology.

I simply shook my head. "This is something I have to do myself."

"Yes sir." The officer thumped a salute on his chest, and I acknowledged it with a nod.

Down in the fighter bay, I fastened the closures on my suit. Technically, the Alveron Horde needed the same oxygen-nitrogen mix we did. But if their ship had gone dead, there was no guarantee I could survive without a suit. Not to mention the possibility that the Horde had left behind something designed to hurt any Khanavai who showed up later.

"Are you certain you don't want to take an entire team over, sir?" the technician who strapped me into the fighter jet asked.

"Not yet. After I do an initial survey, I'll open it up for your team. You'll get your chance, don't worry."

The tech grinned at me, then closed the canopy. It had been a while since I'd been in one of the jets but flying was always like coming home.

As I made my way to the Hordeship, the silence of space stretched out around me, echoing with the nothingness in between the far-flung stars.

This is what it would feel like to be entirely alone forever.

But with Mia in my life, that would never happen.

Shaking off the thought, I maneuvered through the oddly shaped entrance to the Hordeship's flight bay, docking my ship and engaging the magnetic locks.

The Horde, unlike humans and Khanavai, functioned with a base-eight system, and that extended itself out to the whole ship.

Octagons everywhere.

Humans had called it a *honeycomb* the first time they had seen it, and the name stuck with me. Apparently, it had something to do with a food-producing bug on Earth.

Human eating practices were strange.

For an instant, I wondered if Mia liked honey, or if the thought of bug goop made her stomach turn the way it did mine.

I shook off the thought, forcing myself to focus on the job at hand.

The ship itself seemed dead. As I walked across the bay, the magnetic soles of my boots clicked in odd echoing noises around me.

I wondered if the Horde believed in ghosts.

If they did, the ship would be full of them.

CHAPTER FIFTEEN

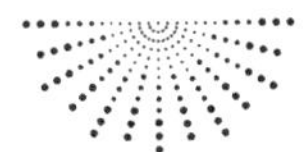

MIA

I ran into trouble halfway to Medical. The attack on the station had sent everything in the central area flying—people, tables, plates, chairs. Humans and Khanavai were staggering to their feet, some of them with wounds, others simply looking dazed and confused.

I paused to help a human male to his feet. He cried out when I touched his shoulder.

"You're hurt," I said. "Come on—I'm headed toward the medbay. Let's see if we can get you some help."

Inside Medical, it was pure chaos. Med techs called out to one another as they tried to triage a steady stream of patients.

I glanced around, looking for Amelia, hoping to find a friendly face—or even a familiar one.

A Khanavai male stopped in front of me, scanning me with a handheld device. "What's wrong?"

"Nothing—I'm fine. This man has a hurt shoulder, broken or dislocated or something."

"If you're not hurt, you need to go back to your quarters," the tech said brusquely.

"What can I do to help?" I asked.

He gave me a narrow-eyed stare. "Do you know how to read a med scan?"

"Just the basics—first-aid kind of stuff." I shrugged. The kinds of things I had learned as a parent, though I didn't say that part out loud.

"That'll work." He handed me the device he was carrying. "Do a general scan of each patient—you know how to do that?"

I nodded.

"The scan should tell you if someone needs immediate help or if they can wait. If they can wait, send them to the seating area over there." He pointed off to our left. "Emergencies, send to intake. I'll send a tech trainee to get those people in for help as soon as possible."

"And what about the guy I came in with?"

"Mid-level cases. He won't die in the next fifteen minutes—or even an hour or two—so he can wait. As soon as we have room for anyone else, we'll get to those cases."

Okay. I could do this. It was straightforward enough—the kind of decisions I made every time Josiah fell down and skinned his knee.

Another shudder went through the station, the walls around us creaking. The tech reached out a hand to steady me. "Thank you," he said. "We appreciate the help."

And then he was gone, and I was left with the stream of frightened, hurting people as they made their way to the medbay.

When Cav and Zont came racing into Medical carrying an injured Vos, with Amelia barking out orders and Natalie making sure they were followed, I knew that was my moment.

While everyone focused on the Games Director, no one paid any attention to me. I slipped away to the storeroom in the back, where I'd seen medtechs gathering supplies all night.

The station had stopped shuddering from weapon blasts. This fight was almost over—I had to hurry if I was going to take this opportunity to get replacement translation-trackers.

I had just realized that all the cabinets were closed with the same kind of wristcom locks everything on the station used when one of the med techs entered the room.

"What are you doing here?" A purple Khanavai male demanded.

I cast about frantically for something to say. "I'm looking for an arm sling. There's a man out there with a broken arm and I want to stabilize it until someone can help him."

The tech frowned, then punched in a number on his wristcom. A series of supply cabinets popped open. "I'm not sure which cabinet it will be in. But it should be somewhere there." He gestured at the cabinets, and then he bent down, gathered supplies of his own, and left the room.

My mouth hung open as I stared after him.

I don't fucking believe it. I think the gods are on my side tonight.

Quickly, I began shuffling through the open cabinets.

For one long, miserable moment, I was convinced the tech had given me access to only first-aid supplies.

But then I found them. An entire cabinet full of neonatal and surgical supplies. And a box of brand-new chips.

Quickly, I grabbed several and slipped them inside my bra. I didn't know if they were programmed yet, and really I didn't care. I could find someone on Earth who could do that.

Before I left, I snagged a sling, too. Closing all the cabinets behind me, I slipped back out into the main triage room.

No one was watching, and the stream of injured coming in had slowed to a trickle.

The man I had helped in still waited, clutching his arm miserably.

"Here," I said, pulling the sling from its package and sliding the brace under his arm. "This should help until someone can take better care of you."

He blew out a relieved breath. "That does feel better. Thank you."

"You're welcome." I glanced around to make sure one of the actual medtechs was nearby. "See that green guy over there? He'll be with you in just a minute."

No one needed me right now. I had done what I had come to do, both by helping and by getting the implants I would need once I returned to Earth.

Just keep watching. You'll see your chance, I promised myself.

I hoped I could believe my inner cheerleader.

CHAPTER SIXTEEN

ELDRON

The Alveron Hordeship would give me nightmares later. I was sure of it.

The octagon halls were a uniformly dark gray, with none of the bright colors that decorated Khanavai ships. Our scientists had speculated that perhaps the Horde didn't see the same color spectrum that humans and Khanavai did.

Worse, though, everywhere I went, those odd, paper-thin husks remained, as if they had been performing actions and had simply slipped out of their skins and disappeared, leaving behind only crumbling shells of what they had been.

On what I presumed was the bridge, several of them stood with forelimbs stuck to the instrument panels, held there by some biological glue, like the bodies of bugs on a wall.

I had hoped that by getting here immediately after a battle, I might gain a better sense of what we were dealing with. For all that the

Khanavai had been fighting the Horde for decades, this was all we had ever found on their ships—empty bodies and dead instruments we could not make work.

"Zagrodnian hells," I cursed, slamming my fist through one of the Horde bodies. It crumbled away into dust.

We had at least three dead Hordeships just like this one, and not one of them had ever given up its secrets to us.

I punched a few instruments randomly, hoping to learn something, *anything*, from one of them.

Suddenly, something behind me spun up with a loud whirr. With another curse, I jumped and spun around, barely refraining from shooting my drawn weapon.

"Watch your six, you bumbling idiot," I muttered to myself. Apparently, my angry, random instrument pounding had started something. I made my way across the bridge to examine a series of blinking lights on the screen.

I stared at it blankly for a moment, and then it seemed to resolve itself into a familiar schematic.

That was Station 21.

And those lighted dots moving around the screen? Those were people.

Specific people, not just life-signs—there were many more station inhabitants than were showing up on this screen.

I began counting and trying to match the numbers of dots to any particular Station 21 group.

"Humans," I said aloud.

More than that, human females. The number of dots on the screen matched up with the number of human females on Station 21.

What, by all the Blordl death goddesses, were the Alveron Horde doing tracking human females?

Maybe it really did have something to do with destroying all Khanavai means of reproduction.

Was one of those dots Mia? Could she be the one moving down the Bridal Suites hallway even now?

No. I told her to remain in her rooms. She has no reason to be out.

Then again, human women had garnered a reputation of not always being the most compliant of females. Not that anything in Mia's actions had ever suggested that she wasn't perfectly well behaved—except, of course, for that wicked gleam I occasionally caught in her eye.

My stomach clenched at the thought of the Hordeship targeting my mate.

All our mates.

I will protect her, no matter what.

I watched the dots move around on the station for a while longer, then pulled myself away and moved through the rest of the ship, checking to make sure there really wasn't anything else alive.

At least we have one more piece of information than we had before, I consoled myself when I couldn't turn on any other instruments, no matter where I went.

The longer I spent in this ghost ship, the creepier it seemed.

After hours alone, I finally decided there was nothing left to be learned and was about to head back to the hangar bay, when inspiration struck.

I hadn't been banging indiscriminately on panels on the bridge when the human-tracker had come to life.

I slammed my fist through one of those creepy alien bodies, and it crumbled to dust. *Then* I hit the panel—presumably with that dust still on my glove.

Could it really be that simple? Our scientists had attempted various chemical interactions with the Alveron Horde instrumentation, always to no avail.

I need to test this theory before I make a fool of myself by sharing it with anyone else.

Instead of heading back to the docking bay, I turned again toward the bridge.

There, the dead Horde members still stood sentinel. Swallowing down my revulsion, I made my way to the instrument panel that, had I been guessing, I would have assumed controlled propulsion. With a quick motion, I swiped my hand through the nearest husk-body, gathered the crumbling dust in my hand, and began moving my hand over the panel.

Lights began blinking to life.

I was right. Something about the dust their bodies produced really did help power up the ship.

I resisted the urge to continue experimenting.

I didn't want to slam the Hordeship into Station 21 if I could help it. *That would not be a fitting legacy*, I thought wryly.

There would be plenty of time to experiment when I got an actual engineering team over here.

The fact that the horde was tracking human females made me that much more determined to learn what they were doing and why—and that started with learning how they use their technology.

This time, as I headed back to the docking bay, excitement warred with disappointment. I would need to spend the next few days working with that engineering team to see what we could figure out about how the Horde used its own bodies to control the ship.

Which was all well and good—and I really was excited about it. Except for one thing: it meant I wouldn't be able to spend much time with Mia over the next few days.

I hoped she would understand.

CHAPTER SEVENTEEN

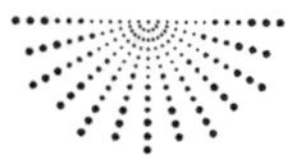

MIA

Almost three days.

That was how long it had been since I had seen Eldron.

I shouldn't care. I told myself that over and over, trying to convince myself I wasn't disappointed by his absence.

After all, if I'd had the opportunity to transport back to Earth, I would have taken it without hesitation.

But if I had to be stuck on Station 21 with no easy way to contact Josiah, I would have preferred to spend my time with the commander.

He, however, was busy analyzing the Hordeship the Khanavai had captured. Which meant I ended up helping Natalie prepare Amelia and Zont's wedding.

I'd been right—Natalie really was good at getting people to do whatever she wanted them to do.

And now I was preparing to be a bridesmaid in a wedding broadcast across the whole galaxy.

God, I hope Frank isn't watching.

Natalie and I marched into the small, mostly undamaged room we had commandeered for the wedding. As we walked up the aisle created by temporary seating, we dropped petals from both Earth and Khanavai flowers on the floor.

Zont, dressed in his kilt-like *chavan* uniform, waited for Amelia at the front of the room—but I couldn't stop staring at Eldron, who had been pulled from his scientific inquiry long enough to perform the ceremony as the senior officer on the station.

At the front of the room, we turned back to face the doorway, and Amelia stepped into the doorway, vidglobes floating around her.

Zont gasped when he saw her, and I couldn't help but smile at how obviously smitten he was with her.

Cav stepped up and offered his arm to escort her the short distance to her groom.

Drindl and Plofnid, Natalie's two bridal assistants, took up the rear of the tiny procession, and at the last minute, one of the station medics pushed Vos Klavoii into the room on a floatchair.

After I left Frank, I swore off the whole idea of marriage.

But I couldn't help but feel a swell of emotion as Zont and Amelia promised to love and honor each other, and to protect one another, allowing their infinite love room to grow.

As I watched Zont and Amelia exchange their vows, I swallowed hard, glancing up at Eldron, wondering if maybe—just maybe—marriage to him would be different than my life with Frank had been.

Could Eldron save me?

Oh, God. I hope so. The thought flickered through my mind before I could quash it.

Tears sprang to my eyes, and I blinked them away before he noticed.

What should I do?

Running wasn't an option. Amelia had tried that, and she'd ended up here on Station 21, mated to and marrying the alien who had chosen her.

At least she'd had the option of either agreeing to be with Zont or going through the Bride Games. Vos Klavoii hadn't given me a choice in the matter—he was determined to have another series of Bride Games with several grooms vying for my affections.

Of course, Eldron and I hadn't had sex, and rumor had it that Amelia and Zont had been together before they even made it up to the station, that he had actually mated her without her knowledge—whatever that meant. The Khanavai were pretty cagey about how the mating process worked. When I'd asked Eldron about it a few moments before the ceremony, he'd simply caressed my cheek and said, "I promise I'll tell you all about it. But not until we're officially paired."

Every single day since I met him, I had thought about that moment in the corridor outside the hangar, when I had been about to board the Earth-bound shuttle.

I thought I'd escaped being given to an alien warrior. I was wrong.

God. I was less than an hour away from washing out of the Alien Bride Games.

None of the Khanavai warriors had chosen me, and I was scheduled on the next shuttle off the filming station.

My secret was still safe.

I mean, I'd been on television. The whole world had seen me participating, even though I tried to keep a low profile. But I couldn't count on not having been seen. When I got back home, I'd have to run.

Again.

Change my name, get new ID cards.

Get the new translator-trackers implanted.

I shuddered at the thought of another back-alley procedure. They were dangerous at best, and I knew I was risking getting caught by the authorities by going back.

Worse, taking the risk of getting a new tracker might put me right back on the Bride Lottery list.

But then a bright red alien passed me in a hallway. A whole long line of women waiting to board the shuttle, and a Khanavai warrior had stopped, sniffed the air, and turned to scan all of us.

I ignored him, staring at the floor and huddling down into myself, trying to avoid any attention at all—just as I had during the entirety of the Bride Games up until now. Even during the pageant and interviews, I had mumbled my responses, hoping to make myself as boring as possible.

But then the cherry-red giant made a beeline toward me. He placed one finger under my chin and gently raised my face so he could look me in the eye.

"You're beautiful," he whispered. Then he leaned down, those luscious lips of his aiming for mine.

And the next thing I knew, we were all over each other. He picked me up and I wrapped my legs around his waist. His tongue plundered my mouth, leaving me gasping, his kiss making my head spin.

I inhaled the scent of him, something dark and heavy with a swirl of sweetness to it, like chocolate or coffee. Everyplace his body touched mine—which was everywhere—sparks of sheer lust shot through me, spinning me into a world where only the two of us existed.

If not for the shouts and cheers of the other brides in line, I probably would have let him fuck me right there.

Instead, I reluctantly pulled away from the kiss, and he set me on my feet.

When he said, "Come with me," and held out his hand, I followed him.

One of the vidglobes had caught it all, and it had been broadcast live—complete with commentary from Vos Klavoii, as I'd learned later.

Now, the memory of his kisses sent a shiver down my spine, and Eldron glanced down at me, taking my hand in his and bringing it up to his mouth long enough to drop another spine-tingling kiss on it.

I smiled up at him, unwilling to let him know how anxious I was.

Bad enough that my name had been drawn in the Bride Lottery.

Now, even though they were supposedly over, I was back in the Games. And not the usual ones, either—a whole new set of challenges, just for me.

Guess it'll make for good television back home.

I sent up a silent prayer to any god who might be listening that I could resist my attraction to Eldron long enough to get back to Earth, to the people I love.

Back to the people I needed to save.

And that I would be able to keep him from learning my most desperate secret.

The odds aren't looking good, though.

Afterward, Plofnid and Drindl rushed out while everyone else was congratulating the newlyweds, returning with station employees bearing a table, chairs, and a meal for everyone to share, including an astounding number of bottles containing a pale, fizzy Earther alcohol.

Eldron waited until everyone was eating and turned to Zont. "I had a conversation this afternoon with Command Central," I said. "And we have a proposal for you."

Zont tilted his head in interest. "Yes?"

"We are considering opening up a permanent station on Earth for a Khanavai diplomatic corps. We think you might be a good fit to act as our military liaison."

"Me? Really?"

Eldron gave him a wink. "We would also like to have a Special Ops presence there."

Amelia leaned around her mate to speak to the commander. "Would this be a long-term posting?"

"Why yes, yes it would." Eldron smiled, pleased at his ability to offer the couple this gift.

He really is a kind man.

Zont glanced at his new bride, checking with her before he replied. "I would be happy to take the position, sir."

"That was nice of you," I whispered, slipping my fingers into his large, red hand.

How could I possibly leave him? He was a good man.

For Josiah.

I met Eldron too late. There was no room for him in my life.

I'm leaving.

Then I saw my chance.

With a distracted air, Eldron took off his wristcom and set it on the chair next to me as he stood to dance with Amelia.

Making sure no one was watching, I picked it up and dropped it into the evening purse I'd chosen to carry.

As soon as my giant, red alien stepped off the dance floor, I took his hands. "Could you escort me back to my quarters? I'm afraid I had a little too much champagne. I'm tired. We could meet again for breakfast tomorrow."

It wasn't fair to let him walk me back to my room, kiss me goodnight, and make plans for the next morning, all the while planning to be gone within an hour.

But I did.

CHAPTER EIGHTEEN

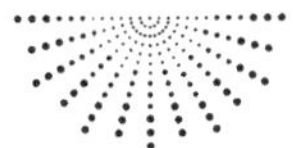

ELDRON

Outside her door, I wrapped Mia in my arms. "We start our Bride Games tomorrow," I reminded her. In anyone else, I might have taken the tiny twitch of her body to be anxiety about my embrace. But somehow, I knew that Mia was nervous about the next day. "I'm sorry I was not able to get Vos to agree to simply allow us a wedding like Amelia and Zont."

She rested her cheek against my chest, her skin brushing lightly against mine. "That's okay."

Anxiety thrummed through her body, as if it vibrated from her soul into mine.

"Would you like to talk about what's bothering you?"

She shook her head. "Just nerves."

I didn't believe her, but I couldn't think of any way to get her to open up to me. There was something going on with her, something overwhelming, but she didn't know how to tell me about it.

She didn't trust me.

That's all right, I reassured myself. *By the time we are mated, she will trust me with everything.*

I leaned down to kiss her, and she responded as if it were the last time we would ever be together. Her mouth pressed against mine, and she wrapped her arms around my neck tightly, clinging to me as her tongue probed my mouth—the first time she had ever taken the lead in any of our kisses.

Through her shirt, her nipples pebbled into hard buds, like points of pure desire pressing against the skin bared by my *chavan* and the *vandenoi* strap that crossed my chest.

My need for her surged through me, bringing my cock to life. Our bodies yearned toward one another, living conduits of the mating bond craving completion. I moaned deep in my throat and tightened my arms around her waist, lifting her up off her toes.

Eventually, I pulled my lips from hers just enough to whisper against them. "Amelia and Zont didn't wait, you know. There are no other grooms vying for your hand. We could follow their example."

I knew it was too much, too soon, but I couldn't help asking, hoping maybe she would realize I would never hurt her.

Hoping she would know we belonged together as instinctively as I did.

With a whimper, she pressed herself against me, deepening the kiss until we were both breathing heavily.

Finally, she drew away a little and shook her head. "Not yet," she whispered. "I couldn't stand it if..." Her voice trailed off.

If anything went wrong, I finished her sentence in my mind. "I understand."

Slowly, I set her on her feet again, sliding the front of her body down mine so she felt the evidence of my desire straining toward her. Her eyes fluttered into the back of her head and her breath caught in her chest. Exhaling one long, slow, shaky breath, she reached up to place one hand on either side of my face. I tilted my forehead down until it rested against hers.

"You really are an amazing man." Her voice trembled, and I knew if I pushed, even just a little, she would invite me in.

I couldn't do it.

"I'll see you in the morning." Gently, I dropped a light kiss on her forehead, forced myself to release my arms from around her body, and stepped back as she opened the door.

"Tomorrow," she whispered, and as she stepped into her room, she glanced back at me, her eyes brimming with tears.

I really needed to find out why she was so frightened of the connection between us.

Tomorrow, I promised myself.

HALFWAY BACK TO MY QUARTERS, I realized I left my wristcom in the chair I occupied during the party that Mia had called a "reception"—which, come to think of it, was an odd term, since no one was receiving anything there.

I should never have taken off the wristcom in the first place. But I had been awake and working for most of the previous two days, and the strap had begun to chafe against my skin in an odd way.

Even now, the skin there was slightly discolored and inflamed, possibly a reaction to accidental exposure to some of the Hordedust, as my team and I had taken to calling the disintegrated bodies from the Alveron Hordeship.

I didn't want to put the wristcom back on yet. And I was too tired to be bothered with anything other than falling into bed right now. Even my kiss before leaving Mia at her door had been perfunctory.

Not that I couldn't have been convinced to work up more energy if she had asked me to stay. But as usual, her response had been mixed—part eager passion, part utter terror.

I'll com Cav when I get back to my quarters. He can get the wristcom to me tomorrow.

And as for Mia—our own Bride Games were scheduled to begin in the morning. I would get a full night's sleep and give her my complete attention then.

The Alveron Horde had once again been repelled. I had all the military scientists onboard the station working on Hordedust. I could afford to take some time out to properly court my bride.

When I got back to my quarters, though, it took me a long time to fall asleep.

More than anything, I wanted to have Mia in the bed next to me. I was ready to claim her, make her mine.

Even the thought of claiming her made my cock twitch and grow hard. I ached to hold her, taste her, make her scream in pleasure. I wanted to plant myself inside her.

I fell asleep imagining holding her in my arms, and I dreamt of her.

In that dream, she held a small child. I knew he was ours, somehow—but at the same time, part of me also knew he wasn't exactly mine.

His head rested on her shoulder, his legs wrapped around her waist. His skin was a lighter shade of human brown than Mia's, his close-cropped, dark, curly hair the same shade as hers.

As I stepped forward to take them both in my arms, she receded from me in the way of dreams, until I stood alone in the center of Station 21, desperate to find them again.

CHAPTER NINETEEN

MIA

I had been here for less than ten days, but it felt like forever since I had talked to Josiah.

At least I had figured out where things were, mostly, so I knew where I was going—and when to go. Station 21 ran on a twenty-four-hour schedule, but there was still a kind of a night shift. The Khanavai had figured out long ago that they needed a dark cycle, just like humans did. At any given time, half the lights on the station were lowered, including the living quarters. A smaller part of the station ran on the opposite schedule, so what most of us considered the night shift workers were acclimated to their own "daytime". I just hoped the transporter room would be on the night shift at the same time I was.

I made my way quickly through the public areas of the station, trying to look like I knew where I going, look like I belonged there, among the humans with legitimate business on the station.

When I arrived at the transporter room, I waved Eldron's wristcom at the entry pad and tapped in the code I'd heard him speak into it.

Luckily, the transporter room had been powered down at some point. I didn't know if it was because of the night schedule or because no one was using it at the moment, but I really didn't care as long as I had the room to myself.

Now I simply had to figure out how to work the damned transporters. The terminals were lined up at the back of the room like giant versions of vacuum tubes at bank drive-throughs—only these were big enough for humans and Khanavai, or in some cases, even crates of goods to be delivered to the space station.

For the first time ever, I wondered why the rejected brides were loaded onto a shuttle transport to go back to Earth, when we were all brought here by transporter.

At least I should be able to figure out how to work a transporter more easily than I could learn to fly a shuttle.

Each tube had a control panel on the side, and as I made my way over to the closest one, I heaved a sigh of relief. Khanavai and human technology had merged over the last several years in more ways than I think either race had ever expected.

Granted, the Khanavai didn't allow us to use their transporter technology freely, so it wasn't exactly the same. I studied the panel for a moment.

Power buttons, numbers, detailed controls...

Yeah, it was familiar—much like the control panels that ran most of the electronics on Earth. Not that I had anything as nice as a unit control panel in my crappy old apartment.

But every kitchen I had ever cooked in—even the diner grill —had one.

I can use this. I can go home to Josiah.

But then what would I do? Start running again? Where could we go? Frank knew where I was, knew that I had been living under is an assumed name. He could be heading to get Josiah from Becca right now, for all I knew.

He could have had Josiah for days by now.

And if he didn't have Josiah already? He would track us down again. He would never stop chasing us.

There was no place on Earth that was safe.

I had only one choice.

Decisively, I entered Eldron's code again and pushed the button to turn on the transporter. It flickered to life, bright white lights running up and down the sides as it powered up.

On the touchscreen, a request for input blinked. Nine digits. It wanted the code for a tracker. Without giving myself time to think, I tapped in Josiah's code—not the one he had been assigned at birth, but the one attached to the new tracker I had implanted to replace Josiah's legal one when we had run from Frank.

I pushed enter and stood back to wait.

I might not be able to protect my child on Earth, but I could make sure he was safe as possible, at least for now, by bringing him up to Station 21 with me. I had no idea how I was going to explain this when we got caught—because I knew we would. But Eldron had said he loved me.

He said we were mates, fated to be together for life.

Maybe he means it.

He probably wouldn't want me after this, not after he found out all the ways I lied to him and to the world.

But he was a good man. I was sure of it. He would make sure Josiah and I were protected.

Sobs clogged my throat as the outline of Josiah's body formed in the transporter. It was all I could do to keep from clawing my way in through the tube door before he was completely solid.

I watched impatiently as the curve of his cheek grew more real by the second, the roundness of his tiny body solidifying before my eyes. As soon as the machine slid open, I lunged in and grabbed Josiah, tears streaming down my face. "Josiah! I am so glad to see you. I love you, I missed you," I babbled, squeezing my tiny five-year-old baby boy to myself as I rained kisses on his face.

He had been sleeping when I transported him, still wearing his favorite Spiderman footie-pajamas, his eyes half-closed with sleep. "Mama," he said. "Are you back?" He glanced around, confused. "Where are we?"

"No, baby, I brought you up to Station 21 with me. You're in space. Isn't that exciting?"

"In space?" He looked around at the walls. "Are you sure?"

"I am." I had to give him another squeeze, just to make sure he really was there with me.

"Where's Becca?"

"I couldn't bring her with you. But we will be sure to tell her where you are, so she doesn't worry."

And that was enough for him. He wrapped his arms around my neck trustingly, and I picked him up, unwilling to stop touching him for even a moment.

I didn't know how I would get word back to Becca—she would be frantic when she found him missing.

But it was more important to keep Josiah safe.

Thank God Frank hadn't found them yet.

Now, though? I wasn't even sure what to do next. But I knew I needed to get out of this room. The last thing I wanted was to be caught illegally transporting someone aboard Station 21.

"I want to go back to bed," Josiah grumbled.

With one hand, I reached up and stroked his dark, tightly curled hair. "I'll see what I can do about that. You just rest your head on my shoulder, and I'll carry you."

The warm, trusting weight of him calmed a deep inner part of me that had been screaming in terror ever since I'd been transported aboard the station.

Safe. My baby is safe.

The words kept echoing in my head as I carried him out into the hallway.

I didn't know how long we could stay hidden on the station, but at least right now, there was no way Frank could get to him.

I started to head back to my room. When I reached the juncture that would lead either to the brides' quarters or to the grooms' quarters, I paused, thinking of all the ways Eldron had helped others since I'd been here.

He'd arranged for Tiziani to be stationed here for the next year. He'd made sure Cav and Natalie could be stationed together when it came time for Cav to go to what Natalie called "Spy School." He had done more than anyone else knew to deal with the Alveron Horde attack.

Surely he can help Josiah and me, too.

The thought of going to him terrified me. What if he couldn't see his way to aid us?

Still, it was the best chance we had of getting away from Frank. Eldron might not be willing to marry me once he knew about Josiah, but he wouldn't simply abandon us, either.

Inhaling deeply, I turned toward the grooms' quarters.

It was time to tell Eldron everything.

CHAPTER TWENTY

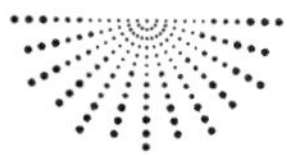

ELDRON

A quiet knock at my door startled me awake, used as I was to years of battle-readiness drills. When I opened the door, Mia stood there with a small child wrapped around her, clinging to her with his arms and legs, his head resting softly on her shoulder, eyes closed.

She looked so much like I had dreamed her that it took my breath away.

"We need your help," she said simply. I pulled the door wide to let her pass inside without a word, even though I was brimming with questions. Who was this child? Why did they need me? What could they need my help with in the middle of the night when our Bride Games started the next morning?

I waited until the door closed behind her, not entirely certain that this wasn't still a dream. I tilted my head toward the boy. "He's yours?"

She nodded. "From my first husband."

My head spun at her words. Married women—even those who had been divorced or widowed—were not placed in the Bride Lottery. "I don't understand."

She moved to the bed, where she placed the boy gently on the mattress, then pulled up the rumpled clothes to cover him. When he whimpered, she sat down beside him and stroked his head gently.

I waited patiently as she settled him, then dragged over the room's single chair until it was across from her and sat.

Speaking softly so as not to wake him, Mia began speaking.

"We married when I was pretty young—almost 10 years ago. His name is Frank Holden. He's a police officer in New Jersey."

At my frown, she explained, "That's a state in the United States."

"So he's an enforcer for Earth laws?"

Her laugh held an undercurrent of bitterness. "He's supposed to be."

I gestured for her to continue.

"He didn't hit me at first." She glanced down at the floor, as if she would find the words there she needed. "But he yelled, said horrible things to me. I thought having the baby would soften him, somehow." Her eyes, when she met my gaze again, were full of dark pain. "I was wrong."

Part of me wanted to hurry her along, get her to explain how she had ended up in the Bride Lottery. But I could tell the story was hard for her, so I forced myself to be still, to keep my hands clasped lightly between my knees as I leaned toward her, when all I wanted to do was gather her up and hold her in my lap, protect her from even the story of her pain.

I clamped down on all those desires, giving her space to tell it at her own pace.

"So you left him?" I finally prompted when she didn't continue.

"Eventually. First I tried to go to the police." That bitter laugh escaped her again. "I had to go to Frank's precinct. It was in his jurisdiction, you see. And that meant telling his colleagues what he had done."

Dark anger swirled in my chest. "They didn't believe you?" I guessed.

"No. When I started telling my story the two of the officers, one of them turned to the other and said, 'Remember that time your wife filed bullshit claims on you?'"

I clenched my teeth together, forcing myself to remain perfectly still. I wanted to get up and pace the room, demand more details. But that would only frighten Mia—and her child.

"What happened next?"

"Frank beat the hell out of me for trying to report him. And I convinced myself that I was okay, as long as Frank was good to Josiah." She nodded at the boy now sleeping peacefully in my bed.

"I take it that didn't last?"

"No. The day he came home and tried to kick Josiah for making too much noise—that was the day I reached my limit."

A fierce protective instinct pushed me to my feet with an inarticulate noise of rage. Mia flinched, and I managed to stop myself from stomping to the door and heading straight to Earth to find this monster who had hurt my mate and our child.

Her child, I reminded myself. But the mating bond didn't agree. He belonged to Mia. Therefore, he was mine to protect, too.

"How did you get away?" I asked, forcing myself to sit back down.

"I ran," she said simply. "I filed for divorce—got all the paperwork ready and everything. But he refused to sign and demanded custody of Josiah. Without any proof that he was abusive—no police reports or anything, of course—there was nothing I could do to keep him from coming after us."

This time, she was the one who stood and began pacing. "So we ran again. I changed our names, arranged for new tracker-translation chips."

"Mia Jones is not your real name?"

"It is now." She shrugged. "I've gotten used to it."

"And that's how you ended up in Bride Lottery."

"The chip was supposed to be clean—it's entered in all the systems, but it was supposed to look like I'd already been through the Lottery. I guess I should not have trusted that man, either."

I stood, reaching out to take her hands in mine but stopping short of actually touching her. "There *are* males who are trustworthy."

She glanced up at my eyes, and with a sad smile, placed her hands in mine. "I think I've figured that out. It's why we're here. I trust you."

"Where has Josiah been while you have been up here?"

"With a friend—she'll be frantic when she finds out he's gone. But I couldn't leave him down there for a minute longer."

"How did you get him up to the station?" I paused, my mind racing. "Oh. My wristcom."

"I'm sorry I took it. I didn't know what else to do."

I wanted to tell her that she could have come to me at any point, but I wasn't even sure that was true. If she had told me all of this in the beginning, would I have accepted it? Would the mate bond have been strong enough to overcome the fact that she was technically married to someone else?

Maybe.

But that didn't matter. I knew now, and I did not care. "I will arrange for your friend to know that Josiah is safe with you."

"And then what? My divorce isn't final. I can't marry you."

Resolve hardened in my chest. "I'll take care of that, as well. By the time our Bride Games are finished, you will not be married to him any longer. I swear it."

With a sob, Mia fell into my arms, and I wrapped her in them, every cell of my being promising to keep her safe. I led her over to the chair and gathered her into my lap, rocking her as if she were the child.

After she had cried out all the tears she had in her for the moment, I picked her up and carried her to the bed, settling her in next to Josiah and tucking in the covers around her.

"You'll be safe here," I promised her. "No one knows where you are. I'll be back soon—I'm going to see what I can do to sort this out for us. What's your friend's name?"

"Rebecca Chilton," she whispered sleepily.

I brushed her hair back from her face. "Rest now. I'll be back soon."

And then I left to do whatever it took to erase the fear from my mate's heart.

CHAPTER TWENTY-ONE

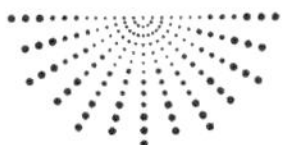

MIA

For the first time since I'd been transported up to Station 21, I woke up with a smile on my face. Josiah was still sleeping, snuggled in my arms, the gentle light the station used to indicate morning just beginning to shine across his cheeks.

As I stretched, I realized Eldron was in bed with us, too, his enormous bulk a comforting presence at my back.

I was safe, Josiah was safe, and I was absolutely certain Eldron would not let anything happen to us.

Quietly, I slipped out of bed. I had to get Thorvid in here to spend the day with Josiah—it would mean drawing the Poltien into our web of secrecy, but I had come to believe I could trust it with my life. Keeping Josiah's presence secret might have been easier if I'd had two handlers —one to watch Josiah and the other to help me figure out what I needed to do—but working through what to wear on my own seemed a small enough price to pay for having Josiah with me.

I had managed to pull on my clothes from the night before, having slept wrapped in Eldron's *chavan*—the uniform that looked so much like a kilt—when Josiah's voice piped up from behind me. "Mama, there's a giant red man in the bed with me."

I laughed aloud and spun around. "I know it, baby. That is Commander Eldron Gendovi. He is a Khanavai warrior and is a very nice man. He's going to take care of us today."

Josiah frowned and leaned in close to examine Eldron's sleeping face. "Are you sure? I think maybe he's a giant."

My heart lightened at the sound of his sweet voice, and I laughed again. "I'm absolutely certain."

Eldron opened both eyes and gazed gravely at Josiah. "It's nice to meet you." Sleep graveled his voice.

"Yep," Josiah confirmed. "He has a giant's voice, too. I don't think he's a Kavan…Khana…"

"Khanavai." Grinning, Eldron sat up, moving slowly as he got out of the bed.

Josiah's eyes grew wide as he watched the alien warrior stand up. "Do things look different from up there?" he asked, wonder threading through his voice.

"Maybe you'd like to sit on my shoulder and find out?"

Josiah whipped his head around to stare at me. "Can I?"

"Yes, you can. Just be careful."

"Mama says I can, but you have to be very careful with me. She doesn't like it when I get hurt," Josiah explained as he scrambled up to stand on the mattress and hold his arms out to Eldron.

"I can't blame her for that," Eldron laughed. He lifted Josiah carefully and placed him atop one broad shoulder. "I would not like it very much if you got hurt, either."

"That's really good," Josiah confided. "Mama worries sometimes."

"I'm sure she does."

They paraded around the room for a few seconds before Josiah was clamoring to be let down again. "I want to see the rest of the station. Can we, Mama?"

"Oh, sweetheart, I am so sorry. But not today. Maybe some other time."

Josiah's face fell. "Why not?"

"Commander Eldron and I have to go be on television today."

Josiah's eyes grew wide again. "On TV? Can I watch?"

"I am going to let Thorvid decide that." I would leave it up to someone else's judgment for once.

A few minutes later, the Poltien answered my call by showing up at the door.

"Technically, the two of you are not supposed to spend the night together before you have been officially matched and mated by the committee," Thorvid was saying as it walked into the room. Its words stuttered to a halt when it caught sight of Josiah, and the lizard-like rill on the back of its neck fluttered.

Josiah seemed equally as awestruck by the sight of a humanoid creature not much bigger than he was. "What are you?" he asked.

Thorvid burst out laughing. "I'm a Poltien. My name is Thorvid, and I think your mother might have something to tell me." The Poltien tossed an arch glance in my direction.

"This is Josiah. He's my son—and he's the reason I wanted to go back to Earth."

"How did you get him up here?"

"I stole Commander Eldron's codes," I admitted.

"Well, this is going to be an interesting story."

"It is," I agreed. "But it needs to be one that I tell you later. Today, I need you to keep an eye on Josiah during the filming."

Thorvid considered us all for a long moment before nodding. "And I assume you don't want anyone else to know about him yet?"

"Please. That would make my life much easier."

"For a minute," Thorvid muttered.

"I've started the process of finalizing your divorce, even without Frank's signature," Eldron said quietly as we headed toward the Bride Games studios.

Hope flared in my chest. "How did you manage that?"

His smile made me want to sing. "I have connections. An Earther judge will sign off on it today—you won't have to do anything."

Tears welled up in my eyes again. But this time, they were happy tears, the result of a weight lifting from my heart. Reaching down, I wound my fingers through Eldron's. "Thank you," I said simply.

He paused outside the studio door and turned to face me. "There's nothing I wouldn't do for you."

"I don't even have words for how much this means to us."

Leaning down, he gently kissed my lips. "There will be some other details we have to figure out, but I am certain everything will work out as it should."

Before I entered the studio, I sent up a silent prayer that he was right to be so optimistic.

CHAPTER TWENTY-TWO

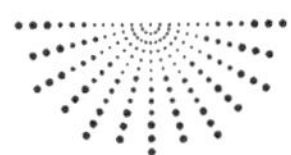

ELDRON

As we made our way into the soundstage Vos had sent us directions to, Mia practically vibrated with happiness. I didn't know exactly what kind of strings I would need to pull to get her out of her current marriage—though by all accounts, she had done everything she needed to in order to complete a divorce. Her ex-husband simply had refused to sign the paperwork.

And there would probably be some legal hurdles ahead to deal with custody and visitation.

For all that the Khanavai were a warrior race, we were gentle with our children—no Khanavai male who attempted to physically assault his own child would be welcome in anyone's home.

Our legal system would support my attempt to gain custody of this Frank's child.

He doesn't deserve to call himself a father.

At most, I would arrange for Frank to have supervised visits with the boy, though even the thought of it made a growl rise in my throat.

I was so wrapped up in my own thoughts about Josiah that it really didn't dawn on me that the soundstage had been turned into a kitchen studio until the door shut behind me.

Cooking?

I was a terrible cook.

Also, I wasn't at all sure how Mia was going to feel about traditional Khanavai dishes.

I had to snicker to myself, though. I was pretty certain I knew exactly how she would feel about traditional Khanavai dishes when I cooked them. If she had any sense at all, she'd feel horrified.

Mia, on the other hand, seemed to light up at the site of the kitchen.

"Am I going to get to cook?" There was a thrill in her tone that nothing else had put there before.

Not even Josiah. When she spoke to him, I heard love and devotion, even joy.

But apparently, *excitement* was reserved for cooking.

Good. One of us needs to enjoy it, at least.

"Shall we get going?" Vos asked, coming toward us with his hands out to welcome us.

Turning toward the camera, he officially introduced us to two worlds.

AS MIA BEGAN COOKING, my mouth fell open. She moved through the kitchen with the grace of a dancer, the joy that I had seen lighting her up earlier suffusing her every movement. She sang as she worked, alternating between vocalizing and humming under her breath. When I stepped closer to her, however, I recognized a few of the words as the names of Earth-style ingredients.

She was cooking from memory, something complicated and precise, and was singing the steps to herself.

It was not just a song, though—and not just a dance, either. Somehow it all blended together into some kind of glorious symphony of a performance. She lost herself in the joy of creating that meal.

After watching for a while, I retreated to a chair in the corner, content simply to see her happy.

I wondered how Josiah and Thorvid were doing back in my room, delighted at the thought of Josiah seeing his mother so content.

When Mia placed the dish in front of me at the table and then joined me herself, I leaned over to inhale the amazing aroma. "What is this?"

"Coq au vin."

Chicken in wine? I thought chicken was a bland human food. Also...

"I thought you cooked breakfast at a meal dispensary," I said.

My mate raised one eyebrow. "I do now."

There was a story to be had there, as well. Who was this human female I had fallen in love with?

As I took a bite of the meat dish, though, I decided I didn't care. "This is amazing," I said with my mouth full.

Mia laughed aloud and clapped her hands before standing up and leaning over the table to plant a kiss on my lips, full mouth and all. For a moment, I completely forgot that the entire galaxy was watching us. I would have happily swept the food off the table and claimed Mia right there.

I glanced down at the dish in front of me.

Well. Maybe I would have carefully moved the food, anyway.

As it turned out, Vos didn't require me to make a Khanavai dish. Apparently, the reports on his numbers were good enough that he was willing to let us simply come back the next day for the next Bride Game.

"Would you like to see the studio we'll have our challenge in tomorrow?" I asked as we left the kitchen stage.

"Absolutely." Mia practically glowed, her day in the kitchen combining with the knowledge that Josiah was safe in my room with Thorvid to leave her perfectly content—the first time I had seen her truly happy since we met.

I led her along the studio hallways until I got to the one I had bribed Anthony to tell me about.

This studio was very different from the last one. Instead of the kitchen, we made our way into a traditional Khanavai bathing room.

"Is that a swimming pool?"

"A bathing pool," I corrected.

Mia spun around to stare up at me, her dark eyes huge. "Bathing? They expect us to *bathe* together on television?"

I grinned. "Traditionally, a bride and groom first bathe together completely clothed. You can think of it as something like swimming, if you like."

Mia put her hands up to her cheeks, as if attempting to compensate for feeling flushed. "How dressed is *completely dressed*?"

"We will be wearing clothing that covers more than a human-style bathing suit," I assured her, fighting to hold in a laugh.

"Then I'm looking forward to it."

Mia stood on her tiptoes and kissed me.

I could do this forever.

CHAPTER TWENTY-THREE

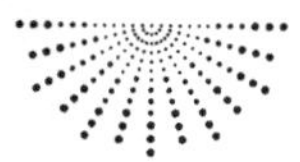

MIA

"I'm going to go back to my room and gather some clothing," I told Eldron as we headed back to his quarters.

"Would you like me to accompany you?"

"No, thanks. I would love it if you told Josiah and Thorvid where I am, though."

Eldron nodded his agreement, and we split up in the common area.

Now that we were all staying in Eldron's room, there was no one living in the Brides' Quarters, I realized as I came around the corner into the long hallway. The automated lights had dropped down to minimal, and it was, I decided, a little creepy.

I was halfway to my door when a figure stepped out of the shadows.

"There you are."

I froze at the sound of his voice.

Frank.

Oh, God. No. What was he doing here? I spun on my heel to run, but I simply couldn't move fast enough.

Although he wasn't nearly as big as any of the Khanavai warriors, Frank was not a small man, by any means. He shot out one muscular arm and grabbed me, fisting his hand in my hair and jerking me backward off my feet. I started to let out a scream, but he slammed his other hand down over my nose and mouth.

"Don't you dare let out a sound," he growled in my ear. "You need to be absolutely silent, or I will make you disappear, and no one will ever know what happened to you."

I didn't mean to, but I let out a small noise of dismay—one he took as disagreement. "Don't think I can't do it. I have contacts on the station. How do you think I got here? Now, promise me you'll be quiet."

My heart pounded in my chest, but I nodded, trying to breathe around his hand. He pulled it tighter, reminding me for just a minute that he had control before he loosened it enough for me to drag in a breath.

"Where's Joey?"

I clenched my jaw shut, irritated by the nickname I had never used and unwilling to tell him where Josiah was.

He tightened his fist in my hair, ripping some of it out by the roots. "Where is my son?" he demanded.

I whimpered, and Frank used his grasp on my hair to shake my head. "You're going to take me to him now."

He began steering me back down the hallway. If I could just get someone's attention, get some help, I could get out of this. But the hall was entirely empty.

“Where’s your room?”

“That’s where I was headed,” I gritted out through my teeth.

“Lying bitch.” Frank shook my head again, snapping my neck back and forth. “They put you in the Brides’ Quarters, nowhere near here.”

My stomach clenched. Maybe he really didn’t have contacts on the station. If he had, he would’ve known I wasn’t lying. Then again, he almost certainly had some help—as he’d said, how else could have gotten up here?

That had always been the problem with running from an abusive police officer—he had contacts everywhere. The one time I had tried to report him for hitting me, his coworkers had banded together.

I couldn’t leave him openly.

Running had been my only option. I had known it then, and I knew it now.

But this time, I had someone to run *to*—I would simply be running from my abuser, but maybe I could count on being able to run to a savior, too.

I didn’t have a chance, though. He opened a door and shoved me into a darkened room. I stumbled and fell to my knees.

At the sound of a whimper next to me, I called out, “Who is that? Who’s there?”

“Mia?”

“Becca?” I scrambled around in the dark until I found my friend and threw my arms around her. “How did you get here?”

“Frank. He came to ask me where Josiah was. I had just heard from your commander—I didn’t think it would hurt for Frank to know now.” She sniffled. “I think he didn’t want me to tell anyone he was on his way up here.”

"It's okay," I comforted her. "I'll get us out of here."

I would, too. I just didn't know how yet.

Then, in the darkness of the room, Eldron's wristcom, still on my arm from the night before, pinged.

CHAPTER TWENTY-FOUR

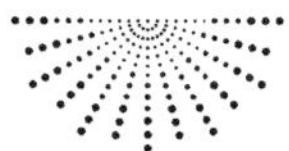

ELDRON

"Where the hell is she?" I muttered to myself.

Behind me, Thorvid and Josiah sat on the bed playing some complicated handshake game that Josiah was teaching the Poltien.

I rang my wristcom again, hoping Mia still wore it.

This time, the screen unfolded to show Mia's face, lit by the com's vid. "Don't say anything," she ordered in a harsh whisper. "Just listen."

The com's light went out. I couldn't see anything, but I could still hear.

A door opened, and then a male voice said, "I did a little recon. Maybe you weren't lying after all. So let's go to your room, if it's really on this floor."

What the Zagrodnian hells is going on?

Then Mia spoke. "Okay, Frank. Whatever you say. Becca and I will go anywhere you want."

Frank and Becca?

I had spoken to Mia's friend the night before.

But now, apparently, Mia's ex-husband—and he really was her ex now; I had checked to make sure the paperwork had gone through—had come looking for Mia and Josiah.

And they were headed back to her room.

Fury burst through me, but a glance in the mirror at Josiah reminded me to keep it under control until I was out of his sight. "I'm going to get your mother," I said casually, calmly standing up from my seat in front of the mirror.

"Okay," Josiah replied with the insouciance of childhood. "Can we play when you get back?"

I nodded, anxiety coursing through my veins, urging me to hurry to save Mia. But I continued to move slowly for Josiah's sake. At least until I closed the door behind me.

Once the door shut, though, I put on a burst of speed, ducking around anyone in my way, racing to the lift and sliding into the tube. A single phrase beat an insistent tattoo in my head, over and over again in time to my footsteps. *Save Mia. Save Mia. Save Mia.*

I slid around the corner into the Brides' Quarters hallway, slamming to a halt outside my mate's door.

I tried to open it, but it was locked. Without my wristcom, I couldn't override the system or call anyone else for help.

Some commander I am, rushing headlong into a dangerous situation without proper assessment.

At least no one onboard Station 21 had weapons—not outside the shuttle bay, where we were all required to check them in.

If Frank had transported aboard, any weapons on his body would have been left behind. So he was almost certainly unarmed.

I leaned my ear against the door, hoping to hear something that would help me decide what to do. Go for help? No. Frank was a violent, dangerous male. Unless I couldn't figure out any way to get into the room, I would not leave Mia with him, not if I could help it.

"Tell me where he is," I heard Frank's voice say.

"He's not here, I told you," Mia replied. "I don't know why you think Josiah is on the station, but he isn't."

She had him talking. That was good.

But then I heard the crack of a fist against bone. "Tell me where he is!"

I had been in battle before. I knew the feel of battle lust, a Khanavai trait that made us great warriors. And I had heard that the mate bond could cause a similar kind of rage.

Everything I had heard was wrong.

It wasn't similar at all.

Mate-bond rage was a million times stronger, like comparing a single ray of light to the strength of a burning star.

My protective fury swelled inside me, erupting from me as a roar that echoed up and down the hallway.

Even as I reared back and slammed my shoulder into the locked door, from inside the room, I heard Frank exclaim, "What the fuck was that?"

The door flew open, its broken lock whirring as it stopped halfway.

I wrenched it the rest of the way open and strode into the room to find a human male—bigger than most, but not as large as a Khanavai warrior—with one hand fisted in Mia's hair, tugging her head backward, the other raised above her, preparing to strike her again.

The man was pale-skinned compared to Mia, but his own rage had turned his face a shade not far from my own.

In the corner, a round woman with golden hair huddled with her arms over her head, her cheek purpling in a bruise. Becca, I assumed.

Frank quickly shifted his hold on Mia, tugging her in front of him to use as a shield. “Come one step closer and I will snap her neck,” he warned.

I skidded to a halt, eyeing the tableau warily.

Slowly, Becca began shifting toward something under the bed. She glanced up at me and put a finger to her mouth.

“Let her go,” I said to Frank, as much to distract him from Becca’s motions as out of any sense that he would do what I told him too.

“You’re the son of a bitch trying to steal my family from me,” Frank growled.

“No. You lost them long before they ever met me.”

Behind Frank, Becca slowly pulled the blue gym bag out from under Mia’s bed.

“I don’t care what happens to me,” Mia said to me, her eyes pleading. “Just don’t let him get Josiah. Don’t let him hurt my baby.”

“Shut up, bitch,” Frank snarled, shaking her a little.

Becca pulled one of the paint guns out of the bag. Under the guise of calming Frank, I held out one hand, straight in front of me.

“Everything is going to be okay,” I promise Mia.

Then I flicked my gaze toward Becca.

With a nod, she stood up and tossed the paint gun to me. In one smooth motion, I flipped it around and shot the paint directly into Frank’s eyes.

He screamed and grabbed his eyes, releasing his hold on Mia, who darted directly to me. I slung her around behind me and tackled

Frank to the ground. Holding him there, I instructed Mia, "Contact security. Get them here now."

Frank lay on the ground writhing and cursing, but I held him there with one hand.

"You must be Becca," I said to Mia's friend. "Nice to meet you."

"That was amazing thinking," Mia said to Becca.

"After he hit me, he wasn't watching me at all," Becca said.

So it *hadn't* been Mia he had hurt.

I glanced up at my mate, who had retrieved the second paint gun and was holding it aimed directly at her ex-husband's face.

"I guess Frank didn't learn one very important lesson from you," I observed.

Mia's gaze flickered toward me for long enough to frown before going back to watching Frank warily. "Yeah? What's that?"

"He needed to learn to watch his six."

An hour later, we had given our statements to station security.

I let them think that I had brought Josiah up to the station. I had the authority to approve that, after all.

Becca was in medical, having her bruised face seen to. They were going to keep her overnight to make sure she didn't have a concussion.

I had commed Thorvid to let it know that we were okay and headed back.

And I was ready to make Mia my mate in truth and in all ways.

"Oh," said Thorvid, taking one look at our faces when we walked into my room, "Josiah, would you like to go on a tour of Station 21?"

"Yes, please!" Josiah exclaimed, jumping up. "Can Mama and Commander Eldron go with us?"

"Not this time," Thorvid said placidly. "We'll bring them back something to eat from the common area in a little while though." It turned to me. "I'll com you before we return."

"Thanks," Mia said with a small laugh. "I'll see you soon, okay, baby?"

Josiah put his tiny fists on his hips. "I'm not a baby anymore, Mama. You need to call me something else."

She gave a salute. "Will do, ba—buddy."

He nodded seriously. "Buddy is much better." Then he turned and gave me the same salute his mother had given him. "Take care of my Mama, Commander Eldron. We will return soon."

I gave him a Khanavai heart salute. "Yes, sir."

And then they were gone, and I was free to make Mia my own.

CHAPTER TWENTY-FIVE

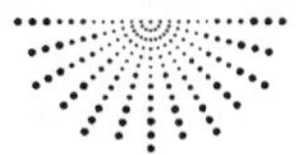

MIA

We tore at each other's clothes as if their very presence offended us, our mouths frantic against each other's skin.

When we were fully naked, Eldron tried to slow things down, placing me on the bed and moving his mouth to my breast. I writhed against him. "No," I said. "I don't want to wait a second longer. Please, Eldron, please make me yours."

With a groan, he slid up to cover me, his enormous cock pressing against my opening. I bucked against him, needing to feel him filling me, and he accepted my body's invitation, pushing into me steadily.

"Oh, gods and goddesses, you're so tight," he said.

His words made my muscles clench, and as if the tightness itself drove him on, he withdrew just a little, then flipped us over so I was on top and pulled me down hard onto his cock.

When he'd driven all the way into me, burying his cock to the hilt, he paused, holding me tight against him.

I could feel his cock filling me up, swelling, growing, and I ached with it. He paused, apparently having to stop himself from coming inside me. "You feel just right," he whispered, his voice rasping.

Eldron's enormous hands, those hands I had started counting on to save me, wrapped around my waist and slid down as he stroked my ass.

The sparks of arousal roared into an overwhelming flame, the heat of Eldron's body against mine and the feeling of his hand stroking from the hollow of my waist to the curves of my ass cheeks making my back arch as I rocked against him.

Eldron groaned, his fingers playing my skin as my nipples tightened. We found a rhythm together without words, just as we had during our first kiss.

I shouldn't be doing this.

Not until I was truly free from Frank.

But Eldron had promised the paperwork he'd filed had freed me from any obligation to Frank in the eyes of the Khanavai law.

That would have to be enough.

"Thank you," I murmured as I bent down to kiss him.

"I will always give you anything you need," Eldron replied in between kisses. "You are free—and I am yours."

And he knows what I need to hear, without me even having to say it.

My response to him built in my deepest core as he slid into me, filling me up, stretching me out, making me want more of him. I found myself throwing my head back and whimpering with the need to come and the desire to draw this out forever.

In the end, the need won.

I began rocking my hips, meeting Eldron stroke for stroke, barely forcing myself not to beg for him to go deeper and harder, to give me more.

But as if he heard me, he began slamming his cock deep into me, reaching between us, his big fingers rubbing my clit, making me slicker and wetter, while the pressure built up in my abdomen, coiling tighter.

The wetter I got, the harder he fucked me. And the harder he fucked me, the more I met him thrust for thrust.

The head of his cock slammed into something deep inside me, prompting me to cry out with ecstasy.

The sensation spiraled up inside me, sending me higher and higher. I wanted to stop it, to draw this out forever, but I couldn't. I couldn't quit moving to the rhythm Eldron set, couldn't quit feeling the sensations washing over me. And then, as the feelings broke over me like waves, I came harder than I ever had before.

I screamed with the pleasure of it, and all the muscles in my lower body clenched as the hot wetness of my orgasm sluiced through me.

As my muscles tightened around Eldron's cock, he gave one enormous final thrust, crying out my name as he came inside me, holding me tightly against him.

We stayed like that for a long moment, and then I collapsed against his chest.

"I love you, Mia," he said.

CHAPTER TWENTY-SIX

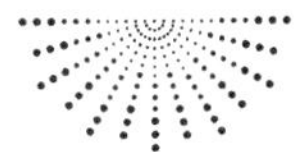

ELDRON

s we lay together, still entwined, I felt my mating cock emerge from the softening skin of my primary cock—a new experience for me, but unmistakable.

Startled, Mia raised her head to meet my gaze. "Again?" she asked, surprise threading through her voice.

We'd known each other only a few days. It was far too early to start tossing around words like *love* or *mate,* but I knew that's what this was.

"This...will be different," I tried to explain. "If we continue, we'll be mated. It's not like human marriage. This will truly be forever."

She swallowed, fear flashing through her eyes.

"Our life together will be different from your time with Frank. I will never hurt you." I kept my voice soft, even as my cock, still inside her, grew harder and harder.

“Promise?” Her tiny question, so full of worry, brought out every protective instinct within me.

“With everything I am and everything I have, I will protect you—and Josiah. I will make sure you are loved and cared for. Forever.” My words spilled out directly from my heart.

“Then…make me yours. Now. Please.”

Without another word, I wrapped my arms around her waist and flipped her over on the bed, a possessive growl erupting from my throat. For an instant, I worried that I might have scared her, but then Mia giggled.

I found myself joining her in laughter, even as I slid deep into her, determined to do exactly as she requested.

By the time this night was over, she would be mine.

CHAPTER TWENTY-SEVEN

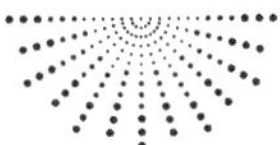

MIA

Somehow, Eldron's mating cock filled me even more than his first cock had. Everything about it was hot, making me ache with desire like nothing ever before.

Eldron pulled me up to him, making sure he stayed embedded in me, buried up to the hilt, but I could feel him shivering, trying not to come.

"Oh, God," he groaned. "You feel so hot and tight."

I shuddered at his words, and his reaction to my body moving around him was to moan again. He began moving. His strokes were like fire, sliding into the deepest part of me—the part that only he could touch.

Soon, the build-up of pleasure began swirling in my stomach, throbbing and aching, but in a way that made me want my alien to touch me more, not less.

"My perfect, beloved mate," he said, rocking me back and forth on his cock. "You are mine."

His mating cock grew even bigger and hotter inside me, stretching me as he moved toward an explosion, and the feel of it touching that most intimate part of my body sent me spinning out of control.

I came hard, waves of orgasm running through me over and over until I sobbed with it.

My orgasm triggered his, and he trembled inside me for a long time afterward.

As he slipped from me and gently settled me on the bed next to him, still breathing hard, he said, "Mia? Now that we're officially mated, I have a very important question to ask you."

I turned on my side to face him, running my fingers lightly over his muscled chest. "What's that?"

He flipped over so he faced me, as well, and gave me a serious, intense stare—one that was belied by the glint of humor in his expression. "What, exactly, is your name?"

I burst into laughter. "How did you manage to get my divorce finalized without that information?"

"I might have run it through the Khanavai courts first so it will simply need to be registered on Earth."

"It's Naomi…well, I guess it can be Naomi Gendovi now, if you'd like. But you can still call me Mia."

"I think maybe I'll continue to call you my *vanata*."

"What does that mean?" I asked.

"Heart's most beloved."

"It's perfect," I said, preparing to snuggle down into his arms.

But then a chime dinged from Eldron's wrist. "It's Thorvid," he said, checking it, "on the way back with food—and Josiah."

"Guess we'd better get up then," I sighed.

Eldron wrapped me in his arms for one last hug. "Absolutely. I am ready to begin our lives together, my *vanata*."

EPILOGUE

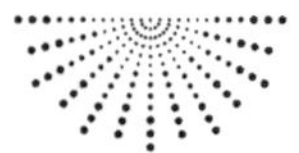

EARTH, SIX MONTHS LATER

BECCA

I climbed down off the witness stand, wiping tears from my eyes.

I hadn't expected to cry as I testified to everything Frank Holden had done the night he tried to take Josiah from station 21.

I was the last witness in the sentencing phase of Frank's trial. He'd already been found guilty of kidnapping and assault. He'd had the option to be tried by a Khanavai judge. Apparently, he had taken one look at their harsh punishment for spousal abuse and decided to take his chances with a human jury on Earth.

As I took my seat next to her, Mia reached out to pat my hand. Commander Gendovi reached around her and covered both our hands with his own enormous one, giving us a gentle squeeze.

Mia is so lucky.

Or Naomi. Whatever her name was now.

Of course, she had gone through hell before finding that luck.

She was blissfully happy now, married—and mated, as the Khanavai said—to the man of her dreams. Not to mention pregnant with her second child, too.

I was happy for her, really I was. But seeing them together, I couldn't help giving a little wistful sigh.

It would be so amazing to have a relationship that strong.

I was pretty sure human men were not up to the task of being the kind of spouses the Khanavai men were.

And as far as I knew, the only way to get a Khanavai man was through the Bride Lottery.

If only I could figure out a way to sneak in somehow.

TWO HOURS LATER, the sentence came down.

Fifteen years.

"And by then, Josiah will be an adult and able to decide what he wants to do about a relationship with his father," Mia said as we walked out of the courtroom and onto the courthouse steps.

"And in the meantime, he has an amazing male role model," I said, taking Mia's arm in mine and leaning in close as if I were confiding something secret. I could tell by the commander's grin that he heard, though.

"Josiah will grow to be a fine male," the commander stated, managing to sound both placid and proud.

"I am starving," Mia said, patting her burgeoning belly. "Let's go meet Thorvid and Josiah and get something to eat before we head back to Station 21."

"Now this is done, are you heading back to Khanav Prime?"

"Yes," the commander said. "I need to get back to work—there are some new theories about the Alveron Hordeships that I would like to incorporate into potential battle scenarios."

"And I want to be there before this baby appears," Mia added.

"Well, then, before you go, I might have a favor to ask."

"What's that?" the commander asked.

"I was wondering if maybe you could pull some strings with the Bride Lottery for me…"

The commander smiled and tilted his head, clearly seriously considering my request as the three of us headed away from the courthouse, leaving this unpleasant chapter of our lives behind.

ENJOYED THIS STORY? Be sure to leave a review! Keep an eye out for Becca's story in *Betting on the Alien Bride Lottery*. You can also preorder Wex's story in Enemy of the Alien Bride Lottery, book four of the Khanavai Warrior Alien Bride Games series. If you've missed any Bride Lottery books, you can read the rest of the series starting with Entered in the Alien Bride Lottery.

CHRISTMAS FOR THE ALIEN BRIDE LOTTERY

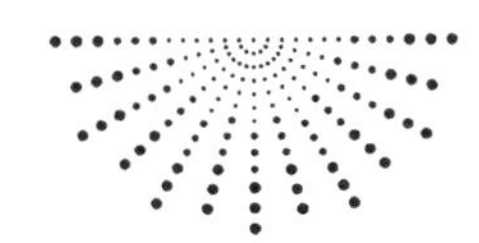

ABOUT CHRISTMAS FOR THE ALIEN BRIDE LOTTERY

When Lola graduates from college a semester early, she's left without a job or even any real prospects. She takes a holiday position working as a Christmas Elf at the local mall, only to learn to loathe all things Christmas.

So when her name is drawn for the Alien Bride Lottery's new "Holiday Special," she's almost relieved. Until she meets Valtin, the Khanavai warrior who has decided to make her his own. He's fascinated with human holiday traditions, especially Christmas.

Can a cranky Christmas Elf and an overeager alien male find the magic of the season together?

CHAPTER ONE

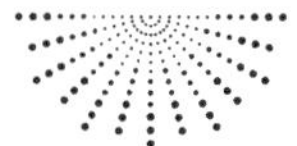

LOLA RICHARDS

You know what's the best part of getting a holiday job as a Christmas Elf in Santa's Village at the local mall?

Nothing.

Not a single damn thing.

Every day, I got up, got dressed in my silly candy-cane-striped tights and ridiculous too-short green dress, the one my boobs always tried to spill out of. The costume definitely wasn't made for curvy elves. It was, however, perfect for the pervy dads who tried to see down it when I was trying to get their kids to smile for Santa.

I couldn't roll my eyes hard enough at those guys.

About half the time in the mornings, I got out to my car without the stupid hat or obnoxious curly-toed shoe covers—both made of cheap felt and festooned with tiny jingly bells. On those days, I cursed aloud and headed back into my apartment.

Mrs. Gardner, the old lady who lived in the unit next to mine, inevitably pulled back the vertical blinds and peered through her open sliding glass door to give me the evil eye when that happened.

December twenty-fourth was one of those days. Mrs. Gardner was still glaring at me when I got back out to my car with all my absurd elf gear.

One more day.

By this time tomorrow, I'll be jobless again.

I gave Mrs. Gardner a fake-cheerful smile and wave as I backed out of my spot, wishing I had the nerve to flip her off instead.

Seriously? I went to college for this?

At the mall, parents with small children were already lined up waiting to see Santa, even though we didn't open for another thirty minutes.

Worse, Penelope had gotten there before me, so she'd grabbed the register to start her shift, which left me wrangling kids onto Santa's lap to get them ready to have their pictures taken.

"I haven't had coffee yet," I complained as I clocked in on the other computer.

"Better go grab some before Molly gets here, then." Penelope smirked at me, pleased that she'd managed to snag the primo spot to start the day.

Not that I didn't like kids. But let's face it—forcing children to go sit in some old, fat bearded guy's lap and tell him what they want him to bring them for Christmas is a creepy fucking tradition.

It's no wonder so many of the little ones ended up bawling their eyes out. But that meant it was my job to wipe their tiny noses and then dance and sing and try to get them to smile for the camera—usually while their parents "helped," usually making the kids cry even more.

Fifteen minutes later, I gulped down the coffee I'd stood in line too long to get, burning my tongue in the process.

Fuck, fuck, fuck. What a shitty day. Already.

Glowering at everyone I passed, almost daring them to say "good morning" to me, I stomped back toward the makeshift Santa's Village in the center of the building, right in front of Macy's.

"You're late," Molly, my manager, said as I arrived.

"I was here. Already signed in." I waved at the second computer. "Besides, we can't start until Santa arrives. Who is it today?"

"Jeff." Molly rolled her eyes as she said it, and I groaned aloud.

"Prepare to be groped," Penelope said to me, smirking again.

"I'd rather report him to my manager," I said, pointedly staring at Molly. As usual, she pretended not to hear me.

If I didn't need this job so much, I'd report you, too.

Then Jeff the Groping Santa arrived, and my shift from hell officially began.

Four hours later, I was waving a small teddy bear dressed like an elf —*his costume is less revealing than mine, and he doesn't even have on pants,* I thought—trying to charm a wailing baby and counting down the seconds to my lunch break, when all the lights in the mall flickered.

"What the—" Penelope smashed several keys on the keyboard, and suddenly every screen in the mall went blank for a second. Then they flashed back to life, showing Vos Klavoii, the administrator for the Alien Bride Lottery, in all his green glory, his shock of white hair standing out against the neon tint of his skin.

"Hello, people of Earth," he announced, his voice booming out from every electronic device in the world. "And welcome to this Special Holiday Edition of the Bride Games!"

"What the hell?" I muttered, totally forgetting about all the children standing in line nearby. Several of the parents covered their children's ears and glared at me. I ignored them, moving to stand by my coworkers as they stopped to watch the screen.

"Is this new?" Penelope asked. "I didn't think they did holiday specials."

She was right. They didn't.

The Bride Lottery only happened once a year—or at least, that had been true until now. Every unmarried woman of childbearing age was put into a giant lottery, and if her name was drawn, she had to go compete to be a bride for a Khanavai warrior. All this was in return for the Khanavai keeping us safe from the Alveron Horde, another race of aliens who wanted to take over our planet.

But this year's Bride Games had already happened, just a few months ago.

Of course, they'd been interrupted by the Horde actually attacking Station 21, where the games were filmed, and the brides were chosen.

Still, that shouldn't have led to *more* games, right?

On the screen, Vos was still talking about this "Very Special Holiday Show, featuring a whole new cast of brides and grooms!"

A strange frisson of fear shivered up my spine.

I wasn't even surprised when he said, "Let's begin the drawing! Our first Bride Lottery winner is... Lola Richards!"

Penelope and Molly both stepped away from me as if I'd just announced I had the plague.

My eyes widened, and I had just enough time to say, "Well, fuuuu—" before a bright white light surrounded me, the scene around me wavered, and everything went black.

CHAPTER TWO

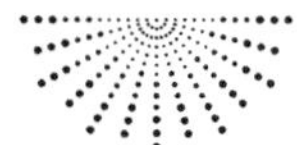

VALTIN VALENOX

"A Christmas Special? Really?" I knew I sounded far too excited, but I couldn't help it. Earth traditions had always fascinated me.

Especially Christmas.

Growing up, my best friend Kein's family had celebrated Christmas. He was half-human, and his mother always said Christmas was the one holiday she wasn't willing to give up when she moved to Khanav Prime.

I loved going over to their house during their holiday season. Kein's mother had decorated in the closest thing to Christmas she could find on Khanav Prime. Khanavai blefnar plants, with their red needles and green berries, substituted for her traditional Earthen Christmas tree. She always said, "At least they're the right colors for Christmas."

As all this flashed through my mind, Commander Colpint nodded. "They're calling it a 'Holiday Special,' but I do believe it's based on the human Christmas holiday, yes."

"I'm in." Part of me knew I should be more concerned with finding a mate than with participating in a holiday special of the Bride Games. But I wasn't all that concerned with choosing a mate; I was still young and there were plenty of brides in the stars. I'd either match with one or I wouldn't.

But this was possibly my only chance to participate in a human Christmas celebration...with humans, no less. No way would I miss out on this.

"I suspected you would agree." My commander grinned at me, and it was all I could do not to laugh aloud in joy as I headed to my quarters to pack.

When I stepped off the transport shuttle onto Station 21, I was disappointed not to see human Christmas decorations.

"Are you Valtin Valenox?" a yellow Khanavai male demanded as I paused to glance around the station.

"I am," I said. "Nice to meet you."

"You're late," the irritable attaché barked at me. He was probably one of the permanent appointees to the station, part of our military who never saw combat but were essential to both the smooth running of the Bride Games and the success of our battles against the evil Alveron Horde.

It always astounded me that our culture valued front-line warriors above support personnel, when those of us on the front lines could not do what we needed to do without their help. Because of that, I always tried to be particularly nice to those soldiers who made my life better—even when they were not especially polite to me.

The yellow male rolled his eyes and gestured for me to hurry up. "Come on. We don't have much time before Vos begins his explanation of the new games."

I worked to keep my expression affable, but part of me wanted to dress him down for his attitude.

Does he not realize how lucky he is to get to spend so much time with humans?

As he led me through the station via a route I had memorized from maps and vids on the way out, I saw several humans out on the station, just going about their business.

They have no idea how wondrous they are.

I didn't know if they realized they were the salvation of the Khanavai race. The longer the Bride Alliance held with Earth, the more integrated into our DNA humanity became. Which was absolutely necessary since our own females' ability to reproduce had been destroyed when the Horde had attacked our planet with a mutated virus. The Horde were monsters, and humans were our saviors.

Humans agreeing to send brides to us in exchange for planetary protection from the Horde meant that our people would survive.

Sure, there had been some purists who wanted to reject all things human—but as they refused the chance for human brides of their own, they had begun to die out.

They were all idiots. Humans are amazing.

My cranky yellow guide pulled up short in the center chamber of the station, home to a food court on one side and the entrance to the station gardens on the other. The games arena was down one of the far hallways. I assumed that's where we were headed.

The guide turned to glance at me with a critical eye. "We don't have time for you to freshen up." His tone suggested he thought maybe I should change my appearance—even though I had recently bathed and had even changed into my dress uniform before I arrived.

"Leave your luggage with me and I will have it stored for you," he instructed.

"Sure. What's your name?"

"Tiziani," he said shortly.

"Well, Tiziani, where are we going?" I asked.

"The arena. Vos will be addressing all of you there."

The arena? Were there that many of us here? I'd been given to understand this was a small group, a test run for how well a larger set of holiday bride games might be run in other cycles.

Years, I reminded myself. *Humans call them years.*

I handed my bag to Tiziani, who led me down the hallway, and then opened a door and gestured me in.

Everything I had hoped to see in the way of Christmas decorations when I exited the shuttle had clearly been put up here.

It was a Christmas wonderland, a beautiful array of red and green, with silver and gold sparkling lights and tiny shimmering streamers. White shavings of something littered the floor, probably to evoke the feeling of ice and snow—though it was nothing like the snow I had experienced in the Battle of Hoffnons.

I wanted to spin around to take all of it in.

Then I caught the most amazing scent in the air. It was like Calderon spices and lifneg flowers, all rolled into one.

It was perfect.

And it smelled exactly like I had always imagined an Earth Christmas would smell.

"Oh, my God. It looks like Christmas threw up in here."

When I turned to see who had spoken, I realized the amazing scent emanated not from any of the decorations, but from a woman who had just entered the arena.

A perfect woman.

She was tiny, round, and beautiful, with hair the color of the Lorishi desert—deep brown with gold streaks. She wore it pulled to one side in a clip so that it hung over her shoulder.

Her eyes matched her hair, right down to the gold streaks.

I could fall into those eyes forever.

The rest of her was all luscious, ripe curves, from the delicate line of her cheek to the fullness of her breasts. I found myself wanting to grab her hips and pulled her against my suddenly hard cock.

No. That amazing smell wasn't the scent of Christmas. It was the scent of my mate.

She's mine.

As she moved into the room, she muttered something I couldn't make out. Then she glanced up into my eyes and stumbled—straight into my arms.

CHAPTER THREE

LOLA

When I staggered out of the weird transporter thing, my stomach heaved, but I managed to swallow it down.

Glancing around, I discovered two brightly colored aliens—one green, one orange—in skirts.

No. That's not a skirt, I remembered. *It's a uniform. A ...* I cast about for the right word. *A chavan.*

Beside them stood a tall, thin, silver-colored chick, and a tiny... person...with a blond braid hanging out of one nostril.

But there wasn't a single, solitary Christmas decoration anywhere.

So that's a plus, I thought.

Then I leaned over and vomited.

"It's no problem," the silver woman trilled at me in her bell-like voice as she led me toward the first meeting. "The transporter often affects humans like that."

That explains the toothbrush and paste they had on hand.

"I'm sorry we didn't have time to get you changed for this," her short, nose-braided companion—a Poltien, I remembered, a race without specific genders—added. "But Vos will love your Christmas-themed attire."

I realized the Poltien had been right when we entered the arena. Clearly whoever had created this atrocity had a thing for Christmas.

"Oh, my God. It looks like Christmas threw up in here," I said aloud before I could stop myself.

At my words, a Khanavai man a few steps ahead of me spun around to stare, his nostrils flaring as if he were an animal scenting something.

His skin was a bright purple, a color I had never seen on any of the Bride Games transmissions. A color that would clash with all the Christmas decorations. Horribly, in fact.

But I didn't care.

Still feeling a little lightheaded from the transporter, I had an overwhelming urge to rush over, throw my arms around him, and start licking, like he was grape-flavored candy or something. The thought made my mouth water, and I had to swallow.

He was more muscular than any human I had ever seen, with washboard abs that could have done the laundry for a whole city in one day. His broad shoulders towered over me, tapering down to a perfect waist, and his piercing turquoise eyes made my knees go weak.

And he was huge.

"I suddenly want to go mountain climbing," I muttered under my breath.

"What was that?" The Poltien asked.

"Nothing." I shook my head to dispel the image of trying to climb the giant purple man.

Then I made the mistake of trying to look up at his face and walk past him at the same time.

I've never been terribly graceful, and those eyes of his boring into me like I was the only woman he'd ever seen before made me lose my train of thought entirely—along with my balance. Like someone in a stupid romcom, I tripped and fell, literally into his arms.

In one motion, as if I weighed nothing, he scooped me up, so my feet dangled off the ground. His arm tightened around my waist, and my breasts brushed against his bare chest. My nipples hardened into tight, sensitive pebbles.

We stared into each other's eyes for a long, silent moment before the yellow Khanavai man standing next to Gorgeous Purple Dude cleared his throat. "Vos is beginning," he said, motioning us forward.

"Right," the purple Khanavai muttered as he set my feet back on the ground. But he didn't remove his arm from around my waist as we moved toward a group of people in the center of the over-decorated arena, where Vos Klavoii was already talking.

"We are changing the format of the Bride Games for this holiday special," Vos said. "Rather than dozens of brides, we have narrowed the field down to just three. Similarly, we have a small number of grooms participating—only six. As usual, any brides who match with one or more grooms will be expected to participate in the games." He raised one eyebrow as he gazed around the room, as if daring anyone to object.

No one said anything. I think all three of the human women were still too shellshocked by the surprise drawing to say anything. I knew I was, anyway. Plus I still had a Khanavai's arm wrapped around me.

"However, we have changed the games, as well. This series will run as a special, so it won't be as varied as our regular Bride Games. In fact, there will be only one game, designed to confirm any matches—but it's a longer game than usual."

As far as I knew, this was completely different from anything they had ever done before. The Bride Games were usually convoluted, a little bizarre, designed to eliminate suitors rather than approve them—and recently, apparently designed to titillate the audience as well, given the spanking ceremony one of the brides had gone through in the last set of games.

Also, it looked like this time, they were working to make sure *all* the brides got matched and sent home with a Khanavai groom.

Suddenly, I didn't care, as long as I got matched with the purple guy.

He's the only one I might consider going home with.

I shook my head to dispel the thought. Go home with him? From a bar for a one-night stand, maybe. But forever? That was a completely different story.

"For this holiday game, each bride and her groom contestant or contestants will be expected to create the perfect Christmas holiday—together. And you have one Earth day to make it happen. Starting now."

I groaned aloud.

More Christmas crap? Seriously?

I glanced down at the elf costume I still wore from my work shift at the mall.

Well, at least I'm already dressed for it.

CHAPTER FOUR

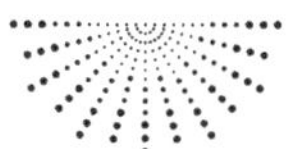

LOLA

Before we were allowed to leave the arena, Vos had us do an abbreviated version of the Bride Pageant. Unlike previous Bride Games, this one wasn't live. It was being filmed ahead of time and would be edited into a special episode to be shown the next night—Christmas in North America. I wondered for a moment if the Khanavai understood about different time zones on Earth. But it didn't seem wise to bring it up.

The other two brides caught up in these games had spent the hour since our transportation getting dressed up in evening gowns.

They looked gorgeous—one was a tall blonde from New York City who could have been a model. They had her in a slinky red sequined dress. In her high heels, she looked like someone who would actually be an appropriate match for a Khanavai warrior—they could walk down runways together and look perfect. The second woman was an equally slender, but not quite as tall, woman from Japan.

They both seem delighted to be participating in the Bride Games.

I still wasn't sure how I felt about it.

Don't get me wrong—that purple guy was steaming hot. I just wasn't sure that was enough to commit my life to.

Supposedly, the Alien Bride Lottery was chosen at random. But as the other two women stepped up onto the dais and spoke into the microphone as Vos interviewed them, I realized we all had something in common.

None of us had any family back on Earth.

Hell, I didn't even have a *job* waiting for me back home.

I had to wonder if that was on purpose. There had been some complaints recently about all the women who had been taken from their families and convinced to marry Khanavai warriors.

But notably, as the press had pointed out more than once, there had been no complaints from the brides themselves.

The whole thing made me suspicious. Were *none* of these women unhappy when they got to Khanav Prime?

A small knot formed in my stomach.

What if this is a trick of some sort?

I glanced over at the six warriors who had been brought in to compete as grooms. The purple one drew my gaze, of course.

God, he's gorgeous.

But the others? They looked… intimidating.

Scary.

Maybe even cruel.

But Beautiful Purple Guy had been gentle when he caught me and kept me from falling on the floor. His arm around me had been possessive, but somehow I also knew I could walk away at any moment.

Something was drawing me to him.

This entire thing was panic-inducing.

And for me, panic almost always came out as sarcasm. So when I stepped up onto the dais for my turn, it all spilled out.

"Tell us something interesting about yourself," Vos said. It was exactly the wrong thing to ask at that moment.

"I am a recent graduate of the College of Art and Design. I have no job prospects in my field. My parents died in a car wreck seven years ago. I have no family, and actually, no job at all now that I've been pulled away from being an elf in a mall—which is why I'm wearing this." I gestured at my outfit. "And I'm guessing all that makes me a perfect candidate to be swept off my planet and taken away to someplace I've never been before to be married off to a hulking alien." I stopped to catch my breath.

Vos laughed, but he shot me a look that was pure venom. "I know you haven't had a chance to properly meet any of our warriors, but what your first impression?"

"They're kind of terrifying." I glanced up at Beautiful Purple Dude in time to see it as his face fell. For a moment, he looked absolutely despondent.

"Except for the one who caught me when I almost fell down earlier," I amended.

No need to give them *all* a reason from the very beginning to decide not to match with me.

Vos looked happier at my second comment and wrapped up the interview as quickly as he could.

Then my two handlers came to whisk me off the stage.

“Let’s go get you dressed for your Christmas development outing,” the silvery one trilled.

Christmas development outing?

“By the way, my name is Plofnid, and this is Drindl,” the Poltien added. “We’re here to help you in any way we can.”

“Perfect,” I said. “The first thing I need to know is this: Is there any chance any of us—the three brides—will go back to Earth?”

Drindl hushed me. “We’ll talk about it later,” she said, glancing around furtively.

Yeah. That’s what I thought.

The only way I was leaving Station 21 was married to an alien.

CHAPTER FIVE

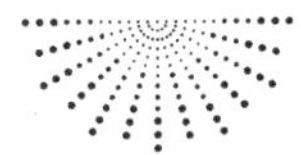

VALTIN

I spent the time we were separated growing increasingly anxious that Lola might end up with someone else.

Rather than the usual grooms' quarters, the six of us were taken to a single room that Vos called the Green Room—I didn't know why, though, because there was nothing green in it, other than one of the other Khanavai warriors.

"Have a seat," Vos said, gesturing around the room. "My assistant, Anthony, will queue up the brides' information on the comscreens. I presume you had a chance to scent the females. However, in case you didn't, there is an aroma enhancer next to each bride's picture."

As soon as the screen popped up in front of me, I scrolled to Lola's image. The aroma link took me to a synthesized version of her scent. It wasn't nearly as overwhelming as her real scent had been in person, but I still found it enticing.

Out of curiosity, I clicked on the other two brides' aroma links as well.

Neither of them interested me at all.

I was glad to have that confirmed, and wasted no time filling out the portion of the paperwork that would allow to match with Lola.

I only hoped that none of the other grooms had reacted to her the same way I had.

Those odds were lessened when one of the other grooms heaved an unhappy sigh and stood up. "None of these brides are a match for me," he announced, and left the room.

Excellent. One less competitor.

The other four warriors still remaining discussed the brides avidly. "What do you think of Lola Richards?" a green Khanavai male asked the room at large.

Unable to stop myself, I stood halfway out of my seat and growled at him.

He burst into laughter and held up his hands in surrender. "So that's how it is, huh? She's all yours."

One of the other warriors, a pink Khanavai male said, "I liked her answer in the interview. And her scent is nice enough."

My fists clenched and rage clouded my vision, but I forced myself to sink back down into my seat.

If it came down to it, I would kill any other male who dared compete for her.

But for all I knew, he was tweaking me, trying to get a rise out of me.

I would simply have to wait to see what happened next.

LOLA

"We are taking you to a dressing room," Drindl said as she turned to move down the hallway. When we rounded the corner, she glanced around. "There aren't any cameras here," she whispered. "Some of the hallways and the deepest part of the garden are almost the only places on the station that don't have cameras. To answer your earlier question, the three brides for this particular version of the games were carefully chosen. As were the grooms. You're supposed to match up with at least two of them according to a new DNA analysis program that Vos had a team develop. So no. There's really no way you won't be matched and mated."

Plofnid shot her a glare. "That is classified information," it reminded her.

"I don't care," she replied. "I think it's important for her to know that she really should make the best possible choice."

"And if I don't?" My voice sounded almost as worried as I felt.

Plofnid shrugged. "If it's any consolation, all of the brides chosen by Khanavai warriors end up very happy."

I narrowed my eyes. "How do you know?"

Drindl let out a trilling laugh. "We've been working to help brides for more than one of your Earth's decades." She gestured at Plofnid. "And every bride the two of us have worked with has ended up with a mate she truly loves. I think you will, too."

Plofnid rolled his eyes but nodded. "She's not lying to you. Even though she shouldn't be telling you any of this at all."

Drindl waved us forward. "We have to hurry. It's almost time for you to start your next segment."

She hurried down the hall and I followed, thinking of everything she had said.

If they were happy, these women who married Khanavai warriors, then perhaps I could be, too.

It was a novel thought. The only time I had really been happy in my life was when I was drawing or painting. Creating things.

I didn't have to be on Earth to do that. I could choose one of these giant males and at least I wouldn't have to worry about being a Christmas elf at the mall ever again.

I snickered to myself. Okay, so maybe that was a pretty mercenary view of choosing someone to marry. But if I didn't have any other kind of choice, that I might as well go with it.

My mother, before she died, had always said that I was the most practical artist she had ever met.

I would do whatever I had to in order to make sure I survived. And in the end, I could look at this as simply another job.

One that might include a gorgeous purple Khanavai male.

Right?

I ignored the tiny voice in the back of my head that suggested I had never been willing to prostitute myself for my art before.

Shut up, I told it.

But it kept whispering to me, all the way to the dressing rooms.

When we reached those rooms, Drindl had me sit in front of the mirror and pulled up the comscreen in front of me. "These are the grooms you have to choose from."

I didn't hesitate. "That one," I said.

Plofnid grinned. "I thought that was the one you would pick. Valtin Valenox."

"The two of you clearly have a connection," Drindl agreed.

"What happens next?" I asked.

"The judges decide if they approve the match, and then you and any grooms who choose you undergo the games."

"What if the one I chose didn't choose me?"

"You'll probably be paired up to do some of the games, anyway." Randall frowned. "But I don't think there's any real chance that he wouldn't choose you. Not the way he was holding on to you in the general meeting."

"But if we choose each other, can't we just make it official somehow?"

"Oh, no," Plofnid said. "There have been a few occasions where the judges decided that a bride and groom who had chosen one another would not suit, after all."

"Why would they do that?" My heart thudded in my chest at the thought of any of the other males getting close to me.

"Well," Drindl began.

Plofnid shot her an irritated glance.

"She deserves to know," Drindl said. "They all do. I think the information should be published on Earth." She turned back to face me. "The brides are here to save the Khanavai culture by interbreeding."

I nodded. That was common enough knowledge.

"Sometimes the DNA match isn't strong enough. The judges check for that. Khanavai mating is serious business. So any cross matches that would not ultimately provide healthy offspring are… discouraged."

"So even if a bride and groom are determined to be together, if they can't have babies, they're not allowed to be together?"

Grendel nodded. "It's presented as being all about love. But really, the Bride Games are absolutely mercenary."

See? I told the voice in my head. *Everyone in this whole Bride Lottery thing is out for themselves. I'm not the only one.*

But that didn't help the knot that formed my stomach.

VALTIN

When he returned moments later, Vos announced the matches.

I waited, my heart pounding, to learn what had happened.

I had matched with Lola, of course. But Lola had also chosen me. My heart leaped in my chest, and I wanted to start singing Earth Christmas carols out of pure joy.

I thought of the tree my friend's mother had decorated every cycle with a tiny, glowing figure atop it.

An angel, she had called it. A messenger of all good things.

Lola was *my* Christmas angel.

She would be going home with me.

As my mate.

"And finally," Vos said, "Wex Banstinad has chosen Lola Richards."

The green Khanavai male who had mentioned her earlier smirked at me.

It was all I could do not to jump up and attack him right there. But I managed to keep my reaction to a low growl.

Lola was mine.

And I would prove it.

Let the games begin.

CHAPTER SIX

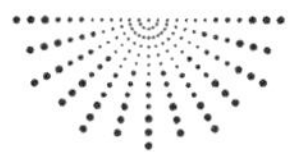

LOLA

Apparently, Vos was obsessed with Christmas decorations. Because that was our first task—to find a Christmas tree and decorate the room we would be having our gift exchange in.

At least, I assumed it was a gift exchange. Vos kept calling it the "Christmas ceremony," whatever that meant.

They had set up some kind of market in the center of the station, between the garden and the food court. Our task was to choose a tree and go shopping together. I wasn't certain what this had to do with choosing a lifemate, but there you have it.

At least they had gotten the idea of Christmas being a commercial holiday completely down.

And here I was, accompanied by two giant Khanavai males. One was purple, gorgeous, and delighted to be surrounded by all things Christmas. The other was green, scowling, and apparently determined to piss Valtin off.

We hit the trees first. Tiny aerial video globes darted around the trees and markets, following us to catch all the video footage possible.

Valtin dashed to the biggest tree in the impromptu tree lot. "What about this one?" he asked, staring up at the tree that towered over even him.

"It's too big for the room," Wex said.

Technically, Wex was right. I'd seen the dimensions of the rooms, and artistically, this would overwhelm the space.

Not to mention the fact that we would have to all but clear out the market to get enough items to decorate it.

Despite how irritated I had become by all things Christmas, I suddenly felt like indulging Valtin's whims. His enthusiasm was contagious.

"No," I said. "I think I like that one."

Wax rolled his eyes in irritation, but Valtin laughed aloud and clapped his hands together.

"Perfect," the purple alien announced. "We'll have it delivered."

Wex snarled something unintelligible and whipped around to walk away from us. As he did, his shoulder caught the edge of the tree. It began to topple over, and Wex jumped out of the way—leaving it headed directly toward me.

Without stopping to consider his own safety, Valtin jumped in front of it, catching it and holding it with his bulging arms.

The first thing he did was turn his head toward me. "Are you all right?"

I swallowed but nodded. "I am. Thank you."

Several other Khanavai males, all smaller than Valtin, rushed over to help them set the tree back upright. He gave them a few directions about delivering it to the room we would be using that night.

Then he turned to take my arm. "Are you sure you're well?" he asked. "Not too frightened?"

"I'm good."

"Good enough to shop for decorations now?"

"Sure."

"Where did Wex go?"

I glanced around to find the green warrior picking through decorations in the stalls. I didn't want to join him. But I was afraid if we didn't, there might be some weird repercussions later.

"I've chosen our decorations," the green alien announced when we joined them.

"Let me see?" I asked.

He opened the bag he carried over his shoulder to show a jumble of mismatched ornaments. "I simply grabbed some things. We should go decorate our tree now."

I frowned. I did not like his high-handed manner.

"I think Lola should choose the decorations," Valtin said. "After all, I chose the tree."

Without another word, I turned and began perusing the decorations. Perhaps unsurprisingly, they were not limited to the traditional red and green of Christmas. The Khanavai loved color, I was beginning to figure out. "I think we should have a theme," I said, irritated by Wex enough to want to get back at him a little.

"Perfect," Valtin said. "What kind of theme?

I caught his eye and grinned. "I think silver and purple would be a lovely color theme for this Christmas."

With a muttered curse, Wex dropped the bag he was holding. "I see how it is," he snarled. "You prefer purple."

I gave him a hard stare. "Right now, I certainly do."

With a snort of irritation, he took a step back. "Fine. I'm out."

"Good," I said as he strode away.

I glanced up at Valtin to see him fighting back a grin.

"Pretty pleased with yourself right now?" I teased.

"Actually, I am surprised to be pleased with *him*," Valtin said, gesturing after the retreating Wex.

"I am, too," I murmured, taking Valtin's hand and drawing him toward the nearest stall with purple decorations. "Let's see what we can find to cover that enormous tree of yours."

Valtin snickered and I found myself blushing at my unintended double entendre. But I didn't correct myself.

I was getting more and more curious about that enormous...*tree*...of his.

Three hours later, I stood back to admire our handiwork in the room we'd been assigned. It had come with a boxy sofa and a kind of electronic fireplace with a mantel. And now it was also half taken up with a giant Christmas tree decorated in silver and purple.

I had fun doing this.

I hadn't had fun at Christmas since my parents had died.

And Valtin was the reason.

I was about to tell him so, when the door opened, and my two handlers appeared.

"It's time to change for the caroling," Plofnid announced. I glanced over at him and nodded. With the exception of the nostril braid, the Poltien made me think of Christmas elves—real ones, not freaks in costumes in malls like I had been.

"I'll see you again soon," I said to Valtin, then headed out the door without waiting for an answer.

Back in the dressing room getting ready to try to sing Christmas carols, I realized that I wanted Valtin.

Not just because he was gorgeous and sexy.

I didn't just want him sexually. No. I wanted *him*. All of him. The thought of any other woman ending up with him made my heart ache.

This is stupid, my inner voice told me. *Love at first sight is not a thing.*

Maybe not. But in one outing, I'd learned quite a bit about him. He was protective and strong. He was kind and generous, and he valued my input.

He was a good man.

There was no getting out of being a bride. As long as Valtin was the groom, I was good with it.

I simply needed to make sure he was the groom I went home with.

I had the beginnings of a plan to make that happen.

And if it doesn't work?

No, I told myself. *Failure is not an option.*

Time to get to work.

"So if we don't have access to the DNA profiles, how can we tell if it's a good match?" I asked Drindl.

She grinned. "A Khanavai male's mating cock only appears with his true mate. And all true mates are good matches."

"Mating cock?"

"It's a special appendage," Plofnid supplied, brushing my hair in long strokes.

Mating cock.

Well. This was going to be interesting.

And it meant I had a question to ask Valtin before we went to sing carols.

"I have an idea about that dress you wanted me to wear tonight," I said. "Do you think you can make some changes to it while we're out singing? I have one more favor to ask, too…when we're on our way to the caroling."

Valtin

"LOLA," I called out as she entered the room, ignoring the fact that Wex, the ugly green bastard, got to her first. She smiled at him and said something, but then ducked out from under his arm and made her way to me.

The aerial vidglobe followed her, only to be waylaid by Drindl, who began chattering into it about the process of getting Lola ready for our Christmas ceremony tonight.

"What did Wex have to say to you?"

"Him?" Lola glanced back toward the other warrior. "I think he wanted to apologize, maybe? I wasn't really paying attention."

I had to smile at that.

She grabbed me by the hand, her touch sending shivers up my arm. "Come with me." Pulling me to the side of the arena, behind one of the more elaborate decorative trees, she bit her lip. "Can I tell you something important?"

"Anything."

"When I got here, I wasn't sure I wanted to be a bride at all—but if it was going to happen one way or another, I decided I would rather it be you than anyone else."

I nodded.

"But now…I *want* to be with you. I can't stand the idea of ending up with Wex."

I growled aloud at the thought of any other male touching my mate. "No one else will have you."

She laughed. "Good. But Drindl and Plofnid say it's not a given. If we choose each other, the judges can make us not be together, can they?"

"I'm afraid the judges can do whatever they want to."

Lola paused, her eyes narrowed in thought, as if trying to decide how to say what she had in mind. "I have heard of…well, of something called the Khanavai 'mating cock'."

I nodded. "It's something human males don't have, right?"

"No, human men have only one penis." Her eyes danced with amusement. "So here's my question. If you use your mating cock while we're together, is there anything they could do to us?"

I shrugged helplessly. "I don't know. I don't think so—but I have never heard of a groom mating a bride before they were confirmed."

"Drindl told me it has happened before." Lola glanced around to make sure no one was listening, then stood on her tiptoes and pulled my head down toward hers to whisper in my ear. "I want you to fuck me with that mating cock of yours. Make me yours. Don't let them separate us."

Her breath against the shell of my ear, slightly damp and burning hot, sent an ache down into my balls.

Not to mention the reaction her actual words caused. My cock hardened, straining to reach her, and I wasn't sure I would ever *not* be erect when she was around.

"Lola? Valtin?" Plofnid peeked around the tree we hid behind. "It's time to begin the singing."

Christmas caroling with a hard-on.

I wondered if we could make that a new holiday tradition.

CHAPTER SEVEN

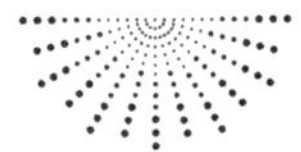

LOLA

When Vos had suggested we go Christmas caroling, I hadn't realized that the Khanavai didn't know any Christmas carols. We all had epaper with the songs on them. But the Khanavai didn't know the words to the songs *or* the music. So as we all moved in a group from office to office in the station, our carols were horrible.

Despite that, Valtin sang with enthusiasm—loudly, slightly off-key, and absolutely adorable.

But then we got to "The First Noel." And to my surprise, Valtin seemed to know that carol. As we sang, he reached down and took my hand.

Wex, on the other side of me, took the other. That lasted for about two songs before I shook him off.

As we left one office and headed through the central area toward another, I asked Valtin, "How do you know that song?"

"My best friend's mother was human, and she used to sing it during Christmas."

"So you already knew some of these Christmas traditions?"

He nodded. "I grew up with Kein on Khanav Prime. His mother decorated once a year—though with nothing as authentic as the decorations we have here. She settled for having the right colors of green and red."

I wrapped my arm around his, my hand curving around his enormous bicep. "I like our choices better. I think purple and silver look really good together."

"Even though my trees too big for the room?"

I snickered. "Yes. Despite that, I think we have the best decorations of all."

He threw his head back and laughed. "We haven't seen any of the others' decorations."

I shrugged. "I don't have to. I know what I like."

He paused for just a second, long enough to stare into my eyes as if trying to figure out what I meant.

"Come along," Vos said, leading us past the now-cleared market space.

I glanced around, trying to figure out if what Drindl and Plofnid had told me about cameras was true.

It was. I could tell which panels they were behind from the way they reflected the light, just as Plofnid had told me.

This was going to make my plan for later more difficult — but not impossible.

I can do this.

. . .

Valtin

LOLA DIDN'T NOTICE when Wex left the caroling group, and I didn't point it out to her.

He had already forfeited his chance with her, as far as I was concerned.

So when I left her to prepare for our holiday evening ritual, my heart was singing.

She's mine. My mate. My love.

An hour later, I arrived in our designated—and beautifully decorated—room before she did. Carefully, I set my tiny, wrapped gift under the tree. I had spent my time since the caroling researching Earth holiday traditions.

This would be perfect. I hoped.

I glanced up and gasped as Lola entered the room.

She wore nothing but a giant, red satin ribbon wrapped around her body and tied in a bow that barely covered her luscious breasts. My cock stood at attention.

"You know we have a tradition of opening gifts on Christmas, right?" she said, sounding almost shy.

I swallowed, my mouth going dry at the thought of unwrapping this particular gift.

"You know the cameras are watching us," I managed to say in a raspy voice.

"Then I guess we'll have to go someplace more private to finish opening all our presents." She winked at me.

"I'm afraid I didn't bring you such an exciting gift."

Her gaze dropped to take in the length of me, especially my cock jutting out against my chavan. "Oh, I think I can manage to unwrap something interesting."

"Right." The word came out strangled as her smile sent a shiver of anticipation up my spine. A slow smile spread across my face. "And I know just the place."

"Where?"

I glanced up at the cameras and held out my hand. "I don't want them to meet us there. Come with me."

She placed her hand in mine trustingly, and I led her out the door. As soon as we hit the hallway, I started jogging.

I was fairly certain Vos Klavoii would send someone to stop us if he could—after all, he preferred to have the Bride Games be the final arbiter of which couples could mate.

But I wasn't going to take that chance. Lola was mine—and I was hers.

Now we simply had to make it official.

"Let's go." I took her hand and led her out of the door, slamming it shut and closing the vidglobe inside.

With a laugh, she followed me, and we ran down the corridor.

Straight to the garden.

"Oh," Lola said in wonder as I led her into the depths of the garden. "Drindl told me there were no cameras in parts of this area of the station."

We left the path and pushed through to a small clearing. "Exactly. I memorized the station maps before I got here."

I realized Lola was trembling.

"Are you sure you want to do this?" I asked gently.

"More sure than I've ever been," she said. "But I think we'd better hurry."

At her words, my cock pushed out against the chavan. As if in wonder, she reached out and touched it through the fabric.

"How does this 'mating cock' thing work?" she asked. "Because I see only one here."

"May I show you?"

She nodded wordlessly.

Carefully, I raised my chavan, exposing myself. Slowly, she ran a hand over my cock, sending a shudder through my entire body.

I took her hand, guiding it to the ridges that ran the length of me. "Feel that?" When she nodded and continued to stroke along the ridges, I swallowed hard before I could speak again. "During an actual mating, after I orgasm once, these ridges collapse, allowing my mating cock to emerge."

"From inside your penis?" Lola asked, fascination threading through her voice.

"Yes."

"From here?" She circled the tip of the head with one finger, sliding across the opening as my cock jumped at her touch.

"Yes." My voice was strained as I fought to maintain control of myself.

"What does it feel like when that happens."

"No idea—I've never mated with anyone before."

She turned her gold-flecked eyes toward me. "Never? Can you be sure it will happen now?"

"I'm certain." I couldn't tell her how I knew, but I did. Lola was my mate, the one for me. Unable to wait any longer, I pulled her to me, kissing her deep and hard, our tongues tangling, our heated desire urgent.

"You say you have to come once before the mating cock appears?"

"That's what I learned in our sexual education courses, yes."

"Then lie down," she whispered. "Let's make that part happen."

Pulling off my chavan, I spread it out on the ground, then stretched out naked on it under her hungry gaze. She knelt beside me, then leaned over to lick the tip she'd just been touching. My cock jumped toward her again.

"I want to feel your mouth on me," I groaned, my cock straining up as if to meet her lips. Lola smiled a slow, hot smile, then ran her tongue in a circle around my belly button. My cock leaped up, bumping against her chin, and I heard her give a low chuckle.

And then she was taking the length of me into her mouth, softly at first, her tongue undulating against the underside, sweeping up and down the ridges until unbidden, a deep sound of satisfaction echoed from me. "Yes," I whispered. "More."

With that, Lola pulled my cock as far into her throat as it would go, until she'd taken me balls-deep into her mouth. I could feel the very tip of my cock pressed against my mate's throat, and as I rocked against her, trying to drive myself even deeper, a swirling heat centered itself in my abdomen, rushing down to my balls, pulsing and aching to explode.

"I'm about to come," I gasped out, and Lola's hand came up to caress my balls as if she were milking them into her mouth.

It was enough to send me hurtling over the edge, the heat drawing into a white-hot pinpoint of sensation, then exploding outward. I cried out in ecstasy and pumped into her as Lola first sucked, then swallowed, then gently stroked my cock into her mouth, until the sensation was too much to take, and I pulled out of her to collapse, breathing hard.

Lola stretched out on her side, watching me. After a few moments, I rolled over to face her. She wore a slight smile. "Ready for the rest of it? Are you ready to make me your mate?"

I would have said I was completely spent, but at her words, I felt my inner cock—my mating cock—spring to life and emerge.

"Goddess, yes," I breathed. "Please."

CHAPTER EIGHT

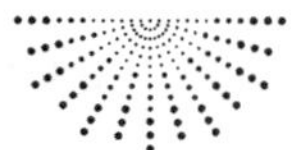

LOLA

Valtin ran his forefinger along the underside of my breast peeking out from beneath the red ribbons crisscrossing and winding around my body. As the edge of his finger brushed against my skin, goosebumps popped up along my arms. My nipples tightened and my breath caught in the back of my throat.

He was utterly silent, watching me intently as he slipped one arm behind my shoulders and lifted me atop him. As he pulled me in tighter against him, his mating cock jutting up between us, he pulled me down and brushed his lips against mine.

My attention split between concentrating on the feel of his mouth against mine and the stroke of his fingertips as they drifted downward, tracing a line from my hardened, sensitive breast down to the exposed skin around my belly button. There he used his fingers to circle my navel for several seconds before sliding them along the edge of the ribbon that circled my hips.

At every point he touched, the contrast between the slightly roughened skin of his fingertips and my own soft flesh sent chills racing out across every inch of me.

When he grazed his lightly stubbled chin across my cheek and took my earlobe in between his teeth, the sensation made me moan aloud.

He reached up to the bow on my chest, but I stopped him, whispering, "Not yet."

Valtin was big—enormous—all over. It was a wonder I'd been able to take him into my mouth. And somehow, his mating cock was even bigger.

Placing his hands on my waist, he lifted my hips. "Are you ready?"

I nodded, still nervous, but unbearably aroused. "Yes."

I slid down onto him, the sheer size of him forcing me to move slowly to accommodate him. As I settled him into my body, I could feel the head of his mating cock pressing against the most intimate part of me, where no one had ever reached before, touching me in a way that brushed up against the border of pain and pleasure.

I closed my eyes to concentrate.

Even when I had settled all the way down, the base of his shaft pressing against me and every inch of his cock buried inside me, my knees didn't quite touch the ground on either side of his hips. Instead, I pulled my feet up onto his legs and hooked my toes between his thighs, pulling my own legs even further apart, as if I could sink down against him even further.

Leaning my hands against his chest and using my feet as leverage, I lifted myself up high. Finally, I opened my eyes to catch his gaze with my own, and slid down him, faster this time.

Valtin rested his hands against my hips without really holding on, letting his palms slide up and down as I moved against him.

"Now," I said, "unwrap me."

With a single tug of the ribbon, he untied the bow and began pulling off the ribbon it had taken Drindl and Plofnid a full hour to get right.

I moaned in pleasure, and that single sound was enough for him to begin matching our movements stroke for stroke. And as we moved together, I felt my orgasm building inside me. He reached up between us and ran his thumb gently across my clit, over and over again, until I felt I couldn't take any more.

I tumbled over the edge, convulsing around him, coming harder than I ever had before. Valtin's mating cock began pulsating inside me as his hands gripped my hips and pulled me down hard against him, our cries mingling as we came together.

Afterward, I collapsed against his chest as he stroked my back and murmured, over and over, "My beautiful, amazing mate."

Vos was going to be furious, but I didn't care.

This had definitely been the right choice.

The very best decision I had ever made.

"Merry Christmas," I whispered.

"Merry Christmas," my amazing, giant, purple Khanavai warrior mate replied. "And if I have my way, all the rest of our days will be merry and bright."

EPILOGUE

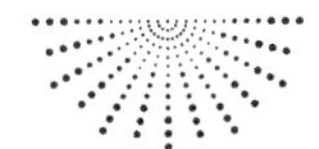

WEX

"What in all the Zagrodnian hells have the two of you done?" Vos ranted as he marched up and down behind his desk.

Valtin shrugged. "We mated. That's the whole reason for the Bride Lottery and Games, right?"

Vos seethed. "You were not supposed to join with her. Wex was the one we had chosen for her."

Valtin's new mate raised one eyebrow. "But he's not the one I chose for myself. And as I understand it, this is something you cannot take back, right? This whole mating thing?"

Vos spun to glare at her.

"It's fine," I said. "These two belong together, Vos. And I know you had plans for me. But…" I glanced at Valtin and Lola. "You two are right. Lola wasn't the one for me."

Vos turned his glare on me. "So I guess you think you have a better idea?"

I nodded. "Yes, but you're not going to like it."

He threw his hands up in the air and turned his glare back to Valtin and Lola. "Well, it certainly won't be the first thing I haven't liked today."

I had to fight to suppress a snicker at that. I had known from the moment I saw Lola that, despite what Vos had told me, I wasn't going to end up mated to her.

No. I had already met my mate.

And if Vos thought he didn't like Lola and Valtin together, he was going to like this even less. I inhaled, then spit it out. "She's a woman I met on Earth when I was on the search team for Zont's mate."

Vos spun around from glaring at Valtin and Lola to stare at me again. "Why didn't you mention that sooner?"

"Because I didn't think it was possible for her to be a bride."

"Why not?"

"She is currently in an Earth prison for having attempted to violate the Bride Alliance Treaty."

For a moment, I thought Vos was going to explode. But then he took a deep breath, visibly calming himself down, and leaned forward to rest his hands on the desk.

"You two," he said, jerking his chin toward Lola and Valtin. "Get out of here. Go enjoy the end of the festivities."

"So you will register our mating?" Valtin asked.

Vos heaved a long-suffering sigh. "Yes. Just go."

Neither of us said anything until the couple had left the room.

Vos turned to me. "You seriously want a chance to mate with an Earth woman who violated the Bride Alliance Treaty?"

I felt a smile growing across my face. "I do. And I believe it will make for some amazing programming."

Vos narrowed his eyes at me, bit his lip, then picked up an epen and held it poised over the epaper in front of him, ready to take notes. "Tell me more."

This is going to be amazing.

ENJOYED THIS STORY? You can preorder Wex's story in Enemy of the Alien Bride Lottery, book four of the Khanavai Warrior Alien Bride Games series. You can also read the rest of the series, starting with Entered in the Alien Bride Lottery.

ABOUT THE AUTHOR

USA Today, Wall Street Journal, and *New York Times* bestselling author Margo Bond Collins is a former college English professor who, tired of explaining the difference between "hanged" and "hung," turned to writing romance novels instead. Sometimes her heroines kill monsters, sometimes they kiss aliens. But they always aim for the heart!

Want to hang out with the author, win book prizes, see the cool covers first, and support Margo's books on social media? Join The Vampirarchy, Margo's street team on Facebook!

If you'd love to hear about brand-new science fiction romances, you can sign up for the Science Fiction and Alien Romance newsletter.

You can also sign up for Margo's general newsletter here for news about all her books, plus freebies and more.

JOIN MARGO ONLINE

www.MargoBondCollins.net
Bookbub
Facebook
Twitter
Instagram
Amazon

READ MORE OF MARGO'S BOOKS

KHANAVAI WARRIORS ALIEN BRIDE GAMES SERIES

Entered in the Alien Bride Lottery

Captured for the Alien Bride Lottery

Claimed for the Alien Bride Lottery

Enemy of the Alien Bride Lottery

Volunteer for the Alien Bride Lottery

Betting on the Alien Bride Lottery

INTERSTELLAR SHIFTERS

Star Mate Matched

Star Mate Marked

THE ALIEN WARRIORS' REPARATION BRIDES SERIES

An Alien of Convenience

ALIEN ROMANCE BOXED SETS

Stolen and Seduced

Captured and Captivated

Alien Embrace

REVERSE HAREM ALIEN ROMANCES

Snatched

Her Alien Crew

Tiny and Fierce

Theirs by Destiny